The FIFTH ASSASSIN

ALSO BY BRAD MELTZER

The FIFTH ASSASSIN

BRAD MELTZER

GRAND CENTRAL
PUBLISHING

NEW YORK   BOSTON

Copyright © 2013 Forty-four Steps, Inc.
Ace of spades drawn by Daniel Pelavin
Map © Map Resource

Grand Central Publishing
Hachette Book Group
237 Park Avenue
New York, NY 10017

HachetteBookGroup.com

Printed in the United States of America

RRD-C

First Edition: January 2013
10 9 8 7 6 5 4 3 2 1

Grand Central Publishing is a division of Hachette Book Group, Inc.
The Grand Central Publishing name and logo is a trademark of Hachette Book Group, Inc.

The Hachette Speakers Bureau provides a wide range of authors for speaking events. To find out more, go to www.hachettespeakersbureau.com or call (866) 376-6591.

The publisher is not responsible for websites (or their content) that are not owned by the publisher.

Library of Congress Control Number: 2012951523
ISBN: 978-0-446-55397-1

For my dad,
Stewie Meltzer,
who lived loud,
loved hard,
and always knew
where to find a good deli

ACKNOWLEDGMENTS

Here's what I love: I love sitting at my desk, staring at the blank screen, and beginning that conversation with my imaginary friends. But no matter how many books I write, here's one of the few things I know for sure: Imaginary friends are indeed vital, but when it comes to actually writing these books, it's my *real* family and friends, including you, dear reader, who make it possible. So tremendous thank-yous to the following: My first love and first lady, Cori, who made me dig deep during what has been one of the hardest years of my life. My love for her is truly profound. Jonas, Lila, and Theo are my best blessings of all. To quote a dear friend: "Nothing in life lives up to the hype...except being a parent." Especially to these three. I love them with everything I have. Jill Kneerim, the friend and agent who took me in when I was twenty-four years old, and who has been with me since; Hope Denekamp, Caroline Zimmerman, Ike Williams, and all our friends at the Kneerim & Williams Agency.

Here's what else I know for sure: With the loss of my parents, this book had no choice but to be about growing up. So let me thank the one person who grew up next to me: my sister, Bari, who reminds me of every insane and wonderful thing our parents taught us. Also to Bobby, Ami, Adam, Gilda, and Will for standing there with us.

Of all the people in here, there's one who needs to be singled out: Noah Kuttler. Noah plots with me, schemes with me, argues with me, and basically spends every free moment challenging me to be the writer I wish I was. Thanks, pal, for always pushing the

ACKNOWLEDGMENTS

craft and for never *ever* letting me down, intellectually or person-ally. Ethan Kline has stood by my side since we first used the Xerox machine at work to make copies of *The Tenth Justice*. He, along with Dale Flam, Matt Kuttler, Chris Weiss, and Judd Winick are the vital readers who take my early drafts and help me find the actual book.

When it came to researching Presidents and their assassins, I owe major thanks to the following: First, President George H. W. Bush, who was generous and kind enough to again answer all my questions, the most macabre ones I've ever asked him. Special colonial shout-out to the man himself—George Washington—for inspiring so much in here. Archivist of the United States David S. Ferriero is one of the nicest and most welcoming hosts around. Also at the National Archives, which everyone should go visit, Paul Brachfeld, Susan Cooper, Matt Fulgham, Miriam Kleiman, and Trevor Plante again helped me conjure my inner Beecher. I both-ered them over and over, and they never complained. Our friend-ship has been the best result. Special thanks to Michael Guidry, who protects so many and for whom I have so much respect; Brian White and all my friends at the Department of Homeland Secu-rity's Red Cell program for again helping take this idea even further, and Eljay Bowron, Jim Mackin, Max Milien, Robert Pearce, and Larry Sheafe for making me respect the Secret Service even more.

Additional thanks to Michael Rhode and the staff of the National Museum of Health and Medicine for letting me hold the bones of John Wilkes Booth; John Nolan, John Piper, and John Ryan for help-ing me explore my inner break-in artist; Alan Brown, whose honesty helped me see life from a wheelchair; Hayden Bryan and Senior Min-ister Dean Snyder invited me into their churches; Ron Decker and the American Playing Card Company made me look at cards in new ways; Bob Gourley, Bob Flores, Roy Judelson, Marc Marlin, Adam Mey-ers, Adam Mikrut, and Jeff Phelan were the best tech experts; Pat-rick Canavan, Jogues Prandoni, Richard Warsh, and Steve Baron for the St. Elizabeths details; my confidants Dean Alban and Arturo de Hoyos for their great historical insight; my first history teacher, Ellen

ACKNOWLEDGMENTS

Sherman; and the rest of my own inner circle, who I bother for every book: Rabbi Steven M. Glazer, Jo Ayn Glanzer, Jason Sherry, Mark Dimunation, Dr. Lee Benjamin, Dr. David Sandberg, Marie Grunbeck, Nick Marell, and Brad Desnoyer; special thanks to those who anonymously taught me about Camp David. More Archives research came from Kimberly Gentile, Richard "Chip" Sandage, Morgan Zinsmeister, the memory of John E. Taylor, and all the archivists who sent me cool stuff. The books *The Manner of Man That Kills* by L. Vernon Briggs; *Stalking, Threatening, and Attacking Public Figures*, edited by Meloy, Sheridan, and Hoffmann; *Murdering McKinley* by Eric Rauchway; *The Trial of the Assassin Guiteau* by Charles E. Rosenberg; *Assassination Vacation* by Sarah Vowell; *A History of Playing Cards* by Catherine Perry Hargrave; and my favorite, *Manhunt* by James L. Swanson, were vital to this process. Yes, Grace is a homage to the real Grace Hopper. Finally, Anne Twomey, Farris Rookstool III, Jeff A. Benner, Paul Bardunias, and Laura Simo, along with the great people at Mount Vernon, lent their expertise to so many different details; our family on *Decoded* and at HISTORY, including Nancy Dubuc, Dirk Hoogstra, and Russ McCarroll for giving me the opportunity of a lifetime; Rob Weisbach for being the first to say yes; and of course, my family and friends, whose names, as always, inhabit these pages.

I also want to thank everyone at Grand Central Publishing: David Young, Emi Battaglia, Matthew Ballast, Sonya Cheuse, Martha Otis, Bruce Paonessa, Karen Torres, Lindsey Rose, Caitlin Mulrooney-Lyski, Evan Boorstyn, the nicest and hardest working sales force in show business, Bob Castillo, Mari Okuda, Thomas Whatley, and all my dear friends there who have spent so much of their lives changing mine. I've said it before, so here it comes again: They're the real reason this book is in your hands. Special mushy thank-you to Mitch Hoffman, who helps ask the hardest questions and who is always family. Finally, I want to thank Jamie Raab. In the current publishing industry, it's so easy to do the same thing over and over again. Jamie never does. She continues fighting the most vital fight of all: the fight for what she loves. I owe her for so much. Thank you, Jamie, for your faith.

The FIFTH ASSASSIN

PROLOGUE

Washington, D.C.

Some funerals are filled with questions. Others are filled with answers. This one was filled with secrets.

The funeral was set for 9 a.m., but it was running late. Everyone knew why.

Shifting in the packed pews, over two hundred mourners tried to be nonchalant, but they still kept glancing toward the back of the church.

They weren't looking for the coffin. Dr. Stewart Palmiotti's dark wood coffin had already been rolled to the front of the church, by the pulpit. They weren't looking for Palmiotti's family. His ex-wife, who had caused so much heartache, and his girlfriend Lydia, who had given him so much happiness, were both in the front row, on opposite sides. Relatives, friends, and coworkers filled in the rest. Typical funeral.

Here's what wasn't typical: Each mourner was forced to walk through a metal detector before they were allowed inside.

This was Washington, D.C. Everyone knew what that meant.

He was coming. The only *he* that mattered.

The President of the United States.

Naturally, the Secret Service waited until everyone was in their seats. Then, with no warning at all, the back doors closed, then popped open.

"Your speech, sir," one of his aides whispered, handing him a binder with the eulogy.

1

Gripping the binder and annoyed that the aide had been seen by the mourners, the President stepped forward as every head turned his way. Usually, when he entered a room, they'd play "Hail to the Chief." Today the room was silent.

Clenching his jaw and keeping his famous gray eyes staring straight ahead, President Orson Wallace walked alone down the main aisle, as if he were in a wedding of one.

He was used to being stared at. That was part of the job. But as he headed farther down the aisle, even the most powerful man in the world wasn't ready for the sudden breathlessness that overtook him. The reality of the moment pressed against his chest. This was the funeral of his best friend.

It's one thing to be stared at by strangers. This was a roomful of family and friends, people who used to call the President by his first name.

Growing up in Ohio, Palmiotti and Wallace went from grade school, to high school, to college at the University of Michigan, always together. When Wallace was elected governor, Palmiotti followed. They were together on that night they never talked about anymore. And when Wallace won the White House, someone mentioned that when George H. W. Bush was elected President, he appointed a dear friend as White House doctor, understanding that sometimes the best medicine was simply having someone to talk to. Especially someone who knew you well. And knew your secrets.

The President liked that. On the day of Wallace's Inauguration, Dr. Stewart Palmiotti was made head of the White House Medical Unit, with an office adjacent to the West Wing.

"All those things you did for him...You know he loved you," Palmiotti's girlfriend Lydia whispered as the President finally reached the front row. Her voice...her body...everything was shaking as she stood from her seat and embraced Wallace.

Returning her hug, but staying silent, the President slowly made his way to the far end of the front row, pretending he didn't see their twelfth-grade history teacher in the crowd.

But the President's real pain didn't come from spotting old

friends. It came from the certain knowledge that he was responsible for all this.

True, the President didn't pull the trigger. But it *was* the President who sent Palmiotti after the archivist: Beecher.

It was Beecher who had learned what the President and Palmiotti had done on the worst night of their lives, back in college, twenty-six years ago. It was Beecher who found out that they had buried a baseball bat and car keys into the face of a man from their hometown. And that Palmiotti and the future President, along with Wallace's sister, had shattered the man's eye socket, punctured his face, and driven bits of his skull into his brain, causing irreversible brain damage.

Worst of all, it was Beecher—and the group he worked with—who would never let it go...never stop searching...not until they could actually prove what happened that night years ago.

Beecher and his so-called Culper Ring.

They were the ones who could do the real damage—the ones who knew Wallace and Palmiotti's secret. Yet that wasn't the only secret the President was keeping.

Taking his seat at the far end of the aisle, the President of the United States eyed his best friend's coffin.

Almost on cue, his phone vibrated in his pocket. Looking down, President Wallace pulled it out just enough to read the newest text onscreen:

How's my funeral going? Dr. Stewart Palmiotti asked.

PART I

The First Assassination

"What will Miss Harris think of my hanging on to you so?" Mary Lincoln asked, holding her husband's hand.

"She won't think anything about it," Abraham Lincoln replied.

They were the last words Lincoln spoke before John Wilkes Booth put a bullet in his brain.

1

Today
Washington, D.C.

The Knight knew his history. And his destiny. In fact, no one studied those more carefully than the Knight.

Rolling a butterscotch candy around his tongue, he pulled the trigger at exactly 10:11 p.m.

The gun—an antique pistol—let out a puff of blue-gray smoke, sending a spray of meat and blood across the wooden pews of St. John's Church, the historic building that sat directly across the street from the White House.

"Y-You shot me..." the rector cried, clutching the back of his shoulder—his collarbone felt shattered—as he reeled sideways and stumbled down the main aisle.

The blood wouldn't stop. But the Knight's gun hadn't delivered a killshot. At the last minute, the rector, who'd been in charge of St. John's for nearly a decade, had moved.

The Knight just stood there, waiting for him to fall. The stark white plaster mask he wore ensured that his victim couldn't get a good look at his face. But the rector still had his strength.

Sliding his gun back in his pocket, the Knight moved calmly, almost serenely down the aisle, toward the ornate altar.

"Help! Someone...*please*! *Someone help me!*" the rector, a sixty-year-old man with rosy cheeks, gasped as he ran, looking back at the frozen white mask, like a death mask, that followed him.

There was a reason the Knight had picked a church, especially

9

this church, dubbed "the Church of the Presidents" because every President since James Madison had worshiped here.

It was the same with the homemade tattoo on the web of skin between his own thumb and pointer-finger. The Knight had finished the tattoo last night, using white ink since it was invisible to the naked eye. It took five needles, which he bundled together and dipped in ink, and four hours in total, puncturing his skin over and over, wiping away the blood.

The only break he took was right after he had finished the first part—the initials. Then, from his pocket, he had pulled out a yellowed deck of playing cards, thumbing past the hearts, clubs, and diamonds, stopping on...*Spades*.

In the dictionary, spades were defined as shovels. But when the four suits of cards were introduced centuries ago, each one had its own cryptic meaning. The spade wasn't a tool to dig with. It was the point of a lance.

The weapon of a knight.

"*I need help! Please...anyone!*" the rector screamed, scrambling frantically and making a sharp right through the double doors and down the long hallway that led out of the sanctuary.

The Knight's pace was perfectly steady as he followed the curved hallway back toward the church offices. His breath puffed evenly against the white plaster mask.

Up ahead, from around the corner, he heard a faint *beep-beep-boop* of a cell phone. The rector was trying to call 911.

But like his hero, who had done this so long ago, the Knight left nothing to chance. The plastic gray device in his pocket was the size of a cell phone, and could kill any cell signal in a fifty-yard radius. Cell jammers were illegal in the United States. But they cost less than $200 on a UK website.

Around the corner, where the main church offices began, there was a dull thud of a shoulder hitting wood: the rector realizing that the doorknob had been removed from the front door. Then the loud thunderclap of an office door slamming shut. The rector was hiding now, in one of the offices.

In the distance, the faint sound of police sirens was getting louder. No way was the rector able to call 911, but even if he was, the maze had nothing but dead ends left.

Looking right, then left, the Knight checked the antique parlor rooms that the church now used for AA meetings and for the "Date Night" services they held for local singles. This side of the building, known as the Parish House, was nearly as old as the church itself, but not nearly as well kept up. Throughout the main floor, every one of the tall cherry office doors was open. Except one.

With a sharp twist of the oval brass doorknob, the Knight shoved the large door open. The sirens were definitely getting louder. In the far left corner, by the bookcase, the rector was crying, still trying to pry open the room's only window, which the Knight had nailed shut hours earlier.

Moving closer, the Knight glided past a glass case, never glancing at its beautiful collection of fifty antique crosses mounted on red velvet.

"You can't do this! God will never forgive you!" the rector pleaded.

The Knight stepped toward him, taking hold of the rector's shattered shoulder. Under the mask, he rolled a butterscotch candy around his tongue. From his belt, he pulled out a knife.

One side of his blade had the words "Land of the Free/Home of the Brave," etched in acid, while the other side was etched with "Liberty/Independence." Just like the one his hero had over a century ago.

Taking a final breath that gave him a sense of weightlessness, he clenched his butterscotch candy in the vise of his back teeth.

"W-Why're you doing this?" the rector pleaded as the sirens grew deafening.

"Isn't it obvious?" The Knight raised his knife and plunged it straight into the rector's throat. The butterscotch candy cracked in half. "I'm getting ready for the President of the United States."

*   *   *

2

There are stories no one knows. Hidden stories.

I love those stories. And since I work in the National Archives, I find those stories for a living. But at 7:30 in the morning, as the elevator doors slide open and I scan the quiet fourth-floor hallway, I'm starting to realize that some of those stories are even more hidden than I thought.

"Nothing?" Tot asks, waiting for me outside our office. The way he's rolling his finger into his overgrown beard, he knows the answer.

"Less than nothing," I confirm, holding a file folder in my gloved open palms and double-checking to make sure we're alone.

Aristotle "Tot" Westman is my mentor here at the Archives, and the one who taught me that the best archivists are the ones who never stop searching. At seventy-two years old, he's had plenty of practice.

He's also the one who invited me into the Culper Ring.

The Ring was started by George Washington.

I know. I had the same reaction. But yes, *that* George Washington.

Two hundred years ago, back during the Revolutionary War, Washington built his own private spy ring. Not only did it help him win the war, but it helped protect the Presidency. The Ring still exists today, and now I'm a part of it.

"Beecher, you knew he wasn't gonna make it easy."

"I'm not asking for *easy*; I'm looking for *possible*. It's like there's nothing to find."

"There's always something to find. I promise."

"Yeah, you've been making that promise for two months now," I say, referring to how long it's been since Tot and I started coming in at 7 a.m.—before any of the other archivists show up—privately digging through every presidential file we can find.

"What'd you expect? That you can look under P and find everything you need for *Evil President*?" Tot challenges.

"Actually, *Evil President* would be filed under E."

"Not if it's his *first* name. Though it does depend on the record group," Tot clarifies, hoping the bad joke will lighten the mood. It doesn't. "The point is, Beecher, we know the hard part: We know what Wallace and Palmiotti did; we know how they did it; and when they were done with their baseball bat and razor-sharp car keys, we even know they put a young man into a permanent coma and left him to die. Now all we have to do is prove it. I'm thinking we should start picking up the pace."

As Tot says the words, he runs his fingertips down the metal strands of his bolo tie, which he doesn't realize is as socially extinct as the Scottsdale boutique where he bought it back in 1994. The thing is, I know Tot. And I know that tone.

"Why'd you just say we need to pick up the pace?" I ask.

At first, Tot stays quiet, rechecking the hallway.

"Tot, if you know something..."

"One of our guys," he begins, using that phrase he saves for when he's talking about other members of the Culper Ring. "One of them spoke to someone in the Secret Service, asking what they knew about you. And y'know what the guy in the Service said? *Nothing.* Not a sound. You know what that means, Beecher?"

"It means they're worried about me."

"No. It means the President already knows how this ends. All he's doing now is working on his cover story."

Letting the words sink in, Tot again rechecks the hallway. I tell myself the proof is still in the Archives...somewhere...in some file. It's no small haystack.

The National Archives is the storehouse for the most important items in the U.S. government, from the original Declaration of

13

Independence to Jackie Kennedy's bloody pink dress...from Reagan's original "Evil Empire" speech to the tracking maps we used to catch and kill bin Laden. Over ten billion pages strong, we house and catalog every vital file, record, and report that's produced by the government.

As I always say, that means we're a building full of secrets—especially for sitting Presidents, since we store everything from their grade school report cards, to their yearbooks, to, the theory goes, old forgotten medical records that might prove what President Wallace really did that night twenty-six years ago.

"Have you thought about ordering his marathon files?" Tot asks.

"Already did. That's what came this morning."

For two months now, we've sifted through every puzzle piece of President Wallace's medical history, from back in college when he was in ROTC, to the physical exam he took when his daughter was born and he bought his first insurance policy, to the X-rays that were taken back when he was just a governor and he ran the Marine Marathon despite having a hairline fracture in his foot. That fracture brought Wallace national attention as a politician who never quits. We were hoping it'd bring us something even better. Yet like every medical document related to the President, everything comes back empty, empty, empty.

"He can't hide it all, Beecher."

"Tell that to FDR's medical records," I reply. Tot doesn't argue. Back in 1945, forty-eight hours after Franklin Delano Roosevelt died, his medical records were stolen and destroyed. No one's found them since.

"So if Wallace's marathon X-rays were a bust, what's *that*?" Tot asks, pointing to the file folder that I'm still holding in my open palm.

"Just something I pulled from our Civil War records. A letter from Abraham Lincoln's son talking about his years in the White House." Tot knows that when I'm nervous, I like to read old history. But he also knows that nothing makes me more nervous than the most complex history of all: family history.

"Your mom called while you were down there, didn't she?" Tot asks.

I nod. After my mom's heart surgery, I asked her to call me every morning to let me know she was okay. My father died when I was three. Mom is all I've got left. But as always, it wasn't my mom who called. It was my sister Sharon, who lives with and takes care of her. Every two weeks, I send part of my check home, but it's Sharon who does the real work.

"Mom okay?" Tot asks.

"Same as always."

"Then it's time to focus on the problem you can actually deal with," Tot says, motioning toward the main door to our office and reminding me that whatever President Wallace is planning, that's where the real damage will be done. But as we step inside and I spot two men in suits standing outside my cubicle, I'm starting to think that the President's even further along than we thought.

"Beecher White?" the taller of the two asks, though the way his dark eyes lock on me, he has the answer. He's got a narrow face; his partner has a wide one that he tries to offset with a neatly trimmed goatee. Neither looks happy. Or friendly.

"That's me; I'm Beecher. And you are ...?" I ask, though neither of them answers. As Tot limps and ducks into his own cubicle, I see that both my visitors are wearing gold lapel pins with a familiar five-pointed star. Secret Service.

I glance over at Tot, who smells the same rat I do.

"You mind answering a few questions?" the agent with the narrow face asks as he flashes his badge, which says Edward Harris. Before I can answer, he adds, "You always at work this early, Mr. White?"

I have no idea where the bear trap is, but I already feel its springs tightening. Last time I saw President Wallace, I told him I'd do everything in my power to find the evidence to prove what he and his dead friend Palmiotti did. In return, the most powerful man in the world leaned forward on his big mahogany desk in the West Wing and told me, as if it were an absolute fact, that he would personally erase me from existence. So when two Secret Service agents are asking me questions before eight in the morning, I know that whatever they want, I'm in for some pain.

"I like getting in at seven," I tell the agent, though from the look on his face it isn't news to him. I make a quick mental note of every staffer and guard downstairs who saw me hunting through presidential records and might've tipped them off. "I didn't realize coming to work early was a problem."

"No problem," Agent Harris says evenly. "And what time do you usually get home? Specifically, what time did you get home last night?"

"Just past eight," I say. "If you don't believe me, ask Tot. He drove me home and dropped me off." Still standing by the door with the priceless Robert Todd Lincoln letter in my hands, I motion to Tot's cubicle.

"I appreciate that. Tot dropped you off. That means he doesn't know where you were between eight last night and about six this morning, correct?" the agent with the goatee asks, though it no longer sounds like a question.

It's the first time I notice that neither of these guys has the hand mics or ear buds that you see on the Secret Service agents around the President. These two don't do protection. They're investigators. Still, the Service's mission is to protect the President. In the Culper Ring, we protect the Presidency. It's not a small distinction.

"Were you with anyone else last night, Beecher?" Agent Harris jumps in.

From his cubicle, Tot shoots me a look. The bear trap is about to snap shut.

"Do you always wear gloves at work?" Agent Harris adds, motioning to the white cotton gloves.

"Only when I'm handling old documents," I say as I open the file folder and show them the mottled brown Robert Todd Lincoln letter that's still in my open palms. "If you don't mind..."

They step away from my cubicle, but not by much.

As I squeeze inside and carefully place the Lincoln letter on my desk, I notice the odd slant of my keyboard and how one of my piles of paper is slightly askew. They've already gone through my stuff.

"And do you take those gloves home with you?" Agent Harris asks.

"I'm sorry," I say, "but are you accusing me of something?"

They exchange glances.

"Beecher, do you know someone named Ozzie Andrews?" Agent Harris finally asks.

"Who?"

"Just tell me if you know him. Ozzie Andrews."

"With a name as silly as *Ozzie*, I'd remember if I knew him."

"So you never met him? Never heard the name?"

"What're you really asking?"

"They found a body," Agent Harris says. "A pastor in a church downtown was found murdered last night around 10 p.m. Throat slit."

"That's horrible."

"It is. Fortunately for us, just as the D.C. Police got there, they nabbed a suspect. Named Ozzie. He was strolling out the back of the church right after the murder. And when they went through Ozzie's pockets, this killer had *your* name and phone number in his wallet."

"What? That's ridiculous."

"So you don't know anything about this murder?"

"Of course not!"

There's a long pause.

"Beecher, how would you describe your opinion of President Orson Wallace?" Agent Harris interrupts.

"Excuse me?"

"We're not asking your political views. It's just, with St. John's Church being so close to the White House...you understand. We need to ask."

I turn to Tot, who doesn't just smell the rat anymore; now we see it. Two months ago, as the President buried his best friend, he swore he'd also bury me. I thought it'd come in the middle of the night with a ski mask. But I forgot who I'm dealing with. Tot said the President already had the bull's-eye on my forehead, then suddenly two Secret Service guys show up? This is Wallace's real revenge: Tie me to a murder, send in the Service, and keep your manicured hands clean as they snap my mugshot.

"Where is this Ozzie guy now?" I ask. "I'd like to know who he is."

"I'm sorry, I didn't realize suspects get to make their own demands."

"So now I'm a suspect? Fine, then let me face my accuser. Is he still in jail?"

For the first time, both agents go silent.

"What, you let him go?" I ask.

Again, silence.

"So you found the murder suspect and already let him walk? And now you think you can come here and pin it on me? Sorry, but unless you're here to arrest me, we're done."

"Can you just answer one last—?"

"Done. Goodbye," I say, pointing them to the door. For thirty seconds, they stand there, just to make it clear that it's their choice to leave, not mine.

As the door slams behind them, I hear Tot whispering behind me.

"You're the best, Mac. I appreciate it," he says from his cubicle.

It's the first time I realize Tot's been on the phone the entire time, and when I hear the name *Mac*, I realize how much danger I'm really in.

When George Washington first created the Culper Ring, he picked regular, ordinary people because no one looks twice at them. His only other rule was this: that even he should never know the names of all the members. That way, if one of them got caught passing information, the enemy would never be able to track the others.

That's the real reason why the Culper Ring has been able to exist to this very day—and why they've had a hand in everything from the Revolutionary War, to Hiroshima, to the Bay of Pigs. Before the OSS, or the CIA, these guys wrote the book on keeping secrets. So when it comes to other Culper members, there's only one besides

Tot that I've met face-to-face. He's a doctor; they call him *The Surgeon*. That's it, no name. He took four pints of my blood in case of emergency. But there's one other member I've been warned about.

Tot calls him *Mac*—which is short for *The Immaculate Deception*—which is short for *when it comes to hacking, if we need something, Mac's the one who'll get it.* The only thing he asks in return is that we buy Girl Scout cookies from his niece.

"You owe me another box of Samoas," Mac says through Tot's cell.

"Y'mean Caramel deLites," Tot says.

"I don't care if they changed the name. They're Samoas to me," Mac says in the text-to-speech voice generator that draws out every syllable in the word *sa-mo-as* and makes him sound like a 1960s robot.

No one's ever heard his real voice.

From what Tot says, Mac was one of the Seven. In case of a national emergency, if the Internet and our computer infrastructure go down, seven people in the U.S. government have the capability to put it back up again. Five of the seven need to be present to do it. Mac, before he left the government behind, used to be one of them.

Cool story, right? It's not the only one. According to the Surgeon, Mac isn't a retired tech genius. He's a nineteen-year-old social misfit who, like every talented hacker who gets *caught* by the U.S. government, is hired to *work for* the U.S. government. The Girl Scout cookies are really for his sister.

I don't care which story is true. All I care is that when trouble hits, no one's faster than the Immaculate Deception.

Tot hands me his phone over the cubicle partition. Onscreen is a photo of a man with buzzed black hair, standing against a light gray wall. My accuser Ozzie's mugshot. He looks about my age, but it's hard to tell since his face…his right eye sags slightly, making him look permanently sleepy—and the way his face is lumpy, like it's coated with a shiny putty…I think he's a burn victim.

Then I notice his eyes. They're pale gold like the color of white wine.

19

Behind me, the door to our office opens as one of our fellow employees arrives. I barely hear it. My skin goes so cold, it feels like it's about to crack off my body.

There's only one person I know with gold eyes. And as I study the photo, as I look past the burns...No. It's impossible. It can't be him.

But I know it is.

Marshall.

3

Twenty years ago
Sagamore, Wisconsin

Marshall didn't hear the rip.

Like any fifth-grade boy, he was moving too fast as he kicked open the passenger door. Even in the small and usually slow town of Sagamore, even before his dad put the car in park, Marshall was out in the cold, racing around to the back of the car and using all his strength to pull his dad's wheelchair from the trunk.

Barely ten years old, the youngest in his grade, Marshall was always told he was chubby, not fat—that his weight was perfect, but his height just needed to catch up. He believed it too, anxiously awaiting the day that God would even things out and make him more like his fellow fifth graders: tall like Vincent or skinny like Beecher.

Marshall was a polite kid—almost to a fault—with a mom so strict she taught him that if he had to pass gas, he had to leave the room. Discipline ran deep in the Lusk household, and the central discipline was taking care of Dad.

"At your service, sir," Marshall announced, making the joke his dad always cringed at as he rolled the wheelchair to the driver's-side door.

"On C," his father said, turning his body and giving the signal for Marshall to lock the chair's wheels and hold it in place. "A...B..."

"C...!" Marshall and his dad said simultaneously. Marshall's father used all the strength in his arms to pivot out of the driver's seat, toward the wheelchair, swinging what was left of his legs through the air.

In medical terms, Timothy Lusk was a double amputee. On the night of the accident, as he drove his pregnant wife to the hospital, a brown minivan that was being driven by a woman in the midst of an epileptic fit plowed into their car. Blessedly, Marshall was born without a scratch. Timothy's wife, Cherise, was fine too. The doctors cut off Timothy's crushed legs just below the knees.

"Careful..." Marshall said as his dad's full weight tumbled from the car and collided with the wheelchair. He hated it when his dad rushed, but his father was always annoyed and impatient at being cooped up in snowy weather. Even though neighbors helped to shovel the Lusks' walk, it didn't mean they could shovel the entire town. For anyone in a wheelchair, winter was a bitch.

"Are you holding it?" his dad barked as his landing in the seat sent the chair skidding back slightly, sliding across the last bits of slush on the ground. The stump of his left leg slammed into the metal base of the armrest.

"I got it," Marshall called back, readjusting his thick glasses and maneuvering the chair to mount the curb. Twenty years from now, every new street would be outfitted with a curb cut, and wheelchairs would weigh barely twelve pounds. But on this day, in Sagamore, Wisconsin, the curbs were unbroken and the wheelchairs weighed fifty.

In one quick motion, Marshall's father popped a wheelie that tipped him back.

Gripping the wheelchair's pushbars, Marshall angled the front wheels onto the curb. Now came the hard part. Marshall wasn't strong, and he was overweight, but he knew what to do. With his palms underneath the pushbars, he shoved and lifted, gritting his teeth. His father pumped the wheels, trying to help. Marshall's palms went red, with little islands of white where the pushbars dug in. It took everything they had...

Kuunk.

No problem. Up the curb, easy as pie.

"Galactic," Marshall muttered.

From there, as his dad rolled in front of him, there was no plan for where they were going. His father just wanted *out*—strolling down the main drag of Dickinson Street…an egg sandwich at Danza's…maybe a stop in Farris's bookshop. But all that changed when Marshall's father said, "I gotta go."

"Whattya mean?" Marshall asked. "Go where?"

"I gotta *go*," he said, pointing down. But it was the sudden panic in his father's voice that set Marshall off.

"You gotta poop?" Marshall asked.

"No! I gotta *pee*."

"So don't you…?" Marshall paused, feeling a rush of blood flush his face. "I-Isn't that what the bag's for…?" he asked, tapping the outside of his own left thigh, but motioning to the leg bag his father wore to urinate.

"It ripped," his father said, scanning the empty street and still trying so hard to keep his voice down. "My bag ripped."

"How could it rip? We haven't even—" Marshall stopped, glancing back at their car. "You tore it when you got out of the car, didn't you?"

Racing behind his dad and grabbing the pushbars, he added, "Now we gotta get back in the car and go all the way home…"

"I won't make it home."

Marshall froze. "Wha?"

His father stopped the wheelchair, keeping his head down and his back to his son. He'd say these words once, but he wouldn't say them again: "I can't make it, Marshall. I'm gonna have an accident."

Marshall's mouth gaped open, but no words came out. For most of his life, because of the wheelchair, he had been nearly at eye level with his father. But he'd never noticed it until this moment.

"I can help you, Dad." Grabbing the pushbars, Marshall spun the wheelchair around, running hard up the sidewalk. The closest store was Lester's clothing store.

His father was silent. But Marshall saw the way he was shifting uncomfortably in his seat.

"Almost there," Marshall promised, running hard, his head tucked down like a charging bull.

There was a loud *krunk* as the legs of the metal wheelchair collided with the concrete step.

"*I need help! Open up!*" Marshall shouted, rapping his fist against Lester's glass door. The small bell that announced each customer rang lightly at the impact.

"Dad, tip *back!*" Marshall yelled as Dad popped a wheelie, and one of the employees, a thirtysomething woman with bad teeth and perfectly straight brown hair, opened the store's front door.

"It's an emergency! Grab the front of the chair!" Marshall yelled as the woman obliged, bending down. He jammed his own palms underneath the pushbars. "On C..." he added. "A...B..."

There was another loud *krunk* as the back wheels of the chair climbed the first step, wedging just below the second.

"Almost there! Just one more!" Marshall said.

"I'm not gonna make it," his father insisted.

"You'll make it, Dad. I promise, you'll make it!"

"Sir, you need to stop moving," the employee added, getting ready to lift again.

"Here we go," Marshall insisted, his voice cracking. "Last one. On C...!"

"Marsh, I'm sorry...I can't."

"You can, Dad! *On C...!*" Marshall pleaded.

His father shook his head, his eyes welling with tears. As he clutched the armrests of his chair, his hands were shaking, like he was trying to claw his way out of his skin...out of the chair...Like he was trying to run from his own body.

"A...B..."

With one final *krunk*, the wheelchair slammed and bounced over the store's threshold, a wave of warmth embracing them as they rolled inside.

In front of them, Marshall saw a crush of customers, almost all of them moms with kids, weaving between the rows of clothes racks, all closing in on them.

It was all okay.

"Hold on, I think something spilled," the employee announced.

The sound was unmistakable. A steady patter that drummed against the wood floor. When he heard it, Marshall didn't look down. He couldn't.

"Oh God," the employee blurted. "Is that—?"

"Pee-pee..." A five-year-old girl began to giggle, pointing at the small puddle growing beneath Marshall's father's chair.

From where he was standing, behind the wheelchair as he clutched the pushbars to keep standing, Marshall could see only the back of his father. For years, he had wondered how tall his dad actually was. But at this exact moment, as his father shrank down into his seat, urine still running down and dripping off the stump of his leg, Marshall knew that his father would never look smaller.

"Here..." a quick-thinking customer called out, pulling tissues from her purse. Marshall knew her. She worked with his mom at the church. The wife of Pastor Riis; everyone called her Cricket. "Here, Marshall, let us help you..."

In a blur of guilt and kindness, every employee and customer in the shop was doing the same, throwing paper towels on the mess, making small talk, and pretending this kind of thing happened all the time. Sagamore was still a small town. A church town. A town that, ever since the Lusks' accident, always looked out for Marshall...and his mom...and especially for his poor dad in that wheelchair.

But as the swell of women closed in around him, Marshall wasn't looking at his father, or the puddle of urine. The only thing he saw was the blond boy with the messy mop of hair staring at him from the corner of the store, back by one of the sale racks.

It was one thing to be mortified in front of a roomful of strangers. It was quite another to be mortified in front of someone you know.

"Marshall, we called your mom. She's on her way," the pastor's wife leaned in and told him.

Marshall nodded, pretending all was okay. But he never took his eyes off the blond boy in the corner—his fellow fifth grader named Beecher, who wouldn't look away.

There was concern and sadness in Beecher's eyes. There was empathy too. But all Marshall saw was the pity.

4

Today
Washington, D.C.

W ait, you know him?" Tot asks as I stand in his cubicle, staring down at Marshall's mugshot. My legs are stiff, my body's numb, and my skin feels like all the blood in my veins suddenly went solid.

"Beecher—"

"His name's not Ozzie. It's Marsh. Marshall. In seventh grade, we used to call him Marshmallow."

"When was the last time you saw him?"

"Not since junior high."

"And did he know *her*?" Tot asks.

I look up from the phone. I thought this was a trap by the President. But from Tot's question, he's also worried it's a trap by *her*—the other person who happens to come from our small town.

Clementine.

My childhood crush, my first kiss, and the girl who, two months ago, was the one who uncovered the President's ruthless attack and tried to blackmail him with it.

I know. I need better taste in women.

"You think Clementine—?"

The door to our office opens behind us. The other archivists are starting to arrive. I scratch the back of my blond hair and hold up a finger. Time to take this outside. As we head back into the hallway, it's now swirling with the morning crowds. The Secret Service

26

agents are long gone, but we both stay silent, beelining for the metal door that takes us into the dark library stacks at the heart of the National Archives. Motion sensor lights pop on, following us as we pass row after row of book-filled shelves.

"You think Clementine had something to do with this murder?" I ask, still keeping my voice down as I make a sharp left, following behind Tot as he stops at our usual hiding spot, a rusty metal table at the end of the row.

"She had something to do with the last one, didn't she?" Tot asks. "Last time she showed up, she used your access at the Archives to blackmail President Wallace. Then she shot and killed Palmiotti, disappeared with the proof of the President's attack, and nearly destroyed your life in the process. You really want to see what she does for an encore?"

"You don't know there's an encore."

"Beecher, her father is Nico Hadrian," he says, referring to the assassin who once tried to put a bullet in a President and now has a permanent room at St. Elizabeths mental institution. "You know Clementine's coming back. She knows about the Culper Ring. So if she's still going after the President—"

"She didn't *go after* him. She was blackmailing him for information about her dad."

"And you believe that? Didn't she also say she was dying of some newly discovered cancer, and that your own dead father is actually alive?"

"She was lying about my father!"

"I know she was, and I also know how much that one hurt. Clementine isn't just a manipulator, Beecher—she's a hunter, no different than her dad. She went after the President, she killed Palmiotti, and she'll happily do it again. The only reason she reached out to you is because she needed a fall guy. Just like now," Tot says, his gray beard glowing in the darkness of the stacks. "C'mon, you knew it was just a matter of time. Clementine wasn't blackmailing the President for money. She wanted information about her own dad, which you know she's still craving. So if she's trying to offer something to the President, or simply to take a crack at you for stopping her last time, wouldn't this be the perfect way to do it: help the President get you caught up in a murder that you can't get out of? All she has to do is connect with her old friend Marshall—"

"They're not old friends," I say.

"They didn't know each other?"

"If they did, they weren't close."

Tot thinks on this, digesting the information. "You do realize that your hometown is full of crazy people, right?"

I nod, still holding Tot's phone and staring down at Marshall's mugshot. From the puttylike texture that makes his face droop, to the way his right eye sags, Marsh looks at least ten years older than me. And the victim of ten times the suffering.

"So if Clementine doesn't have a hand in it, you think the President put Marshall up to this?" Tot asks.

"I have no idea. All I know is, two minutes after you tell me the President's about to kick me in the face, I'm suddenly being accused of a crime that should be handled by the D.C. Police, but is magically in the hands of the Secret Service. And did you hear what those agents said? The cops arrested Marshall for murder, but he's somehow already out on the street? Doesn't that seem a little smelly to you?"

"Maybe he posted bail?" Tot offers.

"He didn't post bail," a robotic voice says through Tot's phone. Immaculate Deception.

I shoot Tot a look. "You let him listen the entire time?"

"There's no record of bail being posted," Mac interrupts. "All it says is *released*. Either they had nothing on him, or Marshall's got big friends who don't mind calling in big favors."

Tot doesn't have to say it. This is it. The President's hitting back.

When I started at the Archives, I learned that good archivists follow the rules, while great archivists follow their hunch.

"They said he killed a preacher?" I ask, still staring down at Marsh's mugshot.

"Yeah, with your name in his pocket. Why?"

"No reason."

Tot's blind in one eye, but he still sees all. "Beecher, I know that look. And I know that brain of yours never lets anything go—it's what makes you a great archivist. But whatever you're thinking with Marshall, you need to stop remembering. This isn't your childhood friend anymore."

Of course, Tot's right. I look at Marsh's burned face now, almost like a mask. Then my mind flips back to Wisconsin, scouring old memories and searching for connections. Maybe this is another trap by Clementine. Or the President, who wants to shut me up and still blames me for the death of his best friend. Or maybe he's after the Culper Ring. But as Marsh's dead eyes stare back at me—

"I can get us into the crime scene," Immaculate Deception announces through Tot's phone.

He acts like it's good news. And it is. The more information, the better. But in my head, I'm still replaying Tot's earlier warning: that the President already knows how this ends. So as we rush out of the stacks and the automatic lights pop on in our wake, I can't shake the feeling that everything we're now doing...

...is exactly what the President wants.

5

There's a band of yellow police tape covering the side door. Tot's too old to duck under it. He tugs it aside, letting it flap in the air like the tail of a kite. I follow slowly behind him, into the scene of the crime.

As we enter St. John's Church, it looks like an old colonial house filled with office furniture.

"Y'mind signing in for me?" a friendly voice calls out.

On our right, a guy with tightly cropped blond hair and an athletic build that stretches his dark suit approaches us with such an authoritative stride that even Tot takes a step back.

"We're here to see Hayden Donius," Tot says, though I don't recognize the name.

"Just sign in. Clipboard's over there," he says, pointing to an antique side table, his arm muscles flexing from the motion. "Here's a pen; don't steal it," he jokes, shoving a blue-and-orange University of Virginia pen into Tot's hands.

In a blur, he's gone, leaving Tot and me alone with...

"Hayden Donius..." a tall man with a soft voice and an out-of-date, gray, three-piece suit says. With an anxious both-hands handshake, he introduces himself as the executive director of the church. "And you're the friend of—"

Tot nods, cutting him off. The two men exchange a long glance, and I remember what Tot said when he first invited me into the Culper Ring. Their membership is small, but their friends are many.

"I-I truly...we appreciate you coming..." Hayden says, his voice shaky as Tot breezes past the side table, ignoring the sign-in sheet and eyeing the wide window on our right.

I see what Tot's looking at. Through the window, past the barren trees of Lafayette Park, there's a perfect view of the city's most famous landmark. The White House. Home of President Orson Wallace.

"Pretty darn close to the murder," I say with a glance.

Tot nods, well aware of how fishy this is—and how familiar.

Two months ago, it was Clementine. Today, it's Marshall. Two murderers, both from my same tiny hometown, and both this close to the President of the United States. It gets even worse when I think about how fast they let Marshall out of jail even though he's supposedly a murder suspect. Even if Tot didn't tell me the President was gunning for me, how many people have pull like that?

"We should get started," Tot says, knowing that the only way to stop the President is to prove what he's really doing.

Leading us inside, Hayden looks tired, like he's been up all night.

I glance around. There are barely six offices in the entire church. This place is small. The rector who had his throat slashed wasn't just some coworker. He was Hayden's friend.

"Sorry, fellas," a young black policeman says as we approach the office at the end of the main hall. "Detectives said no one gets inside until they're back from lunch and the techs are done."

"But that's my office," Hayden protests. "I need to be able to do my job."

The officer nods but doesn't budge. "They say *no one*, they mean *no one*. I don't make the rules until they give me the suit and tie."

He waits for us to argue, but from our spot near the doorway, we can see everything inside: Two evidence technicians—one Asian, one bald—flit around the office, making notes and taking a few final photographs. In the corner, a few yellow plastic evidence placards are marked with a directional arrow that shows the blood spatter sprayed across the bookcase and the window. That's where the killer slit the rector's throat.

It's all in the police report that Mac got for us on the way here. One shot in the back; throat slashed in the front. Hayden heads up the hallway toward the actual church and pews, but it's not until we reach a set of open double doors, with a strip of yellow police tape across them, that he suddenly slows down.

To bring us in here, he's breaking the rules. Breaking the law. Luckily, he knows that some things are more important.

"Promise you'll be fast," he begs as I lift the police tape and rush inside. The ceiling rises, revealing ornate balconies, the wide dome, and the stained glass windows that fill the Church of the Presidents with a kaleidoscope of morning light. The room stretches back with half a football field worth of pews, but it's the familiar church smell of rose candles, old books, and stale air that takes me back to childhood and fills me with memories of my own dead father.

"They think the killer started here," Hayden says, leading us up the aisle. On both sides of us, on the armrest of each pew, a small gold plate identifies donors. Every pew is spoken for, except for the one that's about a third of the way from the altar: Pew 54. The gold pew plate reads simply, *The President's Pew*.

"I'm surprised the President doesn't sit in the front row," Tot says.

"Blame James Madison," Hayden explains. "When he was President, they gave him first dibs on one of the pews, but he said, 'Pick one for me.' So they put him as a person of the people. Right in the middle, like everyone else."

"And President Wallace abides by that?" I ask.

"He's only been here once. Some leaders worship more than others. But even Presidents want to be a part of history." As he says the words, he points inside the pew. On the floor, there are four kneelers with needlepoint cushions for people to pray on. Each cushion has a different name in bright gold letters: *George W. Bush. Barack Obama. Leland Manning.* And an ancient one—the very first one from two hundred years ago—that says *James Madison.*

"Where's the one for President Wallace?"

"You only get it when you leave office," Hayden says, still anxious to keep us moving as he strides toward the back of the room. In every pew are more kneelers. Ronald Reagan. Woodrow Wilson.

Bill Clinton. Harry Truman. At one point in time, every single one of them came into this room and bent a knee to God. It should be humbling. But as I picture our current President—and the power he threatened to level against me—I don't even want to think about it.

As we reach the very last row, the last two pews are roped off by more police tape, where the killer took his first shot at the rector. More placards with little arrows on them mark the blood spatter along the pews and wood floor. This time, though, I know the pew we're looking at—the one that's more famous than all the others combined.

The Lincoln Pew.

It's the last pew, the very last row. Back in the 1860s, Lincoln used to walk across the street from the White House, sneak into this pew in the back, and then disappear before the church service was over. The gold plaque on the wall reads: *He was always alone.*

"So the killer shot at the rector from this pew?" Tot asks.

Hayden says something, but I don't hear it. I study the pew... the wooden bench... the hardwood floor. But the closer I look... Something's not right.

"Okay, you've seen the pew. Now can we go?" Hayden begs.

I don't move.

"Beecher, what's wrong?" Tot asks. "You see something?"

I don't answer.

Next to me, Tot rolls the pen he's still holding against the tip of his beard. Following my sightline, his good eye scrolls along the bench, up to the stained glass window that hangs above it, then over to the back wall of the church, which is flush with the back of the pew. He still doesn't see it.

"We need to go," Hayden says. "The detectives made me call all our employees. They said everyone had to stay home, so if they find you here..."

"Hayden, I need two minutes," I tell him.

"You said you'd be quick!" Hayden says to Tot.

"*Hayden,*" I bark, raising my voice just enough that he turns my way. "Listen to me. Do you know who Joseph B. Stewart is?"

Hayden pauses, confused. "Who?" he asks, checking over his shoulder. "Is that a congregant?"

"*Listen to me,*" I insist. "On the night that Lincoln was shot in Ford's Theatre, Joseph B. Stewart was the only member of the audience who actually got up out of his seat and chased after John Wilkes Booth. Think of it a moment. The President is dying. A single metal ball is shot into Lincoln's brain and lodges behind his right eye. Of course, hundreds of people start screaming, but in that moment, Joseph B. Stewart keeps his wits, gets up from his front-row seat, and jumps across the orchestra pit to try to grab Booth as the assassin darts across the stage. Stewart actually hopped across the chair tops as he ran after him. And yes, Booth got away. But for those first days after the shooting, it was Joseph B. Stewart who was America's hero."

"I don't see your point," Hayden says.

"The point is, he's now forgotten by history, but when he was faced with that challenge, he did *what was right*. So now it's your turn, Hayden. I need two minutes here. You really want to kick us out?"

Hayden stands there, motionless, digesting every word.

"Just please…" Hayden begs, once again checking over his shoulder. "Be quick."

6

I dart toward the back of the church and head past the police-taped area, into the small anteroom that leads out to the public entrance.

"Beecher...!" Tot calls out, speed-limping behind me.

I don't slow down.

"Beecher...will you—? What'd you find?"

"Tot, on the night of Lincoln's assassination in Ford's Theatre, John Wilkes Booth didn't just come in and pull the trigger. Tell me what you know about the precautions he took."

He knows the story. "He drilled a hole in the door."

"Exactly. Hours before the play started, Booth went up to Lincoln's box and drilled a peephole in the right side of the door so he could see inside and make sure there were no guards. And what else?" I ask.

"He took a long, narrow piece of pine—the neck of an old music stand—and he hid it in the box so that once he was inside, he could use it to bar the door."

"And what about the weapons?"

"Forty-four caliber, single-shot Derringer pistol. But since it only had that one shot, he also brought a knife that—" Tot cuts himself off, knowing what it said about the rector in the police report. Shot once in the back; throat slit in the front. "Wait. You really think—?"

"Look for yourself," I say, reaching up toward an old framed watercolor that hangs on the wall. The picture shows the church back when it and the White House were the only two buildings on the block. But as I pull the frame from the wall...

There it is.

35

Just under the nail that holds the picture in place is a small round peephole. Even from here, I can tell it goes through the wall and into the Lincoln Pew.

"That's when I started looking for *this*..." I add, pointing to the church's main doors—and the metal urn that serves as an umbrella stand. There are two stray umbrellas in there. Plus one long, narrow piece of pine.

"Oh my," Hayden whispers.

"So you think your friend is a John Wilkes Booth copycat?" Tot asks.

I stay silent, still sifting through the details. Between the time of death...the way it was set up...and all that preparation to make it just right... This is more than a copycat. This is a full-on *re-creation*. And if it's a re-creation...

No.

Pulling out my phone, I scroll through my emails.

Tot watches me carefully, tapping the pen against his beard. "Beecher, tell me what you're not saying."

"On that night that John Wilkes Booth pulled the trigger, every single detail—large or small—is accounted for," I say, still scrolling through my phone. "How Booth planned it...the coconspirators he worked with...the type of drink he had at the saloon next door..."

"Whiskey with water," Tot says.

"But what's the one detail, the only one in nearly a hundred and fifty years that no one—and I mean *no one*—can account for?"

Tot doesn't even pause. "How Booth got past the White House valet."

"Bingo. How Booth got past the White House valet."

Reading the confused look on Hayden's face, I explain, "Back then, security in Ford's Theatre was beyond pathetic. The police officer who was supposed to be guarding Lincoln's private box actually left his post so he could get a better view of the play. So when Booth finally made his way up there, the only one standing guard was Charles Forbes, Lincoln's White House valet. Historians agree that, at that moment, Booth stopped and spoke to the valet. They agree that Booth showed the valet a card. But the one thing no one knows is what was on the card. What'd Booth show him? What'd it say?"

"Some say it was a letter," Tot points out. "Others say it was Booth's business card, which, since he was a famous actor, would certainly open doors."

"But again, the reason the valet stepped aside and let Booth into Lincoln's private box was because of whatever was on that magic card."

Tot knows me long enough to know I'm not done.

"Don't tell me you know what's on that card, Beecher."

I shoot him a look, motioning down to my phone. "Remember that thing that they found in the suspect's pocket?"

He nods. I'm talking about Marshall having my name and phone number.

"Well, I take notice when people have that on them. So when we were driving here, I had Mac send me the full list of his belongings. Look what else he had with him . . ."

I push a button on the phone, and an image pops open onscreen. I hold it up to Tot, making sure he gets a good look.

Tot squints. Hayden leans in.

"Old playing cards?" Hayden asks.

"A full deck of them," I say. "Nineteenth-century, from the look of them."

"I still don't see what this had to do with John Wilkes Booth's mystery card."

"Well, God bless the D.C. Police for cataloging each and every item, because when I went through their full list, there was actually one card missing from the deck: the ace of spades."

7

B eecher, you lost me," Tot says.

"The deck of cards," I say. "It's missing its ace of spades. He's carrying a deck of cards where one card is missing!"

"Okay, so unless we're fighting the Riddler, is that supposed to mean something?"

"Look around . . . !" I say, pointing from the peephole, to the pine bar in the umbrella stand. "This guy—"

"You mean Marshall."

"We don't know it's Marshall. But whoever he is, he's meticulously re-created every last detail of Abraham Lincoln's murder, which, let's be clear, only happened because John Wilkes Booth was let inside the building after flashing some mysterious long-lost card. And now the one guy we're looking at happens to be carrying, of all things . . . long-lost cards."

"Can I just say," Hayden interrupts, still struggling to follow, "even if this is the historical card you're speaking of, who would he even give it to? The church was locked last night. No one was here."

"What about this morning?" I ask. "He could've left it for someone. Were you the first one in?"

"I'm always the first one in. And I told you, when they called me last night, I notified every employee and asked them all to stay home today."

"What about the guy with the sign-in sheet?" I ask.

"Excuse me?" Hayden says.

"When we walked in . . . the guy . . . the one in the cheap suit . . ." Tot says, holding up the pen he gave him. "He told me we had to sign in."

"I thought he was—" Hayden stops. "Hold on. He's not a detective?"

My shirt sticks to my chest. "They said all the detectives were at lunch," I point out.

Tot looks down at the pen. I'm not sure what he's staring at. I may know Lincoln history, but he's been at this far longer than I have. On a hunch, he unscrews the pen as fast as he can. The front half holds the thin metal pen tube. But in the back half...there's a small red wire connected to an even smaller transmitter. A microphone. We've been holding a microphone the entire time.

Tot shoots me a look.

I run full speed, racing back down the aisle of the church and toward the staff offices in back. Whoever this guy is, he couldn't have gotten far.

8

*W*hen we walked in . . . the guy . . . the one in the cheap suit . . ." the older man known as Tot said. *"He told me we had to sign in."*

"I thought he was— Hold on. He's not a detective?"

Crossing through the slush on H Street and entering the well-plowed edges of Lafayette Park, Secret Service agent A.J. Ennis kept his pace slow and steady, barely even registering the "cheap suit" comment. Instead, following his training and staying focused on the problem at hand, he turned up the volume on the thin receiver that was tucked into his jacket pocket.

For A.J., it was simple enough to slip them the pen with the transmitter. He'd actually stolen the idea from an overwrought mystery novel he read a few years back where some plucky investigator did the same.

In the novel, the investigator saved the day and, naturally, rode off into the sunset. But A.J. knew that life, especially his current life, was no longer that simple.

"Dammit," he muttered to himself, seeing the *No Signal* message on the receiver and running his hand along the back of his buzzed blond hair. They had found the transmitter. Most people never found it, which told A.J. that what they warned him about was right. Beecher and Tot weren't novices. But then again, neither was A.J.

There was a reason A.J. had been sent to the church. It was the same reason A.J. was the one who accompanied President Orson Wallace out to Camp David, and on that off-the-record visit back in Ohio that tested his loyalty to the President. Luckily for A.J., he had passed.

It wasn't all luck, of course. As a kid in Johnson City, Tennessee, A.J. Ennis used to dream of being Jacques Cousteau. But when his father got sick and his mother went bankrupt, young A.J.'s dreams became far more realistic.

Not for long. After Business School at Duke and three tedious years as an investment banker, the explorer once again reemerged, knowing that there were more exciting things to chase than money. As he applied for the Secret Service, luck had nothing to do with his getting hired or promoted, or how quickly he made his way over to the President's Protective Detail. The Service knows talent when it sees it.

What it didn't know was that thirty years ago, A.J.'s father was one of President Orson Wallace's dearest friends from law school. A.J. never pointed out the connection or took advantage of it, but he knew it made him lucky.

It made the President's best friend, Dr. Stewart Palmiotti, even luckier, since after the funeral, A.J. was the one who helped Palmiotti set up his new identity.

Yet the luckiest of all?

A.J.'s phone vibrated in his pocket. Caller ID said "King's Copiers," a copy shop in Maryland that had closed at least two years ago. Maybe even three.

"A.J. here," he said, picking up.

There was silence on the other end.

"You were right about the church," A.J. said.

There was no reply.

"They're both there. I saw him. It was definitely Beecher." Before another bit of silence hit, A.J. added, "I know it's not ideal, sir. But it doesn't mean it's a total disaster. We can still—"

There was a click. The President of the United States hung up.

With a flurry of tapping, A.J. dialed another number.

The phone rang once...twice...

Palmiotti picked up without even saying hello. "Where've you been?" he asked. "Do you need me down there? I can be there in—"

"Don't come down here."

"But I can—"

A.J. wanted to scream at him. But in these past few months, he knew what Palmiotti had been through, and what he'd sacrificed to keep their secret safe. With the fake funeral, Palmiotti now had a second chance. That's how he saw it. This was his chance to make it all right.

That didn't mean it was easy. The physical recovery took longer than expected; Clementine had shot him straight through the neck. Plus, there was that incident when he asked if he could contact Lydia—his girlfriend—to say a more proper goodbye. But A.J. knew how Palmiotti was when it came to President Wallace. Palmiotti didn't just *love* Wallace. He *needed* him. That was the right word. *Need*. And the President needed him back.

"We can definitely use your help. He needs your help," A.J. said, leaning hard on the word *He*.

"And he'll have it. I can fix it," Palmiotti promised.

"That's what you said a week ago."

Palmiotti stopped at that. "So the church— Is it really that bad?"

"Bad enough that *he* called *me*."

"He called *you*?"

"Look around, Doc," A.J. said, standing at the southern end of Lafayette Park and turning from the tall marble columns of the White House, back toward the double-tiered bell tower of St. John's Church. "Do you have any idea what you've unleashed?"

9

orget it, Beecher. He's long gone," Tot says, slowly making his
way down the brick steps to join me outside. Up the block,
there's nothing but passing cars along H Street.

"You think he's our killer?"

Tot shakes his head. "Sneaking back into his own crime scene
with cops in the building? Even crazy people aren't that crazy."

"So he's police?"

"He's a fed. Or something worse. Look," he says, tossing me the
two pieces of the microphone pen. "Motion-activated so it doesn't
need a battery. Hairline mic that amplifies through the pen chamber. You don't buy that at the local spy shop."

"Fed money," a mechanical voice says through Tot's speakerphone. I didn't realize his phone was even on, much less that
Immaculate Deception was listening in. "Ask Santa. I bet he can
tell us where it's from."

Two weeks back, I heard them mention *Santa*. At first, I thought
Tot was being facetious. But I'm thinking I just found another
Culper Ring member: Santa, the guy who brings them the best
high-tech toys.

"Mac," I call out, "how many Thin Mints will it cost me to have
you look up details on my old friend Marshall?"

"I've been looking since you found that John Wilkes Booth
peephole. You're a bigger nerd than I thought, by the way. Nice job,
though," Mac replies. "Marshall's got no credit cards...no phone
records...and he files his tax return through a P.O. box. Guy definitely likes his privacy."

"What about his cell phone?" Tot asks.

"Already tried. He's using a Trustchip."

"What's a Trustchip?" I ask.

"Encrypted. Expensive. Usually for big companies or government contractors," Mac explains. "Whoever he is, he's not playing around. I can't see calls or messages in or out."

"Can't you just turn on the phone's speaker and we'll listen in?" Tot asks.

"Checked that too. Headphone in."

It was the first trick Mac taught me when they brought me into the Culper Ring: In any smartphone, it's easy for someone to remotely turn on your speakerphone. But if you want to thwart it, you plug something into the headphone jack since speakers get disabled when headphones are enabled.

"What about a home address?" I ask.

"Apartment in Crystal City, Virginia."

"Then there we go," I say. "Next stop: Crystal City."

"And that's your big idea? Just walk up to Marshall and ask him if he's the murderer?" Tot asks.

I shake my head. I haven't seen Marshall in over a decade. I have no idea if he's working with Clementine, or the President, or even if he's the one imitating John Wilkes Booth. But right now a man is dead—and since it was my name that was found in Marshall's pocket, I'm now tied to whatever the hell is really going on here.

"I know there's something you're not saying about this guy, Beecher. And I appreciate you trying to be proactive, but if Marshall's our killer, he's gonna be dangerous. You can't just go knock on his front door."

I totally agree. "Who says we're gonna knock?"

PART II

The Second Assassination

"I thank you, doctor, but I am a dead man."

—President James Garfield, while being treated on the floor of the train station where the assassin, Charles Guiteau, shot him in the back

He was the second President murdered in office.

10

President Garfield was scheduled to be on the 9:30 a.m. train. Like most Presidents, he was running behind schedule. It was hot in Washington—every summer was always brutal in its own way—and on top of that, Garfield was exhausted. Though he'd spent barely four months in office, he already knew it was hard being President.

And so he was making this train trip. His first stop would be at his alma mater, Williams College, to attend commencement. And then he was heading to northern New England for a well-earned vacation.

He never made it out of the station.

At 9:20, his carriage pulled up to the Baltimore & Potomac Railroad Depot at what is currently Constitution and 6th Street in downtown D.C. Behind him, in a second carriage, were his two sons, Harry and Jim.

Realizing he had a few minutes, Garfield decided to stay in the carriage, catching up with his friend and secretary of state, James Blaine. During the election of 1880, both Blaine and Garfield were among the Republican nominees, but it was Garfield who was picked as the true compromise candidate—the man who would unite the various party factions.

As they sat there in the carriage, Blaine was calm, playing with his cane and tossing it over and over in the air. At the time, the

Secret Service wasn't in charge of presidential protection yet. With his top hat and gray traveling suit, the President eventually stepped down from the carriage, leading his friend and family into the station.

Inside, among the Cabinet members who were waiting to see him off was Robert Todd Lincoln, the eldest son of the first slain President.

Entering the nearly empty station with a few minutes to spare, President James Garfield was calm. He was relaxed. And he had no idea that a slight five-foot-five-inch man named Charles Guiteau had arrived an hour earlier and was hiding in the washroom.

Unlike John Wilkes Booth, Guiteau wasn't an actor. He hadn't prepared any final, memorable lines.

Waiting for the President to pass, Guiteau was silent as the two-hundred-pound commander in chief marched through the station. Without a word, Guiteau rushed the President from behind, pulled out the small, snub-nosed British Bulldog pistol that he'd bought a month earlier, and fired at the President's back.

The first shot seemed to graze Garfield's arm, so Guiteau stepped closer and fired again.

That shot hit President Garfield in the back, above the waist. The President sank to the floor. His top hat was crushed, his gray traveling suit covered in blood.

Still silent, the assassin Guiteau tucked his gun into his pocket and walked quickly to the exit. Outside, a D.C. cop heard the two shots. Racing to investigate, the officer yanked open the door just as Guiteau slammed into him. The officer didn't let the flustered man pass.

"I have a letter to send to General Sherman!" Guiteau blurted, speaking his first words. Within seconds, a ticket taker and depot watchman grabbed Guiteau from behind, tackling the man who had just shot the President.

Inside, Garfield's younger son, Jim, was bawling, the older son trying to comfort him. People were screaming, begging for a doctor as blood spread across the station floor.

By noon that day, as the news of the shooting traveled, President Garfield, who just months earlier had been put in office as a result of political compromise, was suddenly a leader of enormous stature.

The nation prayed that Garfield might live—and he did, though he never recovered. Dwindling from two hundred pounds down to a hundred and twenty, President Garfield died in bed two months later.

At the time, some said God was judging the nation. Others said Guiteau was part of a grand, power-grabbing plot.

The assassin Guiteau never hid the truth: He told them he was trying to prevent another civil war. No one believed him.

But he was right—and he said it best: "God makes no blunders... He selects the right man every time for the right place; and in this He always successfully checkmates the Devil's moves."

John Wilkes Booth had done his job as the Knight of Spades. And now the Knight of Diamonds had completed his task.

11

Today was a perfect day to kill a President.

The Knight knew it as he stood in the cold on the corner of 16th and P Streets, ignoring the passing cars of early commuters and staring at the wooden double doors of his newest destination, the massive Neo-Gothic castle known as Foundry United Methodist Church. This would go better than the mess last night at St. John's.

Without a doubt, he could've waited—could've pushed it back a day... but now... with Beecher already involved... No. History had already been written. It couldn't be changed.

President Garfield was shot at exactly 9:25 a.m.

The Knight glanced down at his watch. Less than an hour to go.

That's how it was written.

That's how it had to end.

Diagonally across the street, a lanky black man in a puffy black-and-red winter coat approached the huge 1904 granite building with its limestone trim and wood-framed windows. At the front door, he pulled out a set of keys. Church custodian, right on time.

Twirling a sucking candy around his tongue, the Knight watched as the custodian disappeared through the right-hand door just like he did every morning. It'd take him at least ten minutes to enter the PIN code, shut off the alarm, and walk through the building, turning on the lights. Otherwise, Foundry Church was now open.

52

Walking calmly across the street, the Knight couldn't help but appreciate his current location. By definition, a foundry is a factory for casting metal, which is exactly what Henry Foxall was doing when he built cannons and guns for the U.S. government in the early 1800s. But it wasn't until the War of 1812 that Foxall had his moment with God. As the British were burning the White House, the rumor was that their next target was Foxall's munitions factory. So Foxall made a vow that day: If God would spare his operations, Foxall would build something in God's honor.

That night, a violent thunderstorm appeared from nowhere, stopping the British from advancing any farther. Two years later, Foundry Church was born.

Over the years, it became the place where FDR took Winston Churchill for Christmas services in 1941, and later it was the Methodist home for Bill Clinton when he was President. But to this day, its greatest role was as the true church of Abraham Lincoln.

Since St. John's was right across the street from the White House, Lincoln used to duck into it for quick prayers. But it was the Foundry, straight up 16th Street, one mile from the White House, where Lincoln became an official church director.

The Knight liked that. God's message couldn't be clearer.

Climbing the concrete steps outside, the Knight reached for the front door, but as he gave it a tug, a burning bolt of pain seized his right shoulder. His newest tattoo was still sensitive, and unlike the small spade and the JWB initials, for John Wilkes Booth, that was on the web of his hand, the marking on his shoulder—the one worn by the second Knight, the assassin Charles Guiteau—was far more complex: the shield, plus the fabled bird . . . and of course the red diamond. It took hours, and over thirty needles, to reproduce the mark.

But again, that's how it was written. That's how it had to end.

Inside the church, he climbed another short set of steps and made a quick left, scanning the empty desks and cubicles in the narrow church office that sat behind a long wall of glass. The custodian was still on the far right side of the building, opening the chapel.

The Knight knew this place even better than St. John's. And this time, he wouldn't be limited to a one-shot revolver. In his right pocket, he felt the British Bulldog pistol. It had a white ivory inlaid grip and five bullets in its chamber.

Back in 1881, on the day Guiteau bought his gun, the owner of the shop told him that he could save money if he bought the same pistol without the white ivory handle. Guiteau wouldn't hear of it. He knew that when the act was done, this was a gun that would be on display. The elegant inlaid grip was the only choice.

From there, Guiteau left nothing to chance, spending nearly a month trailing President Garfield and learning his schedule. He even followed Garfield to church, peering through the window to see if he could shoot him in his pew.

Today, the Knight was no different. In less than an hour, history would be made. He'd put in the time. And bought the antique gun. And paid for the specially made inlaid handle. Most important, he'd mastered every detail of Foundry Church, from the building's layout to every employee in it.

On his left, as he reached the end of the hallway, the Knight peered into the office suite, eyeing his eventual destination—the private office of the new pastor, who everyone knew came in at exactly 9 a.m.

On his right, he shoved open the door to the men's room and made his way to the back stall, which had a sign reading *Out of Order* on it. He had put the sign there two days ago. Lifting the tank cover off the toilet, he pulled out the plastic bag that held a white plaster mask—a duplicate of the death mask made from Abraham Lincoln's face, but with eyeholes cut into it—that he'd hidden during the dry run.

A glance at his watch told him he was right on time. In sync with his predecessor. In sync with God's plans.

At 9:25, the next lamb—perhaps the most vital lamb—would take his fall.

Until then, the Knight would do exactly what the assassin Guiteau did when he was in the train station waiting to put a bullet in President Garfield.

Kneeling down on one knee, the Knight reached into his pocket and pulled out a small round tin and a horsehair brush that was about the size of a chalkboard eraser. With a twist of the metal tin, the bitter chemical smell of shoe polish filled the air. Dipping the brush into the tin, he dabbed a swirl of black shoe polish onto his loafers. *Small circles... then brush*, he reminded himself. *Small circles... then brush*.

It was no different with the Knights.

Small circles were the strongest circles.

12

St. Elizabeths Hospital
Washington, D.C.

Nico didn't like the new building.

"Nico, you're gonna love the new building," the heavy male nurse named Rupert Baird called out. "It's beautiful, right?"

Walking through the gravel parking lot, Nico didn't answer. He preferred the old building—the redbrick John Howard Pavilion—which for decades had housed the most dangerous of the NGIs. Not Guilty by reason of Insanity.

Today, the John Howard Pavilion was being closed, and all of its patients were being moved to the brand-new facility that had been built directly next door.

"Wait till you see inside," Rupert said. "New rooms...new TVs... a relaxation garden...You're gonna think you're at a damn hotel."

Nico glanced up at the modern building. It was squat in shape and had only three floors, and from the flat shine on the windows, Nico could tell they were high-impact glass, maybe even bulletproof.

"*I don't like it either,*" added the dead First Lady, whom he killed a decade ago.

Nico nodded at her, but didn't reply. He knew what the nurses thought about him talking to his old victims.

"All your stuff, it's being transferred as we speak," Rupert added, leading him around the side of the building, near the loading dock that said, *New Patient Intake—Ambulance Parking Only.*

Nico knew why Rupert was being so nice. Just like he knew why they were entering through the loading dock instead of the main lobby. With all the VIPs and reporters who were watching during the grand opening, the last thing the hospital needed was to have their most famous patient—the man who, a decade ago, tried to kill the President—making a scene during his transfer.

"It smells different than the old building," Nico said as they climbed the concrete steps that ran up to the loading dock.

"That's kinda the point," Rupert said, approaching a high-tech keypad and swiping his ID. There was a loud *ca-chunk* as the double doors popped open, swinging toward them and revealing a brand-new U-shaped desk at the front of the still-empty Intake Office. The desk and the surrounding chairs were still covered in plastic. As they reached the hospital's main hallway, there wasn't a staffer in sight.

"You should ask to see your room," the dead First Lady said.

"I'd like to see my room now."

"You will, Nico. But first they want you in—"

"You're not listening. I want to see my *room*," he growled. To make the point, Nico stopped in the hallway, refusing to move.

"Nico, I am so not in the mood for your nuttiness today. They're waiting for us in TLC," Rupert said, raising his voice as he referred to the Therapeutic Learning Center.

Nico still wouldn't budge.

Rupert grabbed him by the biceps. "Can you for once not be a pain in my rear?" Tightening his grip, he added, "Y'know how many of us got fired to pay for this building? We used to have orderlies running the juice cart. Now I gotta do all that, *plus* haul you to TLC, *plus*—!"

"You need to let go of me," Nico warned in a calm voice.

"Or what?" Rupert challenged, making sure Nico got a good look at the small electronic device—like a miniature walkie-talkie—that Rupert held in his left hand.

Nico had heard rumors that the new building would have those. To be used during patient transfers. It was called a "man-down system." If a staffer dropped it, or their body went horizontal, an alarm would ring through the building, while the hallway's cameras would immediately zoom in within twenty feet of the device.

Nico checked both ends of the hallway. Brand-new cameras—encased in unbreakable glass cubes—on each side.

Nico stayed silent. Two years ago, he would've jammed his thumbs in Rupert's eye sockets and pressed hard enough to hear the pop in his brain. But Nico's therapies...all the drugs... He was a new man now. A cured man, is what the doctors called him. Cured. With a soft exhale, Nico unclenched his shoulders. Even the dead First Lady didn't argue.

Smiling and still holding Nico's biceps, Rupert steered him up the—

"What do you think you're *doing*!?" a southern voice shouted behind them.

Following the sound, Rupert and Nico spun to find a tall man with tight curly black hair and a fine gray wool suit. Around here, only doctors wore suits. And among those doctors, only this one wore a vintage 1950s King Kong tie.

"Rupert, you have half a second to get your hands *off him*!" Dr. Michael Gosling barked.

"Sir, you don't understand," Rupert pleaded, letting go of Nico's bicep. "I was just taking him to TLC—"

Gosling's hand shot out, gripping Rupert by his own bicep and tugging him aside, just out of Nico's earshot. "Was he putting himself or anyone else in danger?" Gosling challenged in a tense, low voice.

"That's not the point."

"It's *always* the point. We have rules here, Rupert—and first among them is, don't put your hands on the patients...especially the ones who're making actual progress." Turning to Nico, Gosling forced a smile and added, "You okay, Nico?"

"I want to go to my room."

Rupert could barely keep from rolling his eyes. Every doctor was careful with Nico, but Gosling was one of the few who built a career on it. A decade ago, Gosling had been the junior member on Nico's team—and the doctor credited with persuading Nico to stop plucking his eyelashes and using them to form tiny crosses that only he could see.

These days, Gosling was one of the hospital's top administrators, in charge of not just the new facility's operations but also making sure it opened without incident. And though Gosling insisted that his vintage movie ties were a way to seem accessible to the patients, everyone knew that he preferred the King Kong tie over the others. That's how he saw himself: King Kong. *The biggest of them all.*

"Take him to his room, then you can go to TLC," Gosling told Rupert.

"I want my calendar, and my book too," Nico said, his voice back to its usual steady monotone.

"We'll get those both to you," Gosling promised.

"He will," the dead First Lady said. *"He means it."*

Nico's chocolate brown eyes, set so close together, stayed locked on Dr. Gosling.

"Keep up the beautiful progress," Gosling added, patting Nico on the back and heading up the hallway.

"You're supposed to take me to my room now," Nico told Rupert.

"I heard him," Rupert said as he led Nico toward the elevators.

"Let me know if there's anything else you need!" Dr. Gosling called out.

Nico looked down at his watch. 9:25 a.m. The exact time Charles Guiteau shot President Garfield.

Nico's lips curved into a thin smile. After all these years, he would finally have everything he needed.

13

Pastor Kenneth Frick wore a little digital monitor on his left shoe that counted his steps. Two hundred and twelve steps for him to get dressed, comb his sandy blond hair, and mix his Cheerios with blueberry yogurt in the morning. Twenty-three steps to get from his kitchen to the front door of his small Capitol Hill townhouse. Then the full 1,958 steps that it took him to walk the three miles from Capitol Hill to the front door of Foundry Church every morning. Unlike St. John's, the site of last night's attack, across the street from the White House, Foundry Church was in a struggling neighborhood, not one most people walk to.

The monitor wasn't Pastor Frick's idea. It came from the church's insurance company, which for every step he (or any of his employees) took gave a wellness discount (up to a total of twenty thousand steps per month). If he expected his staff to do it, the pastor had to lead the way.

It was the same when he was a boy. He wasn't from an overly religious family, yet Frick was the one who used to drag his mother to Sunday sermons, making him the only five-year-old in their poor Indiana town who could tie his own tie. Back then, Kenneth was drawn to the church because it was the only place his father wouldn't lay hands on them. But as he got older, Frick was captivated by the *mystery* of the church—the way it could broaden life beyond what you can touch, feel, and grasp.

"Anybody here besides God?" Frick called out with the same old joke he used every morning. He knew the answer. Except for the custodian, he was always the first one in. Right at nine, which was now his custom.

It'd been barely four months since Frick—only an associate pastor in title—had been assigned to the church, taking over while the head pastor was traveling in New Zealand. Frick felt blessed to be selected, but it took him over a month to work up the courage to cancel the free fruit smoothies that brought in parishioners to the late Sunday service. This was still Lincoln's Church. Wearing a digital monitor on your shoe for an insurance discount was one thing. Bribing people with fruit smoothies was another.

Down the main hallway, with the bathroom behind him, Pastor Frick entered the main office suite, made his way through the maze of desks, and headed for his office in back. Through the frosted glass doors, he could tell the lights were off inside. The glass was too old and thick to see anything else.

Every pastor has rituals. At 9:05, as he stepped into his office and the door closed behind him, Frick did what he did every morning: He hung his coat—always on the middle hook—grabbed his Bible off the bookshelf, and began his morning prayers. For nearly twenty minutes, he stood praying and looking out the wide glass window that was directly behind his antique maple desk. He could see the reflection of his round face and dimpled chin in the window.

On his left was a door that led to his private bathroom. It was usually open. This morning, for some reason, it was shut.

Frick didn't give it a thought. In the midst of his prayers, he looked down at the digital counter on his shoe—not to count his steps, but to see what time it was.

Onscreen, it clicked from 9:24...

...to 9:25.

On the floor, a needlepoint carpet covered with green and yellow leaves kept the office warm and mostly silent. The oak floor creaked from a nearly imperceptible shift in weight.

Then the Knight pulled the trigger. Twice.

The pastor's body convulsed as one of the bullets entered his back.

Another mission complete. For the second time, history had repeated itself.

14

Six days ago
Ann Arbor, Michigan

S ir, you ready to order?" the thin black woman with splotchy skin asked from behind the counter.

"Not yet. I'm waiting for someone," Dr. Stewart Palmiotti replied from the bright red booth as he again scanned the small fast-food restaurant located just inside the entrance of Target.

He knew why she had picked it: It was well lit and safe, with plenty of people watching them. Plus, by doing it in Ann Arbor—Wallace's alma mater—the message was clear. If the President didn't deliver, she'd take apart every piece of his life.

"You need to try the hot dogs," a female voice eventually announced behind him. "They're better than you think."

Before Palmiotti could turn, a woman in a stylish brown overcoat was standing over him, looking down. Her hair was short and dyed blonde. But he knew that grin: same as her father, the presidential assassin known as Nico.

"Y'know, after your funeral, I read your obituary. They made you sound nicer than you really are," Clementine said, sliding into the empty seat across from the President's oldest friend and most trusted doctor. "By the way, I mean it about the hot dogs," she added, pointing to the counter, where a dozen thick hot dogs twirled on the grill's treadmill. She was enjoying herself now, which annoyed Palmiotti even more.

Both A.J. and the President had warned him about this. Everyone thought that Nico was the monster, but it was his daughter who had tried to blackmail them, threatening to expose their secret unless she got the information about her father. And in the end, during her escape, it was Clementine who fired the shot that nearly killed Palmiotti.

But Clementine was different from Beecher, and far more dangerous. If they had any hope of containing this, they needed to make peace, not war.

"The blonde hair looks good," Palmiotti offered. "Quite a change from the black."

"Same with yours," Clementine said, pointing at his own dye job. "Though I also like the scar on your neck. Isn't that where I shot you?"

Palmiotti cupped his hands, intertwining his fingers, refusing to take the bait. "Y'know, I remember the last thing you said to us: about the cancer that was eating at your body. I lost a niece to brain cancer. She was four years old. When her hair fell out, she used to cry, 'Why can't I have pigtails?' So you can talk as tough as you want, but I'm a doctor. From your skin alone... I'm guessing oral chemo, yes? I know what it does to you. I'm sorry for that."

Across the booth, Clementine studied him, her eyes narrowing. "Did you bring what I asked for or not?"

"Of course I did." From underneath his coat on the bench, Palmiotti pulled out a thick manila envelope.

From the back of her pants, Clementine took out a similar envelope that looked slightly thinner, with a water stain on it.

"And this is everything you found?" Palmiotti asked, lifting the flap, where he saw a familiar name typed on the file folder that was tucked inside. *Wallace, Orson.*

True to her word, this was everything: the complete file that, two months ago, Beecher had tracked down in the Archives. As far as they knew, this was the only proof of what he and the future President did all those years ago, when they attacked and eventually took the life of that man with the eight-ball tattoo.

"How do we know you won't say anything, or that you didn't make copies for yourself?" Palmiotti asked.

"You don't," Clementine said as she reached for the envelope that Palmiotti had brought in return. Undoing the figure-eight loop, she added, "How do I know this is his real military file?"

She waited for an answer. Palmiotti didn't give her one. But he didn't deny it was.

Back by the counter, one of the hot dogs sizzled and popped, spitting a fleck of grease against the protective glass. Clementine smiled. With enough pressure, everything pops. Even a President.

Freeing the brown accordion file from its envelope, she read the name that was typed on the peeling blue-and-white sticker in the corner. *Hadrian, Nicholas.* Her father.

"You know Beecher's been looking for you," Palmiotti warned as she started flipping through the file.

Clementine nodded, licking her finger and flicking to a new page. She'd waited too long not to take a peek. But what caught her eye was the logo at the top of the page: an eagle gripping a metal anchor. The logo of the U.S. Navy. It made no sense. Nico wasn't in the navy.

"Beecher's not searching alone," Palmiotti added. "He's got help."

"Who? Tot?"

"And some others," Palmiotti said, resealing his envelope.

Across from him, Clementine was flipping faster than ever, skimming through the pages—letters of recommendation...physical profile...record of induction—glancing through details of her father's lost life. But as she read the date of Nico's induction into the military, three years before she was born, Palmiotti saw the way her hands started shaking.

For so long now, Clementine had waited for this moment: to have details...documentation...the proof of what they did to him, and by extension, to her. Whatever they put in Nico's body, it was the only way to explain the unknown cancer that she had today. Her doctors said they'd never seen anything like it. That her type of cancer...that it didn't exist...it was a new mutation. But as

Clementine thumbed to the pages labeled *Psychological & Medical Records*, she felt a swell of tears that surprised even her.

"You okay?" Palmiotti asked.

Clementine looked up, caught off guard by the question. He already had what he wanted.

"What does he have on you?" she blurted.

"Excuse me?" Palmiotti asked.

"I meant it before. I read your obituary. To do what you did, to let the world think you're dead ... You had to leave your wife—"

"Ex-wife."

"—and two kids—"

"My kids haven't spoken to me in years."

"But your *life*," Clementine said, her eyes back down on the file. "You left your entire life behind, and for what? For a President? For one man? What the hell does Wallace have over you?"

"You're questioning *me*? What about your own life? You're hiding in Michigan. You have no home. And for what, Clementine? To get Nico's files?"

"He's my *father*."

"Don't play the wounded child. We all know that's not why you did this," Palmiotti challenged. "All the hurt you caused...that wasn't for your *father*. That was for *you*, Clementine. You did all that for *you*. And now that you got the files and everything you wanted, you really think it matters how we got here? You wanted something so you did what you had to do to get it. The only thing you have to ask is, *was it worth it?*"

Clementine stared down at the file folder, rereading the peeling blue-and-white sticker with her father's name. She thought about how she still had two more days in her chemo cycle, which meant the tingling in her toes, the hideous nausea, and the loose diarrhea would only be getting worse. So. Was it worth it?

"Depends what I find," she shot back, slapping the file shut and sliding out of the booth. As she was about to leave, she turned back and added, "No matter how much of a piece of garbage your boss is, I'm sorry you lost your life over this."

"Yeah..." he whispered as Clementine headed for the stable of red shopping carts and disappeared out the front door. "Me too."

For a full two minutes, he sat there, alone in the bright red booth. And then, in that moment, Dr. Stewart Palmiotti had a brand-new idea.

From there, he made one call. Directly to A.J., who would take it directly to the President. "I know what to do about Beecher," he said.

15

Today
Crystal City, Virginia

A little over an hour later, I'm outside Marshall's apartment building out in Virginia. Standing halfway down the block, I stare down at my phone, pretending to text. It makes me disappear just enough so that passing drivers—including the pasty-faced lawyer in the black Acura—don't bother to look my way. That's the lawyer's first mistake. Actually, I take that back. His first mistake is the personalized license plate that says *L8 4 CRT.* His second mistake comes as he turns into the driveway at the back of Marshall's building.

Of course, I tried going in the front door first. But as I approached the double glass doors of the modern apartment building, I saw what was waiting inside: a miserable-looking doorman at the front desk, plus one of those high-tech intercom systems where a well-placed camera lets residents see who's there before they buzz you in.

If I want Marshall's real reaction, better that he doesn't see me coming.

Which brings me to the Acura driver's third mistake: thinking that just because his building has an underground garage with a code to keep strangers out, it'll stop me from sneaking in.

Still fake-texting on my phone, I walk casually down the block, timing it so I'm crossing right behind the Acura as Pasty Lawyer leans out the window and enters his six-digit PIN code on the garage's keypad.

151916.

I keep walking as the garage door rolls open, then closes. When he's gone, I double back to the keypad, tapping in *151916*.

There's a loud metal *rr-rr-rr* as the garage door again rolls up, saluting me with a dark black entryway. Bits of dust, lit by the sun, hang in the air. But as I take my first step down the slight decline that leads inside, I notice two shiny black shoes and perfectly pressed slacks standing in my way. Even before the garage door fully opens, I know who it is.

"Do I look blind?" the guard from the front desk challenges. "I saw you checking out the front of the building!" His ID badge says Lance Peterzell. From his beefy build and his tight buzz cut, military for sure. "You really think we wouldn't have cameras back here?"

In the corner of the garage, I spot the camera—miniature, like a voice recorder. I've seen cameras like those, when you check into the White House.

"What do you think you're doing!?" he shouts.

I try to make an excuse, but he plows forward. I stumble backward up the driveway.

"I-I was just trying t—" I trip on my own feet, nearly falling backward.

"I can have you arrested for trespa—!"

Standing over me, he cuts himself off, suddenly silent. He's not focused on me anymore. He sees something...

Behind me.

I turn just as a navy blue SUV pulls up, perpendicular to the driveway. As the passenger-side window rolls down, I spot the driver: a man with a strict part in his black hair, and a face that sags. His drooping eyes are the color of white wine. I recognize him from the mugshot. But I've known him for a long time.

Without a word, Marshall shoves open the passenger door, motioning for me to come inside.

I hesitate.

"Isn't that why you came here, Beecher? To find me?" Marshall calls out in a raspy voice that sounds as burned as his face.

Tot would tell me to walk away. That nothing good can come from getting in Marshall's car. But when it comes to Marshall, that's the thing Tot will never understand. In life, there are many reasons why we become who we are. Marshall played a minor but memorable role in my childhood. But what I did to him...on that night in the basement...I altered Marshall forever.

"So you came all this way, and now you're just going to stand there?" Marshall challenges. He takes a deep breath through his nose, like a bull. If I thought he had forgiven me after all these years, I was wrong.

From inside the SUV, his gold eyes lock on me with an odd calm that makes me feel like I'm the only person in the world. Even from here, I can see how meticulous he is—how he holds the steering wheel with just the tips of his fingers.

But as his stare drills down, I realize he's not *talking* to me. He's observing me. He's not impatient, though. He's waiting for me to make my decision.

Once again, I can hear Tot screaming for me to stay away. And I should.

In the road map of my life, Tot represents where I'm trying to go. Marshall represents where I used to be. But that's the thing about the past: No matter how dangerous or disturbing or inconvenient it is, you don't get to move forward until you deal with what's behind you.

Plus, if I want answers, there's only one way to get them.

I dart for the SUV, quickly climbing into the passenger seat.

Still holding the steering wheel with just his fingertips, Marshall backs us into a sharp three-point turn, then hits the gas as we dive down the ramp and disappear inside the underground garage.

I look behind us as the garage door lowers, locking me in the lion's den. But as I spot that flat grin on Marshall's face, I can't help but think that whatever he's really up to, he's just getting started.

*   *   *

16

One hour earlier
Foundry Church

He'd read in some magazine that when you're hit by a bullet—when it punctures and burns through your skin—you don't feel it. That the shock overwhelms any pain.

Facedown on the needlepoint carpet, Pastor Kenneth Frick now knew that wasn't true.

For a moment, he'd forgotten how he got here. He looked around, blinking hard. His heartbeat pumped all the way to his ears. He must've blacked out. In his mouth, his tongue—*ptt, ptt*—it was covered with lint from the carpet.

Turning on his side, he heard a squish. The carpet was soaked. He couldn't see it yet...but down by his hips, a dark puddle was growing, blooming beneath him and slowly engulfing the carpet's green and yellow leaves.

Feeling a sudden blast of cold air, the pastor looked up, spotting the wide-open window that led out toward the street. The room swirled. He couldn't ignore the sharp burning pain in his stomach, like someone was using a hot poker to burrow out from inside him.

He clenched his jaw so hard, he thought his teeth would crack. He'd been through worse...in the army...plus with his mother... to watch what happened to her...

Through the frosted glass, a light went on outside, in the main part of the office. Mina Pfister. The youth director. Always right on time.

The pastor struggled to get up on his knees, determined to crawl to the door. The heartbeat in his ears kept getting louder.

He knew that smell...the smell of charred skin...it was coming from him.

He didn't care. He focused on his mother...what he'd seen...

Closing his eyes, he whispered a prayer—the prayer he came back to more than any other. *Be strong and courageous! Do not tremble or be dismayed, for the Lord your God is with you wherever you go.*

"Mina..." he shouted, though he couldn't tell if any words were coming out. "Please...somebody...*someone help me...!*"

17

"Just a few more steps," his mother said, giggling.

She was actually giggling as she cupped her hands over her young son's eyes and walked him into the snow-covered backyard.

Of course, even at eleven years old, Marshall had known they were about to surprise him. He knew it earlier in the week when he caught his mom on the phone, whispering, *"He's here...gotta go..."*

Kids aren't stupid. Christmas was only a week away. And after eleven years of being the only kid in their small town with an unemployed father who also happened to be in a wheelchair, well... Marshall was accustomed to the extra thoughtfulness that came this time of year.

Five years ago, the town pitched in to redo the rotted wood wheelchair ramp that led up to their front door.

Three years ago, when his mom lost her job, they bought new clothes and a new backpack for Marshall to wear to school.

Two years ago, they bought Marshall a new bike to replace the one he'd outgrown.

This year? Had to be a dog, Marshall decided. He'd mentioned a dog a few weeks back. But the fact that they kept him at church... stalling him so long—and that he was now blindfolded and being led into the backyard—?

With each step, the icy snow snapped like fresh popcorn under his feet.

He could hear the buzz of dozens of imperceptible whispers. He could feel their...their *energy*?...their *presence*?...whatever it was, he could feel it against his chest. There was definitely a crowd here. But it was coming from...

Above.

"On C..." his father called out. "A...B..."

"*SURPRISE!*" the crowd yelled as his mom removed her hands.

Following the sound and readjusting his glasses, Marshall craned his neck up at the giant mulberry tree, where at least a dozen kids, plus a few parents, were out on the porch of the— In his head, he was about to use the word *treehouse*. But this— It looked like a real house, with a pitched roof and a *porch*. This wasn't a treehouse. It was a—

"Welcome to the *Watchtower!*" Vincent Paglinni, a meaty eleven-year-old with furry eyebrows, shouted. "*Get up here, Marshmallow! You gotta see this!*"

"It was the pastor's idea," Marshall's mom said, pointing to Pastor Riis, who was pushing Marshall's dad in his wheelchair.

"Give it a whirl," his dad added, looking prouder than ever.

Marshall darted for the ladder rungs that were nailed to the tree.

"No! Grab the rope! Take the elevator!" Vincent Paglinni yelled from above.

Following where everyone was pointing, Marshall headed for the thick rope that dangled down, a baseball-sized knot at its end. As Marshall grabbed the rope, he looked up and saw the pulley that was attached even higher than the roof of the treehouse.

"Ready for liftoff...!" James Wert, a heavy kid from his class, called out. Without warning, Wert leaped off the side of the treehouse and gripped the rope, wrapping his legs around it like he was sliding down a firepole.

The pulley began to spin; the rope pulled taut.

Like a bottle rocket, Marshall shot into the air, where a crush of hands grabbed him, tugging him onto the porch of...

"It's the greatest damn treehouse of all time!" Vincent Paglinni shouted as the crowd of kids cheered.

Marshall knew he was right. This wasn't something built by a dad. This was built by a town. Ushered inside, Marshall saw that the doorway had a real frame—and the way the roof was sealed so perfectly on all sides . . . No doubt, it was watertight.

"Lookit this!" Lee Rosenberg, who always wore Lee jeans, called out. "Beanbag chairs! Comic books! Foldout beds!" he said, pointing to two cots, which folded down from the wall. "There's even working windows!" Lee added as someone pushed the large Plexiglas window that had a hinge on top and swung out like a huge doggie door.

"If it's raining, you prop it open and still get fresh air," Eddie Williams's dad, who sold wholesale Plexiglas, pointed out.

"Plus . . . look! A carpeted floor!" Lee shouted, motioning at the pale blue carpet. "Carpets are the Cadillac of treehouse options!"

"No, *here's* the Cadillac!" Vincent Paglinni interrupted, pointing to a bottle opener that was built into the wall. *"For beer!"*

"For orange soda and root beer only!" one of the brave mothers up there insisted as the whole group laughed.

For Marshall, that was the best part. Not the beanbag chairs, or the working window, or even the bottle opener. It was the laughter. And not *at him*, for once. *With* him.

Sure, he spotted friends like Beecher in the corner. And Jeff Camiener, who he always ate lunch with and was the only one who never called him Marshmallow. But most of the kids here were kids he never talked to . . . who he was too afraid to talk to, like Vincent Paglinni, who usually focused his attention on what rock concert shirt he'd wear the next day. But there Paglinni was, as excited as the rest. They were all thrilled for him. Like friends.

"Check it out, Mallow! The pastor's looking up your mom's skirt!" Vincent called out as the mob of kids rushed out to the porch to see Marshall's mom climbing up the tree's ladder rungs, with the pastor right behind her.

The pastor looked down quickly. He wasn't looking up her skirt.

Still, the kids were laughing. So was Marshall. They were *all* laughing. Together.

Forget the treehouse. For Marshall, this sense of *belonging* made his chest swell so large, he thought it would burst open. To have so many friends, their mouths all open with laughter...

This was the greatest day of his life.

Even as he looked out the Plexiglas window and saw his father, in the wheelchair, looking up at him—even that couldn't ruin it.

"You gotta see this!" Marshall called out, pushing the Plexiglas outward and letting in a wisp of cold air.

"Already did!" Marshall's dad called back, pumping a fist in the air.

"Awesome, right!?" Marshall shouted, not even catching his dad's lie.

No matter how well the treehouse was built, there was no way his father would ever make his way up there. Not today. Not ever.

But at this moment, surrounded by so many new friends, Marshall wasn't being naïve, or insensitive. He was just being eleven years old.

He smiled and pumped his fist back at his dad.

From this height, Marshall could see over his house, over the telephone poles, over everything.

Nothing could ruin a day like this.

18

Marshall's silent the entire ride down.

But as his SUV moves deeper and deeper down into the underground garage, what's far more discomforting is this: If Marsh is really the one who killed that rector last night—if he's the one carrying around old playing cards and thinking he's John Wilkes Booth—why's he taking me inside?

And more important, why am I letting him?

For both questions, I tell myself it's because he's clearly not a murderer. I know that Marshall used to have Muppet sheets on his bed. I remember thinking his house smelled like werewolf. And I remember, when we were twelve, being at his mother's funeral, right before his dad moved them out of town.

But as the SUV curves down another level, I keep glancing over at him, waiting for him to say something. He never does. I try to play it cool, but I can't stop staring, especially at his face.

In the mugshot, his face looked shiny, like it was coated with putty. But up close, even in this bad light, the lumpy texture of it makes his forehead and cheeks look like a melted candle. His skin isn't red, it's pink. Whatever happened, it was years ago. But he was burned badly. His nose is square at the tip from whatever surgery put it back together. His eyebrows are tattooed on. His black hair covers what's left of his ears. I can't even begin to imagine what he's been through.

I try to say something, but the only thing I can think of is just how much I don't know this person anymore.

As Marshall continues steering the curve of the ramp, I try to picture the chubby kid with glasses from the treehouse. He's not there. Today, the new Marshall's posture is perfect, his shoulders square and unmoving. Even through his wool peacoat, I can see he's compact, but all muscle. And somehow, there's an ease about him, like a poker player who already knows the order of all the cards in the deck.

The thing is, as I notice his flat grin, something tells me that even if he didn't know the order of the cards, he'd still be just as confident. No matter how much I was trying to surprise Marshall, it feels like he always knew I was coming.

"So how long have you lived here?"

Marshall stares straight ahead.

I've lived in Washington long enough to know what people do with silence. The CIA uses it as an interrogation technique, knowing that the longer you stay quiet, the faster you get people to talk. Reporters do the same. So if that's the game Marshall's playing, he's about to learn that there's no one more patient, or more comfortable in their own silence, than an archivist.

My ears pop as the ramp dumps us on the fifth level underground. As we pull into one of the many open parking spots, I don't know why he took us down this far. Whoever else is in this building, most of them are gone.

Still silent, Marshall hops out, his pale, bumpy face peering back at me through the car's front window. I follow him in silence as he shoves open a red metal fire door, and we enter a fluorescent-lit concrete room with a dull metal elevator. He's got his back to me, but now that we're both standing, I see he's shorter than I am.

I remember him always being a few inches taller. It messes with the perspective of my memories, like when you go home and see how tiny your childhood room looks.

"How did you know I was looking for you?" I ask as the doors of the elevator stretch wide.

He doesn't answer as we step inside. He waves his hand in front of the small black rectangle that's set just above all the elevator's call buttons. He's got a key fob in his hand that allows access to the building.

The button for the twelfth floor lights up automatically, and we rise quickly.

"Marsh, I asked you a—"

"I go by *Marshall* now," he interrupts, forcing his grin back into place.

"Marshall," I correct myself, making note of the sore spot. "Listen, Marshall—I appreciate the Clint Eastwood silent thing you've got going, but c'mon . . . how often do you get drop-in visits from people you haven't seen since puberty?"

He laughs at that one, making the waxy skin on his neck wriggle.

His peacoat is open now. I notice how his burns continue down his neck, into the collar of his pristine white dress shirt. Is he burned all over his body?

I look down at his hands, and for the first time realize he's wearing gloves. A small pool of sweat fills the dimple of my top lip, and I wonder if the decision to come here was one of the stupidest of my life.

"You're staring, Beecher."

I don't look away.

"If you want to ask about my burns, just ask."

I pause, staying with him. "How'd you get burned?"

"By a fire," he says, his eyes narrowing into a grin.

"I just want to know how you're doing, Marshall."

The elevator doors open, but we're not in a hallway. It's a small entry with a single wooden door. This is a private elevator, in a very private building.

With another wave of his key fob, there's a click, and Marshall pushes the door open, revealing a long and narrow loft. There's a slightly outdated white Formica kitchen on the right, overlooking a sparse and just as outdated 1990s-era IKEA living room. On the left, an open door reveals what looks like a bedroom.

Stepping aside, he pats me on the back, motioning me to go first.

He's still grinning as I step inside.

19

Eighteen years ago
Sagamore, Wisconsin

Listen, here's an even better one…" Beecher said, tucked into the treehouse's worn beanbag chair, his nose deep in the newspaper. "Guy's name is Albert "Alby" Eliopoulos. Died at the age of seventy-two. And according to this—oh my jeez, listen to this—it was *his* unit that raised the flag at Iwo Jima, but they did it without him! Two days before, Alby *broke his collarbone* and was sent to some hospital unit, missing the whole thing! Mallow, you listening to this?"

"Of course I'm listening," Marshall insisted, lying back on one of the foldout beds and flipping through the thick stack of bra ads that he'd collected from over six months' worth of newspapers. It was summer for the two twelve-year-olds, but with the Plexiglas window open, the treehouse still got a good cross-breeze. "Some guy was at Iwo Jima. Sounds galactic."

"He wasn't just *at* Iwo Jima. He *missed* Iwo Jima! By *two days*! He's part of one of the most famous units of World War II…but he pops his collarbone, and it's like…it's like you're about to be selected for the biggest moment of your life, but instead you're sitting on the can, so you miss it. Can you imagine being that close to history and it passes you by!? How do you ever come back from that!?"

Marshall was silent.

"Mallow, you paying attention, or you still drooling on the bra ads?" Beecher asked from behind the newspaper.

"Beecher, why do you come here?"

"Whuh?"

"Here. To the treehouse. Why do you come here?"

Confused, Beecher peered over the top of the newspaper. Marshall was cleaning up, tucking the stack of bra ads back into the Lucky Charms cereal box that he kept in a milk crate under the bed.

"You don't like the obituaries as much as I do, do you?" Beecher asked. He didn't take it personally. He'd been reading the obits since he was almost four, when his dad died. Since then, he loved reading the stories of all those lives of people who, just like his dad, he'd never see. Lives that could've been.

"I mean it, Beecher. Why do you come here? I mean, I *like* you coming here, but... All these years, it's not like we really talked much...or even *ever*. We don't even eat lunch together. We just— I didn't think we were friends."

"What? Of course we're friends."

"We *are*?"

"Mallow, if we weren't friends, why would you sit here every day and listen to me read from the obituaries?"

"I dunno," Marshall said with a shrug, leaning back on his bed. "Sometimes it's just— I kinda thought you'd stop coming here if I didn't listen."

Sitting there, frozen in the beanbag chair as the newspaper floated down to his lap, Beecher stared across at the chubby kid he forever knew as Marshmallow. "Mallow, tell me this: What do *you* like?"

"*Like* for what?"

"When you're bored...when you're sitting around... When no one else is looking, what do *you* like?"

"You really wanna know?"

"I do. I want to know."

Marshall's mood shifted in a split second, tumbling from *confused*, to *shocked*, to a cautious smile. Excited to answer the question, he pointed toward the Plexiglas window, at the stars that lit the black sky. "Space."

"Y'mean *outer* space? Like *Star Wars*?" Beecher asked. "Time out. Is that why you always say that things are *galactic*? Because you like *Star Wars*?"

"*Star Wars* is fiction. Imagine if you could do it for *real*."

"Yeah, I can totally picture that. You'd be a perfect astronaut." Beecher laughed. "Haven't you had like every eye disease known to man?"

Pushing his glasses up on his face, Marshall kept staring out at the sky. "But imagine, Beecher. To go that high...to escape everything... Don't you ever wonder how far we can go?"

Beecher sat up in the beanbag chair, suddenly excited as he waved the newspaper. "No, I *know*! That's *exactly* why I like obituaries! When you see what people have accomplished... They're proof of how far we can go—of what we're capable of on our very best days."

"I guess," Marshall said, thinking it over. "But obituaries are weird."

"You wish. Outer space is weird."

The two boys looked at each other. For a moment, the treehouse was silent.

Hopping off the bed, Marshall raced for the treehouse door.

"Where you going?" Beecher asked.

"To fart. My mom said it's rude t—"

"How old are you? Six? Fart here! No one cares!"

Standing there, Marshall kept his hands at his side and did exactly that.

It was a quiet one.

"You do realize," Beecher said, leaning back in the beanbag chair, "it's conversations like these that make people not wanna hang out with us."

Marshall laughed at that. A real laugh.

"But with space, and the obits, it's also why we *will* escape," Beecher added. "From here...from Wisconsin. We'll be the only ones who get out of here."

"I'm not worried about getting out of here," Marshall replied, sitting on the edge of the foldout bed and glancing down at his house below them. "I'm just worried about who'll take care of my dad."

Beecher fell silent, but not for long. "I bet we can find someone to take care of him too."

In that moment, as Marshall focused his attention back on the treehouse...as he scooched back on his foldout bed and thought about how many people had been packed in here just eight months ago...as he looked past the Plexiglas window and the super-cool bottle opener, Marshall Lusk realized that when it comes to treehouses, the only thing you really need...is a friend.

"I just farted again, Beecher."

"I know. I can smell, dumbass."

20

Six days ago
Ann Arbor, Michigan

Sometimes, when the stress felt overwhelming, Clementine would imagine—would practically feel—her chubby ginger cat making figure-eight loops around her ankles.

She was doing it now as she drove back along the highway. In her lap, she had the file that Palmiotti had given her, propping it open and letting it lean against the steering wheel.

Clementine wanted to pull over, to just read it on the side of the highway. But the thought of Palmiotti, or anyone else, catching her by surprise... She knew she had to wait.

She couldn't. She'd been waiting for so long—for her whole life, really. So as she focused on the calm that her cat brought, she stole quick glances at the file.

It was hard to read, especially at this speed—and there was so much to go through, from the physical and mental profiles to the documentation of her father's service. As she kept glancing down to fish through the papers, she stopped on the very first thing that looked easy to skim.

It was a single, pink page, right at the front. The word *commendation* stood out.

It was just a letter. From the typewriter font, it looked like one of the oldest documents in there. Scanning the first paragraph, she kept glancing up at the road, then back to the text. According to the letter, her father—Nico Hadrian—*was instrumental in ren-*

dering valuable assistance during battlefield operations modeling at Headquarters.

There was a loud *tunk-tunk-tunk* as her car drifted left out of its lane, plowing over the reflective road studs along the highway. Looking up, Clementine tugged the wheel, bringing the car back on course.

She tried to breathe, but her chest...it felt like someone had reached underneath her ribcage and wedged their fist up into her throat.

It was a simple letter. A commendation. From Commanding Officer Bryan Burgess...*rendering valuable assistance*... It said he did something *good*.

In her lap, the file folder fell to the right, spraying paper across the seat.

The swirl of emotions caught her by surprise. Her eyes became watery. But what she was feeling wasn't sadness. Or even relief. Holding tight to the steering wheel, Clementine felt the fist in her throat growing heavy, sinking down into her belly. This was anger.

With a jerk of her foot, the ghost of her ginger cat dissipated like a rolling cloud.

Palmiotti was right. The real reason she had searched for this file...and risked so much to get it...was so she could get answers about her cancer. About her health. About herself. Her future.

But to see this commendation...to see what they wrote about him...

They always said he was a creature with no redeeming attributes. But here, this was proof. Proof of what could've been. Of what should've been.

Proof that Nico—her father—wasn't born a monster. They turned him into one.

*   *   *

21

Here you go, Nico. Welcome home," Nurse Rupert announced, throwing open the heavy wooden door to Nico's new room, which wasn't much different than the average college dorm room, right down to the institutional furniture and the thick concrete walls.

Stepping inside, Nico noticed that instead of doorknobs, there was a metal latch that you push, like you see in hospital rooms. But unlike hospital rooms, next to the latch was a small metal switch. Nico knew what that was. If a nurse flipped the switch, instead of opening *inward*, the door would open *outward*, ensuring that as a patient you can't barricade the door.

"*They put your calendar up,*" the dead First Lady pointed out as Nico turned toward the only item on the otherwise bare walls: his Washington Redskins calendar that was already hanging above his nightstand, just like in his old room.

"*The light switches are new too,*" the dead First Lady added.

Of course Nico noticed that. In the old building, patients used to unbend paper clips, jam them into the light switch, and use the live wire to light their cigarettes. But now the light switch in Nico's room was covered with a bulky porcelain switchplate that was snug around the switch and didn't allow anything inside.

"It's childproofing for really *big* kids," Rupert joked. "So whattya-

86

think? Does your unbridled happiness make you committed to stop being such a pain in my keister?"

"Where's my book?" Nico blurted. "They brought my calendar, but where's my book?"

"I dunno. Check the dresser...or one of the drawers..."

Slowly opening the drawers on his nightstand, Nico saw a copy of his Bible, his red glass rosary, and a few other knickknacks from his drawers in his old room. But not the—

"My book isn't here," Nico insisted.

Before Rupert could argue back, the door opened behind them. "Just checking in to make sure everyone's—" Dr. Gosling took one look at his star patient and could read the stress on his face. "Nico, what's wrong?"

"They didn't send my book," Nico growled.

"I'm sure they sent it. We'll find it," Rupert insisted, frantically yanking open the drawers of the dresser.

"You mean this book here?" Dr. Gosling called out, pulling a book from the top of the wardrobe that was bolted to the wall.

"There!" Nico said. "My *book*."

"Where'd you find that?" Rupert challenged.

"Right here. It was sitting on top of the wardrobe," Dr. Gosling replied, his King Kong tie swaying just slightly.

"I-I must've missed it," Rupert apologized.

"I didn't see it up there either," Nico blurted as Rupert looked over at the top of the wardrobe. As Rupert knew, Nico never missed anything.

"Maybe now you can take him down to TLC," Dr. Gosling said, referring to the therapy center downstairs.

"Yeah...that's what I was thinking," Rupert said, motioning Nico out into the hallway.

Following a few steps behind the oversized nurse, Nico was already flipping through the pages of the leather-bound book with gold writing on the cover. It was an old book, a novel called *Looking Backward*. He stopped on page 122, where his bookmark was.

"C'mon, Nico, they're waiting for you," Rupert called out.

Nico stayed silent, his head down. He was already lost in his book, which he cradled in his left hand. In his right, he pulled out his makeshift bookmark: a shiny new playing card.

The dead First Lady smiled as she saw it.

"I'm right behind you," Nico said, rubbing his thumb against the ten of spades and knowing that after the spades came the diamonds.

22

Tell me what I'm looking at," Tot said, staring as the browser on his computer screen loaded its video image. "These security cams?"

"Traffic cams," Immaculate Deception's computerized voice said through Tot's phone, which sat on the desk of his cubicle in the Archives.

Sure enough, onscreen, the video came to life. The images weren't perfect, but they were clear—and in color—showing an intersection that Tot recognized as 16th and H Streets in downtown D.C., not far from the White House. "I'm surprised Homeland Security lets you get this close."

"They don't. You never get a clear shot of the White House. But *one block from it*, the Department of Transportation runs feeds over the Internet so commuters can avoid the traffic snares that come with motorcades and other delays."

"God bless America."

"No. God bless paranoid people," Mac said. "See the site you're on?"

"EyesOnWhiteHouse.com?" Tot asked, reading the URL.

"After 9/11, everyone wanted to know who was walking the streets near the White House. So one site started recording *all* the traffic feeds, cataloging and stocking the footage so you can view it whenever you want—like your very own DVR. This shot is from 9 p.m. last night."

In the left corner of the screen, Tot saw a clear shot of St. John's Church.

The still image refreshed every three seconds, like he was

watching bad stop-motion animation. Cars appeared, frozen—then...*blink*...they were ten feet ahead and then...*blink*...they were gone.

Leaning in, Tot put on his reading glasses and studied the front steps of the church, waiting to see the killer.

"If you're waiting for the killer to enter, he doesn't," Mac said. "Police report said he entered from the back. But here's where the fuss is..."

Tot's cursor, controlled remotely by Mac, clicked a button, and the video fast-forwarded to 9:30 p.m., then 10 p.m. There were still cars on the streets, but not many people.

Until 10:19 p.m.

Onscreen, a man's shadow entered first, and then...*blink*... there he was: on the steps, leaving the church. Like a ghost. The church's tall columns obstructed the view, so Tot could only see him from the waist down.

He had a glove on his left hand, and his other hand was stuffed into his coat pocket. Taking a step down and coming more into frame, he looked left...*blink*...then right, like he was worried he was being watched.

Blink.

He was down on the second-to-last step, by the curb. But as the light hit his face...

Blink.

Tot's eyes went wide.

"You seeing that?" Mac asked, freezing it right there.

Tot didn't answer. He stared at the screen—at the killer. There he was.

On his face was a white plaster mask.

Leaning toward the screen, Tot squinted. Even on a webcam, even under the bad light, even though he couldn't see much else... some faces are unmistakable.

No question, it was Abraham Lincoln.

*　　*　　*

23

Marshall keeps his hand on my shoulder and follows behind me as we enter his apartment. He's unnervingly calm, as if he's been expecting me for weeks.

In the living room is a dark gray starter sofa from IKEA with matching gray IKEA chairs. It's the same with his glass-and-metal coffee table, which match his glass-and-metal end tables, which match his glass-and-metal entertainment center. Everything's from a set—and not the expensive set either, which makes me wonder if he's on a government salary like me.

But as I scan the room, what really stands out is just how little this so-called living room looks lived in. The chairs are untouched. The sofa doesn't have a crease in it. On the tables, there're no books, or framed pictures, or any of the other knickknacks that are proof of life. I feel like I'm in a play, and this is the furniture for the "living room scene." Or even worse. I look around.

Please tell me this isn't a safehouse.

I think about the safehouse I was in a few months ago—used by the government to hide diplomats, witnesses . . . or even for a private conversation with the President of the United States.

I look around again. Except for a neat stack of mail on a nearby desk, and a bowl of blueberries on the kitchen island, the only personal touch in this whole place is on the long wall behind the sofa. A simple white frame holds an elegant . . . at first I thought it was a photo . . . but it's a canvas. A painted canvas slightly bigger than an iPad. I walk closer to see it.

It's a painting of a woman, though her features are blurred. Her eyes aren't really there. Her mouth either. And as she enters this soothing, turquoise body of water, her legs...her arms...her whole body seems to dissipate, spreading outward from her waist as if she's becoming part of the water.

"Nice painting," I tell Marshall to break the silence.

"Flea market," he says, blowing past me and beelining toward his bedroom. "I need to use the restroom," he adds, thinking I don't notice that as he cuts through his bedroom, he's still wearing gloves.

He zigzags quickly around his bed, crossing into the bathroom. I pretend to keep staring at the painting, but I can see him back there. He takes his gloves off. And throws them...did he just throw them in the trash?

As he closes the door to the bathroom, I look back at the painting. I work with enough priceless documents to know archive-quality matting when I see it.

Reading the signature at the bottom—*Nuelo Blanca*—I type it quickly into my phone, adding the words *painting for sale*. The first hit that comes up is a gallery in Los Angeles. For a painting called *WaterFall 5*. Price tag? $22,000.

Okay, Marshall—an artist that sells for 22K? This item clearly isn't from a flea market.

"You got a call?" his throaty voice asks.

I jump, spinning at the sound. Marshall's standing right behind me.

He motions down at my phone, which is still in my hand. "You got a call?" he repeats with a verbal shove.

"Just checking messages," I say, staying where I am.

His eyes narrow. "Most people can't get cell phone reception here," he says.

I look down at the phone Tot gave me two weeks ago. Souped up by Immaculate Deception. Built just for the Culper Ring.

"It's a good phone," I say, verbal shoving him right back.

Marshall licks his lips and I notice that the left side of his tongue is a lighter shade of pink than the right half. It almost looks like it's plastic. His tongue was burned too.

"Do me a favor," Marshall says. "Tell me why you're here."

I continue to look right at him. "I'm here to see what *you* wanted to talk to *me* about."

"Pardon?"

"When you got arrested yesterday, you had my name in your pocket."

He cocks his head, watching me. "I get it. The police called you."

"Of course the police called me. They found my name and number in your pocket."

His shoulders stay square. His grin's back in place. I look down, noticing his perfectly shined shoes. "Why else would I have your number on me, Beecher? I wanted to talk to you."

"Really."

"Isn't that what old friends do? I ran into Craig Rogers last week. Remember him?"

"I know who Craig Rogers is. I see him on Facebook."

"Then you know he has your phone number. Which he gave to me and said I should call you. I didn't even realize you lived here in Washington."

I nod and take a look at that $22,000 painting. "Marshall, you know someone was killed in that church, right?"

"So I gathered. Apparently that's why they arrested me."

"What were you doing there, anyway?"

"What does anyone do at a church, Beecher? It's nearing the anniversary of my mother's death. You know how much prayers meant to her."

"You were there *praying*?"

"I was there praying."

"At ten o'clock at night?"

"The sanctuary is open till midnight. Apparently there are some very religious people who work across the street."

It's a perfect story. No holes in it. "They said you also had a pack of old playing cards on you. With a missing ace of spades."

"I always have them on me. I travel a lot. They're good for solitaire."

"And the ace of spades?"

93

Without warning, he hits both his front pockets. From one, he pulls out the pack of playing cards and tosses it at me. From the other, he pulls out his phone. I didn't hear it ring or vibrate, but as he looks down at it, this is clearly a call he can't miss.

"Beecher, you'll have to excuse me a moment. I need to take this." Heading back toward the bedroom, he adds, "This is Marshall . . ."

He closes the door quietly, leaving me alone in the kitchen.

I study the playing cards. The box is yellowed and severely worn. On the back of the pack is a classic hand-drawn American eagle with spread wings. But instead of its head raised high, the eagle ducks down, its head lowered, like it's ready to bite something.

I glance back at his closed bedroom door. Underneath it, Marshall's shadow paces back and forth. Whoever's calling him, he's caught up in it.

Before I can talk myself out of it, I head for the nearest cabinets. When we were kids, I remember Marshall's dad kept all his medication in the kitchen drawers, since he could reach them from his wheelchair. If I'm lucky, maybe Marshall does the same. But as I hunt through the drawers—silverware in one, spatulas and wooden spoons in another . . . nothing to speak of.

The overhead cabinets are the same. The first has dishes, bowls, cups, and glassware.

The next has wineglasses . . . coffee mugs . . . a few thermoses . . . but again, nothing revealing. The mugs are all plain, same as the thermoses. No school logos, team logos, work logos—nothing. And for the second time, I start wondering if this sterile place is really a safehouse.

But as I open the biggest cabinet—looks like the pantry—the first thing I spot are large boxes of breakfast cereal.

I scan quickly. Of course, there's no Lucky Charms. It's all healthy now: Raisin Bran . . . Special K . . . and one of those fancy oat ones you buy at Whole Foods. My brain flips back to the treehouse . . . and the hiding spot for every nudie pic we could find.

I grab the box of Raisin Bran, ripping it open. Nothing. Same with the Special K. And the fancy oat one. Nothing and more nothing.

Closing the cabinets, I turn back to the bedroom. Marshall's still pacing. Time for one last attempt.

On my right, where the cabinets run in an L-shape around the corner, there's a section of the counter that's built like a desk, but with no drawers. It's where Marshall threw his keys. There's also a neat stack of mail and a few boxes from J.Crew.

Tossing his pack of cards on the counter, I flip through the mail. Electric bill . . . something from a wine-tasting organization . . . coupon circulars . . . His name's on all of them. But the address—it's not the same as the address here. They're all addressed to the P.O. box that Immaculate Deception found earlier. It's the same with the J.Crew packages. But as I lift the rest of the mail off the final box—

The flaps on the box pop upward. It's already open. There's no address on it. No return address either.

I look back at the bedroom. He's still busy.

As I push back the flaps and peer into the box, staring back at me is a shiny white face, with no eyes.

I jump at the sight.

A mask.

It's a plaster mask. White, like chalk. It looks like . . .

It's Abraham Lincoln.

I pull out my phone and try to take a quick pic, but my hand's shaking. I can't steady it.

I look again over my shoulder. Marshall's still pacing in the bedroom.

My phone makes the fake *cha-chick* as I snap the picture. Tot needs to see this. I forward the photo to him, with a note: *Found in Marshall's place.*

Quick as I can, I fold the box shut and put the stack of mail back on top.

I have no idea why Marshall would have his own Abraham Lincoln mask—but considering we're looking for John Wilkes B—

Over my shoulder, there's a low steady sound, like someone breathing.

I don't even have to turn around.

Marshall's right behind me.

24

There are certain moments that change a person's life. For some, it comes quickly and violently, in the form of a car crash. For others, it comes from bad news at a doctor's office.

For Clementine, as she sat Indian-style at the kitchen table in her small rental apartment, papers spread out in front of her, she assumed it would come with Nico's file.

She finished reading the file days ago. She read every word. Every report. Every review.

She read the commendations—six in total. One called her father *sober, industrious, and of impeccable character.* Another commented on his attendance record, and noted that he had accumulated hundreds of hours of unused sick leave. Another said that Nico had *rendered invaluable assistance* when there was a fire on base.

She read the scolding letters of reprimand too—all of them coming in the later years, when whatever they did to him was already long done. Doctors warned of sudden *long periods of silence,* then of his *disregard for the safety of himself and others,* and finally of his *aggressiveness and inability to distinguish fantasy from reality.*

But as Clementine flipped through the file again and again, there wasn't much more than that. Yes, the file showed that her father...that Nico...had been inducted into the military three years earlier than his public records say. And yes, if she was piecing

96

it together correctly, that some of that time was spent with the navy, despite the fact he was an army man. Aside from that, as she tried to rebuild the file in chronological order, there was no other paperwork from any of those first three years. They were gone. Three entire years—totally unaccounted for. No commendations, no letters of discipline, no nothing.

Until Clementine could unlock those years, she'd never know what really happened, never know what her father went through. Most important, assuming she was right that the experiments on *him* had been passed to *her*, she'd never be any closer to understanding the cancer that was currently eating through her own body.

She told herself she shouldn't be surprised. What'd she expect? That the President would hand her a smoking gun wrapped in a big bow? *Here you go . . . even though we've kept it hidden for two decades, here's that top-secret info about your dad that you kept asking for.*

The truth was, the file already told her the answer. Or part of the answer. Those three years—by the mere fact they were missing—that's when the damage was done.

Unfolding herself from her Indian position and sliding one leg under her, Clementine continued flipping through the file. In front of her, on the table, she made four different piles—one for each of the "acknowledged" years that Nico served in the army.

Page by page, she distributed the papers, assigning each document to its appropriate year. Most of the commendations came in the early years, the reprimand letters in the later years. But for the most part, it was the same as before: nothing.

That is, until Clementine flipped through a set of paper-clipped documents and noticed a pale pink sheet that was stuck inside. Of course, the pink color stuck out. She'd seen these sheets before: immunization reports. The army took vaccinations seriously, and Nico had a form like this for all four of the years that he'd—

Wait.

Cocking an eyebrow, Clementine stared at the piles on the table and counted again. Nico already had four of these.

This was a fifth.

Staring down at the sheet, she double-checked the date. The page started shaking in her hand. This was from one of Nico's missing three years.

She was reading fast now. There wasn't much to it. *Request for . . . Nicholas Hadrian . . . to receive influenza vaccination . . .*

It was a request for a flu shot. So easy to overlook. But unlike the other immunization reports, this one was . . . *Approved.*

For whatever reason, someone had to specifically approve this flu shot.

Her hand still shaking, Clementine looked at the bottom of the sheet. There it was, in thin black pen: a muddled signature. The signature of the doctor who approved it. Dr. Michael Yoo.

From there, the next half-hour was easy. An Internet search with the terms *Dr. Michael Yoo* and *army* brought back only two candidates. One died last year, at the age of forty-two. Too young.

The other lived in San Diego, California.

Ten digits later, Clementine had her cell phone to her ear, listening as it rang once . . . twice . . .

"Hello . . . ?" a soft older man's voice asked.

Clementine didn't say a word.

"Hello? Who's there?"

"I'm looking for Dr. Michael Yoo," Clementine blurted.

"Who's this?" he countered.

For an instant, Clementine searched her brain for the best way to keep him talking. But all she came up with was, "I think you know my father. Nico Hadrian."

There are certain moments that change a person's life. For some, it comes in the form of a car crash. For others, it comes at a doctor's office.

For Clementine—as she sat there, her hand now steady—it came from a stranger on the other end of a phone call.

"You must be Clementine."

*　　*　　*

25

Today
Crystal City, Virginia

I spin around. Marshall's almost nose to nose with me.

"I hope your call wasn't bad news," I say.

"Now you're wondering about the mask," he says, calm as ever.

"Listen, Marsh—"

"*Marshall*. And I'm not mad, Beecher. You saw the mask. You should have some questions. Especially considering it came from the crime scene."

"The mask did?"

He makes a mental note, tracking the fact that, at least for me, the mask is a new piece of the puzzle. "Where do you think I found it?" he asks.

"So now you *found* the mask?"

"Please don't take that tone, Beecher. If my story didn't check out, you think the detectives would've released me last night? I know how investigations go. I do them for a living. And I know how often they incorrectly grab the first suspect just because they're the closest suspect."

"Just tell me about the mask, Marshall."

"I found it two blocks away. In a garbage can on the corner of 17th Street."

"Why'd you even go looking for it?"

"You're joking, right? If you really have friends who are D.C.

Police, you know how overwhelmed they are. If they're accusing me of murder—which thankfully, they aren't anymore—you better believe I wanted every piece of evidence that proves my innocence."

"So why didn't you tell the police about it?"

"I did. Called them last night. Then again this morning, which is when they finally assigned a detective to the case. Check their call log; you'll see. They asked me to handle it only with gloves, pack it up in bubble wrap and bring it in today."

I glance over my shoulder at the closed box that holds the mask and the bubble wrap. Another perfect story.

"What kind of investigations do you do?" I ask.

"I was about to ask you the same," he counters, reaching for the deck of playing cards and sliding them back in his pocket. "I mean, for you to be looking into this . . . to track me here . . . Who you working with these days?"

"Uncle Sam," I reply, watching him carefully.

"Funny. I have that exact same uncle," he replies, watching me just as carefully.

My brain starts making guesses. CIA . . . NSA . . . FBI . . . In this town, the acronyms are endless. But if he's telling the truth—if he's really on the same side I am— No. Nonono. There's no way this is all just coincidence.

"We really should grab a drink sometime," he says, putting his gloveless hand on my shoulder. It's scarred even worse than his face. Whatever he was reaching for in that fire, he wanted it desperately.

"I didn't realize I was leaving."

"Sorry. I need to deal with this phone call," he says, steering me to the door.

"Well, let me at least give you my email, and my phone at the Archives," I say, going for one of my business cards. But as I reach for my wallet . . .

I pat my right back pocket. Then my left. Then my front pockets . . .

"My wallet!" I blurt, already mentally retracing my steps. "Maybe it fell out in your car . . . ?"

"You check your coat pockets?" Marshall asks.

I pat my coat pockets. Right one. Then left. Sure enough, there it is. Left coat pocket.

"I do that all the time," Marshall says as I stare down at my wallet.

The thing is, I never put it in my coat pocket. Ever.

"Let's grab that drink ASAP," Marshall says, opening the front door, his grin now spread across his face.

As he ushers me into the hallway, I'm still staring down at my wallet. I flip it open. My cards, my ID: Everything's perfectly in place. I look up at Marshall, then back down at my wallet.

"Really glad we got to see each other, Beecher. Let's do it again real soon," Marshall says as the elevator pings behind me and he steps back into his apartment.

I jam my foot in his doorway, preventing it from shutting.

"Beecher, I really have to run..."

"One last question," I tell him. "Do you remember a girl named Clementine?"

He squints, his glance sliding diagonally upward. "Clementine...?"

"Clementine Kaye," I remind him. "From that night... With the closet..."

He presses his lips together, shaking his head. "Sorry, Beecher, I don't. Remember, I left when we were still little."

With a final slam, he's gone.

I stare at his closed door. Whatever Marshall's up to—whatever really happened last night at the church, and whether this has anything to do with Clementine—there's only one detail I know for sure: I don't know this guy at all anymore.

But he also doesn't know *me*.

In the elevator, I pull out my phone and hit the speed dial for Tot's office. It rings once...twice...then clicks.

"Please tell me Marshall wasn't home and you're driving back here right now," Tot says.

"Tot..."

"Don't *Tot* me, Beecher. Was he there or not?"

"What're you going so nuts about?" I ask.

"Because I just got off the phone with Mac, who just got off the phone with a source, who just got off the phone with someone at the White House. Guess who your pal Marshall Lusk really works for?"

26

As he entered the Chinese restaurant known as Wok 'n Roll, Agent A.J. Ennis headed for a booth in the very back.

It was the opposite from Secret Service protocol. In most restaurants, especially where they were guarding a VIP, agents were stationed by the *front* door so they'd have first crack at anyone who raced in.

Today, A.J. was happy in back. Glancing down at his watch, he saw it was—

Ding, the small bell above the door rang.

Usually, doctors were notoriously late, but with this one . . . considering everything going on . . . Right on time.

Clearly upset, Dr. Stewart Palmiotti threw himself into the seat across from A.J., his back to the front door.

"Why'd you pick this place?" Palmiotti growled.

"Wok 'n Roll? He told me you liked it," A.J. said. "Said you had history here."

Palmiotti sat there, his mind tumbling back over two decades— before Wallace was President . . . before he was even governor— when they took a road trip to Washington during law school. With no money in their pockets, cheap Chinese food was always a good option. But the reason the President first brought them here? As the bronze plaque outside the restaurant pointed out, back in 1865, Wok 'n Roll was originally Mary Surratt's boarding house, where all the Lincoln conspirators, including John Wilkes Booth, plotted to kidnap Abraham Lincoln.

"I just figured . . . y'know, with this Booth thing—"

"*Is this a damn joke to you!?*" Palmiotti hissed.

"Doc, chill out..."

"Or maybe you think it's a game! Like we're playing Monopoly, and you're the race car, and I'm the dog...and you just move me around the board—"

"Doc..."

"I lost my life! I don't have a life—!"

A.J.'s hand shot across the table, like a viper. *"Listen to me,"* he growled, gripping the underside of Palmiotti's wrist and squeezing hard enough to compress all the blood vessels and nerves. Hard enough so Palmiotti stopped talking. The few customers around them stopped staring and went back to their meals.

Palmiotti unclenched his jaw, trying to swallow. He was in pain.

"Listen, Doc—I know what you gave up," A.J. whispered, leaning into the table and easing his grip. "I know. And *he* knows. So if it makes you feel better, the only reason he told me to take you here is because you liked it."

Seeing the doctor's calm return, A.J. released his grip and sat back in his seat. From the wooden bowl between them, he stole a handful of crunchy Chinese noodles, tossing them back one by one and studying the man who was across the table from him.

Palmiotti was the same age as President Wallace. But over the past month...these new lines on his face...plus the way he stared down at the empty table... The bullet wound had taken its toll. He looked twenty years older.

"Doc, your friend needs you right now. *The President needs you,*" A.J. added, sitting straight up and no longer reaching for Chinese noodles. "To pull this off...especially with Beecher so close..."

"I can do it," Palmiotti whispered.

"You sure?"

"I can do it. I'm already doing it," he insisted. "He knows I won't let him down."

"Not just *him. Us,*" A.J. said. "All of us. We're all in it. Like a team."

Palmiotti nodded. Slowly at first. Then faster. The words made him feel better. *Like a team.*

At that moment, a busboy came by, putting two water glasses on the table. The two men didn't say a word until the busboy was gone.

"So you hear anything else from Clementine?" A.J. finally asked.

Palmiotti shook his head. He was staring at the water glasses, watching drops of water swell and skate down the sides of the glass. Like tears.

"But you think the rest is going well?" A.J. asked.

Palmiotti nodded. "This'll be a big win for us."

Now A.J. was the one nodding. That's what he needed to hear.

From the bowl, Palmiotti took a single crunchy noodle. "A.J., can I ask you a question?" Before A.J. could even reply, Palmiotti added, "How's he doing?"

"He's doing fine, Doc." There was a pause. "I think he misses you."

"I miss him too. We'll have our time, though."

"You will."

"At the Presidents' Day event. We're still on for that, yes?"

"Absolutely," A.J. promised, putting both palms flat on the table and getting ready to stand.

"Do me one favor, though," Palmiotti urged. "Don't tell him I lost my cool today, okay?"

"Of course," A.J. said, rising from his seat and never taking his eyes off the doctor. "I'd never say a word."

27

J ust tell me who he works for, Tot."

"Not until you get far away from him," Tot warns in my ear. "Your pal Marshall... Promise me, Beecher. This is not someone you want to be around."

"Relax, I'm nowhere near him," I insist, sitting in the pristine 1966 pale blue Mustang, two blocks from Marshall's building. From the angle I'm at, I've got a perfect view of his garage in back. Marshall said he had to run out. Like he had an emergency. So whenever he drives out—wherever he's going—I'm going with him.

"Beecher, please don't be stupid. You think I don't know you're trying to follow him?"

"You just said the killer was wearing a plaster Abraham Lincoln mask—right as I find a plaster Abraham Lincoln mask in Marshall's apartment. You really telling me you don't want to know where he's going right now?"

"No, what I'm telling you, is, you're being reckless. Without any training—"

"Tot, you said the most important part of this job would be me using my brain. I'm using it. If he wanted to kill me, he could've done it in his apartment. Otherwise, I'm the only one here right now. So I either follow him, or we lose him," I say as the door to the underground garage opens. A white Mercedes shoots out with a black woman at the wheel. Not Marshall.

"You're still not listening, Beecher, because when it comes to superpowers, your friend Marshall's superpower is *this*: losing people and getting away."

Up the block, the Mercedes disappears around the corner, and the garage door lowers back into place.

"Just tell me who he is. Navy SEAL? FBI? CIA?"

"Oh, he's far worse than that. According to Immaculate Deception, Marshall Lusk is GAO."

"*Government Accountability Office?*" I say, referring to the guys who do our audits. "They're America's accountants."

"No. That's where you're wrong. Accountants deal with numbers. What the GAO does is look for waste and inefficiency."

"And that's different from an accountant because . . . ?"

Up ahead, the garage door again opens. This time, a light gray Toyota rolls out. Another woman at the wheel. But just as the garage door is about to roll down, it jerks back up.

Another car pokes its nose out. A navy SUV.

Marshall's car. With Marshall behind the wheel.

As he takes off, he's two blocks ahead. I give him another block as a head start. He's in a rush, but I still see him.

Time to find out where he's going.

28

eecher, listen to me," Tot says through the phone as I kick the gas and trace Marshall's path. "You ever hear of something called *pen testing*? Penetration testing?"

Up ahead, Marshall weaves through traffic. But as he makes a sharp left, it's clear he's going straight to the highway—north on 110—back toward Washington.

For the most part, he sticks to the left lane, making good time. I let him keep his lead.

"Long before SEAL Team Six or even the Navy SEALs themselves," Tot explains, "there was a group known as the S&Rs—Scouts and Raiders."

"The first group of frogmen," I say, sticking behind a white van and using it to stay out of sight. "I've seen their files in the Archives."

"Exactly. The Scouts and Raiders started eight months after the attack on Pearl Harbor—made up of army and navy men. And in 1943, these sneaky sons of bitches' graduation exercise was supposedly to kidnap the admiral in charge of the 7th Naval District. During wartime!"

"Did they do it?"

"The point is, that's what penetration testing tells us. When our own guys break in and grab an admiral, that tells us we have a real problem in security. The military's used it for decades: hiring units to try and penetrate our top facilities, from nuclear depots, to Air Force One."

Up ahead, as we approach Arlington Cemetery, Marshall's SUV veers to the right, following the exit toward the roundabout at Memorial Bridge. Time to pick up the pace. "So that's what Marshall does now?" I ask as I pull out from behind the white van and hit the gas.

"It's what *everyone* does now. These days, we have people trying to break into the White House, into the Capitol, even into the cafeteria at the Air & Space Museum."

"Like when you see those news stories about guys successfully sneaking knives onto airplanes."

"Penetration testing," Tot says as I spot the roundabout up ahead. The few cars around us all begin to slow down. I'm now barely five or six cars behind Marshall. He's never seen my car. I pull down my sun visor so he can't see my face. "After 9/11, the GAO realized that it wasn't just useful for the military. It's a test for all of us," Tot explains. "Penetration testing isn't just about *breaking in*. It's about *solving problems*."

"So again, back to Marshall," I say. "He does these penetration tests."

"And does them well. That's how he got out of jail last night. In his line of work, when things go bad, he's got a direct line to the Justice Department, who'll get him out of any mess he gets into. But yes—from what we can tell, he's spent nearly four years in the GAO's Office of Investigations."

"So why do I hear that worried tone in your voice?"

"Because he's the *whole office*, Beecher. There used to be a few of them, but once Marshall came in...that's it. He's all they needed. According to our source, when he first started, Marshall was sent to break into some unlisted military base out in Nebraska, and since the general in charge of the base didn't want to be embarrassed— which is what happens when strangers break into your military base—the general actually broke the rules and told his security guys that Marshall was coming...that they should keep a serious lookout. That night, at three in the morning, Marshall was standing in the general's bedroom—and woke up the general by putting a gun to his head and whispering, '*You lose.*'"

As Marshall's SUV merges onto the roundabout by Memorial Bridge, my thoughts run back to his apartment—to my wallet being in my coat pocket and me telling myself that there's no way Marshall could've pulled it off.

"Now you understand why I don't want you confronting him? Look at the facts from last night: for a guy like Marshall—a guy who regularly sidesteps the best security in the world—for him to get nabbed coming out of a church...by two D.C. beat cops..."

"It was bad timing. Maybe the cops just got lucky."

"No. There's no luck. Not with people like this, Beecher."

"So what're you saying? That Marshall killed this rector and then got arrested *on purpose?*"

Tot's silent, thinking it through. "That's the real question, isn't it? Do you think *you* found Marshall, Beecher? Or did Marshall actually use all this to find *you?*"

The heat in the car is blasting full steam. But for the first time, I'm feeling it. In front of me, as I snake around the roundabout, I'm barely three cars behind Marshall. The white van slides in front of me. I still see the SUV...up by twelve o'clock, where the entrance to Memorial Bridge is. I'm at four o'clock.

"Listen to me, Beecher," Tot says as I twist the wheel. "I know you two go back a long way. And I know there's something about this guy—something that happened with him—that's making you want to believe, with all of your nostalgic heart, that he's not a murderer. But know this: your pal Marshall? He finds weaknesses in things. That's how he breaks into things for a living. And of all the things he's dissecting—when you come chasing him...when you get suckered into his apartment—the thing that he's found the biggest weakness in, and that he's *broken into* the most...

...is you."

With a final jerk of the wheel, I twist the Mustang to the right and slide out from behind the white van. I look to my right, out the passenger-side window, and onto the bridge. The SUV isn't there.

I stay on the roundabout. He's not here either.

I search the next turnoff. There're only three in total. He's not there either.

It's daytime. Light traffic. There aren't many options, but even so...

"You lost him, didn't you?" Tot asks through the phone. "You have no hope of catching a guy like this, Beecher. He's a professional ghost. And y'know what the worst part is? Guess who the GAO reports to?"

"To the legislature. They're the legislative arm of Congress."

"That's right. But the head of the GAO—the comptroller general—guess who appoints him?"

"The White House."

"The White House, Beecher. So you know who someone at Marshall's level really works for?"

I turn the heat down in the car, but it still feels like it's blasting full steam. "The President."

"Or more specifically, President Orson Wallace, who attacked and was responsible for the murder of a man known as Eightball, and who promised to bury you for finding out about it."

I'm still circling the roundabout, still searching for the SUV. It's gone.

Two months ago, this is where I'd bang the steering wheel and give up.

That's because two months ago, I wasn't part of George Washington's secret spy ring.

"Beecher, please tell me you—"

"Of course I did, Tot. I just need to turn it on."

He knows what I'm talking about, and how it works. I need to get off the phone.

He wants me to be careful, but I hang up before he says it.

To Tot, this is Culper Ring business...presidential business... and it is. But for me, think of your best friend growing up. No. I take that back. Think of the friend you hurt the most. Think of what you owe him. Whatever's really going on, I still owe that to Marshall.

Back in his apartment, Marshall was amazed that my phone was getting a signal there. He doesn't know the half of what it can do.

As Tot hangs up, I scroll to an app called Jupiter.

After the Revolutionary War, George Washington was committed to building our country. But in his personal life, his commitment was given to, of all things, *breeding*.

Not kids. Washington never had kids.

He had dogs.

According to his papers, he wanted *a superior dog, one that had speed, sense and brains*. He did it too—after merging a set of hounds that were a gift from the French with a set of tan-and-black hounds here.

His creation was the American foxhound. The ultimate hunting machine.

More than thirty hounds were listed in his journals, with names like Drunkard, Tipsy, Sweet Lips, and of course...

Jupiter.

With a press of my thumb, the screen on my phone displays a map. The circular road shows the roundabout and Memorial Bridge. There's a tiny green pin, which represents me. There's also a red pin. That's the SUV.

When I was in his apartment, Marshall may've grabbed my wallet to pick through my life. But when we were in his parking garage—when I was in his SUV—I dropped a small silver beacon into the plastic well on the passenger-side door.

Marshall's smart. And clearly smarter at this than I am. But he's not smarter than the Culper Ring.

Based on the map, he's making his way toward the Key Bridge, headed to Georgetown.

When I was little, my mom said I shouldn't get out of bed until I said a prayer for something I was thankful for. It's a rule I carry with me to this day. God bless GPS. And Jupiter, the ultimate hunting machine.

Within ten minutes, I see where he stops.

Ready or not, Marshall. Here I come.

*   *   *

29

*D*on't let them put you in it, Nico," the dead First Lady warned. Nodding at her, Nico squinted down at the floor of the redbrick courtyard, where a section of light beige bricks formed a circular maze pattern.

"So it's a maze?" Nico asked, his book—with its ten of spades bookmark—tucked tightly under his armpit.

"It's not a maze. It's a labyrinth," Nurse Karina, a short Asian woman with black statement glasses and perfectly smooth skin, offered, motioning her clipboard toward the bricks. "Do you know the difference between a maze and a labyrinth?" Well aware that she wasn't supposed to let Nico tangle with a problem he couldn't solve, she quickly explained, "A maze is designed to be an obstacle, with dead ends and wrong turns. A labyrinth will never block you— it gives you a winding but totally clear path right to the center and then back again."

"So a bad hospital would have a maze?" Nico asked, still eyeing the wide, circular labyrinth that...no question about it...looked like a twenty-foot-wide maze.

"Yes, a bad hospital would have a maze. In *The Shining*? That's a maze. We have a labyrinth. It's very therapeutic. Now would you like to begin?"

Nico didn't want to begin. It was cold outside, and even though the courtyard was covered, he didn't like the cold. But he did like

Nurse Karina, who always looked him right in the eyes. Most of the nurses never looked him in the eyes.

"I start here?" Nico asked, entering the labyrinth.

"I can hold your book for you. If you like," Karina offered.

At first, Nico hesitated. But then he saw her outstretched hand...and the pale pink polish on her thin, crooked fingers. His mother had fingers like that.

"I want it back when I'm done," Nico said, handing Karina the book as she offered a small smile in return.

He trusted her now. Enough to hand her the book and to step into the labyrinth. Yet as he took his first steps around the outer edges of the circle, Nico couldn't help but notice the double-pane window that looked out onto the courtyard. Through it, he saw a breakroom, where a group of construction workers were watching the local news. In St. Elizabeths, they never let Nico watch the news.

"Y'know back during the Crusades, walking a labyrinth represented a pilgrimage to the Holy Land. For many, they're still sacred places," Karina added, knowing that Nico always responded well to religious references.

Nico barely heard the words. As he followed the zigzag and it led him past the window of the breakroom, his eyes were locked on the handsome news anchor sitting at the news desk. The graphic onscreen said: *Shooting At Local Church*. But it wasn't until the camera cut to video footage of Foundry Church that Nico stopped midstep.

"Nico...?" Karina called out. From the angle she was at, she couldn't see into the breakroom. It looked like Nico was staring blankly at the wall.

"Nico, what's wrong?"

His body was tensed, his arms flat at his sides. He wanted to say something to the dead First Lady, but with the nurse watching, he just stood there, looking in the window, at the screen. There it was. The message he'd been waiting for. Just as the Knight had promised.

"Nico, look at me!" Nurse Karina pleaded, as if she were saying it for the fifth time.

He whipped around, facing Karina. His chest was pumping, though his sniper training kicked in quickly. You don't hold your breath as you squeeze the trigger. You learn to breathe into it.

"Don't move," the dead First Lady agreed. *"Let her get us what we need."*

Nico nodded. There was still so much to do. Beecher...and Clementine...would be here soon.

"Nico, you okay?" Nurse Karina asked.

He just stood there, frozen.

"Nico, please. I need you to say something."

His chest continued to rise and fall. Maybe even a little bit faster. The dead First Lady was right. This was how he'd get what he wanted.

"Nico, I'm serious," Karina demanded. "Please say something."

30

I find Marshall's SUV on a narrow side street in Georgetown, just off the main drag of Wisconsin Avenue. The tracker I hid is still in the car, but it only takes a few footprints in the snow to trail him along the lumpy brick sidewalks.

Up the block, there's a redbrick building with royal blue awnings. The footprints make a sharp left, into an alley just before the building.

I scramble as fast as I can, sticking to the streets so I get a better foothold to run.

With each of my steps, the gray slush leaps from the pavement, arcing up and outward, like synchronized divers. I don't stop until I'm near the blue awnings; then I look to my left to make sure the alley's clear.

Darting from the street and toward the sidewalk, I step through a drift of black snow that doesn't look that deep but somehow swallows my leg all the way up to my ankle. My sock fills with frozen water. I remind myself I'm not a spy. I'm an archivist. A history major.

But that's the thing about history majors. We know the value of what's left behind.

In front of me, the alley's empty. Marshall's gone.

But once again, his footprints—curving around to the right... behind the building—are right where he left them.

Racing forward, I tear around the corner. The alley widens into an open brick courtyard. But the first thing I see is— On my right. There's a door. A propped-open door that's about to slam shut.

It leads into the back of the building. Where Marshall just ducked inside.

I race for the door, catching it just before it closes. With a yank, I pull it open and step inside. A familiar but unplaceable smell wafts through the air. Like I said, Marshall's smart. But I'm—

Uccck.

His fist hits me in the throat first.

He *grabs* me. *My throat—!*

He grips my Adam's apple with the tips of all five of his fingers. Like he's plucking it from my neck. The pain is— It's not just that I can't breathe... My neck...

He's crushing my larynx—!

My knees collapse. My eyes flood with involuntary tears. But I still see him. The melted-wax face. Those gold eyes.

Marshall's trying to kill me.

31

Staring down at his eelskin wallet, Dr. Palmiotti knew better than this. He did. But a few minutes ago, as he left Wok 'n Roll and stood out in the cold—amid the back-from-lunch rush crowd—he couldn't help but watch A.J. walk up the block, back to work.

Back to 16th Street. Back to the White House.

For two minutes, Palmiotti stood there, knowing it shouldn't matter. But it did.

And so there he was, staring down at his eelskin wallet. Or to be more precise, at the fortune from the fortune cookie that was sticking out of that little secret hiding space that, if he were thirty years younger, he would've used to hide a condom. It was the hiding space that you can only get to if you dig at it with your pointer- and middle fingers, which Palmiotti quickly did to pull out the paper fortune.

It wasn't the contents of the fortune that mattered. It was what was written on back.

Two months ago, after A.J. helped him send that text during the funeral, as they were putting his new identity together, Wallace took the little scrap from a fortune cookie and wrote a ten-digit number on it. The President told Palmiotti that if anything went wrong...if there was an emergency and Palmiotti needed to talk...even if he just needed a friend...*this* was the number he should dial. A number that would connect him directly to the President.

Palmiotti knew what that meant. The public was told that Wallace carried a BlackBerry. It wasn't a BlackBerry. Neither was Obama's or any other President's. It was a Sectéra Edge, a phone made specially by General Dynamics solely for the use of the President. The one phone Wallace carried himself.

So you won't be alone, Wallace had promised. *I'm always a phone call away.*

For two months, Palmiotti had never used the number. Didn't even think of it.

Okay, that wasn't true.

He thought of using it during the very first week, when he was watching the Michigan game, which brought back memories of their college years. Then he thought of using it again, later that same week, when he was out for a walk and saw a dog that reminded him of the beagle Wallace had when they were young.

But Palmiotti wasn't dumb. And he wasn't shallow enough to break the emergency glass and place a direct call to the President of the United States simply because he was feeling homesick.

Yes, Palmiotti had known it wouldn't be easy to just walk away from his life. But in those moments of doubt, he'd think back to what his mentor used to tell him twenty years ago when he was doing his cardiac residency: *The bleeding always stops—one way or another.* It was good advice. True advice. And when the advice didn't make him feel any better, Palmiotti would close his eyes and inevitably start making a list of all the other people he now wanted to speak to, including his kids.

But as Palmiotti knew, whether he was alive or dead, his kids didn't want to speak to him. He hadn't even seen them in over a decade. Not since the divorce. Not after what he put them all through.

It was the same with his ex-wife. That's why she was an ex.

Of course, it was different with his girlfriend, Lydia, which is why, on that one night a few weeks back, he (with aid from a far too expensive bottle of scotch) dialed her home number just to hear her voice. When she picked up, he hung up. That was all he needed.

After that, Palmiotti was strong. Committed.

Just like he was when it came to dealing with Beecher. After his conversation with A.J., he knew what the next steps were. He knew how to make it happen. And he knew it would only work if he made it work. But still...as A.J. disappeared around the corner and Palmiotti looked down at his eelskin wallet and the phone number scribbled on the paper fortune...

Orson Wallace wasn't just his best friend. They were brothers. How can you separate brothers? Hesitating, Palmiotti told himself to wait. That he'd be seeing Wallace soon—like A.J. said, at the Presidents' Day event...

Still.

With everything Palmiotti had sacrificed, would one phone call—just a few seconds...a few sentences to say hello—really hurt?

Studying the phone number, Palmiotti replayed his mentor's words: *The bleeding always stops—one way or another.* That was absolutely right.

But as he *also* learned in med school, there was actually a faster way to stop the bleeding: when you take matters into your own hands.

Pulling out the cheap disposable phone that he'd switch every few weeks, Palmiotti looked down at the fortune cookie and dialed the ten-digit number.

As it rang, he knew, on some level, that the President would be pissed. But once he and his friend started talking, it'd all go back to normal. That's what friends do.

In Palmiotti's ear, the phone rang once...twice...

His shoulders lifted at the sheer excitement of reconnecting. Sure, Wallace would be mad, but he'd also—

"*We're sorry,*" a female mechanical voice eventually answered. "*The number you dialed is not in service. Please check the number and dial again.*"

Palmiotti felt a hot, sudden throb in the wound that was healing in his neck. For a moment, he thought he must've dialed the wrong number.

But as the mechanical woman repeated herself...even before he checked the paper fortune...before he redialed...Stewart Palmiotti knew he'd dialed exactly right.

32

Marshall doesn't say anything.

He holds tight to my throat, still clutching my Adam's apple.

I fight to break free, but my eyes feel like they're about to pop.

Without a word, he loosens his grip, though not by much. My lungs refill with air and I unleash a hacking cough. But Marshall doesn't let go. Not completely.

He looks me dead in the eye. His bumpy, burned hand is still on my throat, holding me in place. "If you're not careful who you follow, you *will* get hurt," he says, making sure I hear every syllable.

He finally lets go, letting me catch my breath. "What the hell is wrong with you?"

He doesn't answer.

As I look around—at the silver pots and pans hanging from the ceiling... the industrial stoves and ovens on my left... plus the stainless steel prep areas with the chefs and waiters...

"Why're we in a restaurant kitchen?" I blurt as I finally place the smell in the air. Fresh pasta.

Marshall looks over his shoulder. At first, I assume he's worried about being heard. He's not.

"What're you guys doing?" a heavy chef with a thin gray beard blurts, looking up from a tray of pastries he's filling.

"Mind your business," Marshall barks back, marching through the kitchen, past the rolling prep carts, and heading for the swinging doors at the far end. His tone is so commanding, the chef doesn't even push back at the intrusion. But I see how quickly the chef looks away. It's hard to stare at Marshall's burned face.

With a shove of the swinging door, the fluorescent lights and stainless steel of the kitchen give way to the muted yellow walls, French doors, and plush décor of a fine Italian restaurant.

A few stragglers from the lunch crowd—all of them in suit and tie—turn and stare. It happens in every posh restaurant in D.C.—people checking to see if we're anyone famous. But again, after one look at Marshall's face, they all turn away. What I'm starting to notice, though, is I think that's how Marshall prefers it.

Sticking to the corner, by the bar, he scans the restaurant. On my right, a stack of menus finally tells me where we are. Café Milano.

I know Café Milano. Everyone in D.C. knows Café Milano. From Bill and Hillary, to Joe and Jill Biden, to Julia Roberts, Kobe Bryant, and every honcho in the last decade—in a town that tires quickly of trendy restaurants—Café Milano has managed to feed pols and celebs, while extending its trend. Which is why I've never been here. "Why are we at Café Milano?"

"I'm meeting someone," he insists, still scanning the restaurant. It doesn't take long; most of the lunch crowd is gone. Nearly every table is empty. Yet there Marshall is, his eyes flicking back and forth, like he's memorizing and cataloging the room's every detail. Unlike in his apartment, his entire stance has changed. His back is straight, his chin is up. He's working.

It takes me a few seconds to realize that from where we're standing, we have a perfect view of every entrance and exit.

"Marshall, I know Presidents eat here. And I know what your job is. The penetration testing… Is that what you're doing? You looking for flaws in their security?"

He turns my way, gripping the edge of the bar with a scarred hand. "You figured me out, Beecher. Just before noon tomorrow, as he heads out to lead his daughter's class trip to the Lincoln Memorial, President Orson Wallace will be leaving this dining room, which is when I'll sneak up behind him and use his own steak knife to slit his throat and pull his larynx into his lap." As he says the words, his lips press into a thin smile.

"That's not funny, Marsh. How can you say something like that?"

"Isn't that what you want me to say, Beecher?" he asks, still calm as can be. "Isn't that why you came here—to prove I'm a heartless murderer?"

On our right, the bartender finally takes notice of us. So does the maître d'. Waving them both back with nothing but a dark stare, Marshall walks—slowly, like he owns the place—through the restaurant and out the front door as I walk behind him. No one approaches. They know a wolf when they see one.

Outside, the front patio of the restaurant has a few wrought-iron tables that're covered with snow. There's no place to sit. But at least no one's listening.

"If you want to know something, Beecher, ask me to my face."

"How's your dad doing these days?" I ask.

"He died. Three years ago."

"I'm sorry, Marsh. I had no—"

"He was sick a long time," he says in the sort of elegant calm that comes from someone who's grown accustomed to tragedy.

No surprise, all it does is make me miss my own dad, who died when I was just three. Two months ago, Clementine said she knew the real story of my father's death. I know it was just another manipulation, but that doesn't mean it didn't leave its own scar.

As we linger in front of the restaurant, I wait for Marshall to say something else, but he's still scanning our surroundings, checking the building across the street and every window in it that looks down on us.

"You want to tell me what really happened at that church?" I say.

"I told you what happened."

"So you just coincidentally were there? You were just saying some prayers?"

"What's wrong with saying prayers? When we were little, your mom made us say that morning prayer, for what we were thankful for. You're telling me you still don't do that?"

My shoulder brushes against one of the metal poles that holds up the restaurant's blue awning, sending a sprinkling of snow toward the earth and once again making me think of my own father. "I really did look you up, Marshall. This stuff at GAO—I know how good you are at getting into places you shouldn't be. So stop insulting me. Why were you really in St. John's Church last night?"

His stance is still all business. He keeps staring across the street, dissecting every window across from us.

"Marshall, if you're in trouble—"

"I don't need your help, Beecher."

"That's not true. A man was murdered. *You* were the one arrested for it!" I hiss, fighting to keep my voice down. "This group I work with…instead of being so stubborn and pushing us away…" I swallow my words, amazed at my own rush of anger.

I take a deep breath. "I know I haven't been part of your life for over a decade. But for years, I *was* part of your life. Y'know how many hours I spent with you in that treehouse?"

Marshall is still facing the building across the street. He won't turn my way. But he's no longer checking windows.

His voice is still. He never gets upset. "You know that rector who died at the church last night," he finally says. "The one who got his throat slit?"

"Yeah?"

"He wasn't the first rector who was killed. There was another. One before him."

"What're you talking about?" I ask.

"Two and a half weeks ago. Another pastor died. That's what I was looking into. That's what led me to St. John's."

Kicking at the ground, Marshall pivots his foot like he's putting out a cigarette. But the force he puts behind it, it's like he's trying to dig through the concrete itself. Last time I saw that look, urine was running down his father's wheelchair.

"Why were you looking at that first pastor?"

He kicks again at the ground. The snow is almost gone. "He was someone I knew. From Saggy."

"Wait. You knew him from *home*?"

Marshall nods. "You knew him too."

33

How long's he been like that?" Nurse Rupert asked.

"Almost twenty minutes," Nurse Karina replied, eyeing the beige brick labyrinth, where Nico was still standing directly at the center, his hands flat at his sides. Like a military man.

"Twenty minutes? You're kidding."

"I wish."

"Karina, you're telling me you've watched Nico stand there— *right there*—at the center of that stupid maze—"

"It's a labyrinth. Mazes have dead ends."

"You're telling me that for twenty minutes—" Rupert cut himself off, "If Gosling sees this—" He cut himself off again. "Why didn't you call for help?"

"I *am* calling for help. That's why I called you," she said with Nico's leather book still tucked under her arm. "Tina said he likes you."

"Nico *doesn't* like me. He just does better with male nurses. Always has."

"I don't care if he does better with transvestites. Last time he shut down like this, Tina said he put a mechanical pencil in Dr. Herthel's leg."

Remembering the incident, and the blood that went with it, Rupert snatched the old book from Nurse Karina. Every few months, Nico would find an object of obsession. For a while it was his Redskins wall calendar. Before that, it was his red glass rosary, preceded by a pair of reading glasses that reminded him of a truck driver whose throat he punctured. Today, Rupert knew Nico's current obsession.

Turning back to the labyrinth, he waved the book in the air. "Nico, I got your book."

Nico didn't answer.

"I know you heard me," Rupert called again, refusing to get close until he was sure it was safe.

Nico just stood there, hands flat at his sides.

Rupert took a deep breath, annoyed. Dammit. "Nico, you wanna go to the computer room?"

Nico turned. He knew they'd only offer the computer if they were desperate. That's why he needed to make his stand in the labyrinth. This was what he was waiting for. It was time to get the Knight's new message. "Is the computer room here the same as the old one?"

"Even better," Rupert said, waving Nico out of the maze and steering him with a gentle back pat. "C'mon, you'll love it."

"Can I bring my book?" Nico asked, eyeing the book in Rupert's hands. The book the Knight had sent him.

"Of course," Rupert said, handing it to him. "Bring whatever you want."

34

Still pinching the slip of paper from the fortune cookie between his fingertips, Dr. Stewart Palmiotti used his free hand to redial the President's phone number. Again.

And again.

"We're sorry. The number you dialed is not in service. Please check the number and dial again."

He crumpled the fortune like a spitball but didn't throw it away. He stuffed it in his pocket, not even noticing he was grinding his teeth.

On his left, a few blocks from Wok 'n Roll, a passing woman in a ratty red scarf seemed to be staring at him.

Dropping his head, Palmiotti walked in the opposite direction. With his head down.

The woman with the scarf definitely was no longer looking. *No one's looking,* he told himself.

And that was the problem. No one *was* looking. No one was watching. Despite everything he'd been promised—all the reassurances that the President...that the Secret Service...that everyone would be looking out for him...

Stewart Palmiotti really was out here alone.

Or.

Maybe it was just a mistake.

At the thought of it, Palmiotti's fists unclenched.

It wasn't the craziest explanation. For over three years, President Wallace hadn't cooked for himself...placed a call for himself...he didn't even carry his own wallet anymore. So was it possible that maybe, just maybe, when Wallace wrote down the number, he wrote it down *wrong*?

Certainly *possible*.

Wasn't it?

Besides, if it were a real emergency, he still knew how to get in touch with A.J. and the Secret Service. He did. It didn't matter whether the number was right or wrong.

Palmiotti and the President had gone to elementary school together. They had traded snacks in the lunchroom together. They had buried Wallace's mother. And Palmiotti's father.

No question, the President would *always* look out for him. Always love him. But as his thumb skated across the keypad of the cheap disposable cell phone, Palmiotti knew there was one other person who loved him too.

Lydia. The woman he'd been seeing before all this.

She loved Palmiotti as well.

His cheeks lifted as he began dialing her number. He didn't want to actually talk to her. No. Even he wasn't that stupid. And even if he was, what would he say? *Hey, hon! I'm not dead. I'm alive!*

No. All Palmiotti wanted was to hear her voice on her answering machine. The little singsongy way she said *Lydi-a*, like it belonged in a musical. He knew she wouldn't be there. It was a workday.

The phone rang once...twice... As it picked up, there was that hollow pause that tells you the answering machine message is about to begin.

For Palmiotti, that's all he needed. Just to hear her voice.

"This is *Lydia*," the message announced as the singsong made his heart balloon, pressing against his sternum. "You called. Leave a message."

He hung up before the beep even sounded, soaking in the irrational rush of emotions that comes from any mention of an old lover.

Stuffing the phone back into his pocket, Palmiotti told himself that that was all he needed. Just to hear her voice. That was enough.

And as he felt that lump in his throat and that rise in his pants . . .

It *was* enough.

But then . . . it wasn't.

35

I knew *who*?" I ask, still lost.

"Riis," Marshall says.

"*Pastor* Riis? From our hometown? Pastor Riis is dead?"

"Three weeks ago. Shot in the chest by an old obscure gun."

He says something else, but I don't hear it. My mind's already tumbling back to Sunday school...to Riis's sermons at church... to the fact that he always smelled like peppermint Tic Tacs and suntan lotion...and of course to that night in the basement when Pastor Riis and Marshall's mom—

"Don't look at me like that, Beecher. I didn't kill him."

"I didn't say you did."

"You think I don't know that look? Get it out of your head, Beecher. When Pastor Riis left town—"

"He didn't *leave* town. They *ran* him out of town! What he did with you...and your mom—"

"Don't say those words," he warns as I feel the rage rising off him. He keeps staring across the street, gripping the pole of the awning like he's about to rip it from its mooring. Behind us, two patrons leave the restaurant and steer wide around us, sensing Marshall's anger.

"You don't know what happened back then, Beecher. To me...or my mom. You don't know anything about what happened that night."

"Your mom died, Marshall! She put a gun in her mouth and pulled the trigger! What else do we need to—?"

He whips my way, his fist cocked.

I jump back, holding my hands up to protect my face. But he drops his hands to his sides.

"You think I'd hit you?" he asks, annoyed.

"You did choke me." When he doesn't respond, I add, "I'm sorry for bringing up your mom like that."

He forces a grin, but his skin is stiff and unpliable. Like he's wearing a plastic mask of himself. Still, there's something real in his eyes.

"And I'm sorry for saying that about Pastor Riis," I add.

"I brought him up," he points out. "But Beecher, would I have told you about Pastor Riis if I was the one who killed him?"

"I'm just saying, I know he's not just some guy who means nothing to you."

"That's why I started looking. First at Riis, and then at the other two."

"Two? What two? There's Riis—and there's the rector who was killed at St. John's . . ."

"And then there's the one from this morning," he says, watching me carefully. He was testing me, to see if I knew that one. The thing is, I'm not sure if I passed or failed. Was I supposed to know or not?

"Someone else was killed this morning?" I ask.

"Pastor Kenneth Frick. They found him shot in the back at Foundry Church . . . up on 16th Street. But from what the paramedics said, he's gonna survive—"

"Hold on. Back up. You said shot in the *back*?"

"Yeah. Why? What's special about the back?" Marsh asks. Unlike before, there's no calculus in his question.

I stay silent, replaying the facts.

"Say what you're thinking, Beecher."

"I'm not sure," I tell him, though I have a pretty good hunch. In 1881, President James Garfield became the second sitting President to be killed in office when he was assassinated by a bullet wound . . . in his back.

Last night it was Abraham Lincoln . . . now James Garfield . . . two lethal attacks that have now been re-created within twenty-four hours. I knew we had a copycat killer. But whoever's doing this isn't just trying to imitate John Wilkes Booth—he's imitating, in intricate detail, the worst murderers in U.S. history. The only thing that doesn't make sense...

"How does this tie back to Pastor Riis?" I demand.

"Three murders. All three of them clergy."

I nod. Of course that's how he sees it. He doesn't spot the copycat assassin part. He just sees dead pastors. But as I replay the facts, St. John's is known as the Church of the Presidents. Foundry Church, I'm pretty sure, is where FDR used to take Winston Churchill for services, and where Lincoln was also a member. That means both churches have ties to the commander in chief. "How about Riis?" I ask, trying to fill in my own sketch. "Where did he die?"

Marshall cocks his head at that, his sparse eyebrows fighting to knot together. "You see something in those two recent deaths, don't you?" he says.

"You just told me about them. What can I possibly know?"

He looks back up at the windows across the street.

I wear a key around my neck. I found it back in Wisconsin when I used to work at Farris's secondhand bookshop. It was hidden in an old dictionary, and good things happened on the day I found it—the kind of good things that helped me escape our little town. So, as whacky as it sounds, since that time, I've worn the magic key on a thin leather necklace. The only time I notice it is when I'm sweating bad and it sticks to my chest. Like now.

"Tell me more about Riis," I add. "How'd you find out he was killed?"

"Jeremy Phillip's dad called me," he says. A name from our past. "And did Riis—?"

"Riis didn't work in Washington. Had nothing to do with D.C. churches, if that's where you're sniffing. He was living out in North Carolina. Retired years ago. As far as I can tell, the only thing these two pastors might've had in common was that Riis spent a few years in Tennessee, teaching at Vanderbilt Divinity School out in Nashville. And when I looked at the rector who was killed at St. John's last night..."

"He graduated from Vanderbilt too, from the Divinity School. I saw the diploma when we were at his office yesterday."

Marshall stops at that, still staring across the street. "You still have that amazing memory, don't you, Beecher? No detail too obscure," he says with a smile that actually feels kind.

"So when you were at the church last night," I say, "it really was because you were doing your own investigation."

"You know what I do for a living. It's good government work. And important work. But this one—with Riis—whatever else you think happened with him all those years ago, no one deserves to die like that. So yes, I'm doing this one by myself. But if you have any extra resources, with whatever organization you said you were working with, please jump in."

"And what happens when you catch him?"

He turns away from the street, his gold eyes hooded as he locks on me. "I told you: I'm taking a steak knife and slicing out his larynx."

He doesn't blink. But after a good ten seconds, his lips press into a thin grin.

"I'm joking, Beecher. Can't you take a joke?"

I think about the Abraham Lincoln mask I found in his house, and how he already knows about this so-called "new" murder this morning. But more than anything else, I think about that night in the basement and the real reason Marshall has so much hate for pastors. And for me.

"I don't like jokes like that." I pause, searching his face. "Just answer me one thing: Clementine Kaye. You really don't remember her?"

He taps what's left of his pale tongue against the back of his teeth. "Short black hair. Always wore short skirts. You really think I'd forget who your first crush was, Beecher? I looked her up after you left my apartment. Nice job keeping it from going public—it took nearly every clearance I have to read the report, but...Nico Hadrian's daughter? She screwed you up pretty good too, huh? You never had good taste in girls."

I shake my head. "Why'd you lie?"

"For a smart guy, you know very little. So know this: Just because you had one devil from your past, doesn't mean you now have two."

Before I can reply, my phone vibrates in my pocket. I know who it is.

Tot starts talking before I can even say hello. "You still with Marshall?"

"I am. Everything okay?"

"Not sure," he says, though I know that tone in his voice. "We've got another murder. Some priest got shot in the back. Like President Garfield."

"I heard," I say, eyeing Marshall, who, as he walks back to his car, is still staring at the empty building across the street.

"Here's the kicker, though," Tot says, his voice dropping to a near whisper. "We did some homework on that photo you emailed," he adds, referring to the plaster Abraham Lincoln mask that I found in Marshall's apartment. "I know where Marshall stole it from."

36

Diagonally across the block on H Street, Secret Service agent A.J. Ennis kept his head down as he stood under the awning at the greeting card store and watched Stewart Palmiotti press the buttons on his phone.

It wasn't hard to double back around the block after they ate at Wok 'n Roll. Maybe A.J. was just being paranoid. But as he learned a few years ago when he was paranoid enough to check his fiancée's text messages, sometimes paranoia pays off.

Across the street, from what A.J. could tell, Palmiotti was clearly worked up as he dialed a phone number. A.J. had no idea who Palmiotti was calling. But when you have a guy who's not supposed to be interacting with any parts of his old life, nothing good is going to happen when he's punching at a cell phone.

From his pocket, A.J. pulled out his own phone and dialed a ten-digit number that didn't ring. It clicked.

Click-click-click... Click-click-click...

"You saw him?" the President of the United States answered.

"I saw him."

"He doing okay?"

"Actually," A.J. said, "that's what I'm starting to worry about."

37

"Y ou agree something's wrong with him?" Tot asks as we fight through traffic in the pale blue Mustang.

"I don't know about *wrong*," I say from the passenger seat, still picturing the scars on Marshall's face, and the way his tongue looked like it was rebuilt with lighter skin. "Something definitely happened to him. He's different."

"No, he's not just *different*, Beecher. That job he has...to do what he does...he's missing the part of his brain that tells him to stay away from danger. And in my experience, when you're missing that, your problems are just beginning," Tot says, jerking the wheel and cutting off a muted green Range Rover that wasn't doing anything but going the speed limit. Since the moment I picked him up at the Archives, he's been in a mood.

"Tot, did I do something wrong?"

"Just answer me this: Do you know what the worst part was of what happened with Clementine?"

"I told you, this isn't Clementine."

"I'm not trying to scold you, Beecher. I'm asking you to take a look at who you are. Because to me, of all the things Clementine did, the very worst was this: She showed them your weakness. When she reentered your life, she showed the President and everyone else that when it comes to an old friend or someone you're emotionally involved with, you'll ignore all logic and reason, even in the face of facts that're telling you otherwise."

"That's not true," I say, stealing a quick glance in the rearview just to make sure we're alone.

"Beecher, we're looking for someone who's been killing pastors while wearing an Abraham Lincoln mask and, for some reason, carrying nineteenth-century playing cards. Earlier today, in your friend Marshall's apartment, you found a Lincoln mask that—oh yeah—perfectly covers the scars on his face, plus those same cards with the missing ace of spades. Do you really need the smoke to be twirling out of the barrel of his gun before you'll realize what he's doing?"

"I hear what you're saying, Tot, but aren't you the one who also taught me that even when the whole world is telling you one thing, sometimes you need to follow your gut?"

"Hhhh," he says, turning the small grunt into a full sentence. In the distance, even though it's getting dark, I spot the tall black metal gates on my right. "Beecher, have you ever really looked at the men who've tried to kill our country's leaders? Experts put them into two categories: *howlers* and *hunters*. The howlers threaten us by sending scary notes and calling in bomb threats, but the good news is, they rarely follow through. They just want attention, so for them, howling and making noise is enough. It's different with hunters. Hunters *act on it*. They research, prepare, plot—and follow that path to a goal. But what's most interesting is that howlers aren't interested in hunting. And hunters aren't interested in howling. So now that you spent that time with Marshall, which do you think he is?"

I stay silent, staring at the red taillights of the cars in front of us. But all I see is the hollow smile on Marshall's face as he made his joke about killing the President with a steak knife.

"He had your name in his pocket for a reason, Beecher. And he wears those gloves for a reason. Now *your* prints are the ones all over that Lincoln mask. So in case you hadn't realized it, when it comes to any murder, even the worst hunters know the benefits of bringing along a fall guy."

"I hear you, Tot. And I appreciate the warning."

"Can I ask you a different question?" Tot interrupts. "I know I know the answer to this, but if Marshall *was* trying to kill the President, you sure you're ready to stop him?"

"Excuse me?"

"I'm just saying, we all know how you feel about President

Wallace. So with this second pastor that was shot at Foundry Church... First we had John Wilkes Booth...now Charles Guiteau... This isn't just a single act anymore. It's a pattern of dead Presidents. So tell me, Beecher: If that pattern kept going toward our current President—"

"Who said that's where it's going?"

"You telling me it's not? Someone just meticulously re-created two assassinations," he says, his voice getting slower. "And there are only two more presidential assassinations to imitate. So. If this is going where we both think it's going, and it led to President Wallace having a steak knife at his throat, would you really want to stop it?"

"Would you've really picked me if you didn't know the answer?"

"I said I knew the answer. I'm just trying to get you ready," he says, his voice more serious than I've ever heard him. "I know the President is a piece of garbage, and I hate him just as much as you do, but this is what we do in the Culper Ring, Beecher. Whatever our feelings, we protect the Presidency."

"I'm not a killer, Tot."

"And I'm not saying you are. But you have to admit: If Marshall did have his hand on that steak knife—if you just stood there and watched—boy, that would really kill a few birds with one knife."

For a moment I sit there, my eyes still on the red taillights in front of us. "That's what you really think of me?" I finally ask.

"Doesn't matter what I think. What matters is, based on the direction these murders are headed, this *will* happen, Beecher. And when it does, you need to be ready with your decision."

I'm still silent as he slows the car and veers right, into the wide driveway filled with flagpoles that hold both U.S. and military flags. The black metal gates are already open, revealing a bulletproof security shack that, a year ago, used to be swarming with armed guards. These days, there's just one, dressed in full army camouflage and armed with nothing more than a clipboard. In the grass, on our right, is a sign welcoming us to Walter Reed Army Medical Center, home to one of the country's most famous and respected veterans' hospitals.

"They still haven't shut it down?" I ask as Tot rolls down his window.

"The hospital's closed. They moved most of it to Bethesda. But that's not all they had here." Tossing a smile at the guard, he adds, "We're here to see Dale Castronovo. We should be on the list."

I don't like it here, I think to myself as we drive through the dead-empty streets that snake across what looks more like a college campus than a military base: lots of brick buildings with pillars in front, lots of open green spaces. But no one's in sight. Truly no one. "You sure it's even safe here?"

Tot doesn't answer, and I get the picture. Doesn't matter if it's safe. We need what they have.

Up ahead, there's a five-story 1970s-era gray concrete building with a U-shaped front driveway. As we turn into the U, a light outside the building flicks on, revealing a tall and severely skinny woman. Dale.

Unlocking the front door, she's wearing a preppy plaid sweater, stone-washed jeans from the late 1980s, thick glasses, and three pens clipped in her pants pockets. I know an archivist when I see one. Who better to run the army's private medical museum?

"You got a real ghost town up here, Dale," Tot says as we get out of the car.

"Okeeyeah, you have no idea," Dale replies with a rat-a-tat-tat laugh that sends puffs of her frozen breath through the air. "You ready to see the body of Abraham Lincoln?"

38

Out in the cold and speedwalking up 23rd Street, Secret Service agent A.J. Ennis remembered that when Clementine first reached out and demanded Nico's files, the President told him to *schedule a doctor's appointment*, which A.J. knew meant *have Palmiotti handle it.*

When Clementine wanted the meet-up out in Michigan, the President said, "schedule another doctor's appointment."

And this morning, when everything first went wrong—with Marshall...with Beecher...with everything at St. John's Church—the President kept his same refrain: "Schedule a doctor's appointment."

In A.J.'s mind, President Wallace was being safe. But he wasn't being smart. Sure, to Wallace, Palmiotti was like a brother. But as A.J. learned all too well when his mother died and the fighting started with his siblings, no one can disappoint you more deeply than family.

More important, as A.J. reported back to the President after lunching with Palmiotti at Wok 'n Roll, the doctor wasn't the man he used to be.

Maybe it was the shooting, maybe it was from one too many personal sacrifices, or maybe—as A.J. had seen on so many staffers when they left the White House—Palmiotti's ego simply couldn't handle the fact that the President was moving on without him.

Whatever the case, reassurances from Palmiotti were no longer that reassuring. So when the call came in about another pastor being shot—this time at Foundry Church—A.J. of course brought it to the President. If this was what he thought...if the snowball was already moving this fast...it had to be dealt with. Immediately.

"Sir, just tell me what to do," A.J. had asked in the side room off the Oval Office, where President Wallace kept a small refrigerator and his stash of frozen Snickers bars. "Should I schedule another doctor's appointment?"

Unwrapping a Snickers, the President didn't say anything. Not one word.

A.J. heard him loud and clear.

Twenty minutes later, A.J. marched toward the monstrous beige brick building that took up most of the block. He didn't bother slowing down, even as the automatic doors slid open and a puff of indoor heat warmed his face.

Letting his training take over, he scanned each sector left to right, then up and down: A black granite reception desk up ahead. A single security guard on the right. Back in Beltsville, the very first lessons of Secret Service training had taught him to look for the person who wasn't acting like the other members of the crowd. Find the person who was fidgety, or sweaty, or who was patting his own chest, a well-recognized tip-off that he was carrying a weapon. But right now, the few men and women who were pacing and waiting by the leather sofas all had similar looks of anxiety, even desperation.

He expected as much. Especially here.

"Welcome to the George Washington University Hospital," the woman at the front desk announced. "Are you looking for a doctor or a patient?"

"Patient," A.J. said. "A pastor."

39

Marshall didn't go to the front gate.

The front gate meant a guard, which meant being seen, which meant being remembered. Worst of all, if the guard made a phone call, it would let them know he was coming.

Instead, as the sun faded from the sky, Marshall pulled his SUV around to the back of Walter Reed Army Medical Center. Most people knew Walter Reed for its hospital. A few, like Beecher, knew it housed a medical museum. But what most people forgot was that, like any army facility of its size, Walter Reed also had barracks and apartments. Soldiers lived here. And made a mess here. And needed that mess cleaned up by a privately run garbage service, which, true to army form, arrived and exited through a maintenance entrance around back. There was no guard stationed there, just a gate with a well-hidden keypad. Sometimes, even generals wanted to come and go without being seen.

None of it was news to Marshall. He'd been here two weeks ago, in the exact same spot: standing outside the metal gate, eyeing the keypad.

Electric gates like this all operated over radio frequency, usually between 300 and 433 megahertz. But to get inside, you didn't need to find some top-secret frequency. You simply needed a way into the powder-coated metal access box below the keypad.

Fortunately, Marshall was good with locks. As good as anyone. With nothing more than two slivers of metal, the tiny lock turned and the access box popped open, revealing a circuit board. From there, it was like operating a light switch. When you flip a light switch on, a small piece of metal is lowered into place, connecting two wires. When that connection happens, the power starts flowing.

It was no different here. Holding a strip of eighteen-gauge wire that was thinner than a paper clip, Marshall touched it to two metal screws on the circuit board. As the electricity began to flow, the metal gate jumped, then rolled wide open.

Same as two weeks ago.

Stepping inside, Marshall didn't even attempt to hide. This was a nearly empty army facility. How hard could it be to find a 1966 pale blue Mustang?

40

All around us, the display cases of the museum are covered with white sheets. Cardboard boxes are stacked like crooked pillars in every corner. The museum is in the process of moving. At the center of the room, Tot and I are both staring down, squinting into one of the few uncovered glass cases, like the ones that hold jewelry at department stores. But what's inside is far more valuable than diamonds.

The two circular flat velvet discs have their own glass tops. Little flecks of white sit at the center of each disc: They look like human teeth that're broken in half. There's a larger chunk too.

"Abraham Lincoln," I whisper.

"Abraham Lincoln's *skull*," Dale clarifies, showing that, like every archivist, she's a stickler as she points down at the old bone fragments. "Or at least what's left of it."

"Why do you even *have* this?" I ask, unable to look away.

"That's what we do," Dale says, sounding almost cocky as she runs her fingers down the Def Leppard lanyard that holds her ID around her neck. As she twirls it, I spot a stack of concert tickets tucked behind her ID. I'm not gonna ask. "Back in 1862, when they founded us as the Army Medical Museum, our job was to document the effects of war on the human body. So the Smithsonian was sent all the cultural items. And we were sent all the human body parts, including the pieces of Abraham Lincoln."

"And the shirt with his blood on it. And the bullet," I say excitedly as I race from case to case. Speed-reading as I go, I can't help but think that the exhibit would be better served if it started with—

There it is. The final item in the final case: the small silver slug of metal that resembles a wobbly lead gumball.

The bullet that killed Abraham Lincoln.

"Tot, you need to see this."

He's back by the open doors of the exhibit. "Do I need to close these?" he calls out.

"Doesn't matter," Dale says with a wave. "We're the only ones here." Following behind me, she motions down to the bullet.

I hold my breath as I read the description. *This handmade ball of lead, fired from a Philadelphia Derringer pistol, was removed from Lincoln's brain during autopsy by Dr. Edward Curtis.*

Dale doesn't say a word. Dr. Curtis's own words are laminated on a card just below the bullet, in a letter he wrote to his mother. He explains that when they took out Lincoln's brain to track down the bullet, he was lifting the brain from the skull and *suddenly the bullet dropped out through my fingers and fell, breaking the solemn silence of the room with its clatter, into an empty basin that was standing beneath. There it lay upon the white china, a little black mass no bigger than the end of my finger—dull, motionless and harmless, yet the cause of such mighty changes in the world's history as we may perhaps never realize.*

I'm still holding my breath. On my left, Dale isn't playing with her lanyard anymore. Even today, there's no way to know all the changes to history that came from John Wilkes Booth's actions that day. But whoever's killing these pastors now, if they really are working toward the current President, I can't help but think they've got their own idea.

"Tell me about the Lincoln mask," I say, finally breaking the silence.

Pointing us to the left, toward a nearby case, Dale yanks on the eggshell-colored sheet, revealing another glass museum case. An empty one.

"I came in two weeks ago and—poof—it was gone." From a nearby display case, Dale grabs a file folder, flips it open, and pulls out a blown-up color photo of what used to be in this case: a plaster mask. There's no mistaking who it is—the pointy nose, the high cheekbones—even in full plaster, we all know Abraham Lincoln. But unlike the mask from Marshall's apartment, the one in this photo has plaster over the eyes. Marshall's had holes cut into it. So someone could see through it. More important, this one is yellowed and old. Marshall's was pristine and white.

"Look familiar?" Tot asks, as I replay what Marshall told me. That he supposedly found the mask in a garbage can a few blocks from the crime.

"Dale, if someone stole the mask, how hard would it be to make another cast from it?" Tot adds, already knowing what I'm thinking.

"That was the whole point. Once the cast existed, people could use it to make busts of the President without having to bother him. They even used it to make the big statue in the Lincoln Memorial. What's odd is, ours is just a copy of the original."

"So what you're saying is that this mask isn't even the most valuable thing here?" Tot interrupts in a tone that tells me he already knows the answer.

"Exactly . . . okeeyeah . . . that's *exactly* my point!" Dale insists a bit too enthusiastically as she readjusts her glasses. "Lincoln's bone fragments and the bullet that killed him, those things are priceless. But to take a reproduction plaster mask and some random pieces of Booth. How does that make any—?"

"Booth?" I blurt. "You mean as in *John Wilkes Booth*?"

Dale looks at Tot, then over at me. "Back then, in the 1860s," she explains, "we were sent *everybody*."

"So you also have pieces of John Wilkes Booth," Tot says, full of fake excitement. "And those pieces were stolen too?"

Tot's not stupid. He knew about the Lincoln mask and the Booth part long before we got here. But for him to keep the Booth part from me . . . to hold it back . . . I've known Tot since my very first day at the Archives. In the Culper Ring, I put my life in his hands. Why would he lie about—?

He shoots me a look and I get the rest.

Marshall.

Back at the restaurant, he was worried I'd tell Marshall.

You're wrong, I say to him with just a dirty look.

Doesn't matter, he replies with his own look.

But it does. Trust always matters.

"Can we see it?" Tot asks, motioning for Dale to lead the way.

"Absolutely," she says, her Def Leppard lanyard twirling as she leads us to the last remaining body parts of John Wilkes Booth.

41

St. Elizabeths Hospital
Washington, D.C.

Nico knew all about steganography, which was Greek for *hidden writing*.

He knew of its history in ancient Greece, where they wrote messages on wooden tablets, then covered the tablet in wax, which made it look blank. It wasn't until the tablet was delivered and the wax was scraped away that the hidden message was revealed.

Nico knew that's what made it different from cryptography, which was all about secret codes. Steganography had nothing to do with codes. In steganography, the message isn't scrambled. It's simply hidden so no one knows you're sending a message at all.

"You're joking, right?" Nurse Karina asked as she stood behind Nico.

Nurse Rupert didn't bother to answer, standing right next to her.

Ignoring them both with his back to them, Nico sat at a blond wooden desk, staring blankly at a computer screen, both of his palms flat on the desk. Along the left wall of the room was a working stove, a microwave, a washer/dryer, and a toilet, each item right next to the other.

The room was used for ADL skills—Activities for Daily Living—which meant that patients came in here to learn how to survive in the actual world. Staff taught them how to turn on a stove, wash their clothes, and even the most basic of tasks, like keeping a clean toilet.

For a few patients, including Nico, it also included minor computer privileges.

"And that's what he likes?" Karina whispered.

"That's it. It's his favorite," Rupert replied.

From the angle they were at, they had a clear view of Nico's monitor, which held a YouTube video called "Cutey Cute Lester."

Onscreen, a fluffy and adorable tabby kitten named Lester rolled back and forth across a plush gray carpet, like he had an itch he couldn't reach. In the background, the cat's owner tapped his foot, laughing along with him.

"So the man who shot the President also likes cat videos?" Karina asked.

"Sometimes he prefers one called 'I'm Just a Cat and I'm Doing Cat Stuff.' Though personally, I prefer Lester. Look at that *range*..."

Onscreen, Lester the kitten was stretched out on his back, his front left paw looking like it was waving right at the viewer.

Nico stared at the screen, thinking of ancient Greece, where Herodotus told the story of a secret message that was tattooed onto the shaved head of a slave and concealed by his grown-back hair. The message stayed hidden until the slave arrived at his destination and shaved his head again. Perfect steganography.

Almost as perfect as George Washington using invisible ink and writing between the lines of his own handwritten letters.

Almost as perfect as what Nico—and the dead First Lady—were staring at today. The video uploaded by a user named LedParadis27.

"That's all he does? He sits here and watches cat videos?" Karina asked.

"We call it his *kitty porn*. But yeah—ever since they stopped letting him feed the cats next door, you wanna keep Nico calm, this is how you do it."

"So how long does he—?"

Before Karina could finish, Nico stood from his seat, picked up his book, and headed past them.

"I need to go to the bathroom," he announced, the dead First Lady right behind him.

"I think it's on the left...down the hall," Rupert said, pointing him out into the main section of the clinic. The building was still new to them all. "Oh, and Nico—y'know you can leave the book here if you want."

Nico looked at him blankly. Then he looked at the female nurse.

Saying nothing, Nico headed for the restroom that was just down the hall. Onscreen, the kitty named Lester was still rolling and wriggling wildly, fighting to scratch the itch on his back. All the while, the cat's owner tapped his foot, presumably laughing.

Yes, Nico knew all about steganography. And now, thanks to the Knight, he finally had the newest message.

Flicking his ten of spades bookmark, all he had to do was write back.

42

As the lock clicks and the metal door slowly yawns open, the smell hits me first.

It's bitter, like vinegar mixed with mothballs and the smell of rain. I know it immediately. Formaldehyde.

The sign on the door reads *Wet Tissue Room*. I don't know what *wet tissues* are, but I'm sure this is what they smell like.

"Sorry, I should've warned you," Dale says, reading our expressions. "I don't even smell it anymore."

Before I can reply, the motion sensor lights pop on, and the worst part hits: I see where the smell is coming from.

There are jelly jars of all shapes and sizes—each filled with pale yellow fluid and stacked on shelf after shelf, from floor to ceiling. This is an archive. Just like the one Tot and I work in. But instead of books, these shelves...this whole room...it's filled with—

From inside the jelly jar, a mucusy gray ear is listening to our every word.

"Now you know why we moved all the Booth stuff back here," Dale explains as we reach the back corner of the room. "After the break-in—" She cuts herself off, stopping at a metal map cabinet. Like the ones we have at the Archives, it has a half dozen wide drawers that are only a few inches tall. "We figured, *who'd be sick enough to break into here?*"

I keep my eyes locked on Dale, refusing to see the hundreds of pale yellow body parts that're floating in the jelly jars all around us.

"So you were saying about John Wilkes Booth?" I nudge.

"Yeah. No. Sorry, we had two parts of him," Dale says, pulling open the middle drawer of the map cabinet, which is lined with a thin sheet of white foam board. On it is a clear plastic cube with a brownish-white piece of bone preserved inside. Running diagonally through the bone is a bright, sky blue plastic probe.

"Booth's spinal cord," Tot says as if he's asking a question. But like before, he knows the answer.

This time, though, so do I. After Booth was shot at Garrett's Barn, they did a quick autopsy, then buried him secretly so he wouldn't become a martyr. What I didn't know was that they kept some of his body parts.

"The blue probe shows the actual path of the bullet," Dale adds, handing me the cube. "Many think that's the actual killshot that did him in."

"So this is the prize of the collection," Tot says.

"Exactly, and like before, instead of taking the priceless artifact, they instead stole *this*..." From her file folder, she pulls out a color copy of a dark gray vertebra that's mounted on a round wooden stand.

"Booth's cervical vertebra. He was hit there too," I say, noticing where the bone is jagged and sharp.

"Were there any signs of a break-in?" Tot asks.

"That's the thing," Dale says. "No windows smashed, no doors kicked open, no fingerprints, no nothing. It's like a ghost himself came in and walked off with everything."

Tot glances my way. He doesn't have to say Marshall's name. In the last forty-eight hours, who else have we encountered who knows how to break into a military installation?

"Here's what still doesn't make sense, though," Dale says. "Whoever it was that broke in, why'd they take a random Booth vertebra, but leave the far more priceless killshot?"

"And why'd they take a replica Lincoln mask, but not the actual bullet that killed him?" Tot asks.

"He wants them alive," I blurt.

They both turn my way.

My eyes stare down at the plastic cube and the chunk of spine that's locked within it.

"I'm not following," Tot says.

"You said this was the killshot, right?" I ask, holding up the cube. Dale nods, just as confused.

"And in your display case, the bullet that shot Lincoln. That was the killshot too, right? The bullet from Lincoln's brain."

"He left both of those here," Tot says, starting to see where I'm going.

"But the plaster mask, even if it's a replica...that was made when Lincoln was *alive*," I point out. "And the same with this," I add, motioning to the color photocopy of Booth's stolen vertebra. "Booth was alive when he got hit here."

"So you think whoever broke in is ignoring the pieces from when Lincoln and Booth were dead..." Tot says.

"...and stealing the pieces from when they were *alive*," I point out.

Tot rolls his tongue inside his cheek. He's not there yet. But he's close. "Why, though?"

"Y'mean besides the fact that you have to be utterly insane to steal people's body parts? Think of yesterday at the church," I say, referring to all the work the killer put into re-creating Booth's crime. "Maybe he's not just copying Booth. Maybe...I don't know...what if he wants Booth *alive*?"

"Or wants to *be like* him," Tot points out.

"Or be like *all* of them."

As the words leave my lips, there's a faint noise from outside the closet.

I stand up straight, turning at the sound.

Tot shoots me a look. He heard it too.

"That's just our air conditioner," Dale reassures us, adding a laugh. "It does that every time someone tells an old spooky story."

It's an easy joke designed to calm us down, but it doesn't stop me from feeling like there's a snake coiled around my spine, slowly winding and climbing up my own vertebrae. It's one thing to copy John Wilkes Booth, but to actually want to *be* that monster, or *mimic* him. I'm not sure what bothers me more: the thought of someone sick enough to even imagine such a thing . . . or the thought that that person might be Marshall.

"It's the same with Guiteau," Dale adds, referring to the assassin who shot President Garfield.

"Pardon?" Tot asks.

"What you said, about stealing pieces from when Booth and Lincoln were alive . . . Whoever stole it, they did the same with Guiteau."

On my left, Tot again rolls his tongue inside his cheek. "You have Charles Guiteau's body too." He's trying to act unsurprised. But I see the way he's running his fingers down his bolo tie. He may've known about Lincoln—and Booth—but Tot had no clue that the body of President Garfield's killer was also here.

"Why didn't you tell me that?" Tot asks.

"You asked about Lincoln and Booth. You didn't ask about Guiteau," Dale explains without a hint of apology. Though the truth is, we didn't figure out Guiteau until Marshall mentioned the second murder.

Turning back toward the map cabinet, Dale reaches down toward the lowest drawer. As she tugs it open, it's filled with assassin Charles Guiteau.

Literally.

43

A.J. tried the pastor's hospital room first.

A nurse told him the pastor was downstairs. In the chapel.

A.J. nodded a quick thanks but didn't bother to ask directions. Like most Secret Service agents, he knew the hospital well. George Washington University Hospital was where they operated on Dick Cheney while he was Vice President—and where President Wallace had his gallbladder out.

As for the chapel, A.J. knew it best of all, since it was there that Wallace—right before going under the anesthetic for his gallbladder surgery—signed away his power as leader of the free world and said a teary, just-in-case goodbye to his wife and kids. For the agents and few staffers there, it was a terrifying moment.

But as A.J. looked back on it, what he was doing now was far more dangerous.

Avoiding the elevators and sticking to the stairs, A.J. stayed out of sight until he reached the first floor. As always, he checked each sector of the long hallway, left to right, then up and down. A nurse with a rolling cart . . . a gift shop to buy flowers . . . and at the far end of the corridor: the only door in the whole hospital with blue-and-gold stained glass in it. *Interfaith Chapel.*

As he opened the door and craned his neck inside, there were two voices talking.

". . . forget going to the games—just give me one good reason why anyone would root for the Orioles."

Straight ahead, underneath a wide window that was covered

with broad wooden horizontal blinds, a man and a woman faced each other, talking casually.

The woman sat on one of the room's three cherry benches that was covered with beige padding. The man was in a wheelchair, dressed in a hospital gown, but wearing socks and slippers. He had a round face and a dimpled chin that reminded A.J. of an elf. And a nose that reminded him of a boxer. Pastor Frick.

"May I help you?" the woman asked in a calm voice tinged with a British accent. "I'm Chaplain Stoughton," she said, though A.J. remembered her from the President's surgery.

"I'm here for Pastor..." A.J. looked at the man in the wheelchair. "You must be Pastor Frick."

"I am," he said, surprising A.J. by standing up from the wheel-chair. A.J. expected a quiet old man. This guy was a show-off, but in the warmest of ways.

"Pastor, *please*..." the female chaplain begged. "The doctors told you to take it easy."

"I'm fine—they all know I'm fine. If I weren't a man of God, they would've sent me home hours ago instead of making me stay over-night. They just don't want God sending a lightning bolt through their windows." He wasn't old—maybe in his fifties—but his voice was lush, like a grandfather's. As he grinned, A.J. again spotted the elfish twinkle in his pale blue eyes. But he also saw those old dents in his nose. A.J. knew: Dents like that can come from sports, or a car accident, or from people who fight—but they can also come from a dad who used to put a beating on someone's mother. No doubt, this was a guy who liked righting wrongs.

"Let me guess: You're another detective. A cop?" Frick asked.

"Secret Service," A.J. replied, flashing his badge and approach-ing quickly. "If you're in the middle of praying, I don't want to inter-rupt," he said, looking hard at the chaplain.

"I was just headed upstairs," she said, walking toward the door.

"So the Secret Service," Pastor Frick began as he lowered him-self back to his seat in the wheelchair, gritting his teeth slightly. "I didn't realize this had something to do with the President."

A.J. forced a smile that didn't reach his eyes. "The Service does lots of work that doesn't deal with the President."

The pastor nodded absently. He was still in shock. "Y'know the bullet went right through me. The doctor called it a . . . he said it was a miracle . . . a reward for all my service," he said with a laugh.

A.J. didn't laugh back.

"Anyway, for someone to sneak into our sanctuary . . ." The pastor took a deep breath, readjusting himself in his seat. "I want to help you catch who did this."

"That's our goal too. So. Your attacker. Did you happen to see what he looked like?"

"I saw his legs. And shiny shoes. I know it sounds nuts, but . . . I'm good with smells. His shoes were just polished."

"What about his face? Did you see if he was wearing a mask?"

The pastor shook his head, clearly confused.

A.J. let out a small sigh of relief. If they wanted to keep this quiet—and away from the President—the last thing they needed was another witness.

"And you didn't see him going out the window?" A.J. added, still reading Frick's confusion. "After shooting you, the attacker escaped through the window."

"I remember that!" the pastor blurted, as if he'd forgotten it until that moment. "I heard the window open! And he said something. He had a deep voice and he told me . . . He said what our church did was a *blasphemy*."

"A blasphemy? And do you know what he was referring to?"

"No . . . Our church . . . We pride ourselves on being open to all."

"And you didn't see anything?"

"All I saw was the carpet. Once I got hit, I was— The pain was just—" He cut himself off. A.J. had seen it before. Especially with those who demand a lot from themselves. They kick themselves for not doing more. As A.J. knew, it was no different with Palmiotti, which was why A.J. was now dealing with this mess.

"Help me get out of this chair," Pastor Frick blurted. "My rear end's falling asleep."

A.J. helped him up and watched as Frick took a few steps around the room. He was moving slowly, but he was clearly strong. A pastor in a tough neighborhood has to be.

"You need to be careful," A.J. warned. "Bullet wounds can take the life out of you."

"That's fine, but you have any idea how many congregants will stop believing in the Almighty if I'm not there tomorrow morning when they have their crisis? I'm not joking. As they say: Faith begins with self-interest."

A.J. paused, then: "One more question, Pastor. Do you know the rector who runs St. John's Church?"

44

The skeleton is in hundreds of pieces, yellow bones of every shape and size. But what catches my eye is the jelly jar that's lying on its side in the corner of the drawer. Like the ones around us, it's filled with a milky yellow fluid and a pale gray, spongy mass.

"Guiteau's brain," I say, still listening for any noises coming from down the hall.

"What makes you think that?" Dale laughs, lifting the jar and pointing to the handwritten sticker on it that says, *What is left of brain of Guiteau.*

"He's not as famous as John Wilkes Booth, but he still killed a President," Dale explains. "The jury found him guilty in little over an hour, and since the science back then said that you could actually see insanity in someone's brain, after Guiteau was hanged, the doctors dissected every part of him, trying to prove it. The theory was that people were insane because of the degeneration of gray cells in their brain. They actually find the same thing today in people who are in asylums too long—and in their offspring too," she says as Tot shoots me a look.

"You were saying, about the parts of Guiteau that were stolen..." I interrupt.

From her file folder, she pulls out a final color photocopy, this one of a flat piece of pale brown leather. It's cracked and faded, like it's been in the sun too long. At the center of it is a picture of...

The lines of the drawing are slightly muddy, and the colors are pale red and blue, but there's no mistaking the hand-drawn three-pointed shield with the American flag on front. Gripping the top

159

of it is an eagle with wide wings and a lowered head. Just like the eagle on the package of playing cards that Marshall had in his apartment.

"That's not a canvas, is it?" I ask.

"Skin. It's human skin," Dale says.

The muddy lines. The pale blue-and-red coloring. It's a tattoo.

"That's what he stole?" Tot asks. "I didn't know Guiteau had a tattoo, much less that they saved it."

"What about the symbol?" I ask, staring at the eagle and the shield. I know it's not the eagle from the Great Seal. That one has its head held high, holds the arrows and the olive branch, and came in around 1782. But this one—with its head down for the attack— is a pretty standard eagle from the late eighteenth and early nine- teenth century.

"You'll see it on china, and as a decorative accent on some antiques. Even the Philadelphia Eagles football team used to use a similar one for its logo," Dale offers. "But back during Guiteau's time, this apparently was the emblem of some group."

"What group?" I ask.

Dale purses her lips. "I hadn't even heard of them until a col- league mentioned them after the robbery. They were called the Knights...the Knights in the..."

"The Knights of the Golden Circle," Tot says coldly, still locked on the red-and-blue tattoo.

45

S t. John's? You mean the church down by the White House?"
Pastor Frick asked, slowly walking in a small circle around the
hospital chapel. "I've heard they run a nice service, but the
truth is, we're Methodist and they're—"

"Turns out, the rector at St. John's was found murdered last
night," A.J. interrupted. "It was on the local news this morning, but
happened too late for the papers to pick it up."

"M-My word...I had no... *Oh.*" The pastor's pale round face
grew even paler. He made his way back toward the wheelchair and
held its pushbars to steady himself. "You think the same person who
did that might have been the one who came after me?"

A.J. knew that was the question. Two churches...two pastors...
two places filled with history. "Pastor Frick, does your church have
any ties to Abraham Lincoln?"

The pastor looked thoughtful. "Lincoln was a Methodist. Back
when he was President, he was actually a life member of our
church."

"So he spent time there?"

"Of course. A great deal of time. But none of that— In our neighborhood, we always have a few too many robberies and muggings.
Nothing violent, thankfully. That's part of the territory when you
serve a less affluent population. But that doesn't explain—"

"Sir, I saw that your regular pastor—Pastor Phelps—is away in
New Zealand for over four months now," A.J. said. "Any particular
reason why he left?"

"He has family there. Why?"

"When I spoke to the staff at St. John's, some of the staffers there said that in the weeks before their rector was killed, he took a lot of criticism for trying to update St. John's, instituting a Date Night for singles and things like that."

"Pastor Phelps used to give away fruit smoothies to bring people in. But that's just part of running a modern church," Frick agreed. "Though what makes you think that's tied to Abraham Lincoln?"

"What about our current President?" A.J. asked. "Have you had any interactions with him?"

"I don't understand. What does this have to do with President Wallace?"

"These are just standard questions, sir. That's our job in the Service."

The pastor blinked quickly, taking a seat in the wheelchair. "I've only met the President once, when he came for services."

A.J. froze. Over the years, he knew there were dozens—maybe hundreds—of religious leaders, of every denomination, whom the President had said prayers with. But last year, after the Easter Egg Roll on the South Lawn, President Wallace had gone to services at St. John's. And now it was clear that the President had also attended services with Pastor Frick. "Sir, can you please tell me everything that happened when you were with President Wallace?"

46

It didn't take long for Marshall to find the small silver beacon.

He knew it had to be there. It was the only way to explain how Beecher tracked him to the restaurant in Georgetown. Sure enough, after a few minutes of searching the passenger seat and the floor mats, there it was, tucked into the plastic well of the passenger-side door.

From the tiny size of the beacon, Marshall knew this was certainly as good as anything the government had. Maybe even better, which wasn't a surprise. Years ago, the CIA and NSA had the best research and development shops, producing the smallest and most impressive toys. These days, it was the private sector that led the way, doing the R&D themselves, then selling it at top dollar to the government. For better or worse, industry was no longer about keeping the world safe—they cared about making money. So for tech this good, whoever Beecher was working with, they knew exactly what they were doing.

Marshall made a mental note. He knew what he was doing too. And now that it was dark, it was all so much easier. Still, he had to admit, despite all his planning, even he was surprised by the rush of emotions that came with seeing Beecher.

Following the same path he took two weeks ago, Marshall stuck to the service road and eyed the gray concrete behemoth at the center of Walter Reed. At the front of the building was a wide U-shaped driveway that held two cars: an old white Honda with an *Elliot in the Morning* radio show bumper sticker, and a pristine 1966 Mustang.

Checking over his shoulder one last time, Marshall approached the passenger side of the Mustang, then got down on one knee like he was tying his shoe. Beecher had already done enough damage. Now it was time to return the favor.

47

That's them. The Knights of the Golden Circle. You've heard of them?" Dale asks, revealing just how little she knows Tot.

"We have a few of their items in the Archives," Tot replies, holding the photocopy to his nose and studying the strange eagle tattoo. "I know them from there."

He's not the only one. Back during the Civil War, groups like the Knights were popping up in every direction, providing outlets for all the anger running rampant in the country. But unlike the Freemasons or other secret societies, who were focused on long-time traditions, the Knights of the Golden Circle wanted something far more hateful: for the Union to end so they could run their own slave-based society. Their goal was to create a true, physical "golden circle"—with Mexico and the Caribbean—to build a private part of the country where slavery would continue.

The Knights supposedly had two famous members: Jesse James. And John Wilkes Booth.

"So this tattoo," Tot says, pointing to the top right corner of the photocopied skin. "Any idea what this stands for?"

Dale and I both lean in. Just above the eagle, in the corner, there's another tattoo—a smaller one, of a knife—a dagger, really—that's drawn 3-D style so it looks like it's stabbing into the skin. What Tot's pointing at is the tiny red item on the hilt of the dagger.

A red diamond.

"You guys know better than I would," Dale says. "Maybe Guiteau liked playing cards."

"Maybe so," Tot says, handing me the photocopy.

As I look for myself, Tot drills me with a long stare. I have no

164

idea if John Wilkes Booth really was a member of the Knights. But no matter the answer, one thing seems unarguable: Over two hundred years ago, the only reason Booth got into Ford's Theatre was by showing a mysterious card to Lincoln's valet. Last night, after the rector was murdered at St. John's, the police found Marshall carrying a deck of cards—with this exact eagle on the package—that was missing the ace of spades. And now, as I study the cracked beige skin of the killer who hunted President Garfield, I'm seeing that Charles Guiteau clearly had a tattoo of a dagger with a red diamond on it.

Two presidential killers. Two suits of playing cards.

For a moment, I tell myself to focus on the present and what we know: that there's a copycat killer who's imitating old assassins and slaughtering religious leaders. But if John Wilkes Booth had the ace of spades. And Charles Guiteau had the ace of diamonds. Either we just stumbled onto a hell of a coincidence...

...or throughout decades of history, two of the world's most ruthless hunters were not just organized, not just linked together— they *might've actually been working for the same cause.*

48

O
h, please. Now you're just rewriting history," Tot says a bit too angrily as he tugs the steering wheel and the Mustang rumbles and bounces back onto 16th Street.

"What're you talking about?" I ask as Walter Reed fades behind us. "You've seen what we've found: the mysterious card at Ford's Theatre, plus the missing ace of spades, and now this ace of diamonds..."

"No, Beecher, what we found is someone killing pastors and imitating the most famous presidential killers. Which is twisted enough. What you're saying now is, even though every history book on this planet says otherwise, that somehow all these killers were *what*? Plotting together over the course of a hundred and fifty years?"

"How long's the Culper Ring been around, Tot? Two hundred years? Two hundred and fifty? You're telling me George Washington can create that, but that the Knights of the Golden Circle—"

"The Knights of the Golden Circle were a bunch of racists from the Civil War..."

"...who suddenly disappeared just as John Wilkes Booth put a bullet in the back of Lincoln's head!"

"I know how it played out, Beecher, and I know that every conspiracy nut in the world likes to say that the Knights' real motives went underground with them, but I'm telling you: The Knights of the Golden Circle don't exist today."

"How do you know that?"

Tot licks his lips, suddenly quiet.

"Tot, just say it."

166

Holding the steering wheel like he's about to strangle it, he turns to me with his milky bad eye. "I know because we fought them already. Years ago. And beat them."

"What're you talking about?"

"We—the Culper Ring—we beat them. Years ago. And the last time I heard the Knights mentioned, it was—" He cuts himself off. "Back when I was first recruited." He stops again. "We're talking nearly fifty years ago, back when Kermit—"

"Kermit?"

"Kermit," Tot says, his voice catching. "Kermit was to me what I hope I'm being to you."

As we veer around the traffic circle at Colesville Road and head for the Beltway, momentum pins me against the passenger-side door. I stare at him, appreciating the—

"Don't go mushy on me, Beecher. I'm just saying, when I was younger and Kermit brought me in, like any parent, there was a lot he didn't say in front of me. But that didn't mean I wasn't listening. And back then, what they were always whispering about—like Holocaust survivors whispering about the concentration camps— were the horrors that happened with the Knights of the Golden Circle."

"Did you ever find out what happened?"

"I *know* what happened: We won. We beat them. Whatever they were up to—and I can tell you, it had nothing to do with John Wilkes Booth or ancient playing cards—Kermit made one thing absolutely clear: We stomped them. So the odds of them suddenly being back, and being responsible for murdering these religious leaders, or even working their way up to the President—"

"Are you even listening to yourself? You're part of a secret underground group that's existed for the past two centuries, and you're telling me that there's no way that *another* secret underground group could've done the same?"

Tot hits the gas, the Mustang jerks, and we pick up speed on the highway. "Beecher, y'know how every family has one moment where they weren't at their best?"

"Can you please just spare me the metaphor and tell me what you're really trying to say?"

He pauses, and then: "You have to understand—the Culper Ring, for all our secrecy, we're no different than any other clandestine unit. We're made up of people. And for that reason, the Ring itself always develops its own personality, especially depending on who's in charge."

"You're saying someone bad was in charge back then?"

"Not *bad*. Aggressive. Proactive. In the right situation, those are still good words. Back then, it was exactly what we needed. So when it came to the Knights, and every last person involved with them...anyone they were associated with..." His voice slows down to that tone you only hear at funerals. "The Culper Ring tracked and hunted and slaughtered them all. Like dogs."

As the words leave his lips, he pulls on the steering wheel, exiting the highway at Rockville Pike. At this hour, the roads are quieter and a bit less crowded. But it doesn't bring a single bit of calm.

"You never tried to find out *why*?"

"Of course I tried to find out why. But it was like trying to find out about when your grandfather had an affair on your grandmother. Like I said, there are some things only the adults talk about. I was a child."

"That doesn't mean—"

"It does, Beecher. They're done. The Knights are done."

"You keep saying that, but just remember, all it takes is one crazy cockroach to skitter free."

"I agree. Which is why it's our job to find him. Whether it's Marshall or anyone else," he says as we enter the residential streets of suburban Maryland.

"I hear you, Tot. But after everything we just saw at Walter Reed, plus the way the murderer's meticulously re-creating these crimes—"

"He's not that meticulous. Don't forget, the pastor he shot today didn't die. He survived."

"Then maybe he's even more of a perfectionist than we thought," I counter. I don't have to explain. Tot knows that when President

Garfield was shot all those years ago, he should've never died. What killed him was the medical malpractice of a Dr. Willard Bliss, who stuck his unsterilized fingers into the wound, causing a hemorrhage. "And Tot, wasn't that the same Dr. Bliss who was also there at Lincoln's deathbed? Quite a historical coincidence."

Turning onto my block and stopping in front of my narrow townhouse, Tot doesn't answer. He knows that around every dead President, there's always talk of a greater group at work.

Kicking the car door open and grabbing my brown leather briefcase, I step out into the cold and look back at Tot. "Can I ask you one last question?"

"You want to know who's running the Culper Ring now."

"No. Well…*yeah*, but—"

"It's been two months, Beecher. Give it time."

"I will, but—" I look up at the black sky, then back into the car. "Just tell me, what you said before: about how aggressive the Culper Ring used to be, and the proactive guy who hunted everyone down…" I stare at Tot as the moonlight makes his blue eye glow the color of lightning. "Tot, are you sure the Culper Ring are the good guys?"

His lips curl into a grin that lifts his wizard's beard. "Beecher, I wouldn't be involved if we weren't. But let me also say, if you do wanna look at history, you know that no one can *always* be the good guy."

He takes his foot off the brake, hoping I'll shut the door. I grip it, refusing to let go. Up until two months ago, I used to keep a brass perpetual calendar—a paper-scroll calendar with a built in clock—on my desk at work. But when everything happened with Clementine, and Tot invited me into the Culper Ring, he told me that you have a choice: You can run your life with a clock, or run it with a compass. The next day, I bought an antique Watkins & Hill thermometer-and-compass from the late 1700s. That's what's on my desk today.

"No, Tot. We *need* to be the good guys. *I* need to. Always."

His beard lifts even higher. "I know, Beecher. That's why I picked you."

With a kick of the gas, the Mustang disappears up the block as a cyclone of exhaust spins through the night air.

My brain's spinning just as fast as I fish for my keys and climb the steps to my townhouse. But as I realize that my front door is already unlocked, the spinning stops.

A careful push sends my door swinging inward. The lights in my living room are on. And like the three bears coming home from their walk in the woods, I find a woman with short golden locks sitting in my oversized lounge chair.

Last time I saw her, her hair was black. The silver rings on her thumbs and pinkies are all gone. So's the funky wooden bracelet she used to wear.

But I've known those ginger brown eyes since I was twelve years old.

"I know you want to kill me," Clementine says, palms facing me in the hopes of making peace. "But before you say anything, Beecher, I know what happened to your father."

49

Presidential Wallace was in your church. Were you advising him?" A.J. asked, standing at the center of the hospital chapel and taking a step toward the pastor's wheelchair.

"No. It was this past Christmas —on the anniversary of when FDR brought Winston Churchill there during the war. Every President goes to church on Christmas. That's why President Wallace—" Pastor Frick rolled backward, his face going pale.

"Is something wrong, sir?"

"T-This morning, in my office...when the attacker called it a *blasphemy*... Do you think he was referring to the President's Christmas visit?"

"Did something happen?"

"Nothing terrible...not like this...but if you remember, we took criticism for the visit," Frick explained, his voice slowing down as he relived the moment. "They told us that Wallace was bringing his son and his daughter, so we had everything ready, a beautiful service. But when the President finally arrived, he didn't just have his family with him. He brought other guests too."

A.J. wasn't there, but he slowly remembered, nodding at the pastor. "He brought a rabbi," A.J. said. "And a Muslim leader."

"A rabbi, an imam, and a pastor. If the three of us walked into a bar—" Frick smiled inadvertently.

"So back to your attacker. You think that when those three religions were brought together, he might've seen it as a blasphemy?"

"I'm just telling you that some of my fellow church leaders like a little more *Christ* in their Christmas."

A.J. heard that tone in the pastor's voice. "And how did you feel about it, sir?"

At that, Pastor Frick was silent.

"I'm not trying to criticize the President," the pastor finally offered, "but when they first approached us about the Christmas service, they said that Wallace wanted to bring the three faiths together so we could have a dialogue. That was his word. *Dialogue.* But when it came to actual communication, the three of us—me, the rabbi, the imam—we didn't say a single word to each other. They gathered us together, your fellow agents made President Wallace appear from nowhere, and next thing we know, fifty flashbulbs and camera lights are shining in our faces."

"It was a photo op."

"Of course it was a photo op. But do you know why President Wallace did it? Because on Christmas morning, it's far better for millions of voters to see the President with three different religious leaders than to see him kneeling in church and proclaiming his servitude to Christ. That's not a personal attack. It's just the state of politics and religion in the twenty-first century."

"I'm not sure that's a blasphemy," A.J. countered.

"That's not my word either," the pastor said. "But let's not forget, the people who founded this country were religious men. President Wallace isn't—he attends on the big days. It's not a flaw, but for millions of believers out there, it will take a toll."

A.J. nodded. "What about the rest of the President's visit? Did you get any time alone with him? Did you offer any advice? Say any prayers?"

For the second time, Pastor Frick went silent.

"Sir, if there's something you shared with the President . . ."

"It was Christmas Day. Of course we shared a prayer. But what was said between us . . . forgive me, but that moment is private. Even if he is the President, I promise my congregants—"

"Pastor Frick, I understand how sacred those interactions are. I do. But you also understand—I work for the Secret Service. I wouldn't be asking these questions if I didn't think the President's life was in danger."

Still seated in the wheelchair, Pastor Frick stared at A.J. in horror. "Did I do something wrong?" Frick asked, his voice catching. "If I put President Wallace in danger..."

"This is solely for our investigation, sir. You have my word."

The pastor took a deep breath. "We only had... it couldn't have been two minutes. It was after we took the photo, before I went out on the pulpit. He pulled myself, Rabbi Moskovitz, and the imam into a small circle and told us how vital it was to bring everyone together. He told us he was trying to do the same for our country. So that's what we prayed for. We lowered our heads...we clasped hands. His prayer was to bring the country—to bring all our voices—together. It was a heartfelt prayer."

"And that was it? Did he give you anything or bring any gifts?"

"That *prayer* was his gift," the pastor insisted, a crease forming between his eyes. "After that, his staff stepped in and... You know how they rush him everywhere. By then, the Christmas photo of the three different religions was all across the globe. To some, his blasphemy unleashed."

A.J. felt his phone vibrating. Caller ID told him it was the one call he was waiting for. Holding a finger up at the pastor, he put the phone to his ear and pressed the answer button. "You find it?" he asked.

"They just brought it in—took all day to finish the crime scene," D.C. police officer Saif Carvalho said on the other end. For three years now, Officer Carvalho had been playing cards with one of A.J.'s dear friends, and now he had an application in to the Secret Service. As A.J. knew, everyone needs a pal on the inside.

"You were right about one thing," Carvalho said, referring to the gun that the attacker used on Pastor Frick. "It was definitely an old weapon."

"How old?"

"Museum old. As in over a hundred years old. According to one of the detectives who's a big gun collector here, it's something called a *British Bulldog pistol.*"

A.J. felt the hair on his scalp prickling. After what Beecher found at St. John's, he'd looked up the rest. A British Bulldog pistol was the gun that killed President Garfield.

Sonuvabitch.

What the hell did Palmiotti get us into?

Racing to the door, A.J. didn't say goodbye to the pastor. This wasn't just about imitating old assassins. President Wallace had spent time with Pastor Frick at Foundry Church...and he'd also gone to services at St. John's. Now A.J. knew where the bull's-eye was heading. The pastors were just the warm-up, like target practice. And now, thanks to Pastor Frick, A.J. knew the one thing all the victims had in common: President Wallace himself.

Bursting out from the chapel and into the long hospital hallway, he dialed a new number on his phone. It was time to move the big chess piece.

Running down the hallway and concentrating on his phone, A.J. didn't bother to scan his surroundings. As a result, he didn't see the lone man lingering just inside the hospital gift shop.

The man fit right in at the hospital. He looked like a staffer, or a doctor, especially because of the ID badge clipped to his lapel.

It was from a hospital too. St. Elizabeths.

Sipping from a cup of coffee that he held with two hands, the lone man stood just inside the glass door, studying A.J., and the fact that he was leaving in a hurry, and the urgent way he was whispering into his phone.

Now the Secret Service was definitely involved. They knew the pattern. And most important, they were well aware of the Knight's final target: the President of the United States.

Nico would not be happy about this.

*   *   *

50

St. Elizabeths Hospital
Washington, D.C.

A pple or orange, Jerome?" Rupert called out nearly an hour
later as he pushed the juice cart into the room of the old
man who, in almost two years, hadn't once said hello back,
much less answered apple *or* orange. Tonight was Jerome's first
night in the new building.

"I hear the orange is better tonight. No pulp, no ice," Rupert
added.

But as was always the case, Jerome didn't even look up. He simply stared at the only section of the newspaper he ever read: the
colorful advertising circulars.

"Sleep tight, Jerome. And remember: Your sister loves you,"
Rupert said, keeping the promise he had made to Jerome's family.

Naturally, every family made special requests, and Rupert
couldn't keep all of them, or even most of them. But in Rupert's
eyes, sisters were different.

His own sister was the only person who got him through their
tough childhood in Baltimore. And to this day, his sister was the
only reason Rupert always asked to be staffed on the NGI floors.
With the extra pay that came from working with Nico and the
other NGIs, Rupert ensured that his nephew—his sister's son—
could keep going to the private school for the deaf that his recently
divorced sister would never be able to afford without him.

Was it worth it?

His nephew just got a recruiting letter from North Carolina. For chess. A silent game.

Even Nico couldn't ruin news like that.

"Almost done?" the nurse with the sad eyes called out from the nurses' station at the end of the hall.

Rupert put one finger up, pivoting the juice cart in the short, bright new hallway. On his right was his final delivery, to the room marked *Nico H.*

He paused a moment, thinking whether he should dock Nico his juice for giving Karina such a hard time. But Rupert knew, when it came to Nico, no matter how annoying he was, it was never personal.

Nico had a sickness. Nico was confused. Sure, they'd gotten him to the point where he was no longer talking to the dead First Lady anymore. But that didn't mean he was cured.

Most important, Rupert knew that if he held back the juice tonight, that's a whole different headache they'd be dealing with tomorrow.

"Knock-knock. Apple- and orange-type drinks coming!" Rupert announced, shoving the juice cart into the door and forcing it to swing open. "Who wants sugary—!?"

"—ust thought you'd want it back," Dr. Gosling said, standing by the head of the bed and handing something to Nico.

Dr. Gosling turned at the sound. Nico just sat there, in bed. Already staring at the door. Like he knew Rupert was coming.

"I-I'm sorry," Rupert said. "I didn't realize you were—"

"It's fine...it's fine...it's fine..." Dr. Gosling said as he put on a wide smile and flashed his crooked ultra-white teeth. "Was just checking up on our favorite resident. Had to make sure he has a good first night, yes?"

Rupert nodded, taking an involuntary step backward. In Nico's hands, he saw what Dr. Gosling had given him. A leather book. Nico's book.

"He left it in TLC, in the restroom," Gosling said, his smile still in place. "I just thought he'd want it back."

"That's nice of you," Rupert said, looking at the leather book. The brown leather was the same, and the title was the same: *Looking Backward*. But when Rupert saw it earlier, the bookmark sticking out of it was a ten of spades. He remembered thinking that spades were sort of sinister. But now, the bookmark was a ten of diamonds.

"You bring my apple juice?" Nico demanded.

Rupert nodded, handing it to Nico.

"Apple is better than orange," Nico added. Rupert continued nodding and Dr. Gosling laughed.

"We should really let him get his rest," Dr. Gosling said, putting a stiff hand on the juice cart and motioning Rupert backward toward the door.

Rupert tugged the juice cart back into the hallway, and Dr. Gosling pulled the door closed behind them. As it was about to shut, Rupert saw Nico looking down at his lap. He couldn't tell if Nico was staring at the book or the juice. But there was no mistaking this: that dark, haunting smile. Nico was definitely happy about something.

"He's doing well, don't you think?" Dr. Gosling asked as they both walked back toward the nurses' station.

As the door shut behind the two men, Nico kept his head down, focusing on the quiet that returned to his room.

"*He's doing well, don't you think?*" Dr. Gosling asked out in the hallway.

To anyone else, it'd be too hard to hear. But Nico's hearing was more acute than the average person's. He could hear what others couldn't. And see too.

"*You don't like it when they ignore me, do you?*" the dead First Lady asked, standing in the corner of the room.

"Shhh," Nico whispered, still focusing on Rupert and Dr. Gosling.

"*Nico, do you even know how lucky you got?*" the First Lady asked. "*With all the money they spent on this building, the doors still aren't thick enough to mask the sound.*"

Nico nodded. That'd be useful. "It's good to know when someone's coming."

"*Sure is,*" the First Lady said. "*And it's even better to know about the bang before the bang happens.*"

Refusing to take a sip of his apple juice, Nico looked down at the leather book that he'd intentionally left in the downstairs restroom. Thumbing through it, he stopped on the playing-card bookmark: the ten of diamonds on page 127. Behind it was another card. A new card. The ace of clubs.

Message received. The third Knight was on his way.

51

Tot was tired as he followed the checkerboard floor down the long basement hallway. He wanted to go home. He needed the rest. But right now, in the basement of the National Archives, he needed something else even more. If the Knights of the Golden Circle were truly back...

He picked up his pace. He'd have the answer soon enough.

Checking one last time over his shoulder, he stopped at the room with no room numbers on it—the thick glass door with beige horizontal blinds.

He knew the glass was bulletproof. He knew the treasures that were stored inside. And he knew better than to knock. The hidden camera above the doorjamb already announced his arrival.

Underneath the door, the lights were off. Tot didn't budge.

Sure enough, within seconds, there was a muffled click and the heavy door opened.

"You really are a pain in my ass," a man in a crisp white lab coat said, running a manicured hand over his perfect, brushed-back blond hair. Daniel "the Diamond" Boeckman. The head of Preservation, and a master of ancient documents. "This better be life-or-death," the Diamond added.

From his jacket pocket, Tot unfolded a color photocopy of a mottled and worn ace of spades.

"It is," Tot said as he eased the bulletproof door shut. "Now, how much do you know about playing cards?"

52

Eighteen years ago
Sagamore, Wisconsin

Marshmallow loved sleeping at Beecher's house.

And not because of the food, which, when you're twelve years old, is one of the greatest benefits of a sleepover at a friend's house. Back then, as everyone knew, *Marshall's* house was the one with the best food. Cap'n Crunch... Lucky Charms... Fruity *and* Cocoa Pebbles, plus two different flavors of Pringles *and* you could drink Yoo-Hoo at dinner, not just as a treat. Forever compensating for having a husband in a wheelchair, Marshall's mom made sure her son had it all.

When Marshall slept at Beecher's, he had to slum his way through Honey Nut Cheerios and regular Cheerios.

But as Marshall was all too aware, Beecher's house had the one thing his house would never have.

A teenage sister.

Two weeks ago, right before bed, Marshmallow was coming out of the bathroom just as Beecher's sister Lesley stepped into the hallway. She was wearing a sky blue nightgown that came well below her knees. But Marshall could still see her ankles. He pushed his glasses up on his nose. *Galactic*, he thought to himself.

"If you even say a word to me, I promise your penis will fall off," Lesley threatened.

Keeping his head down and rushing around her, back to Beecher's bedroom, the chubby Marshmallow kept quiet.

He was mortified. And already making plans for the next sleepover.

"Beecher, maybe this isn't smart," Marshmallow whispered, two weeks later, now regretting that decision. "We don't even know if they're coming up here."

"They're coming. They have to," Beecher insisted as the two of them knelt in the dark, peeking out from inside Beecher's sister's closet. "Don't be such a coward."

They heard the rumbling, like thunder, of half a dozen teenage girls racing up the stairs, and then saw the crowd of them burst into the pale pink bedroom, scattering and gossiping as they stole seats on the bed, at the desk, across the carpet with the daisy edges.

Marshall saw her immediately. At the back of the crowd, walking hesitantly. The last girl to enter the room. The girl who had just moved back to town. Clementine.

Now it all made sense.

"You knew she'd be here, didn't you?" Marshall whispered.

Beecher didn't answer, his eyes stuck on Clementine.

"Beecher, can I break the news to you now? She doesn't like you."

"She doesn't even know who I am," Beecher whispered.

"Doesn't matter. You oogle."

"I'm in puberty. I'm allowed to oogle. Besides, you oogle my sister."

Marshmallow pushed his glasses up on his nose, still focused on Clementine. "How'd she get invited anyway? She's not friends with your sister," he whispered, leaning his nose toward the crack of the door.

"My mom felt bad for her—new girl, new school—she told my sister that Clementine *had* to be invited."

"And she came? If Andy Levey invited me to his house, I wouldn't—"

"Shhhh," Beecher hissed as one of the girls—a short and bossy one named Rita—called out...

"Okay, who's *playing*?"

Within seconds, a small circle formed at the center of the room. Girls scooched in, then out, to make more room. In the best childhood games, no one had to discuss the rules.

Beecher's sister reached under her bed and pulled out an empty glass Diet Coke bottle.

"Please, God in heaven, I'll go to church every day if these girls start making out with each other," Marshmallow whispered.

Beecher flicked Marshmallow's ear. He took the hint. Be quiet.

With a sharp twist, Beecher's sister gave the bottle its first spin. A few girls smiled. A few looked terrified. But every girl in the circle shifted with a nearly imperceptible flinch as the bottle twirled past them. Everyone but Clementine, who—as Beecher noticed—was still standing awkwardly, her hands behind her back, by the door.

"*And the winnah is...!*" Beecher's sister announced.

The girls began laughing, clapping, squealing as the bottle stopped and pointed at the short, bossy girl who just a minute ago had called the game to order. Her wavy brown hair was tied in a messy braid that was slowly coming undone. Rita.

"Sorry, sweetie," Beecher's sister sang as Rita got on her knees and crawled into the center of the circle.

From the closet, Beecher saw the forced smile on Rita's face, and the terror in her eyes.

"Who wants to start?" Lesley asked as Rita sat Indian-style in the center of the circle. "What's wrong with her?"

"Your house smells like pickles," one of the girls, a blonde with braces, called out as everyone laughed.

"Your mom drives that dumpy old Mercury Capri," a girl in a unicorn sweatshirt added as Rita pretended to laugh with the group.

"You look better from far away," another called out.

The group giggled at that one, but it caused a pause in the action.

Watching from the closet, Beecher assumed that they were now feeling bad—that they had taken the game *What's Wrong With You* too far. Until...

"You st-st-stutter when you read out loud," a girl with a gold cross around her neck blurted.

"I know you stuffed your bra for Reina Pizzuti's birthday at the bowling alley!"

"You stuffed it for my birthday too!" another girl yelled.

"*Stovetop stuffing!*" the girl with the gold cross added.

"*Stovetop stuffing!*" Lesley repeated.

"St-st-stovetop!" the blonde with braces added, getting the biggest laughs of all.

At the center of the circle, Rita tried to hold her smile in place, but it wobbled. A swell of tears built just behind her eyes.

From the closet, Marshall looked back at Beecher. "Girls are like...evil bitches."

"What was *that*!?" someone shouted.

"From over there!" another yelled.

The crowd went quiet.

Beecher froze, hiding his eyes by staring down at the closet's wood floor, which was a mess of shoes. He held his breath. Marshmallow did the same. No one was pointing at them. Maybe they didn't—

The door to the closet flew open as the burst of bright lights attacked their retinas. "You little rat *fink!*" Beecher's sister screamed. "*You're dead for this!*"

Beecher scrambled backward, deeper into the closet. But with nowhere to go, he was tripping, tumbling, stumbling over the mess of shoes.

"Grab him!" a girl yelled.

Before he knew what was happening, the group of girls were grunting and pulling...

But not at Beecher.

"Get the fat one!" someone shouted.

"Nonono...please...!" Marshmallow pleaded as they dragged him from the closet. The girls were bigger—and two years older. Marshall didn't have a chance. He tried grabbing Beecher's shirt, then the cuffs of his jeans, but at the back of the closet, Beecher was tucked down, curled into his own self-preserving ball.

With a final tug, Marshall was out—literally pulled onto the worn yellow carpet with the daisy edges. The girls didn't have to say a word. The circle formed instantly around him.

"You fat little shit!" Beecher's sister shouted. "I should tell Pastor Riis what you did!"

"Y'know the pastor's screwing your mom!" the girl with the gold cross added.

"That's not true!" Marshall said.

"I heard he's screwing her because your dad's penis is even more broken than his legs," the blonde with braces added.

"That's why you're an only child!" another girl said.

"I bet your penis is broken too!" Rita chimed in as the group let out their collective giggles and laugh.

"Broken penis!"

"Little penis!"

"*No penis!*"

The laughter grew louder as Marshall lay there, curled on the carpet, covering his head like he was in one of those 1950s Cold War instructional videos trying to protect himself from an atomic bomb.

In the back corner of the closet, as Beecher jammed himself against a row of once neatly hanging sweatshirts, he felt the empty clothes hug him, like cotton ghosts.

"They call you *Marshmallow* because you've got those boy boobs too, don't you, fatty?" one of the girls called out.

"His dad has man-boobs too. Bigger than his mom's!"

"Maybe the pastor's screwing your dad too!"

The circle tightened around Marshall, like a gang when they start kicking their victim.

"*Don't cry, fatty!*" Rita threatened as Marshall's body started to shake.

Of course, Beecher wanted to stop them. Wanted to race out and help his friend and scream to stop them all. But he didn't. He *couldn't*, he thought. They were older. And bigger. How could he take on a roomful of—?

"*That's enough,*" a girl's voice interrupted. Calmly. Confidently.

The room turned.

Still embraced by the ghost-sweatshirts, Beecher peered out from the closet. He knew who it was.

Clementine.

"What'd you just say?" Beecher's sister challenged.

"Listen, if it was my little brother, I'd kill him too," Clementine said. "So go kill your brother. But don't think you're all-powerful just because you can pick on the fat kid who can't fight back."

The room went silent.

"Listen, bitch—you weren't even really invited to this party," the short bossy girl named Rita jumped in.

"You think I wanna be here? I'd rather gouge my eyes out than look at some Napoleon-teenbitch who's so insecure she can't remember how much the same thing hurt two minutes ago." Turning to Marshall, Clementine added, "C'mon, get up."

Jamming his fingers underneath his glasses to wipe his eyes, Marshmallow slowly rose to his feet. He didn't say anything. He simply followed Clementine to the door.

Beecher watched it all from the closet. Clementine was incredible. Even more incredible than he had thought before.

But as she disappeared and Marshall trailed behind her, Beecher was still waiting for Marshall to turn back to him. He waited for Marshall to take one last glance over his shoulder.

Beecher kept waiting for his friend to look.

Marshall never did. He didn't need to.

Beecher knew what had happened—he knew he was the cause of this.

And the sad truth was, it wouldn't be the worst pain that Beecher would cause for Marshall Lusk.

53

Today

G et out of my house!" I shout.

"Benjy, listen to me..." Clementine pleads, using the old nickname my mom used to call me.

"Get out!"

"Beecher, before you—"

"Get the hell out of my house!" I insist, rushing forward and swinging my briefcase at her.

She hops from the chair but doesn't take a single step away from me.

Her smell—a mix of caramel and a pinch of peach from her lip gloss—washes over me, reminding me of our kiss two months ago. She's wearing the same tight black sweater from that first day we reconnected. It's not nearly enough to make me forget what happened after that.

"Beecher, just listen."

"*Listen!?* You're a liar. You're a manipulator. And the last time we were together, you—oh yeah—*you murdered someone!*" I yell the words so loud, they burn my throat. "I'm calling the cops. They're going to arrest you," I tell her coldly as I reach for my phone.

"No. You won't," she challenges. "That doesn't help either of us."

I dial 911 and hit—

Her hand whips out, slapping the phone from my grip. It rockets

186

against the armrest of the sofa and ricochets off the floor, skittering under the coffee table.

"Are you insane!?" I ask. Then I remember who her father is. Of course she's insane.

I dart for the phone. She grabs my wrist.

I try to pull away. She's holding so tight, her nails dig into the underside of my wrist.

"*Get...off!*" I shout, fighting to pull free and giving her a hard shove that slams her in the shoulder, catching her off balance and sending her stumbling backward.

Her feet hook on the carpet and she falls like a cut tree. The back of her head hits the edge of one of the lower shelves on a nearby bookcase, and her head snaps forward. A few picture frames sky-dive from the higher shelves, crashing next to her.

Heading for the coffee table, I reach for my phone.

"Beecher, can you please calm down a second?"

Thankfully, my cell's not broken.

"I'm serious, Beecher! You need to listen!"

Again, I dial 911.

"You really think I came here without a good reason?" Clementine pleads. Her voice is desperate now.

I hit *send* and wait as it rings.

"I didn't come here empty-handed!" she says, struggling to sit up. She reaches behind her back like she's pulling something from her waistband.

If she has a gun—

"You need to pay attention," Clementine says, pulling out a...

...folded-up sheet of paper.

No gun. In my ear, 911 rings for the second time.

"Beecher, you need to see this. It's written by your father."

"Everything you say is a lie, Clementine."

"Not this time, Beecher. It's a letter he *wrote*."

"And that's how you planned to hook me in? That's as low as you could go? By using a letter that my dead father supposedly wrote to me?"

187

"He didn't write it to *you*. He wrote it to your mother."

On the third ring, I hear a click as the operator picks up. "Emergency Assistance. What is your location?"

"What're you talking about?" I ask. "It's a love letter?"

"No," Clementine says. "It's his suicide note."

54

Most people made small talk with Julie Lyons. She knew why. It's not that they liked her. They knew where she sat, and what she was in charge of.

Back during the President's term as governor in Ohio, Julie—a fifty-four-year-old, square-faced woman who, around her neck, wore gold charms with her kids' names on them—did all of Wallace's scheduling. Today, her job was exactly the same, making her the only person who sat in the small room that connected to the Oval Office—and more important, the official gatekeeper for anyone who wanted to see the President.

"Hey, Julie—how's it going?" most staffers asked.

"You do something new with your hair?" the real suck-ups would add.

"How's your daughter doing at Dartmouth?" the smart ones said.

But as A.J. stepped into the cramped office and approached Julie's desk, the last thing on his mind was small talk.

"Ma'am, we need to speak with him," A.J. announced, using the word "we" even though he was alone. *So Secret Service.*

"Sorry. He's on the phone," Julie said, pointing A.J. to the wing-back chairs across from her desk.

A.J. didn't move. At all. "Ma'am, we need to speak with him. Right now."

Julie stared up at A.J. It was easy saying no to staffers, and interns, and even to Secretary of Education Prebish, who brought his new wife and stepkids to the White House. But that's different from saying no to the Service.

Squeezing around her desk, she headed for the curved door that

189

connected to the Oval. A.J. couldn't help but notice the blown-up photograph that filled the wall behind her desk. It was a shot—a private one—of the President (in profile and in full suit) pitching a whiffle ball to his eight-year-old son as the two of them played on the South Lawn. Even in profile, it was easy to see the joy on Wallace's face. Yet like any Secret Service agent, A.J. knew his protectee. He could also see that deep wrinkle that ran from his nose to his chin and burrowed a dark parenthesis around the President's smile. It was a worried wrinkle—the kind of wrinkle that came with knowing the peace wouldn't last. As A.J. was well aware, that crease was only getting deeper.

On his left, Julie popped open the curved door. President Wallace was at his desk, on the phone. But as he glanced over at Julie, he could see who was standing right behind her.

A.J. didn't have to say a word.

"Conrad, let me call you back," the President said, hanging up the telephone.

With that, A.J. stepped into the Oval and the curved door closed behind him.

55

I know you're lying," I insist.

"I can't always be lying, Beecher. Not about everything."

From my phone, I hear the 911 operator asking what my emergency is. I tell her I dialed wrong—that there's no emergency—even though I see one standing right in front of me.

"Just read the letter," Clementine pleads, holding it out and trying to hand it over.

I don't reach for it. I can't.

"Just read it, Beecher. Judge for yourself."

I still don't move. Across from me, Clementine waves the letter like a white flag. She can soften herself all she wants with the blonde wig and all; it's still the same person living in that body. But the most compelling part of Clementine's argument has nothing to do with her.

"It's your *father*," Clementine says, still offering me the white flag. "How could you not at least read it?"

I glance down at the inside of my wrist. Her nails left crescent indentations. They'll fade soon. My questions won't.

"You'll only regret it if you *don't* read it, Beecher."

I snatch the sheet from her hand. From the poor quality of the photocopy, it looks like a fax. I try to read it immediately, scanning it once, then again—but the words don't make sense. My hands start to shake, and I feel like a teenager trying to read the directions for a home pregnancy kit.

Dear Teresa,

My mother's name. But what makes my body numb—what makes it feel like there's a thin plastic sheet between my outer layer of skin and my inner layer of skin—is when I see the starkly printed "T" in front of the scribbly cursive "eresa."

My father died when I was three years old. He wasn't around long enough for me to know his handwriting. But to this day, my mother keeps the last card he sent her—a Valentine's card with Snoopy on it—in the giant hat box that she has in the corner of her bedroom and stores all of our loose photos and Polaroids in.

My mom didn't believe in photo albums. She wanted the photos out, so you could sift through them at any time. As an archivist, the disorganization still kills me. But as a son, I appreciated the opportunity to study the old Valentine.

It didn't say much. My dad wrote *To My Valentine Teresa* at the top, then let the card do the talking. But the way he wrote *Teresa*—printed "T," cursive "eresa"—I studied that card for hours, down to the UPC barcode on the back and the price that was ninety-nine cents. I know that card. And I know my father's handwriting when I see it. Blinking hard, I fight to read it.

Dear Teresa,

You win. As you always have. I still hear your words from that morning at the bus station. You were so scared I wasn't coming back. I swore you were wrong. But I'm now all too aware that is not the case.

I grieve for the pain I know this will cause you. And the damage to our babies. When you tell stories of me, please always mention that I loved them. I always will.

I wish I could have made a better life for you. But with my passing, my menace to them—and to you—is gone.

Please have Pastor Riis officiate at my funeral. And if this reaches you before Beecher's birthday, please buy him something big and stupid.

—Albert

My entire life, I was told my father died in a car accident on a bridge in Wisconsin. The plastic sheet that feels like it's between my layers of skin now seems like it's expanding, cleaving me in half. My hand starts to shake even harder.

Clementine, standing now, reaches out to comfort me.

"Don't touch me," I warn her. "Where did you get this?"

"Beecher, before you—"

"Where'd you get it?"

"Beecher, please. I know it's hard. When you helped me find Nico—"

"I didn't help you find Nico! You found him yourself and then came to me, pretending you were clueless! Now what the hell is going on!?"

She takes a half step back. "Did you look at the date?" she asks.

I stare down at the note. My father died on July 20th. But this suicide note, or whatever it is, it's dated July 27th. One week after he supposedly died.

My tongue swells in my mouth. I try to breathe but nothing comes out. I know it's a lie. Everything she says is a lie. "My father didn't commit suicide," I insist.

"I'm not saying he did, Beecher. But don't you—?"

"He didn't commit suicide! He wouldn't do that!"

"Beecher, I know this is a wrecking ball for you, but you have to—"

"Don't tell me what I *have to do*! You didn't know my father! You never met him! He wouldn't leave us like that!"

"Beecher—"

"He wouldn't leave us!" I explode. "It wasn't his choice! So for you to come here—to...to...to make a fake letter like that...I knew you were a monster, Clementine! But to use my dead father to manipulate me like that."

"I swear on my life, I'm not manipulating—"

"You're a liar! It's always a lie!" I shout, shoving the sheet of paper back in her hands. She tries to hand it back, but I push it toward her. *"You lied about Nico! You lied when you first approached me.*

And then all that crap about having cancer and how you're dying? What's *not* sacred, Clementine? What *won't* you lie about? *It's like the bullshit wig you're wearing right now!*" I shout, grabbing at her phony blonde hair.

"Beecher, get off!"

"Why? What's wrong with some truth for once?" I grab at her hair again, this time getting a grip on it. It goes cockeyed on her head. "What's wrong with revealing the true you—?"

I yank the wig from her head. But instead of revealing short black hair, she...she's...

Completely bald.

56

I'd say eighteenth century—y'know, if I were a guessing man," the Diamond said.

Tot's good eye narrowed. "Daniel, don't do that. You never guess."

"Agreed. And I never said I was guessing here," the Diamond teased, waving the color copies that held pictures of the old playing cards, and tossing them onto the nearby light table.

Tot didn't care for show-offs. But he did care that when the Archives had to manually reweave the frayed corners of the original Bill of Rights, Daniel was the only man trusted to do the job. In the world of document preservation, no one was tougher than the Diamond.

"I'd date them to somewhere in the 1770s, maybe 1780s," the Diamond added. "But if you had the actual cards—or even that missing ace of spades..."

"What's so important about the ace of spades?"

"That's where cardmakers used to sign their work. Think of the cards you played with when you were a kid. The ace of spades used to have the company's name on it: *US Playing Card Company*, or the guy on the old bicycle, or whoever it was that made it. In the eighteenth and nineteenth centuries, it's where the printer signed them too. Depending on the year, though, these cards you have here might even date back to the... Hmmmm." Spinning on his heel, the Diamond headed for the corner of the room, toward a bank of map cabinets and storage units. He stopped at one that held two stereo-binocular microscopes and an array of tools and brushes, all lined up in size order, of course.

"By the way, she said *yes*," the Diamond added, pulling open the lower drawer of the file cabinet. Tot knew who he was referring to. The only thing that the Diamond loved more than old artifacts: Tot's officemate. Rina.

"We're going on a date. A real one. Next Tuesday night."

"Tuesday night?" Tot asked. "Tuesday nights aren't dates."

"It's a date. Whatever you said to her, it worked. I owe you and Beecher big."

Tot hadn't said a word to Rina. Neither did Beecher. But in the world of the Archives, where nerdy librarian love was far more common than people thought (*You* like old books? *I* like old books! Let's date!), Tot knew better than to get in the way.

"Where do you think I should take her?" the Diamond asked. "Are wine bars still considered cool?"

"Daniel, can we please focus here? You were saying about the ace of spades..."

"Of course, of course," the Diamond said, kneeling down at the open bottom drawer of the cabinet and fingerwalking through the hanging files. Toward the back, he opened one and rummaged through it. Tot saw what was inside. Tons of loose...

"Playing cards? Is there anything you're not hoarding down here?"

"You kidding? I've got Thomas Jefferson's left shoe down here. If you put it on and it fits, you get to be President."

"Daniel..."

"Playing cards. Got it. Anyway, most of these are from that exhibit we did on cards a few years back—back when Bill Clinton was playing hearts all the time. Turns out, he wasn't the only card player. Back in World War II, the government used playing cards to send secret maps and messages to our POWs in Germany, since cards were one of the few things the enemy let them have. If the tax stamp was crooked on the pack, that meant it was a fixed deck. So our troops would soak those cards in water, then peel them apart, revealing secret maps to help them escape," he said, pulling out a nine of clubs that had been peeled open. "In fact, years later, in Vietnam—"

"Daniel, I know that playing cards have been used throughout history. What's this have to do with the ace I'm looking for?"

Still kneeling at the file drawer, the Diamond stopped, staring up at Tot. "Tot, you know I never mind helping you, especially in these cases I know you can't tell me about. But don't talk to me like I'm some college-kid researcher."

Tot took a deep breath, staring at the peeled-away nine of clubs. "I apologize, Daniel. I've just . . . It's been one of those days."

"Is this like before? Are you and Beecher—? You hunting another killer?"

Tot didn't answer. He'd known the Diamond for years, for decades even. But he never talked openly about the Culper Ring. Or about the Ring's real history and all the things he didn't even share with Beecher. As always, though, the Diamond never missed a detail.

"Tot, if you're in danger, I can help you."

Tot stared back at him. "Sorry, you were about to say something. About my missing ace of spades . . . ?"

The Diamond shook his head, knowing better than to argue. "Y'know, Tot, you're the reason people don't like the elderly."

"Do you have the information or not, Daniel?"

Reaching into the back of the file folder, the Diamond pulled out one final item—a single old playing card in a clear case. It had sharp corners rather than modern rounded ones. Yet what made the weathered ace of spades so memorable was the familiar symbol on it: the hand-drawn American eagle with wide wings and a lowered head.

Tot's chest tightened as he studied the image. It was the same eagle from the pack of old cards they had found on Marshall. The eagle from Guiteau's tattoo. And the same eagle that was the symbol of the Knights of the Golden Circle, a group that Tot's mentor swore didn't exist anymore.

"Like the magician says," the Diamond added with a grin. "Is this your card?"

57

Clementine steps backward, her bald head down, her hand shielding her eyes.

"Clemmi, I—I'm sorry. I didn't mean—"

She looks up. It's her glance that interrupts me.

To see her like this, so pale, with no hair. Her face looks longer.

In my hands, her wig feels dead, like a mound of straw. I hand it back. Holding it, she just stands there as I stare.

"You really have cancer."

"I told you, Beecher. Not everything's a lie."

The light in the living room reflects off her forehead. Her bald head looks so small. So fragile. And though she stands up straight and offers a half-smile, it's like looking at any woman in a cancer ward. Since they have no hair, you can't help but focus on their eyes—and then all you see, imagined or not, is the vulnerable sadness within them.

"Have they given you a prognosis?" I ask.

She shakes her head. I expect her voice to be quiet. It isn't. "No one knows what it is. They said they've never seen anything like it. That's why I've been searching so hard for"—her jaw shifts off center and she again hands me the letter from my father—"for Nico's files. That's how I found what your father wrote. The s—"

"Don't call it a suicide note," I interrupt.

"I won't."

"And it doesn't mean that's how he died."

She studies me, not saying a word.

I scan the letter that's supposedly from my dad. The teeny letters running across the top say *FedEx Office* with a 734 area code.

"What were you doing in Michigan?" I ask.

She doesn't answer.

"Clementine, I'm feeling bad for you right now, and because of that—despite everything you did—I'm actually considering whether to listen to you."

"I was hiding, Beecher. I was going through the file I stole from the Archives, and I was hiding. First in Canada. Then I snuck into Michigan."

"And that was it?"

"What else do you want there to be? How bad a person do you think I am? Oh, that's right, you already told me. You used that word, the one they use for my dad. *Monster*."

I feel bad as she says it. And I feel even worse seeing her bald with cancer. "You still killed Palmiotti," I tell her.

She doesn't speak, but I see that familiar wicked twinkle in her eyes.

"What? How is that amusing, Clementine? You killed him. You shot him."

"Palmiotti's not dead."

"I *saw it happen*! I saw you pull the trigger!"

"And I saw him six days ago in a Target in West Bloomfield, Michigan, when I traded him the President's file. They dyed his hair. He has a scar on his neck from where I shot him. And he still thinks pleated khakis count as a fashion statement. But he's breathing just fine."

A burning pain stabs my chest, like someone just jammed a shovel in it and started digging. I look around, but the world is blurred. All I see is Palmiotti. When he was shot, I saw the blood . . . his neck . . . he was— *How can*—? "*Oh no* . . ."

"*Oh yes*," Clementine says, still smiling.

"Th-That's not possible."

"Beecher, he's the best friend of the President of the United States. Anything's possible. And if it makes you feel better, without Palmiotti giving me Nico's file, I'd never have been able to track down the doctor."

"What doctor?"

"The military doctor. His name was in Nico's navy records. Dr. Yoo. I found him in San Diego. All those years ago, he was the one who treated Nico…the one who looked after him while they did their testing. But he also—he treated your father, Beecher. He treated all of them."

"No. No way," I say, refusing to be suckered. My father was older. He didn't…he couldn't have served with Nico.

"They were plankholders together," Clementine says. "That's what the doctor called them. Plankholders. Y'know what that means?"

I nod, feeling numb as I mindlessly stare at the patch of pale freckles on her bald head. I recognize the term from our navy files. "They're the first crewmembers to serve on a ship."

"Yes—but in the army, they're also the first members of a unit. The ones who launch it. Plankholders."

I look down at my dad's handwriting. "So you just found this doctor and *what*? He conveniently told you all his secrets?"

"No, he wouldn't say much. He's old. I think he's sick. But he knew what they did to Nico. He knew it was wrong. And when I asked him for the paperwork… He didn't have much. But he did have *this*," she says, pointing back to my father's note.

"My father didn't commit suicide," I tell her for the third time.

"Maybe not. But to even have a note like that—it's time to ask the questions. Why'd your father write this suicide note? And how'd he write it a week after he supposedly died?"

My brain cartwheels, fighting for balance. I try to tell myself this is just another Clementine trick. But as I look back at her, I know it's not. It can't be.

"Maybe it's something your father wrote and never used," she suggests.

I look at her, confused. "That doesn't even make sense. Whatever you think that note is, my dad died a week earlier. How could they get the date of his death wrong?"

"I don't have the answer. I'm just saying, maybe he wrote the note—or even planned to use it—but then he died first."

"So his suicide note was postdated? Do people even do that?"

"Why wouldn't they? I mean, if you wanted to be prepared for your death, wouldn't you want to write it and...I don't know... work toward it?"

"I don't think so. I think those notes are the *last thing* people do. The *very* last thing. But again: Even assuming it wasn't, if he postdated it and planned to die—and then he somehow actually died right before the big day—doesn't that seem a little ridiculously convenient to you?"

She thinks about that a moment. "Maybe it's something they *made him* write."

"You mean they threatened him to do it?"

"Or required him to do it. Who knows what they needed it for."

I collapse in the lounge chair and wrestle out of my jacket. "In the Archives, I once read about this high-level military program that was organized after the first war in Iraq: a group of UN weapons inspectors. But what no one knew was that they weren't weapons inspectors. They were there to search for and rescue three of our MIA troops that were being held in Mosul. And before they went in, rumor was, their commanding officer had them write suicide notes. That way, if it all went bad and they were killed, they'd still be able to keep their true mission quiet."

"See, that makes sense to me," she says, now excited.

"Yeah, but so does them lying to my mom and telling her it was a car accident just to spare us the horror of a suicidal father," I reply, balancing the note on the edge of my left knee.

Clementine watches me carefully, clutching her wig with both hands and tapping it over and over against her belly. She's more than excited. For the past year, she's been searching for the truth about her father. She's lived her life with questions, so she's not afraid of the answers. But for me, I wasn't aware the questions even existed. I've spent my entire adult life carving the image of my dad into my emotional bedrock. Stories of his unstoppable work ethic are why I still carry his old briefcase every day. His untold adventures—and my obsession with his death—are why I begin each morning reading the obituaries. And when it comes to his impact on my psyche, why else would I work in the Archives, reminding people every day of the power that comes from exploring their past?

But now...to hear that my dad's death might not have been an act of *chance*, but an act of *choice*—that he left my mother and my sisters, that he left *me*, not by accident, but on *purpose*? I stare over at Clementine's empty wig, feeling my bedrock start to crumble. The note in my hands doesn't just undo the construct of my father. It undoes my *father*. It undoes *me*.

"Now you understand why I had to bring it to you, Beecher. For the doctor to send this..."

"I still don't understand. How'd he even have it?"

"I told you, he treated the whole group of them—"

"Group of *who*? What *group*?"

"The plankholders, Beecher. The first members of the unit."

I shake my head, redoing the math. "Clementine, my father was in the military for barely two years. He was a mechanic. How could he possibly serve with Nico, much less be a plankholder with him?"

"I'm just telling you what Dr. Yoo said. He told me they were all brought in together. All three from our hometown."

Three? She reads my confusion perfectly.

"There were three of them, Beecher: Your dad...my dad... and the dad of..." She looks off in the distance, like she's pulling a memory from the back of her brain. "Do you remember a kid—his dad was in a wheelchair—his name was..."

"Marshall Lusk," I whisper.

58

ow bad?" the President asked.

A.J. shook his head. He didn't have to say it.

"So you went to see him?" Wallace asked, sitting on the edge of his desk and careful to never say the word *pastor*. Sure, they were alone in the Oval, with all three doors closed. But it didn't take a copy of the Nixon tapes to know that there were always ears in the White House.

"I saw him. And spoke to him. He said he actually met you."

The President paused at that.

"You don't remember him?" A.J. asked. "He said it was at Christmas. That you said a prayer together. He was with a rabbi and an imam."

"You're kidding, right? You know how many people I say prayers with? Or how many of these I give out?" he added, pointing to the pink carnation on his lapel. It was a trick he stole from President McKinley, who every day used to pluck a carnation from his lapel and hand it as a gift to some lucky citizen. The real trick was that McKinley kept half a dozen carnations in his Oval Office desk.

"Sir, the point is, that's two in two days. And the only thing they have in common is they've both spent time, and said prayers, with *you*."

"So you think whoever's doing this, I'm next?"

"No, but my fear is there'll be a third attack, then a fourth, and after that..."

A.J. knew better than to finish the sentence.

Leaning there on the edge of his desk, arms crossed at his chest, Wallace looked more annoyed than anything else. For nearly four years, he had begun every morning with a private briefing that informed him about the most active threats against the United States. After the first one, he realized there was a whole different world that he never knew existed. By now, he'd gotten used to it.

But A.J. saw the way Wallace rubbed his thumb and middle finger together.

Even to the President of the United States, there was no threat like a personal one.

"And that doctor you've been seeing?" the President finally asked. "He's been no help?"

"Not with this. For this you need a specialist. Maybe even a surgeon."

Wallace thought about that. "What are you suggesting?"

"I think we take you out of here. Get you on the chopper, let us put our hands on this guy, and in the meantime, you'll be safe at Thurmont," A.J. said, referring to the compound known as Camp David.

"Yeah, I'm not doing that."

"Sir...?"

"I've been in this job for almost four years," Wallace said as he headed to the small anteroom on the opposite side of the office. Opening the mini-refrigerator, he scooped a handful of frozen Snickers from a silver bowl. "You know how many threats there've been?"

"I hear you, sir. And I know moving you is a disruption. But if I'm right about this—"

"Did you hear what I said? I'm the President of the United States. I'm not trashing my schedule, panicking my family, and hiding in a bunker just because some nutcase started seeing secret messages in the crumbs from his morning toast."

"But what if it's a nutcase you already know? From high school?"

The President slammed the mini-fridge shut. "What're you saying, A.J.? You think our doctor's become a quack?"

"I'm just saying, whoever's doing this, he seems to know where you've been."

"So does everyone with an Internet connection. My schedule's posted every single day. So go alert the shift leader and tell them what's going on. Time to let the rest of the Service do their job."

"I can do that, sir. I will," A.J. said, trailing the President back into the Oval and watching him toss back one of the Snickers. A.J. had heard it for years: All Presidents were stubborn. But for Wallace to take a risk like this, it made no sense. "Sir, can I just ask: Is this about tomorrow, about Presidents' Day?"

Wallace's gray eyes narrowed. "*What* about Presidents' Day?"

"I'm just saying, I know you want to bring your daughter to the Lincoln Memorial...and I know they're expecting a big crowd, but—"

The President dug his tongue into his back teeth, freeing some remnant peanuts. His voice was as calm as A.J. had ever heard it. "I have full confidence in the ability of the Secret Service to do its job."

"I do too, sir. But that doesn't mean—"

"I have full confidence in the Service," the leader of the free world repeated. "That means get the hell out of here and *find out who's doing this*," he growled.

"Of course, Mr. President," A.J. said, heading for the curved door. "I'll take care of it."

59

Tell me about this card," Tot demanded, gripping the faded ace of spades and studying the familiar crouched eagle on it. The card was heavy and thick, made of a layered card-stock, probably rag paper. "Why's it so important?"

"Forget the card a moment," the Diamond pleaded, delicately taking the card from Tot's hands and placing it on a nearby art table covered with sheer Japanese paper that was used for repairing fine works of art. The gossamer-weight paper was so thin, it was barely visible when applied to the object. "This isn't about a single card. It's about the *history* of cards."

"Daniel, there are lives on the line here. If you're telling a story, tell it quickly."

"What's the most popular book of all time?"

"The Bible," Tot said without hesitating.

"Exactly. In our modern world, where everything is constantly changing, it's simply amazing that the Bible itself has managed to stay pretty much the same—*for centuries*," the Diamond said. "That's how it is with playing cards."

"That's not true. Look at that eagle on the card. Name another pack of cards you've seen that on."

"Forget the eagle and what decorates the cards. I'm talking about what doesn't change. The modern suit symbols: hearts, diamonds, clubs, spades. In Italy, they used to be called cups, coins, swords, and batons. But those modern symbols—hearts, diamonds, clubs, and spades—those were created in France back in the fifteenth century, by a knight named Étienne de Vignolles."

"A knight?" Tot asked.

"Not just any knight. One of France's most famous knights. A man who rode with Joan of Arc herself," the Diamond explained, noticing the change in Tot's posture. "This was a knight who served both church *and* king, and as the story goes—and I'm not saying I believe it—to test his loyalty, each side—church and king—entrusted Vignolles with their greatest secret. Vignolles was the *chosen knight*. So when it came to decorating the cards...his lasting legacy...he picked his symbols with great care. These days, most historians will tell you that the four suits represent the four classes of medieval society: Hearts were the sign of the church; diamonds were arrowheads, representing vassals and archers; clubs were husbandmen or farmers; and spades were the points of lances and therefore represented the knights, and by extension, the king. Others say Vignolles was just inventing a game, or that the symbols were a key to the knight's true loyalty. But there are a few who insist that Vignolles, when he was forced to choose between church and king, used the cards as a vehicle to deliver a hidden message."

"I'm lost. A message to whom?"

"To his fellow knights. To the others who he'd eventually entrust with his secret." Clearing his throat, the Diamond asked, "Have you ever really examined the court cards in a deck? Why does the king of diamonds have an axe, while all the rest have swords? Why are the jack of hearts, the jack of spades, and the king of diamonds the only cards that appear in profile, while all the others are full face?"

"You're telling me that's a secret message?"

"Tot, you of all people know how much gets lost in the march of history. Today, we keep printing cards like this out of habit. But it's no different than when the dollar bill was first designed and someone decided to put a pyramid with the all-seeing eye on the back of it. The designers didn't just pick random symbols. They selected things for their meaning."

"That doesn't mean there are secret messages hidden in playing cards."

"You sure about that? Look at these here," the Diamond added, kneeling back down to the file drawer and flipping through the loose cards in the file, eventually pulling out a modern-day king of hearts.

"In just about every deck in the world, every face card—the jacks, the queens, all the other kings—they all have two hands. The king of hearts always has four—two of which are stabbing him with a sword, like he's stabbing himself. That's where we get the term *suicide king* from. But look closely. His sleeves don't match. He's not stabbing himself or committing suicide. He's being stabbed by *someone else*. Someone so hidden, the king can't see him coming."

Tot pulled the card closer, examining the image.

"You see it now, don't you? They match another card in the deck," the Diamond said, now excited. "Those are the sleeves of the queen of *spades*."

"So the spades kill the hearts?"

"Or as Vignolles designed in his original symbols: the knights— and by extension the king—kill the church."

"But you said the queen—"

"Forget the queen. In the very early decks of cards, there *was no* queen. Women weren't recognized as a part of civil society. Even jacks were introduced years later. So in Vignolles's original deck, and the decks that were passed down generation to generation, it wasn't *king, queen, jack*. It was *king, knight, knave*. That was the warning Vignolles was sending. The real killers of the church were the knights of the king. So if the church's greatest secret was to be protected, a new army had to be formed. A secret army. A sacred group sworn to protect the church. A group of knights who would hide amongst the king's knights and attack when they were needed most...and when no one would expect it," the Diamond explained as Tot glanced back at the antique ace of spades from the deck Marshall was carrying.

Tot eyed the familiar eagle on it: the symbol of the so-called modern Knights—the Knights of the Golden Circle.

"Vignolles knew this battle would outlive him," the Diamond explained. "The battle between church and king has been waged for centuries. It's the ultimate civil war. So for his few secret knights who were loyal to the church, Vignolles hid his warning right there in the images: Without these sacred knights, the king would slaughter the church. The cards were their call to arms—the message hidden right in front of everyone—as a secret signal that would make sense only to those who knew the message was there," he added as Tot thought about the mysterious card that John Wilkes Booth used to get into Ford's Theatre... or the red diamond tattoo on Charles Guiteau's shoulder.

"Maybe it's true, maybe it's all silly folklore," the Diamond continued. "But when you look at a deck of cards, make no mistake, those cards still tell a story. And it's a story that always ends the same way..."

"With a knight murdering the church."

"There you go. Now you see Vignolles's warning—and why he wanted to change that story. When his signal was given..."

"His knights would murder the king," Tot whispered.

"Or murder whatever leader was in charge when there was no king," the Diamond countered.

Confused, Tot asked, "What're you talking about?"

"You think I just keep a stash of antique aces for no good reason?" the Diamond asked, motioning to the ace of spades with the ancient eagle. "Those cards you brought in here—they're the same ones that belonged to George Washington."

60

arshall. You remember him?" Clementine asks, sounding energized as she grips her wig.

"Of course I remember him," I reply weakly. "Marshall was my friend."

"He was? I forgot that," she admits, still not putting her wig on. "According to Dr. Yoo, before Marshall's dad was in the wheelchair, he was a plankholder too. They were young back then, before any of us came along or—"

"Clementine, when was the last time you saw Marshall?"

"I dunno, when did he move away? I think I was . . . maybe thirteen or fourteen?"

"And you haven't seen him since?"

"Where would I see him?"

"What about speaking to him? Have you spoken to him?"

"Beecher, you okay?"

"Please just answer the question."

"Y-You're acting like—"

"Just answer the question, Clementine! Have you spoken to Marshall or not!?"

Clementine's eyes go wide, then quickly narrow and tighten, clicking back and forth like she's frisking me for information.

"You spoke to him, didn't you?" she blurts. "You know something about Marshall."

"I don't—"

"You *do,* Beecher. I know you do. Your left eyebrow goes up when you lie."

"Clementine, I barely saw the guy . . ."

"Hold on. You *saw* him!? I told you! I knew it!" Rushing forward, she grabs me by the front of my shirt, like she's about to attack. "What'd he say to you!? You need to tell me!"

"Are you *high*? Let go of me!"

"Tell me what he said, Beecher!"

"I said, *let go!*"

"*Then tell me what the hell is going on!*" she demands, tugging harder on my shirt and still clutching her wig. It's so close to my nose it smells like wet fur. "*Tell me what Marshall said about Nico!*"

I pull back, confused. *Nico? This has nothing to do with Nico.*

Before I say a word, her eyes flood with tears and her shoulders fall. "I told you everything about your dad, everything I knew," she says, steeling her jaw and refusing to let herself cry. "How can you not tell me what you know about mine?"

"I don't know anything, Clemmi. I swear to you."

"But you saw Marshall, didn't you? You spoke to him?"

"Yes, but when I spoke to him, it wasn't about *Nico*. It had nothing to do with Nico. Or the plankholders."

She looks left, then right, like she can't get her bearings. I've never seen her so rattled. In fact, I've never seen her rattled.

With her hands shaking, she touches her ear, brushing an imaginary curl of hair behind her bare earlobe. At this point, some things are pure instinct. "If this isn't about Nico, then why were you talking to Marshall?"

"Because we're trying to figure out if . . . it sounds crazy when I say it out loud."

"My father lives in a mental institution and tried to shoot a President. I'm used to *crazy*. Just say it, Beecher."

"I'm trying to figure out if Marshall killed someone while pretending to be John Wilkes Booth. There. That looney-tunes enough for you?"

Clementine takes two steps away from me, clutching her wig at her chest. "What'd you just say?"

"I know. And if we're right about what's going on, it's not just Booth. There's also Charles Guiteau, who—"

"I need to go," Clementine insists, finding the tag on the inside of her wig and sliding it back on her head.

"What? Where're you going?"

"I need to go, Beecher." She's patting her blonde locks back into place. Even with the hair, she looks paler than I've ever seen her.

"Clementine, please... What're you not telling me?"

"What you said—about Booth... and Guiteau... Is that true? *Marshall's* copying old killers?"

"I have no idea. Maybe it's Marshall. I pray it's not. But we know that pastors are dying, and whoever's doing it, they're copying old presidential assassins."

"No, Beecher. They're not."

"What're you talking about?"

She covers her eyes with her hand. "Oh, God, it's happening again!"

"What's happening again?"

"You need to listen to me, Beecher. Please," she begs, clearly terrified. "When I spoke to Dr. Yoo, he told me. There was someone else. Someone who did this, who copied John Wilkes Booth... and Guiteau... and all the rest. He did it years ago. And now, this killer you're looking for... He's not just copying the original assassins." She takes a breath, barely able to get the words out. "The killer is copying my father. He's copying Nico."

61

eorge Washington?" Tot asked. "You're telling me these are George Washington's personal playing cards?"

"Washington was a big card player—always playing whist," the Diamond explained. "When it came to these particular cards—with the so-called eagle on them—Washington was, without question, their biggest purchaser. Every few months, he'd order the same deck from the same printer and cardmaker."

"I didn't know that."

"I didn't either—until I had to fill an entire exhibit on the historical significance of playing cards. And what was most interesting—at least to me—was what else was going on as George Washington was buying all these playing cards. Don't forget, we may see the Revolution as this idealized American victory, but not everyone was thrilled with changing the power structure.

"George Washington may've picked a fight with the British, but suddenly there were all these other groups pointing guns at his head: locals who preferred the old way of doing things, Indians who were forced to pick a side, even wealthy families who just didn't want to lose what they had. It affected everyone who had a vested interest in the status quo—including small selfish groups who won't even reveal themselves until their power is threatened," the Diamond said, motioning back at the ace of spades with the eagle symbol.

"You're talking about the Knights?"

"I'm talking about the *church*—or at least a small subset that these sacred Knights were a part of. Even with all the colonials' Puritan values, territories dedicated to self-determination aren't always good for church business."

"So what's that have to do with playing cards?"

"According to the curator at Mount Vernon, Washington knew how many of these factions were working against him. And when it came to that faction within the church, he even knew how they communicated—hiding secret messages in the same way Washington hid his own...in books and in letters... But one of the great tricks of the church was also hiding things in..."

"Playing cards," Tot said, his knees suddenly aching far more than usual.

"In 1777, y'know how many decks of these cards George Washington ordered for himself?" the Diamond asked, his finger hovering above the ace of spades, but never touching it. "Six dozen. That's seventy-two packs! Just for himself!"

"You think he was looking for something?"

"Or that he *found* something—or at least found the way these so-called sacred Knights communicated. Look at how it played out: Right as Washington's big order for cards was placed in 1777, the church suddenly asserted itself, coming to Morristown and asking Washington to issue an order to all his troops. You know what it said?"

Tot nodded. Of course he knew what it said. "It forbade all his officers and soldiers to play cards and other games."

"They said it led to moral indecency—but that's a pretty particular request, don't you think: *no more playing cards?* It's like they didn't want Washington to see what they were doing. Washington had no choice. It was still the church. But have you seen George Washington's diaries at the time? He never stops playing cards. Never. Instead, he keeps writing about *these specific playing cards.* Over and over. Like there was something special about them."

"You think he knew that this faction of the church, that these Knights, were using the cards to send messages?"

"George Washington was not a stupid man. He knew who he was fighting. And he knew how they were communicating. Some say that's when he started to smoke them out. That he even put together his own little spy ring..."

"The Culper Ring."

"Exactly. Some say that's why the Culper Ring was born. To protect Washington and hunt the Knights."

"That's not true," Tot insisted, surprised by his own reaction. "That's not why the Culper Ring was founded."

"It doesn't matter why they were founded. All that matters is that the mission of the Knights never changed. They were watching. And when it came to protecting the church from any perceived 'king,' the Knights knew one thing: George Washington was wielding the power of the state in a brand-new way. And he wasn't going anywhere."

As the Diamond said the words, Tot couldn't help but think of the current President, and of Beecher and Marshall. But he was also thinking of his own mentor, Kermit, and all the stories that Tot only heard in whispers: the stories no one would talk about—of the horrors unleashed by the so-called Knights of the Golden Circle.

"Can I ask you a question, Daniel? Even assuming this whole thing isn't some old campfire tale, assuming that these original Knights, or some variation of them, somehow continued to exist all the way to George Washington's time—you think there's a chance, or more important, any proof, that they could've lasted even longer than that?"

"Define *longer*."

"You said the battle between church and state was the ultimate civil war, so let's say, to our Civil War. To Lincoln's time. Or maybe even to, I don't know . . . 1963."

The Diamond stared across the art table, studying his old friend. "Tot, I'm going to ask you this only one time: This killer you're chasing that you can't tell me about . . . ? Is he trying to kill the President of the United States?"

"Daniel . . ."

"You're mentioning Lincoln, and then the year JFK gets assassinated. How am I not supposed to ask?"

"You *are* supposed to ask. But if I thought that was about to happen, you'd have fifty Secret Service agents in here asking you this question instead of me. All I care about is: Could these Knights, whoever they are, whatever they stand for, could they possibly survive long enough to exist today?"

"Isn't that the point? That's why they picked the symbol."

"What symbol?"

"This one!" the Diamond said, pointing down to the ace of spades.

"Y'mean the eagle?"

"You keep calling it an eagle, but have you actually looked at it?" He taps a finger against the head of the bird. "The tuft of feathers on an eagle's head goes *down*, flat against the neck. The feathers here curve *up*. This isn't an eagle, Tot. It's a phoenix."

"A phoenix," Tot whispered, rolling his finger into his beard and still remembering Kermit's words: that the Knights were gone, completely defeated.

"That's what I'm trying to tell you, Tot. Whoever you're chasing here, it doesn't matter if they were around for Lincoln, or JFK, or anyone else. What matters is they *think they were*. So if these Knights are now trying to take a shot at the current President—and start a new civil war—now you know who you're facing. This isn't a *fight* to them. This is their destiny. In their eyes, like the phoenix and their church predecessors, they're holy warriors who can never be killed."

62

No. That's impossible," I say.

"It's not. It happened," she shoots back.

"But how can—? The killer we're chasing— How could he possibly be copying Nico?"

"Because that's what Nico *did*."

"I don't understand. All those years ago, when Nico shot at the President... It was during a NASCAR race. What does John Wilkes Booth have to do with NASCAR?"

"You're missing what I said, Beecher. When Nico took those shots at the President, that was the *end* of Nico's journey. What I'm talking about is his *beginning*."

Watching me digest the statement, and everything else she's said, Clementine stands by the front door, once again taking off her jacket.

"Was this in the file Palmiotti gave you?" I ask.

"You think they'd give me something like that? No. This was from the doctor."

"Dr. Yoo."

"He wasn't there when the plankholders first started—he came after the experiments began. In South Carolina. In Charleston—at the Naval Shipyard."

"My dad wasn't in the navy. He was army."

"So was mine. But from what Yoo said... this wasn't just about the navy. It was about *privacy*."

I nod, well aware that throughout history, when it was time to brief the President of the United States in true privacy, they'd put him on a ship since it was the one place they could guarantee he'd be alone.

"Nico was barely eighteen," she explains. "Yoo said that even back then, they knew Nico was having trouble adjusting to life as a soldier. That's why Dr. Yoo was brought in. He was an addiction specialist—one of the first to realize that methadone was a good way to help soldiers fight heroin addiction. But when it came to what they were giving Nico, no one had ever seen anything like it. One week, he'd be happy and easygoing; the next week, he'd stop sleeping...stop eating...and suddenly they'd find half a dozen dead possums all around the naval base."

"Possums?"

"No one could explain it. Until one morning at breakfast, when Nico took a spoonful of his morning cereal and calmly announced he was killing them. With his bare hands and a cinderblock. That's when Yoo was called in."

"So what do possums have to do with John Wilkes Booth?"

"Nothing," Clementine says, her eyes following me as I pace. "In fact, everyone thought Yoo had it all under control and that everything was back on schedule. But what they didn't know—and couldn't possibly know—was that a few months later, a hunter in the South Carolina woods was shot in the back of the head at around 10 p.m. while hunting coyote. Police assumed another hunter did it by accident. Then a month after that, a second man was shot in the back of the head—caught him right behind the earlobe—while he was out on a night jog."

"Also at around 10 p.m.?"

"No one thought twice about it, but yes, around 10 p.m. Again, because it was South Carolina, they assumed another hunting accident. But soon after that, there was a third man shot in the back of the head, point-blank, in a local movie theater. Exact time of death was 10:11 p.m."

"The exact time John Wilkes Booth shot Abraham Lincoln."

"Don't you see?" she asks, starting to pick up the books that fell when she crashed into the bookcase. She knows I need the order. "Nico was practicing, Beecher. Working out the details so he could work his way toward the perfect kill."

"And nobody put it together?" I ask, slotting an old red leather book into place. "Were all the deaths out by the shipyard?"

"No. That was the problem," she says, gathering the last few books and a small picture frame. "They were all spread out. The first was over seventy-five miles away in Hampton County. The second was in the opposite direction. And the last one was right outside of Charleston. It got even harder when the fourth body turned up—this time in Georgia. A thirty-three-year-old dental equipment salesman was getting off his Amtrak train, and as the train pulls out of the station, he gets shot in the back..."

"Like Guiteau shooting President Garfield..."

"...and a month after that, up in one of the mountain areas of North Carolina, as the local county fair is shutting down, a drunk soybean farmer has to pee, so he darts behind one of the loading trucks...and gets shot in the belly..."

"Like Czolgosz shooting President McKinley at the World's Fair..." I say, slotting another book into the bookcase.

"The whole thing didn't come to a head until months later, when, back in Hampton County, some poor retired priest—"

"A priest? That's what—"

"I know. Just listen. While the priest was working his garden, he got shot in the back of the head with something called a CE 573—a 6.5-millimeter caliber metal-jacketed bullet. Based on the way the priest's head exploded, they think a sniper picked him off from something like two hundred and fifty feet away."

"Or two hundred and sixty-five feet to be exact."

She nods, cradling half a dozen books and waiting for me to finish. "No one else came close to connecting the killings—until the local sheriff started thinking that a shot like that, from two hundred and fifty feet, could only be made by someone who's military. From there, he started making phone calls to all the local area military bases, where the young administrative assistant who picked up the phone happened to notice that the time of death was exactly 12:30 on the nose. For most people, that wouldn't mean much. It's a standard time. But for this assistant, who was a certifiable JFK conspiracy enthusiast, it was a clarion call. He not only knew that 12:30 was the exact time that President Kennedy was shot, but that a 6.5-millimeter caliber bullet was the exact one that traveled two hundred and sixty-five feet and was used by..."

"Lee Harvey Oswald," I say, slotting a book onto the top shelf. It hits with a *thunk*.

"On a hunch, the investigative folks checked Nico's locker. And his belongings. All were clean. Until they ran a metal detector over his mattress and found, burrowed deep inside it, a Mannlicher-Carcano bolt-action military rifle."

Now I'm the one nodding, recognizing the rifle that Oswald used on JFK. My brain swirls, thinking about the current killer going after rectors and pastors. But that still doesn't explain...

"Why'd they let Nico go?" I ask. "If they knew he did it, how come they didn't tell anyone? Or arrest him?"

"Back when it was open, do you have any idea what the navy used to use the Charleston Shipyard for?"

"I assume to dock our ships?"

"Yes, of course that's where we docked our ships. And when our ships and submarines were there, they'd also clean them, upgrade them, whatever they needed for upkeep. But according to Dr. Yoo, there was also something called the Weapons Station."

"We have some of their files in the Archives. They upgrade the ship's weaponry."

"Again, yes," Clementine says, still cradling the half dozen books that she picked up from the floor. "But even within the Weapons Station, there's a hierarchy. Some places did *regular* weapons. Others did nuclear weapons. And then there was Subgroup 6."

"Subgroup 6? That sounds like a fake name."

"It's real. Look it up. At one point, it was run by Admiral Thomas Coady, whose goal was to take Subgroup 6 and use it to produce the one weapon more dangerous than even a nuclear weapon."

"Which is?"

"The ultimate weapon, Beecher: the human weapon."

At the bookcase, Clementine dumps the stack of books on a chest-high shelf.

"You think that's what our dads were working on?" I ask.

"No, not at all. My dad, your dad, and Marshall's dad were eighteen- and nineteen-year-old grunts. Subgroup 6 didn't hire children. Think about it: When you're putting together your top-secret team, you choose people you know. Veterans with experience. For Admiral Coady to bring our dads there, c'mon, Beecher. You know what they call an eighteen-year-old who's drafted into something that top-secret? They were the *experiments*. The guinea pigs."

Her words pop the imaginary membrane I didn't even realize I kept around myself whenever she's around. I've kept it there as a shield. But as the membrane ruptures and reality seeps through it, there's nothing more emotional than hearing her talk about my own dead father. And the unspeakable things that might've been done to him. No one wants to hear that their dad was in pain.

"I know it's a nightmare, Beecher. It's a nightmare for me too. But now you know why they couldn't let him be arrested. Whatever they put inside Nico—whatever they'd invested in him—if their top lab rat showed up on the front page of the newspaper with a story about how he was a homicidal maniac copying Lee Harvey Oswald, every eyeball in the country would've been staring at Subgroup 6. And that was a risk no one in the program was willing to take."

I look down at the note—the suicide note—that I'm still gripping in my hand. "You think that's why my dad died? Because of some cliché military cover-up?"

"No...I don't think so. From what Dr. Yoo said, your dad died a year later. When Nico flipped, the Subgroup was split up. Nico got punished internally, locked away for nearly a year until they were convinced that whatever they put inside him was out of his system. Everything else was wiped."

"And when Nico shot the President, none of this came out?"

"This is the government we're talking about. You really think they'll admit they created the monster that attacked their own President? Back when they thought Nico was cured, they sent him into the regular army as if he was a brand-new recruit showing up on day one. Your dad and Marshall's dad were sent elsewhere."

"And that's the big finale? They buried the records, hoping no one would ever find them?"

"But don't you see, Beecher? When it came to Nico's records, someone *did* find them! You know this better than anyone. No matter how hard you hide them, or where you bury them, the files are always found. So for someone to be re-creating the crimes of John Wilkes Booth...and killing pastors on top of it...someone clearly knows what Nico did!"

"Or maybe they're just copying the original assassins. Don't forget, when Timothy McVeigh blew up the Federal Building in Oklahoma City, he was wearing a T-shirt that said *Sic Semper Tyrannis*. These assassins have never been forgotten."

"But to kill pastors..."

"Nico only killed *one* pastor."

"No. He only killed one that *we know about*. Look at the similarities, Beecher. You think someone just happened to have the same crazy idea, using the same ancient weapons, targeting the same innocent pastors? This isn't Timothy McVeigh. Whoever's doing it read Nico's files!"

"Maybe," I say, my voice slowing down. "Or maybe they just heard the story from their father."

She looks at me. "Wait. You don't think I—?"

"I didn't say *you*."

"So you think Marshall—?"

"I'm not saying it's Marshall either. And when it comes to who he could've heard it from, from what he told me, Marshall's dad is dead."

"So? His dad could've told him the details before he died," she says, grabbing one of the books—a narrow book about the cartography of battlefields—and slotting it onto the bookshelf.

I snatch it back out. "*It's in the wrong spot,*" I say with a verbal shove.

I wait for her to shove back. She always shoves back. But instead she just stands there, chastised, like she's physically shrinking in front of me. She shifts her weight, and I get the feeling that *this*—right here—is the first real and honest reaction she's shown me. She knows the pain she's caused. But as I study this petite, broken girl who, back in eighth grade, pulled me close and gave me my first real kiss...I can't help it. Even now, even bald, I forgot how stunning she is.

"So what happens now? How do you figure out if Marshall's the killer?" she finally asks.

"You go to the source. The only one who's left." From the way her face falls, she knows who I'm talking about.

There's no avoiding it. We know a third murder is coming. If we want to stop it...

"We need to go see Nico."

63

And if you had to rate the pain on a scale of one to ten?" the doctor with the bald head and thin beard asked.

"Probably a five," Pastor Frick said, walking down the hallway toward his room, on the fourth floor of George Washington University Hospital.

The doctor watched the pastor carefully, motioning for him to walk the hall one last time so he could see how Frick was breathing. "And no shortness of breath?" the doctor asked.

"No. No more problems than I usually had," the pastor joked, though the doctor, like most doctors, didn't laugh. It was late. These were clearly the last of the doctor's rounds.

"What about pain anywhere else?" the doctor asked.

"I told the nurses, I'm sore, but otherwise just fine. The thing I feel worst about is taking this bed. If you need it for someone else—"

"We can spare the bed," the doctor reassured him, motioning Frick back into his room. As Pastor Frick took a seat on the bed, the doctor pulled his stethoscope from his pocket. "I just need to listen to your lungs and we can—"

There was a loud ringing: the hospital phone on the side table.

From the look on the doctor's face, plus the late time, he didn't want Pastor Frick to pick up the phone, but the pastor had been away from the church all day. If someone needed him, or needed help...

"Sorry, it'll just take a minute," the pastor promised. "*Hello...?*" he asked, cradling the phone.

"Pastor Frick, I'm sorry to bother you at this hour, but my name

227

is Tot Westman. I'm working on the investigation of today's shooting and was just wondering . . . is now a good time to chat?"

The pastor wanted to help, was determined to help. But he took one look at the doctor, who held up his stethoscope, not even bothering to hide his impatience.

"Actually, is there a way we can do this a little later, or maybe tomorrow?" Frick said into the phone.

"Tomorrow sounds perfect," Tot replied. "If you want, I can come by first thing in the morning."

"That'd be great." Hanging up the phone and turning back to the doctor, he added, "My apologies. Just trying to help them catch who did this."

"No worries at all," the doctor replied as he pressed his stethoscope against Pastor Frick's chest. "We all have our jobs to do."

64

It's nearly midnight as I head downstairs clutching an old comforter, fresh sheets, and a waffle-thin pillow against my chest.

"Beecher, I really appreciate that you're—"

"Please stop thanking me. And stop pretending we're friends. You have information about my father. And information about these murders—information which I hope will save innocent lives." I dump the sheets and comforter on my black art deco sofa.

"I can stay in a hotel if you want," Clementine says. "I'll be fine there."

She's wrong. It may not be the smartest move to keep her here. In fact, considering she's still wanted for questioning by the Secret Service, it's a pretty dumb move. But to put her in some random hotel room, *by herself*, where there's nothing stopping the killer—or even the President—from taking their own crack at her? I've seen enough movies to know what happens when you let your key witness out of your sight. This isn't the time for taking chances. Especially when we're this close to finally figuring out what's really going on.

As Clementine spreads out the sheet and tucks the pillow near the sofa's armrest, her wig is back on and all once again seems calm. But she tentatively glances back at me.

"Can I just ask you one last thing?" she pleads.

"Only if it's not about psychotic killers or dead parents."

"It's not. It's about— When we were little, did you ever listen to my mom's CD?"

I don't answer. Clementine's mom was a hippie lounge singer whose *only* recording was the "Greatest Hits" CD she made herself. Most people in town never bought a copy, much less listened to it.

But in tenth grade, all I wanted was Clementine. I listened to that album more than even the *Grease* soundtrack. "I heard it once or twice. Why?"

"Y'remember the third song on there?" she asks. "'The Worst Thing You'll Ever Do...'"

"'...Will Be to Someone You Love,'" I say, completing the title.

"You actually remember it!" Her face flushes with excitement. "Beecher, what I did to you, I can't take it back. But when I think about hurting you, all I can say is... My mom sang it right," she adds, reaching out for my forearm. She's so close, I notice her nose piercing, a sparkling silver stud no bigger than the head of a pin. As she puts her hand on mine, her body temperature feels about ten degrees warmer than my own.

Two months ago, that would've worked on me. In fact, if I'm being honest, it's still (slightly) working on me. But not entirely.

"Good night, Clementine," I say coolly as I head for the stairs.

PART III

The Third Assassination

"It is useless, gentlemen, I think we ought to have prayer."

—President William McKinley, his eyes half closed,
six days after he was shot by assassin Leon Czolgosz

He was the third President murdered in office.

65

St. Elizabeths Hospital
Washington, D.C.

Nico knew they were talking about him.

Even from his room, even with the door closed, as he knelt down and meticulously made his bed, tucking the sheets into crisp forty-five-degree military corners, he heard the morning shift of nurses—up the hallway, at the nurses' station— saying his name and bitching about what happened yesterday.

"*They're worried about you,*" the dead First Lady told him, standing behind Nico as he folded another corner of the bedsheet into place.

"They're not worried. They're annoyed."

"*You're wrong. They're worried. You didn't eat your breakfast this morning.*"

"The eggs are runny here."

"*They don't care about the eggs. After your tantrum in the labyrinth yesterday, they're concerned you may be taking a step backwards.*"

Nico glanced over his shoulder, eyeing the First Lady. In his old room, she had always sat in the small alcove, just inside the window. Here, in his new room, she was always standing. She wasn't comfortable yet.

Nico wasn't comfortable either. Especially with what was coming. These next few hours—

He stopped himself from thinking about it, knowing the dangers of overexcitement. The Knight was close now. But there was

235

still so much to be done...so much that could go wrong. Indeed, he'd warned the Knight about rushing. Especially with going back to that unfinished business at the hospital. But the Knight was proud. The Knight was determined. And the Knight saw it all as his personal destiny.

How could Nico possibly argue with—?

"Nico, you dressed?" a voice called out as a loud knock rapped against his door. A warning knock. "Nico...you hear me?" the nurse with the pointy breasts added.

Before he could answer, the door opened. The nurse stepped inside, doing her usual scan of the room. She smiled at the sight of Nico making his bed.

"*See that?*" the First Lady called out. "*Now she thinks you're accepting the new building as your home.*"

Nico fought hard to ignore the First Lady, staying locked on the nurse. "I didn't eat my eggs because they were runny," he blurted.

The nurse just looked at him. "You've got a visitor downstairs."

Still on his knees, Nico stopped making his bed. He didn't get many visitors.

"Is it someone I know?"

"I think so. He's on your list. Someone named Beecher White?"

Nico shot to his feet. At first he just stood there.

"Nico, you okay?"

He blinked three times, then three more times, searching the room for... *There.* He grabbed his leather book—with the playing card bookmark, the ace of clubs—from the nightstand and tucked it under his arm. "I'd like to see Beecher now," he told the nurse as he followed her out into the hallway.

66

Eighteen years ago
Sagamore, Wisconsin

Marshall's mother liked working at the church.

The job, especially when she got to read the early drafts of the pastor's sermons, was interesting. And the pay, thanks to the generosity of a few anonymous donors, was slightly better than the supermarket. Most important, unlike her house, it was exceptionally quiet.

Though some days were less quiet than others.

"Heads up! Coming in! Everyone get their clothes on!" a female voice sang through the closed door that led to the back office.

As the door swung wide, a middle-aged woman with short dyed-black hair, bright coral lipstick, and a matching, far-too-short coral sundress strolled playfully toward Marshall's mom's desk. As she walked, a dozen cheap metal bangles banged like tambourines at her wrist. Penny Kaye. Clementine's mother.

"Oh, c'mon, Cherise. That was funny," Penny teased, smiling wide. Marshall's mom didn't smile back.

"What do you want, Penny?"

"Just dropping these off. Can you give them to Pastor Riis?" Penny asked, handing her a stack of photocopied flyers. "I have a gig next Saturday. In Madison. Ten-dollar cover, but you get two beers. Figured the pastor could give them out to the congregation."

"I'll put them right on his desk," Marshall's mom said dryly, dropping them next to her in-box. But not inside it.

237

Penny shifted her weight and started biting her coral nails. "You're gonna put those straight in the trash the moment I leave here, aren't you, Cherise?"

"And why would I do that?" Marshall's mom asked, now the one smiling. On her left, Penny noticed, in one of the open offices, the pastor's wife was eavesdropping. And smiling too.

"Cherise, what the hell...?"

"Don't bring that language in here."

"...happened to you? We used to be friends."

"That was a long time ago. People change."

"People *don't* change...people *never* change! So you can act as prissy and super-religious as you want, but I know who you are. I remember you sneaking into your mom's purse...and stealing money from her so you could buy silver wire and make all that jewelry you used to sell at my gigs. Wasn't that your dream back then? I'd sing songs; you'd make jewelry? For chrissakes, when you were pregnant, we used to smoke pot at—"

"*Enough!*" Marshall's mom exploded, jumping out of her seat and racing around the desk. "You don't know anything about me!"

"There we go. There's the spitfire I used to know."

"I'm serious, Penny. For you, it's simple to be the hippie chick who never grew up. Even your daughter doesn't care if you're out all night. But have you seen my life!? Do you know what it costs to put hand controls in a car so someone in a wheelchair can drive it? Or how much it is for massage therapists to come in three times a week so that whatever muscles are left in Tim's legs don't cramp?"

"That doesn't mean you have to bury every dream you ever had! Your jewelry—"

"Stop talking about my jewelry! It's been ten years since my—!"

Gripping Marshall's mom by the shoulders, Penny pulled her close and planted a kiss—firmly—on her mouth. For a moment, the two women stood there, their lips pressed together as Penny slid her tongue...

With a shove, Cherise freed herself, pulling away. Penny began to laugh, but it didn't last long. Cherise unleashed with an open-handed slap that slammed Penny across the face.

The room went silent.

On their left, the pastor's wife disappeared, shrinking back into her office.

"*What's wrong with you!? How dare you!?*" Cherise exploded, wiping lipstick from her mouth.

"C'mon, Cherise, I was just having fun . . . like the old—"

"*You're an abomination! Y'know that? An abomination!*" Cherise screamed, shouting the words so loud the whole room shook.

Stepping backward at the outburst, Penny searched Cherise's face, still looking for her old friend.

"I want you out of here," Marshall's mom insisted.

"Yeah, I got that part. But can I just say . . . ? I'm sorry your life got jackknifed. I truly am. But Cherise, you can't take everything you are and just shut it inside yourself. The more you bury it, the more the pressure starts to build, and the more that sucker's gonna blow."

"I appreciate that. Especially since in this town, you're the expert on what blows."

"Heh. A cheap blowjob joke. Good for you on that one," Penny said with a laugh as she walked to the door. "But I'm not just talking about *your* life, Cherise. You're not the only one under pressure. You teach your husband to live like that, and your son to live like that, that's when it tightens. And then one day, when you least expect it, it's your boy Marshall who's gonna go boom."

"I appreciate your insight, Penny. But you don't know what the hell you're talking about."

67

Today

The man carried a clipboard as he walked up the street. The tail of his red scarf waved behind him.

There was nothing on the clipboard, just a few blank sheets. But in any suburban neighborhood, a clipboard meant neighbors wouldn't look twice at a passing stranger, and even if they did, the bright red scarf hid his face.

Eyeing Beecher's townhouse from across the street, he knew Beecher and Clementine were gone. He knew where they were going and the new car they were driving. And last night, as he watched them through the side window until nearly three in the morning, he even knew about Clementine's clumsy attempt to get Beecher into bed, an attempt that most men would've fallen for.

Whoever was training Beecher, he was clearly learning something.

But that didn't mean he'd learned everything.

Faking a quick look at the clipboard, the man stepped over a drift of blackened snow, crossed the street toward Beecher's townhouse, and walked right past the front door. He didn't care what was *inside* the house. Right now, he was here for what was *outside*.

Ducking into the narrow driveway, the man followed the tire tracks in the snow until he saw—

There.

Flat on the ground, its glass face shattered, was the cheap wristwatch he'd left there last night.

It was an old detective trick Jack Nicholson used in *China-*

240

town: Buy an inexpensive, non-digital wristwatch—only $14.99 at Target—tuck it under the tire of the car you're tracking, and when the car rolls over it...*crack*...the hands stop, telling you exactly what time they left.

"Eight-oh-four a.m.," Marshall whispered to himself, staring down at the cracked watchface as he placed it on his clipboard. Beecher should just be arriving at St. Elizabeths.

Readjusting his red scarf, Marshall grinned to himself. He wished he could be there. But right now, now that he knew where Beecher was, there was so much more that needed to be done.

68

Twenty minutes later
St. Elizabeths Hospital
Washington, D.C.

eecher, if anything happens...anything at all," Tot says through my phone, "you call Mac to put the word out."

"I understand. And I appreciate you worrying, Tot," I say as I head through the lobby for the small bank of metal lockers in the corner.

Tot goes to say something else, but instead just offers silence. He knows there's no choice. If we want to know if Marshall's our killer—or worse, whether he's reaching out to Nico—this is the only way to find out.

"Phone and all sharp objects..." the guard says into his intercom, his voice echoing out from behind the thick ballistics glass. Above him, hanging on the bombproof black granite wall, bright silver letters spell out *Saint Elizabeths.*

"Listen, Tot, I gotta go. But when it comes to being safe, I know where you are. You do the same."

"Just do me one favor, Beecher: Keep an eye out for Marshall. You never know where he'll show up."

Refusing to argue, I hang up and follow the guard's instructions.

Last time I was at St. Elizabeths, at the sign-in desk they had a pen with some scotch tape at the back of it that chained it to the counter.

Today, they have me leave my phone and any sharp objects in this bank of shoebox-size lead lockers. Then I'm guided through an X-ray and metal detector, and scanned by whatever chemical sniffer that they think I can't see is hidden and built into the doorframe. By the time I step through the glass doors and into the shiny, well-lit room that serves as the visiting area, it's clear that when it came to this new building, most of their money has been spent on security.

I don't blame them.

John Hinckley, who shot President Reagan, lives here. So does a man who killed his wife and three children, then put them back in their beds, living with their rotting bodies for weeks. But when it comes to their most famous patient . . .

"He's on his way," a uniformed guard tells me as he closes the glass door behind me, locking me alone in the wide meeting area that has all the charm of a workplace cafeteria. There're no pictures on the beige walls. No decorations. It's all brand-new, including the dozen or so empty round tables—all of them built of clear, unbreakable Plexiglas, so that nothing can be snuck underneath.

Last time I saw him, Nico would only call me by my middle name, Benjamin. He told me he was the reincarnation of George Washington, that I was Benedict Arnold, and that God Himself had brought us on this mission together.

I know. It's nonsense. But I can't help but think of what Tot told me this morning about the Knights, the playing cards, and the attacks on the pastors. No question, the killer we're looking for—whether he's part of the Knights of the Golden Circle or not—he's treating this as his holy mission. And right now I'm seconds away from being face-to-face with the chessmaster of holy missions.

On the far side of the room, there's a *krrk* and a *tunk* as a magnetic lock unclenches.

My stomach twists as the heavy door opens.

There's no guard with him. Just a nurse, who sticks her head in and gives a quick glance, making sure all is calm.

"Nico, if you need anything . . ." she begins.

"I won't," he insists, his too-close-together eyes seizing me. He makes a beeline through the minefield of Plexiglas tables. His lips are flat, but there's no mistaking the smile underneath.

"Happy Presidents' Day, Benjamin. I'm so glad you came to celebrate."

69

This was the day—at the Pan-American Expo—that should've been the greatest day of President McKinley's life.

First, the President loved World's Fairs.

Second, McKinley was at the height of his power. Months earlier, he'd started his second term. And just a day earlier, he'd used the Expo to give the speech of his life, calling for "concord, not conflict" and proclaiming, "God and man have linked the nations together"—evoking what many described as the hope and scope of George Washington's Farewell Address.

So after a breathtaking morning visiting the natural miracle of Niagara Falls, the President *was* having a perfect day...until his secretary—a wise man and Culper Ring member named George B. Cortelyou—said that he had a bad feeling about the afternoon's big public event at the Music Pavilion. When Cortelyou suggested that the President skip the reception and enjoy some quiet time, McKinley would have none of it.

"Why should I?" the President asked. "No one would wish to hurt me."

Of course, the President didn't know about Leon Czolgosz, the pale-skinned, blue-eyed twenty-eight-year-old who was now waiting for him inside the wide Temple of Music Pavilion.

Like Guiteau, Czolgosz was short and slightly built.

Like John Wilkes Booth, he wore a mustache.

And like both of them, he was prepared, arriving so early for the event that he had a prime spot right by the stage.

Czolgosz knew this was God's will. Especially when he saw the venue. The Temple of Music. How perfect. A temple.

From there, his plan was simple. He'd stand in line like the hundreds of others who were waiting to shake the President's hand. And when it was Czolgosz's turn, well... His right hand was covered by a handkerchief so it looked bandaged. But underneath the handkerchief, Czolgosz held the .32 caliber Iver Johnson revolver that would end the President's life.

All he had to do was wait.

As McKinley entered the room, the grand organ played the national anthem, and the crowd let out a huge cheer.

The Secret Service weren't nearly as thrilled. One year earlier, an assassination plot to kill the top rulers in the world had been discovered. The first two on the list were already dead. President McKinley was number five.

"Watch every man approaching the President," one of them warned.

They did. But as the long line of strangers and admirers snaked toward the President—as McKinley shook every hand and literally kissed every baby—none of them noticed the man with the slight mustache who was waiting in line so patiently. Dressed in shirt and tie, he looked like everyone else—except for the handkerchief that was covering his hand.

Watching from the crowd, Leon Czolgosz took another step forward. He was almost at the front.

Across the room, the massive organ began playing Schumann's *Traumerei*.

Looking at his pocket watch, the President's secretary asked that the doors be closed—the line needed to be cut off.

Czolgosz never panicked. He took another calm step forward, so close that he could see the carnation that President McKinley always wore in his lapel.

As for the Secret Service, they were focused on the man directly behind Czolgosz—a large black waiter named James Parker. He was the suspicious one. The Negro.

With only one person in front of him, Czolgosz took a breath, knowing this was it.

The President smiled at Czolgosz, reaching for a handshake.

Czolgosz never smiled back. Facing the President, he extended his hand, pressed the handkerchief-covered gun against McKinley's chest, and fired two quick shots.

McKinley stumbled backward, crashing into a potted plant as blood poured out through his shirt.

The handkerchief that held the gun burst into fire from the gunshots.

Fairgoers screamed. People in the room scattered.

Czolgosz tried to fire again, but James Parker, the large black man behind him, smashed the assassin with one hand and grabbed the gun with the other. Within seconds, the Secret Service and other fairgoers tackled him to the ground.

"*I done my duty!*" Czolgosz shouted.

It was the same thing he'd later say to the police. "I done my duty." But when the police asked him to write it as a confession, Czolgosz's hands were shaking too much. So they brought in a stenographer, who typed what Czolgosz repeated over and over: *I done my duty. I done my duty. I done my duty!*

He had.

Behind him, the President collapsed to the floor, blood now soaking his shirt. The first bullet had hit McKinley in the chest, right between his second and third ribs—but it never penetrated the skin, deflecting off a button.

The second bullet did the real damage, hitting the President in the stomach, entering down the front of his abdomen, and burrowing toward his back.

As the pavilion was cleared, the Secret Service agents were still beating on Czolgosz.

"Be easy with him, boys," McKinley called out, trying to protect his attacker even as he fought to stay conscious.

As Czolgosz was taken into custody, he initially told a policeman that his name was Fred Nieman, an alias that came from the word *Niemand*, which in German meant *Nobody*. He was Nobody.

As for the President, a group of hastily assembled doctors, headed by a gynecological surgeon, rushed him into surgery to find the second bullet. Thomas Edison sent an early version of an X-ray machine, though it wasn't used. As heads of state flooded into Buffalo, including Robert Todd Lincoln, who now had the distinction of being near all three assassinations, the nation held its collective breath.

The doctors never found the bullet. The technology at the time couldn't see the extent of the damage. Eight days later, President McKinley was dying from infection.

After singing his favorite hymn ("Nearer, My God, to Thee") and saying his favorite prayers, McKinley's final words were simple: "Oh, dear."

Yet for the Knight of Clubs, the battle had just begun.

Unlike his predecessor, who had murdered President Garfield, Leon Czolgosz wasn't a raving nut. He was calm. Unafraid. In his jail cell, he combed his hair methodically, and asked for a handkerchief, which he would fold and refold over and over on his gun hand.

From the moment he was arrested, Czolgosz insisted on only one thing: He was working alone.

Few believed it.

Government officials pointed to his ties to various anarchist groups.

But those same groups, five days *before* the shooting, had issued a warning in their anarchist publications that Leon Czolgosz was actually a spy working for the government.

Accusations flew in every direction. But Leon Czolgosz remained as calm as he was when he stood in line to kill the President, never losing sight of the bigger mission.

"I don't regret my act," Czolgosz explained, "because I was doing what I could for the Great Cause."

With McKinley cut down, the nation demanded vengeance. Czolgosz was rushed through a two-day trial and immediately sentenced to death. Indeed, the electricity from Niagara Falls, which literally lit the Pan-American Expo where the crime took place, also supplied the current that ran Czolgosz's electric chair.

When he died, a death mask was made of Czolgosz's face. After the autopsy, which found no evidence of delusion or craziness in his brain, his body was placed in a black casket and covered with sulfuric acid. The warden didn't want Czolgosz to become a martyr.

His body disintegrated in twelve hours. His clothes and all his letters were burned.

Except one.

A man named John Grinder came forward with a letter that Czolgosz had written him a few weeks before the shooting. Both Czolgosz and Grinder were members of the Golden Eagle Lodge, which most history books fail to mention was also known as . . .

The Knights of the Golden Eagle.

And so, the question remains: What did Czolgosz write in this final letter, in red ink?

"Brother Grinder, will you send my book to me?"

To this day, no one knows what book Czolgosz was referring to.

But Czolgosz knew.

It was a novel called *Looking Backward*, and it would never be forgotten. Especially by the current Knight and a man named Nico Hadrian.

70

Today
Washington, D.C.

Today was a perfect day to kill a President.

The Knight knew it as he pushed open the door marked *Employees Only*. Entering the dark storage closet and purposely not putting on the light, he smelled the tubs of cleaning supplies and cans of fresh paint that were stacked throughout.

After so much planning, today was finally the day. And such an appropriate day. Presidents' Day.

To be honest, the Knight was hoping he could've moved things a bit faster. But after yesterday, to have A.J. show up so quickly at the hospital...to have him asking all those questions of the previous lamb, plus just keeping track of Beecher...

Adjustments needed to be made.

In many ways, it was no different for his third predecessor. Three days before he killed President McKinley, Leon Czolgosz purchased a .32 caliber revolver and was there as McKinley exited from his arriving train at the Pan-American Expo. Two days earlier, gun in hand, Czolgosz stood right near the President during a speech, but got jostled by the crowd. And one day earlier, Czolgosz couldn't get close enough for a clear shot. Over and over, roadblocks were put in Czolgosz's way. But the Knight of Clubs never lost faith. Indeed, by shifting his plans, Czolgosz found the Temple of Music.

Czolgosz took it as a sign.

And on that day, God's will was done.

Just as it would be today.

Flicking on the light switch in the storage closet, the Knight noticed that so many of the janitorial supplies were labeled *Poison*. Yet the far deadlier object rested in the corner. Pushing aside an empty mop bucket, he revealed a medical rolling cart—marked *Bookmobile*—that was stocked with magazines and used paperbacks.

Kneeling down, he slid open a small compartment and pulled out a brown paper bag labeled *For Pediatric Unit—Do Not Touch*.

Inside the bag was the white plaster Abraham Lincoln mask that he had put there last night.

The Knight checked his watch. Nearly 9 a.m. The same time Czolgosz first entered the Temple of Music. Tucking the Lincoln mask under his jacket and feeling the weight of the .32 caliber Iver Johnson revolver and the specially designed sound suppressor in his coat pocket, the Knight was well aware that Czolgosz had not used a suppressor. But again, like the timing of it all, adjustments had to be made. Tugging open the closet door, he stepped out into the polished hallway that was lined with hospital gurneys.

Keeping his head down to avoid the morning arrival of doctors and nurses, the Knight didn't even register the automated grand piano on his far left that played a slowed-down Musak version of Prince's "Little Red Corvette." Heading right, he stayed focused on his destination at the end of the long corridor: the door with blue-and-gold stained glass in it. The Interfaith Chapel, which was the best place to find Chaplain Elizabeth Stoughton.

The Knight had spotted her yesterday. A chaplain. Like a pastor. And one who had prayed directly with President Wallace.

Like his predecessor, the Knight knew a sign when he saw it. Pastor Frick had served his purpose. There was a new lamb now. A fresh lamb.

With fresh blood.

Taking one last glance at his watch, the Knight wasn't moving quickly. Like Czolgosz, he was calm and focused. But it was for that exact reason that, as he passed the grand staircase that overlooked the main atrium downstairs, he never glanced over the railing or saw who had just stepped inside, one flight below.

"Beecher, if anything happens…anything at all," Tot whispered into his phone as he stepped through the hospital's sliding doors and approached the visitor check-in desk, "you call Mac to put the word out."

"I understand. And I appreciate you worrying, Tot," Beecher replied.

Tot went to say something else, but as the greeter at the check-in desk waved him forward, Tot raised a fake grin and handed over his driver's license.

There was still so much Beecher didn't know—about the Culper Ring, about what was really going on with the President, and even about Tot himself. But Tot had been at this long enough to know that you don't get to treat the minor wounds until you deal with the big ones.

"I'm here to see Pastor Frick. He's on the fourth floor," Tot told the greeter.

The computer clicked as the ID camera took Tot's picture.

"Listen, Tot, I gotta go," Beecher said through the phone. "But when it comes to being safe, I know where you are. You do the same."

Tot nodded, scanning the grand staircase. One flight above, there was no one in sight. An automated grand piano played a Musak version of Prince's "Little Red Corvette."

"Just do me one favor, Beecher: Keep an eye out for Marshall. You never know where he'll show up."

Heading for Pastor Frick's room, Tot had no idea how right he was.

*   *   *

71

I like the new building," I say, glancing around the sterile visitors' room.

"You're trying to look relaxed, Benjamin. It's not working," Nico says, sitting directly across from me at the round see-through table. His hands are clasped—prayer-style—on the Plexiglas. In his lap, he's got an old book with a leather cover. I try to read the spine, but the print is too small.

"We can speak back there if you like," Nico adds, motioning toward the few private rooms in the corner. The signs on them read *Lawyer's Room.* They're for patients to talk privately with their attorneys. But right now, as I look over my shoulder and spy the guard at the X-ray who's staring at us through the bulletproof glass, plus the wide window behind him that looks out onto the sunlit front of the building, I'm happy for the lack of privacy.

"You're afraid of being alone with me," Nico says.

"Not at all," I say, keeping my voice upbeat. "Why would I come here if I didn't want to see you?"

Staring uncomfortably at me, Nico doesn't answer.

"So they still letting you feed the cats?" I add, remembering how much easier he is when he's saying *yes.*

"No. No more cats," he says with a twinkle in his eye. He's gloating. Like he's already won. "Why don't you tell me what you're really here for, Benjamin?"

I'm supposed to ask him about the killings . . . and the Knights of the Golden Circle, but instead . . .

"Did you know my father, Nico? Back in Wisconsin . . . did you know Albert White?"

253

I wait for him to react. But like Marshall when I asked if he knew Clementine, Nico doesn't move. His hands stay clasped prayer-style.

"I don't know who you're talking about, Benjamin."

"You never knew Albert White? You weren't stationed together as plankholders?"

He smiles at that—the same creepy, crooked smile that was on his face when the Secret Service dragged him to the ground after he took his famous shots at the President. "Sorry, Benjamin. I've never heard of Albert White. Or any plankholders."

"What about a man named Marshall Lusk? Do you know anything about him?"

From my back pocket, I pull out a color copy of Marshall's mugshot and place it on the table between us. Nico hovers over it, staring down at Marshall's burned face and never touching the copy.

"His burns are terrible," Nico says.

"Do you know him?"

"His lips are gone. Do you know if his tongue was burned as well?" Before I can answer, he adds, "When burn victims go in for tongue surgery, the night before, they usually record final messages so their loved ones can hear their voice—just in case the surgery goes bad and they never speak again. Have you ever thought what your final message would be?"

I stare down at the photocopy, thinking about the last message my father left me. His suicide note.

"Do you want to tell me what the man with the burns was arrested for?" Nico asks.

"Actually, that's what I was hoping you could help with. Over the past few days, some pastors have been shot in local churches."

"Pastors were shot?" he asks, his crooked smile growing wider. "Why would you think I know anything about that?"

I snatch the photocopy off the table and lean back in my chair, stretching both arms.

"Before, you were frustrated. Now you're angry, aren't you, Benjamin?"

"No. Not really." I stretch my arms up again, like I'm caught mid-yawn. But this time, I'm the one locking eyes with him. "This isn't for you, Nico. It's for *her*."

I extend my stretch all the way to my fingertips.

Nico tilts slightly, staring over my shoulder—through the bullet-proof glass by the X-ray, and outside the glass window that overlooks the front of the building, where a woman with short blonde hair reads my signal and finally steps out from behind one of the building's main pillars.

Nico thinks we're playing the same game we played last time. He's never been more wrong.

From the moment I arrived, I knew Nico wouldn't help. But as Marshall pointed out, when it comes to breaking in somewhere, the key is finding a weakness. In Nico's case, it's always been . . .

"Clementine," he whispers, watching the blonde woman turn down the pedestrian path that leads around the side of the building.

"I assume you'd like to speak to your daughter?" I ask.

Nico stands from his chair and holds tight to his book. To his credit, he's absolutely calm as he marches toward the bulletproof glass. People forget—this isn't a prison, it's a hospital. And Nico still has grounds privileges. "We'd like to take a walk outside," he says to the guard.

"Don't you need a coat?" the guard challenges.

"I don't get cold."

The guard rolls his eyes. Nico's always a pain.

With a quick notation in the system and the press of a button, the bulletproof glass doors open, and I gather my phone from the locker, leading Nico outside. To see his daughter.

72

"Where is she?" Nico asks.

I don't answer. We're halfway around the building, on the pedestrian path that's lined with benches and leads out toward a snow-covered garden. When we first left the lobby, the X-ray guard was watching, but out here, except for a roving guard who patrols the metal fence in the distance, there's actual privacy. A few other patients take their morning walks. Nico barely notices.

"Tell me where she is," he insists, his shoulders hunched forward. With no jacket, he's definitely cold. But that's not why he looks so uncomfortable.

Last time I was here—when he started talking about her—Nico was reduced to tears.

"I need to speak to her!" he hisses, spinning back to face me and clutching his leather book to his chest.

I don't flinch. We both know who's in control.

"She wants to speak to you too," I reassure him as he scans the garden, the path, every nearby bench. They're all empty. He checks the snow for footprints. There aren't any. He's not happy with that. Whether he likes it or not, he needs me.

"Nico, if you want to see her, I need you to tell me what you know."

"About your father? I didn't know your father."

"What about Marshall?"

At least fifty yards in front of us, the path dead-ends at an empty bench beneath a sickly-looking sycamore tree that's propped up by a few wooden stakes. Like before, Nico checks the snow for footprints. No way anyone can see that far.

256

His eyes narrow. He hugs his book even tighter. "I see you, Clementine," he whispers.

"Nico, wait...!"

He's already on his way.

"*Clemmi*...!" I call out.

She sticks her head out from behind the tree, well aware he's coming.

Up ahead, Nico knows better than to run. He eyes the guard in the distance—who's at least a football field away. I race right behind him.

From behind the sycamore tree, Clementine steps out to face him.

As Nico gets his first good look at her, he stops midstep. His mouth tips open and the leather book tumbles from his hands, landing in the snow with a wet thud.

"Why are you wearing a wig?" he asks.

"She didn't want anyone to recognize her," I tell him, picking up the book and offering it back to him.

Nico doesn't take it. He won't face me, won't acknowledge me.

"Is that true?" he asks, still locked on Clementine. "Or is Benjamin lying?"

"It's true. It is," Clementine insists, her voice surprisingly soft and reassuring, like she's worried about him. I don't know why I'm so shocked. It's still her father.

"Here, you look cold. Wear this," she adds, unwrapping her black wool scarf and holding it out for Nico.

When he doesn't reach for it, Clementine steps even closer, draping it around his neck. I hand him back the book, tucking it under his armpit. For a moment, Nico just stands there, staring awkwardly at his daughter—like he's searching her face or waiting for her to say something.

"So are you the one?" he finally blurts.

"Excuse me?" she asks.

"The *one*. The one who's... It is *you*, isn't it?"

"I-I'm not sure I understand," she says, clearly lost. "The one who *what*?"

"The one who sent me *this*," he says, holding out the leather book. "Who sent me the messages."

Clementine takes a half step back. Her father takes a half step forward.

"Tell me, Clementine," Nico says. "Are you the Knight?"

73

"*e? The Knight?*" Clementine asks, her fingertips pressed against her own chest. "How can *I* be the Knight?"

"That's what you call him? *The Knight?*" I ask, remembering what Tot told me about the playing cards.

"But what you did before... *You're not the one?*" Nico challenges.

"The one who *what*? Who's killing pastors? No, are you cr—!?" She catches herself, but it clearly hits home. "I'd never do that! *How could you think I'd do that!?*"

Nico's eyes flick back and forth, dissecting her. He holds tight to the leather book, but also to the black scarf she gave him. Like he's choosing between the two. But what's far more unusual is...

He looks happy.

"I knew it, Lord! I knew you wouldn't do that to me!" he says, staring up at the winter sky as if he's talking directly to God. "*Thank you for making her different from me!*"

"Nico, keep your voice down," I insist, eyeing the guard, who's still in the distance.

"You really thought I was a murderer?" Clementine asks.

Nico's eyes are closed. He's whispering, saying some sort of prayer.

"Nico, I'm serious," Clementine adds. "How could *I* be the murderer?"

Nico's eyes pop open. He turns to her. "You're my daughter. Why should I think you were *different*?"

The words crash into her chest as if they're about to knock her over. But no matter how much they hurt, there's no mistaking the raw concern in her eyes as she studies her father. I came here to find information. Clementine came for something far more personal.

259

"Nico, you're not a monster," she tells him.

He shakes his head. "I have a sickness. That's what put the evil in me."

"You're wrong. I know where the evil comes from. I know about the other killings. I spoke to Dr. Yoo..."

At the mention of Yoo's name, Nico loosens his grip on the black scarf, his hand sliding down it like a fireman on a pole.

"He told me what they put in you—what they did to you," she adds. "All these years...all the things they blamed on you. But it was *them*, Nico. They're the ones who caused this."

Nico's hand slides down to the end of the scarf, dangling at the tip. He won't let go, shaking his head over and over and over. "But the doctors...the nurses...they told me...my sickness... God chose me for this. God made me this way."

"No, God made you like *me*," she insists. "God made you *good*."

Nico blinks hard, a swell of tears taking his eyes. Clementine's too. She needs to hear it just as much as he does.

"Nico, listen to what she's saying," I jump in. "When we first met, you told me that God chooses each of us—that He tests us. Maybe this is your test. If you know what's happening with the Knight—this is your chance to make it right."

Like before, he won't face me. Won't hear me. He stays locked on his daughter.

"Are you helping the Knight?" Clementine asks.

"He doesn't need my help. He wants my blessing."

"Your blessing for what? For more murders?"

Nico doesn't answer.

"You can still help us stop him," I say.

At that, Nico freezes. For the first time, he looks away from Clementine, his close-set eyes sliding toward me. His voice sounds like crushed bits of glass. "You think you can stop this?" he asks. "This can't be stopped. This is fate. It's his destiny."

"His destiny is killing people while copying John Wilkes Booth?"

Once again, he turns away, back to his daughter.

I shoot a look at Clementine. *He'll only answer you.*

"So this is the Knight's destiny?" Clementine repeats. "Killing people while copying John Wilkes Booth?"

Nico licks his lips, then licks them again, like he's hearing the question for the first time. "You misunderstand. He knows he's not Booth. Not Guiteau. Not any of them. But he understands the power of walking their path . . . building on their success."

"Is that why he approached you? So you can guide him on the path?" I ask.

He glances at Clementine, who nods that he should answer me.

"I know you doubt me, Benjamin. But you know the history. Booth. Guiteau. Czolgosz. Even Lee Harvey Oswald. Each murdered a President. But what else do they have in common?"

At first, I stay silent.

"Don't hide it from her, Benjamin. Tell her," he says, though he still won't face me. "We label my predecessors as outcasts and lunatics. But when you look at their lives—truly look—what's the one thing they all share?"

"All four of them believed they were chosen by God," I say.

"Exactly. They all thought they were chosen by God," Nico says. "But here's the real question: What if they were right?"

74

Pastor Frick, you there?" Tot called out, adding a quick knock against the hospital room door.

There was no answer. Shoving the door open, Tot peeked inside.

The hospital room was no different than any other hospital room—but from what Tot saw: no lights...no flowers...no writing on the wipe-off board. Even the bed was perfectly made. Whoever used to be here was long gone.

"You from the church?" a female voice called out.

Tot turned, tracing the voice back to the hallway, to a nurse with a gold cross around her neck, pushing a rolling blood pressure cart. "If you're looking for Pastor Frick, they released him."

"*Released* him?"

"Beautiful news, right? In fact..." She pointed toward the elevators. "If you hurry, they just wheeled him downstairs. He said he was stopping by the chapel first—to say goodbye to the chaplain."

"Do you know if he's headed home after that?" Tot asked, still determined to ask the pastor about yesterday's attack.

"No idea. But if you want, ask Chaplain Stoughton..."

"Only if you think it wouldn't be a bother."

"Don't be silly. She loves everyone. Even the President was impressed when he was here."

Tot froze at the words. "What'd you just say?"

"The President. President Wallace."

Sonuvabitch. "President Wallace was in *this* hospital?"

"Don't you remember? Back when he had his gallbladder out."

"And he met with your chaplain?"

"Even said prayers with her—right before they put him under. Why? Is that—?" The nurse stopped, staring at Tot. "Is everything okay?"

"No, it's just—" Tot spun around, rushing and limping back toward the elevators. "What floor'd you say the chaplain's office is on again?"

75

So that's what this killer thinks?" I ask. "That he's been chosen by God?"

"Not just him. He said the same of me. He *told* me," Nico says, his voice starting to pick up speed. "He told me that what I began—all those years ago... He said it was a revelation for him. That was his word. *Revelation*."

"And that makes you *what*? His inspiration?"

"I see the way you look at me, Benjamin. You want to insist that I'm the cause of this. But what the Knight is doing... the path he's on... This isn't my creation. It's existed for centuries."

"I agree," I say, nodding along with him. Nico isn't just the grand poobah of kooky conspiracies and alternative history. He once shot the President to save the world from evil Freemasons. It's not tough to figure out how to keep him talking. "We know about the Knights of the Golden Circle," I tell him. "And we know how the first Knights—the sacred Knights—used the symbolism of playing cards to hide their commitment to the church."

"Then you know how powerful their legacy is," he says, his voice now at full gallop. "Back in 1994, a man named Francisco Martin Duran tried to kill President Bill Clinton by firing twenty-nine shots at the White House. But on his drive from Colorado to Washington, did you know he stopped in Dallas, Texas, passing the Book Depository... and that when he got to D.C., he even stayed at the Hilton Hotel where John Hinckley shot Reagan? The path is clear to those who see it," he adds, still staring at Clementine and blinking faster than ever. "And when you see the map... Have you seen the map?"

She shakes her head and takes a small step backward. She knows what happens when Nico gets too excited.

"Look at a map...any map," he continues, clutching the scarf on his neck. "John Wilkes Booth was born in Bel Air, Maryland. Guiteau in Freeport, Illinois. Czolgosz in Detroit, Michigan. And Oswald in New Orleans, Louisiana. If the next assassin were born in northern Florida, those five birthplaces—if you draw straight lines between them..."

From his back pocket, he pulls out...it's not a wallet. It's a fat stack of folded papers, all bound with a rubber band. Unwrapping the rubber band, Nico flips through the pile and holds up... "Those birthplaces form *this*!"

"You see it, Benjamin!? A pentagram—*a pentagram!*—across America!"

Next to me, Clementine takes another step back. Something's wrong. Something I'm missing.

"Nico, were you born in Florida?" I ask.

Gritting his teeth to catch his breath, he looks in the distance, at the guard, then over at two squirrels chasing each other at the base of a nearby tree. They're moving so fast, they don't even leave paw prints in the snow.

"It doesn't matter where I was born," Nico growls. "It's the Knight's turn now. He knew all that I'd done. But to see what he's shown me... With the maps alone... I only had the tip of it."

"I'm confused," Clementine jumps in. "If it's the Knight who's doing this— Is his mission different from yours?"

"Now you're seeing it, aren't you? Now you know why he can't be stopped. Mine was a selfish mission—everything for my own purpose. But what the Knight is doing here— Did you see his first slain? To let Pastor Riis be the first lamb..."

My heart clenches as he says the name of our old pastor in Wisconsin. Marshall told me he was looking into Riis's death. But back when we were little, I remember that night in the pastor's basement. Within weeks, Riis was run out of town. And Marshall's mother put a gun in her mouth and pulled the trigger.

"Nico, if you know that Marshall's doing this..."

Nico wraps up his homemade map, stuffing it back into his pocket.

"If you're protecting Marshall, or covering for him," I add.

"I told you, Benjamin, I've never seen the Knight before. He knows better than to come in person. But I do know this: In the case of Pastor Riis, the Knight understands the value of doing for others. And proving one's loyalty."

"Loyalty to who?"

Without a word, Nico lowers his chin and drills me with a dark glare.

From behind us, a determined wind shoves against my back. "You asked the Knight to kill Pastor Riis, didn't you? You pointed him to the first victim."

Staying silent, Nico stares straight at me. "In my experience, Benjamin, you can't make a man do what he doesn't already want to."

As I turn away, my brain tries to fill in the rest. Riis was practice. Then when the copycat murders started . . . first the rector from St. John's . . . then Pastor Frick from Foundry Church. Both of them spent time with the President—but both also studied under Riis. For it all to be tied together . . . "Nico, is that how the Knight found his other victims? What started with Riis then led to—"

"You keep focusing on the lambs. But look at their locations too: Look at the temples—look what he's working toward. His is an act of God."

"Why? Because he thinks he's protecting the church?"

"You keep saying that. You keep insisting that in the playing cards, they're protecting the church. But you're forgetting the real mission of Vignolles and his sacred Knights. From the start, the Knights weren't just protecting the church. They were protecting the church's greatest *secret*."

"And what secret is that?"

Nico tilts his head, looking at me like I'm still arguing that the world is flat. "Isn't it obvious, Benjamin? They protect the real Name of God."

76

In the beginning, the Knight had doubts too. How could he not?
Even now, as he walked slowly down the hospital hallway, toward the chapel at the far end, he thought back to those moments when he first heard the story, about the true Name of God. There was no arguing with what really happened. Or that it happened over and over throughout history.

For Jews, the true Name of God was said only once each year, by the high priest in the Temple. To protect it, the Hebrews used *YHWH*—the four consonants of the Hebrew name for *God*—saying that the vowels should be hidden and the real Name should never be pronounced. To protect it even further, they later replaced it with *Adonai*, which meant *Lord*. In the Christian Bible, God gave Jesus the "Name above all Names," which began as *The Anointed One*, then *The Christ*, then *Jesus Christ*, then *Lord* and *YHWH*. And in the Muslim religion, where God is known as *Allah*, God is said to have ninety-nine names, and that those who know all of God's Names will enter Paradise.

Indeed, the issue remained such a potent one throughout history that as recently as 2008, the Vatican issued a directive that said, when it came to the Name of God, the name *Yahweh* could no longer be "used or pronounced" in any songs or prayers.

It was this essential question that the Knight could not let go of: What power could the Name of God really hold that all three religions still treat it with such reverence, even to this day?

Over the centuries, dozens of theories developed. Ancient healers supposedly used God's real Name to cure the sick. Early grimoires said that the Name of God unlocked untold power. And exorcists and mystics insisted that those who controlled the Name of God could control God Himself.

Even the Knight knew that was crazy. Just as his predecessor in the fifteenth century—Étienne de Vignolles...the Chosen Knight...the Sacred Knight—knew that the true Name of God had nothing to do with magic powers or mystical exaggerations.

Still, century after century, religion after religion, there were always those who sought power by claiming to know God's real Name. But as Vignolles found out when he was trusted by both church and king, great power didn't come from *knowing* the Name of God.

Great power came from *hiding* it.

Over the course of centuries, so many religious answers have been lost. But as for the true Name of God, those answers were purposely hidden.

For thousands of years, so much good has been done in the Name of God. But also, the First Knight was asked, how much harm has been done—by Christians, by Jews, by Muslims alike—because of their assumption of exclusiveness? How many throats have been slit? How many innocents slaughtered? Religions have built empires, launched crusades, and fought some of the world's bloodiest wars based on the *differences* in how they viewed God.

But what if there was *no* difference? How would the followers of Jesus, or Allah, or Adonai react if the real secret of secrets—the greatest secret of all—was simply this: that for every religion, the true Name of God was *exactly the same*? Forget Christian God, Muslim God, or Hebrew God. Think of the power that would be lost if there were just...

One God.

Vignolles was shaken too when he first heard the story. He didn't want to believe it. No one would believe it. But to hear the rumblings from the king's court...from someone so respected...how could it be ignored? Unsure of what to do, Vignolles did the only thing he always did before a battle.

He prayed.

In no time, he had his answer. The story of *One God* was a blasphemy—a lie!—and if the king were to ever bring it to light...

Luckily, Vignolles didn't have to pull his sword. King Charles VII never reached the heights of power that would let him challenge the church.

Still, Vignolles knew this was a problem that would rise again. When it did, a new Knight would be needed. From there, the secret army took shape. Preparations were made. Instructions written. And the symbols—of hearts, spades, diamonds, and clubs—were incorporated into the one place no one would ever think to notice.

For centuries, Vignolles's playing cards would carry his warning of how the king could destroy the church. And for centuries, the chosen Knights would lie in wait, taking on chancellors, emperors, monarchs, tsars, and anyone else whose growing influence and claim of unity might interfere with the primacy of church power. Including, even, a President.

Six centuries later, the current Knight—the Knight of the fifth and final symbol—reached the end of the hospital's long hallway and approached the Interfaith Chapel. A place that treated every religion the same. How perfect.

The plaster Abraham Lincoln mask was hidden inside his jacket. So was his Iver Johnson revolver. Behind him, the slowed-down version of "Little Red Corvette" still echoed on the piano.

From his pants pocket, the Knight pulled out a white linen handkerchief and, like Czolgosz, the third assassin, folded the handkerchief, then unfolded it again, then folded it, and unfolded it again, finally using it to hide the revolver as he tugged it—so carefully—from his jacket pocket.

He checked the hallway one last time. It was quiet back by the chapel. Grabbing the door-pull with his left hand, he held his right hand out, like he was offering a handshake, just like Czolgosz did over a hundred years ago.

Every generation has its Knight. And every Knight knows his sacred mission.

"Chaplain Stoughton...?" the Knight called out, tugging open the stained glass door. As the smell of rose candles wafted past him, he lifted the Lincoln mask into place and couldn't help but think that Nico was right. With each new lamb, he was definitely getting stronger. "Chaplain Stoughton, are you in there?"

77

You're joking, right? The *Name of God*?" I ask.

"Most people don't want to believe it," Nico says.

I glance over at Clementine, who's still digesting it herself. Even for Nico, it's a new level on the tinfoil-hat scale.

"You asked about the Knight's mission," Nico adds, eyeing the two squirrels spiraling around the tree. "Now you won't accept it?"

"So everything you told us…about the Knights and God's Name…" Clementine interrupts. "Is that *true*?"

Nico turns slowly toward his daughter, his crooked smile crawling back in place. "Does it matter if it's true? Or only that the Knight *believes* it's true?"

"And that's why he's killing pastors?" I ask. "He thinks he's on a holy mission?"

"He *knows* he's on a holy mission. Why do you think he'll only kill in temples? Look at his predecessors! Why did John Wilkes Booth pick Good Friday—the most solemn day in the Christian calendar—to take down the king? Why did Czolgosz say that he could've shot his king at Niagara Falls, but instead wanted to shoot him at the temple?"

"Time out. Lincoln wasn't—"

"Lincoln *was* a king! Just as Garfield and McKinley—and JFK—all were at the height of their power! *Just as Wallace is today!*"

As Nico raises his voice, the perimeter guard, who's still pretty far away, turns toward us. When it comes to Nico, they don't take chances. The guard's not just watching anymore. He heads toward the curving concrete path, coming our way.

Nico leans to his left, like someone's whispering in his ear. I almost forgot. His imaginary friend.

272

"Benjamin, do you remember what I told you the first time we ever met?" he finally asks.

"You said I was the reincarnation of Benedict Arnold."

"No. I told you about your *soul*. I told you we all have souls, and that our souls have missions. Missions that we repeat over and over, until we conquer them. That's the battle you're facing here."

"So now this is *my* mission?" I ask skeptically.

"It's *all* our mission. You, me, the President... Do you know what entanglement theory is, Benjamin?" Before I can answer, he's already into it. "Scientists found that when two subatomic particles come in contact with one another, they're forever entangled. Even when they leave each other's presence, if you reverse the spin on one—no matter where they are—the other one automatically reverses its spin. It's the same in life. The moment you meet someone, you cannot be unchained."

Clementine is silent. I can't tell if she's horrified or mesmerized. But she can't take her eyes off him.

"It's why I'm chained to the Knight," Nico adds. "He came to me thinking *I* was the Knight. That *I* was the chosen one. But don't you see? The mission is *his*!"

"Nico, you need to lower your voice."

"Look at the cards—think of the roles that Vignolles picked all those centuries ago: king, knight, knave. Always king, knight, knave. These roles exist forever, Benjamin. Always chained together. King Wallace *rules*. The Knight *slays*. And the Knave— Do you know what the Knave does?"

"The Knave serves. He's the servant."

"No. Look at the original meaning. The Knave is the Trickster— the one who *claims* to fight for good, but brings only darkness with him. That's why the Knave always dies in battle, or causes others to die, Benjamin. So as you leave here—as you try to stop the Knight— don't you see? That's *your* role, Benjamin. *You're the Knave.* You're the one who'll die in battle."

On our left, one of the two fighting squirrels gets a piece of the other, sending him skidding across the snow. But he rights himself so quickly, it's like it never happened.

"Nico, I came here to save innocent lives."

"You say that, but what were the first questions you asked? You wanted to know about your father. Then about the burned man, about Marshall. Which haunts you more, Benjamin? The victims, or your own childhood guilt?"

"You don't know what you're talking about. I'm trying to catch a murderer."

"Then if that's the case, why haven't you asked me one question about the *next* murder? We all know it's coming; we all know who the Knight is building toward. So why haven't you asked one question about how he's going to kill King Wallace?" Nico asks, his voice grinding louder than ever. Clementine swallows hard, glancing at the guard walking toward us. "I'll tell you the answer, Benjamin. It's because, in your heart, you'd be happy to see the President dead. You're the Knave, the bringer of evil. That's why the Knave dies— and causes others to die with him."

In my pocket, I feel my phone vibrate. I don't bother to look.

"Nico, do you really know when the next murder will take place?" I ask.

"I told you: This is destiny, Benjamin. The Knight can't be stopped."

My phone continues to vibrate. I still don't answer. On our left, the guard's getting closer, approaching the curving concrete path. He pulls out a walkie-talkie, but we can't hear what he says.

"Nico, if you know something," Clementine pleads. "Please… Dad… Tell Beecher. He can help you. He can get stuff for you."

Nico turns at the words. He kicks his shoulders back and stands up straight.

"That's not true," I say.

"Nico, everything okay?" the guard calls out.

Nico pretends not to hear. "What can you get me, Benjamin?"

"Tell us what you want," Clementine says.

Nico doesn't even have to think about it. He looks at me, but points at Clementine. "I want to talk to *her*. Without *you*. I want to know why she's wearing a wig."

Clementine stutters. "It's not a—"

"I know it's a wig. I need to know why you're sick," he demands, his voice cracking. Eyeing the guard in the distance, he's fighting to hold it together. At his chest, he clutches his book tighter than ever.

My phone vibrates again, but goes silent when I don't pick up. "We didn't come here to make deals," I say.

"Beecher, it's okay." She turns to her father. "If I stay, you'll tell us when the next murder is?"

I wait for Nico's eyes to narrow. They don't. They go wide. Like a child. "You'll really stay? You'll talk to me about your sickness?"

"I wouldn't have come here if I didn't want to talk to you."

Two days ago, I would've said she's working him. But last night, I saw the tears in her eyes. And those freckles along her bald head. It's still her father.

"Nico, you hear what I said?" the guard calls out from about half a block away. "Everything okay?"

Once again, Nico leans back and to the side. Final advice from his imaginary friend. This time, he disagrees with her.

"Please, Nico," Clementine pleads. "Tell us when the next murder is."

Holding his wrist out, Nico glances at his watch like a proper butler checking teatime. "The murder already happened. Ten minutes ago."

My phone again starts to vibrate. My throat goes so dry, I can't feel my tongue. As I pull my phone out, caller ID shows me a randomly generated number from an area code that doesn't exist. Only one person has that.

"Beecher, you need to get out of there," Immaculate Deception demands in his computerized voice.

"What're you talking about? What's wrong?"

"You haven't heard, have you?"

"Heard what?"

He pauses, leaving me with the high-pitched squeal that leaks from my phone. "Beecher, when was the last time you heard from Tot?"

275

PART IV

The Fourth Assassination

"You know, last night would've been a hell of a night to kill a President."

—*President John F. Kennedy,*
three hours before he was shot

He was the fourth President murdered in office.

78

Ten minutes earlier

Stepping out of the elevator, Tot was thinking about coffee.

Not the taste of it. The smell of it.

He didn't smell it now; hospitals smelled of ammonia and bleach, not fresh-roasted coffee grinds.

But as Tot speed-limped up the first-floor hallway, trying to move as quickly as he could to the chapel in back, he couldn't help but think about the smell of coffee from all those years ago—after his wife's brain aneurism—when she was the one in the hospital. Back when she was first admitted, the doctors said it wasn't that bad, that she'd recover. But when her liver and kidneys began to fail and the paralysis started causing bedsores, Tot didn't need a medical degree to know what was coming.

The doctors wanted her transferred to hospice, but one of the senior nurses in the unit knew Tot from the Archives. Tot helped the nurse find the documents that proved her great-great-grandfather—a slave at the time—fought during the Civil War. She made sure Tot's wife stayed in that private room in the ICU.

Over the course of the next week, Tot would sit at her bedside, staring at the plastic accordion tube that ran down from his wife's neck—the feeding and breathing tube—that was still spattered with blood from where it entered her throat. He watched his wife's weight plummet to less than a hundred pounds, her skin sagging against her cheekbones. She didn't even know Tot anymore. When

281

they could rouse her...*if* they could rouse her...the only question she could answer was, *What's your sister's name?*

But for Tot, the very worst came in those final days, when the nurses began stocking the room with open coffee cans filled with freshly ground beans. At first, Tot didn't understand. Then he realized...the coffee cans were there so he couldn't smell what was happening to his wife's body.

It was that lingering thought—of cheap Chock Full O' Nuts French Roast—that nibbled through Tot's brain as he reached the far end of the hallway and approached the stained glass door of the chapel.

Grabbing the door-pull of the chapel and determined to refocus on the task at hand, he let the memories of his wife dissipate. He tried thinking about what Immaculate Deception had said, that all of the Knight's victims were clergy members who had spent at least some time with the President. As Tot just found out, the hospital pastor—Pastor Stoughton—had done the same when President Wallace was here last year. But as Tot gave the door-pull a tug, the smell of coffee still lingered.

"Pastor Stoughton?" Tot called out, stepping inside and smelling... he knew that smell too...that burnt smell like fireworks or...

Gunpowder.

"Pastor, are you—?"

Tot almost tripped on the coat-rack, a wooden one. It was lying diagonally across the carpet. Like someone had knocked it over.

As he stepped over it, he heard breathing. Heavy breathing. Like someone panting. Or crying.

Feeling time harden into slow motion, Tot headed deeper into the room. It was difficult to walk, as if he were moving underwater. As he looked around to his right, he saw the blood—small drips of it, like a barely spilled soda dotting the light beige carpet. Behind that was her body.

Tot saw her legs first. She wasn't moving. Just from the awkward way her knees were bent, Tot knew Chaplain Elizabeth Stoughton was dead.

She was crumpled on her side—like she'd tried to curl into a fetal position, but never quite made it. At her stomach, a puddle of blood soaked her blouse, still blooming and growing up toward her chest and over toward her right breast.

Next to her body, an older man with sandy blond hair was down on his knees, like he was hit too. He was breathing hard, trying to say something. Tot knew the man—from the photo Immaculate Deception had sent: the pastor who was shot yesterday. Pastor Frick. Time was twirled so tight, Tot barely heard him. It was all still underwater.

Still, Tot saw his hands . . . they were up in the air. Like he was being robbed and someone was pointing a gun at him.

"B-Behind you . . ." Pastor Frick cried, pointing behind Tot.

Slowly turning, Tot looked over his own shoulder.

It was too late.

Pfft.

The silenced gunshot bit like a hornet, drilling into Tot's head. Right behind the ear. Just like JFK.

A neat splat of blood spit against the nearby wall.

Tot tried to yell something, but no words came out. As his knees gave way, he saw the Knight's eyes, and it all made sense.

The world blurred and tipped sideways. His bones felt like they were turned to salt. As Tot sank, deflated, onto the carpet, his last thoughts were still about the smell of coffee. And how good it'd be to finally see his wife.

79

Now

Beecher, I need you out of there!" Immaculate Deception's computerized voice barks through my phone.

"But if Tot's— If he's been shot—"

"You're not listening to me, Beecher! Another pastor—the female one from the hospital—is dead! That's the *third* victim! Tot's the *fourth*! *Four* victims... If we're right, you know who the Knight's going after next!"

My mind leaps back to the President—and to Marshall—and to the restaurant he was casing in Georgetown. "You need to look at Café Milano—see when Wallace is going there," I blurt. "I'll go to the hospital. If Tot needs help—"

"*You can't help Tot now!*" Mac explodes in full panic. "I spoke to the surgeon—the doctors just brought him in, but...the way the bullet entered his head— His heart's beating, but his brain function... I don't think they're finding brain activity. You need to get out of there and—"

"Nico, stay where you are!" the guard yells behind me.

"S-Something's wrong," Nico whispers. "It was just here a moment ago. I saw it."

I spin back to the benches and the sycamore tree. Nico's right where I left him. The guard's a few feet behind him. But as Nico looks down and flips through the leather book he's been holding...

"My card—the bookmark," Nico says. "I'm missing my playing card!"

"Beecher, get outta there," Immaculate Deception says.

"He took it! Benjamin took it!" Nico insists, pointing at me. "He took my card!"

"*What?* I didn't take anything," I say, backing away from Nico, toward the front of the building. "I don't know what card you're talking about."

"The playing card! You *stole* it! Wh-When I dropped my book... you picked it up and handed it back to me," Nico growls, taking his first steps toward me.

"Nico, don't move!" the guard shouts, pulling a high-tech walkie-talkie from his belt. He doesn't talk into it. He just pushes a button.

On my right, through the glass windows that look back into the hospital's main lobby, I see the guard who ran the X-ray rushing through the lobby. A male nurse is right behind him.

As Nico starts plowing at me, I back up even farther, glancing around for Clementine...

"I know you have my card!" Nico shouts.

I check the benches, the trees, even around the corner of the building.

Clementine's nowhere to be seen.

80

Nico, if you don't stop, you're gonna lose ground privileges! Mail privileges too!" the guard yells from behind him.

On my right, the X-ray guard and a male nurse come racing out of the hospital's front doors.

"Rupert, he stole my bookmark! He has my ace of clubs!" Nico yells at the nurse.

"I swear to you—I don't know what he's talking about," I say.

The nurse takes one look at Nico, then turns back to me. "Empty your pockets," the nurse tells me.

"Me? I didn't—?"

"Empty them. *Now.*"

Frozen at the front of the building, I reach into my pockets, pulling out my wallet, keys, and a small thumb drive that carries a backup of my computer. I do the same with my coat pockets. There's chapstick, a set of gloves, and an old taxi receipt, but otherwise...

"Nothing, see? Check them yourself," I say, stepping toward the nurse.

"Stay where you are," the nurse warns, motioning me back.

"He's a liar!" Nico shouts.

"Nico, I need you to get control," the nurse says.

"He has my card! Check his pockets!"

"Please—check them again!" I insist.

"Kid, I need you out of here. Nico, get control," the nurse says, throwing a look to the nearby guard.

Backing away, I'm already past the main doors, toward the concrete path that'll take me to the parking lot. But as Nico starts to follow, the nurse and the guard grab him by the biceps...

"He's the Knave!" Nico growls. "Don't you see!? You're letting the Knave get away!"

Breaking free from the nurse, Nico tries to run, but the X-ray guard has a stronger grip.

I don't care who wins this fight. I sprint toward the parking lot, fishing the car keys from my pocket.

"I know you're the Trickster, Benjamin. I know you have my card!" Nico roars as another guard arrives and they fight to drag him down. I hear an unnerving thud. Someone cries out in pain. As I turn the corner, into the gravel parking lot, I don't even bother looking back.

"Nico—!" the male nurse shouts.

Skidding across the gravel and cutting between two parked cars, I dart for the small silver car I drove here. Clementine's rental.

I glance around, searching for Clementine. Still no sign of her, but I take an odd relief from the fact that if Tot was shot at the hospital at the exact same time that Clementine was here with me...that means she can't be the Knight. She can't. But at just the thought of it...Tot was shot!

Inside my skin, I feel another, smaller version of me shrinking within myself. *Please God, don't let him die.*

With a pop of the locks, I rip the door open and slide inside as momentum sends my phone tumbling out of my grip and into the small gap between the seats.

Stabbing the key into the ignition, I try to start the car, but my hands...my whole body...I can't stop shaking or thinking of Tot.

On my left, a hollow thud hits the driver's-side window. I jump so high, my head smacks into the lowered sun visor.

Tuuuump.

I turn just as Nico's fist collides with the glass. It hits at full speed, his knuckles flattening at the impact. He's trying to punch his way in, though the car doesn't budge. From the sound alone, it has to hurt—like punching concrete. Nico doesn't feel it. But as he winds up for another punch, he's pulled backward, off balance.

The hospital guards grab him from behind, clutching his neck, his shoulders...anything to bring him down.

Nico howls like a captured bear, still trying to stay on his feet.

I slam the gas and a wave of loose gravel somersaults into the air.

"You're letting him go! Don't let him go!" Nico pleads, still scream-ing as I take off and watch him slowly shrink in the rearview mirror.

Skidding out of the parking lot and back onto the unpaved dirt road that runs toward the sign-in gate, I'm still searching bushes... trees...anywhere for Clementine. I know I won't find her.

As I approach the small guardhouse, I slow down and add a friendly wave, praying that the guards who're fighting Nico are still too busy to have put the word out.

From the guardhouse, a uniformed guard waves back, but I still don't take a breath until I reach the end of the dirt road, out of the hospital grounds, and turn back onto the main city street.

Halfway up the block, I hit a red light and the car bucks to a stop. As I clutch the steering wheel, my heartbeat pumps in my fingertips. In the rearview, no one's coming. No one's following. I'm clear.

"Beecher...! Beecher...you there!?" Immaculate Deception's voice squawks from below the seat. My phone's still on. *"Beecher, you okay!?"*

I'm not okay.

Tot was hit in the brain.

Clementine's missing.

And the Knight—if I'm right—is about to try and kill the Presi-dent of the United States.

But as the traffic light blinks green, I keep hearing Nico's words in my head: *I know you're the Trickster, Benjamin. I know you have my card!*

He's wrong about me being the Trickster. But he is right about *one* thing.

Reaching into my jacket pocket, inside one of my gloves, I pull out the single playing card with the familiar black club at the center of it. The one I palmed as I handed Nico his book.

The ace of clubs.

You were right, Nico—I've got your stupid card.

And if I'm right about what's hidden on it—and the fact that he was using it to communicate with the Knight—I may not be able to stop destiny...

But I'll be able to find out where the Knight is headed next.

81

Change of plans—everyone into your gear!" the shift leader called out as half a dozen suit-and-tied Secret Service agents poured into the command post that was just below the Oval Office.

Sitting on one of the benches in the corner of the locker room, A.J. watched as his fellow agents scrambled around him, undoing their ties and kicking off their shoes. For any President, the schedule was set weeks in advance. To make even a minor change meant moving staff, security, press, advance teams, communication systems, and for off-site events—like today's at the Lincoln Memorial—aerial and ground protection. So for the Service to be making all these last-minute changes on Presidents' Day, something big was definitely going on.

"He fighting with his wife again?" an agent with black hair and a chunky gold class ring from Ohio State asked.

"No, this one came from headquarters," another agent replied, pulling off his tie and hanging it in his locker.

At this point, A.J. knew that word hadn't trickled down to the field guys yet. But no question, the emergency cord had been pulled. It had to be. When the higher-ups heard that a third pastor had been killed—plus an old man who was shot in the back of the head like JFK—action had to be taken. The target needed to be moved.

Naturally, Wallace again insisted on keeping to his schedule. He wanted to stick to the Lincoln Memorial event and the early meal that would precede it at Café Milano. But as the director of the Secret Service explained, there's a reason the President isn't in charge of his own protection.

290

"I heard it's a Class 3," another agent called out, referring to the Service's code name for a mentally unstable attacker.

Another agent nodded. Based on where they were headed—to one of the few places more secure than the White House—someone was definitely trying to knock down the old man.

Even so, as the agents approached their individual lockers, they weren't panicking, yelling, or rushing around. They weren't grabbing for guns or weapons or bulletproof vests. There'd be plenty of weapons waiting for them at their destination. In fact, at this moment, as the metal lockers clanged open, the only thing the agents *were* grabbing was a change of clothes. Suits and ties were being replaced by khakis and casual dress shirts, to match the attire of where they were going—the safest place to hide the leader of the free world, the same place they hid George W. Bush during the days after 9/11 and countless other Presidents during times of possible attacks: the private presidential compound known as Camp David.

One by one, A.J. watched as the casually dressed team bolted from the room. The Secret Service was doing their part. And now A.J.—still wearing his suit and tie as he headed upstairs to the Oval—was ready to do his.

82

Nico thinks he's smart.

And he is.

He's smart enough to fool the doctors at St. Elizabeths, and the nurses, and to somehow pass secret messages—and clearly some advice—to the Knight who's been killing pastors and imitating past assassins. And he's smart enough to know that if he wants to keep those secret messages secret, he should hide them in something that no one would look at twice, like a playing card that he uses as a bookmark.

But as I sit at my kitchen table, squinting down at the slightly beat-up ace of clubs and examining the front and back of it, I do everything I can to put Tot out of my mind. Mac said he's still in surgery. He said I shouldn't come to the hospital, that the best way for me to help was *this*—with the card—especially as I think about the leather book that Nico was hiding it in.

I saw it when he first put it down on the glass table in the public meeting area. It wasn't a history book. It was a novel from the early 1900s—a bestseller called *Looking Backward*. In it, a young Bostonian named Julian West goes to sleep in 1887 and wakes up in the utopia of the year 2000. But the only reason I know the book—or why anyone still remembers it—is because, as I learned last night when I looked up the third attack, it was the favorite novel of assassin Leon Czolgosz. *Looking Backward* was the book he read and reread for eight years, right up until it inspired him to kill President McKinley.

Yet as I study the nicked and slightly bent ace of clubs, the only thing I really care about is whatever message I have to believe is

292

hidden in it somewhere. When I first met Nico, he told me he was the reincarnation of George Washington. That was his way of telling me how special he is. But it's also my way of knowing how Nico thinks.

Back during the Revolutionary War, no one was better at sending secret correspondence than George Washington. As the leader of the Culper Ring, he helped invent numbered codes that were so uncrackable, versions of them are still in use by the CIA to this day. He used hourglass-shaped masks that, when placed on top of a handwritten letter, would block out certain sections of the letter to reveal a hidden message.

But George Washington's favorite magic trick was always the same: invisible ink. As I learned when I first joined the Culper Ring, invisible ink dates back thousands of years, from Egypt to China, using organic liquids like the juice from leeks or limes. Indeed, as every kid in a science fair knows, all you need to do is heat the paper, and voilà—you'll see the hidden writing. But as Washington understood, it's not much of a secret when all you need to crack it is a nearby candle.

As a result, Washington and the first members of the Culper Ring got rid of the *heating* process and changed it to a *chemical* one. Washington would write in an invisible ink, called the *agent*. And when the recipient applied a different chemical, called the *reagent*, it'd reveal the hidden message. As long as the British didn't have the reagent, they'd never crack the code.

As I raced back home, Immaculate Deception said that I should pour lime juice, lemon juice, any juice I could find across the front of the ace of clubs. But he's missing the point.

No question, Nico's not doing this alone. Whether Marshall is the Knight or not, Nico must be getting help from someone in the hospital. *Someone* is sneaking these cards to him, or at least sneaking him books with new cards tucked inside them. But that doesn't mean Nico can get whatever liquid or juice he needs at the exact moment he needs it. No, for Nico to really communicate with the Knight, he needs a reagent that's *always* available. And that's when it hits me. Forget lime juice, lemon juice, or even apple juice—even in an insane asylum—there's only one liquid that Nico *always* has access to.

Grabbing a nearby piece of Tupperware, I race to the bathroom and unzip my pants. One short but incredibly satisfying pee later, the Tupperware is filled with warm urine that sloshes in a mini-tide as I carefully make my way back to the kitchen.

Standing over the sink, I lower the ace of clubs into the Tupperware. Nothing happens. Nothing at all. And then...

Pale purple letters bloom upward, like alphabet soup letters rising from the broth.

There's no cryptic warning. No special instructions. Just two words that make me feel like someone's using a hole-punch on my stomach.

I read them again, and again. I don't know if Nico was sending them to the Knight or, more likely, that the Knight is somehow bragging to Nico, but I do know this: These two words were intended for only Nico and the Knight to see—the location where the Knight plans to make his final stand.

Camp David.

83

A.J. watched the entire argument.

Of course, the President didn't participate in the argument. He was at his desk, signing letters with his head down. No, when it came to the big arguments with the Secret Service, Wallace had staff wade into the mud.

Within seconds, those staffers were livid. The heads of the Service weren't surprised. Staff was always annoyed when they heard POTUS wouldn't be where they wanted him.

But as the chief of staff pointed out, this wasn't just about Wallace's safety. It was about the entire country. As they all knew, the President's schedule was published every day for the world to see. So when the press suddenly spots members of the White House Military Office out on the South Lawn, rolling out three giant circles with huge Xs on them...and then a Black Hawk helicopter armed with missiles and countermeasures swoops in, takes the President and his family out of there, and upends said schedule with no notice...there's not a person on this planet who won't know something is intensely wrong.

"But something *is* wrong," the head of the Service pointed out. "We've got an active threat—that's why we need the EA movement," he explained, referring to the Emergency Action that came with the Black Hawk.

"That's fine, but you go running to Camp David with an unannounced EA movement and you know what the press will scream? Terrorist attack," the chief of staff argued back. "From there, financial markets plunge, people panic, and investors start buying stock in ammunition companies and businesses that make body bags."

"If you want, I can leak the details about the assassination threat."

"Oh, that's far better. So the whole world thinks that the President is running like a scared kid?"

At that moment, President Wallace looked up from whatever letter he was signing. Without a word, the argument was over.

Twenty minutes later, A.J. stood outside on the South Lawn of the White House, watching as the First Lady and the President's son climbed aboard the waiting helicopter. As a compromise, it was their standard copter, instead of the armed Black Hawk, which meant the press would see this as a regular administrative lift instead of an emergency one.

And the stated reason for the trip? That was the far more subtle compromise. The press was told that Wallace's son was feeling pressure at school, and they begged reporters to keep it quiet to protect the son's privacy. Of course, reporters wouldn't keep anything quiet. Not anymore. But now Wallace looked like the perfect dad—taking the family to Camp David so he could help his kid through a hard time. As the chief of staff knew, when everything went sideways, there was no better cover than family.

With a muffled *whup-whup-whup*, the blades of the helicopter began to twirl, and the wheels leapt off the South Lawn. On most days, reporters would be watching from a roped-off press area. Today, by the time the first member of the press even realized what was happening, the President's copter had everyone on board.

Craning his head back and squinting against the sudden gust of wind, A.J. watched as Marine One rose into the gray sky. Through the window in the back of the helicopter, he could see Wallace's young son pressing his forehead against the bulletproof glass, looking down at the fire truck that always pulled onto the South Grounds when the helicopter took off.

A.J. knew why the fire truck was there: It was filled with foam in case of a sudden crash.

There could always be a crash.

A.J. couldn't disagree.

And he knew, so soon, that the real crash was about to begin.

84

Mac, he's gonna kill Wallace at Camp David!"

"Beecher, you need to listen to me," Immaculate Deception's robotic voice demands through my phone.

"No, you don't understand," I say, using my cell to snap a photo of the ace of clubs as it floats there in the Tupperware. "The Knight—"

"You mean Marshall."

"Stop saying that . . . you don't know that."

"I *do* know that. Just like Tot knew that. In fact, the only person who doesn't seem to know it is *you*."

My hand shakes as the camera makes a *ka-chick* sound, blurring the photograph of the playing card. Just the mention of Tot's name makes my whole body shrink. My God, if he's not okay . . .

"I get it, Beecher—whatever you did to Marshall all those years ago . . . whatever happened . . . you don't want it to be your old friend. But it's time to be realistic. After all that's happened—"

"Tot's what *happened*! And Camp David is what *happened*! I found the message!"

"I did too," Mac shoots back. "They're pulling the trigger at noon."

My camera phone makes another *ka-chick* sound as I snap another photo. "What're you talking about?" I ask.

"That's the kill time. Twelve p.m."

"I don't understand. How do you—?"

"His medical reports. I've been tracking these YouTube cat videos Nico's been watching. The nurses do patient reports every shift, and those reports get filed online, which means . . ."

"You hacked the reports."

"They're using steganography. Do you know what that is?"

"Hidden writing."

"Exactly. But in today's world, y'know what's even harder to track than hidden writing? Hidden *videos*. Think about it—when it comes to stopping terrorists from sending each other emails, our government tracks certain words across the Internet: *Bomb. Bomb materials. How to make a bomb.* The NSA has the best word-tracking software in the world. But when it comes to videos, there're no words for them to track."

"Can't they see what's in the video?"

"Ah, now you're getting closer. Y'know who Mike McConnell is?"

"He ran the NSA. Then director of national intelligence."

"Exactly. And back during Desert Storm, McConnell was so busy, his daughter kept saying, 'I only see you on national TV—you need to tell me you love me during one of your press conferences.' McConnell said he couldn't. So his daughter told him to do it like Carol Burnett: Tug your earlobe, which was Burnett's secret way of saying *I love you* to her grandmother. So that's what McConnell started doing. During press conferences...on *60 Minutes*...all throughout Desert Storm and his entire career, he'd tug his ear, and his daughter would get the secret message. The one message not even the best NSA software can crack."

"So what's that have to do with Nico?"

"I checked the other videos that Nico's been watching, and if the time logs are right, before the second pastor was killed, Nico watched a video of a cat named Cutey Cute Lester—"

"*Cutey Cute Lester?*"

"I know it's a stupid name, Beecher. But as the cat rolls back and forth, in the background of the video, the cat's owner taps the front of his foot against the carpet exactly nine times...then he taps his heel a quick twenty-five times..."

"The second pastor was shot at exactly 9:25."

"Then in yesterday's video, his foot taps just nine times."

"Nine o'clock," I say, noting the time of the shooting at the hospital this morning. As another pang hits my stomach, I look down at the ace of clubs with the words *Camp David* on it. "Mac, you found another video, didn't you?"

"Uploaded twenty minutes ago. This time, the cat owner taps his foot twelve times, Beecher. Noon today. And when I looked back at the President's official schedule—which yes, they just changed after the shooting—that's the same time that Wallace was scheduled to be leaving with his daughter from . . ."

"Café Milano," I say, referring to the restaurant that I caught Marshall casing yesterday. The one where he said he'd carve out the President's larynx with a steak knife.

"I know you see it, Beecher. That's why Marshall was at the restaurant. He was looking for the best angle to put a bullet in the President's brain. The only question now is, with the schedule being changed, if the President's not going to the restaurant—"

"Camp David," I blurt. "They're taking the President to Camp David."

"You're sure about that?"

"I'm sure," I say, reading from the playing card and still picturing that thin grin on Marshall's face. That knowing grin. The kind of grin that makes me wonder if, from the moment everything started, *this* is where Marshall always planned for it to end. Create a big enough emergency, and they'll always send the President to Camp David.

I glance down at my phone to check the time. It's almost ten. Barely two hours. "Mac, if this is right—we need to let people know!"

"Let *who* know? Tot's in the hospital."

"Then call the other agents! Call every Culper Ring member you can find!"

At that, Immaculate Deception goes quiet.

"What? What's wrong?" I ask.

"Beecher, how many members do you think are in the Culper Ring?"

"I don't know. A lot."

"Define *a lot*."

"Fifty...?"

He doesn't respond.

"Less than fifty?" I ask.

Again, he doesn't respond.

"Less then *forty*?" I add.

"What did Tot tell you?" Mac asks, his robot voice slower than ever.

"Mac, this isn't funny. How many members are there?"

Through the phone, there's a loud click, like a radio being turned off. Instead of Mac's robot voice, a female voice—an older woman—says, "Beecher, my name is Grace Bentham. You need to get out of your house."

"W-What're you—? Who the hell is this?"

"It's Mac," the old woman replies as I realize I'm hearing Immaculate Deception's real voice. "My name is Grace. I'm trying to save your life."

85

Nico didn't realize the guards were there until they grabbed him from behind, clutching his neck and dragging him down toward the gravel parking lot.

"You're letting him go! Don't let him go!" Nico screamed, still kicking wildly.

Beecher punched the gas, his tires spun, and a windmill of loose gravel flew through the air.

"He's the monster! Not me!" Nico howled as the car sped off, fishtailing out of the parking lot.

"Nico, catch your breath!" Nurse Rupert yelled. Between him and the guard, their weight was too much. Like a cleaved tree, Nico tumbled backward.

With a crunch and a thud, his shoulders slammed down into the frozen gravel. Bits of rocks and dust coughed into the air. It didn't stop him from thrashing, trying to free his arms, his legs, anything to break free.

"Guys! Some help!" Rupert shouted.

Within seconds, two more guards caught up to them, joining the fray. Trained in a variety of restraining holds, they weren't punching or hitting Nico. They grabbed at his wrists, going for pressure points.

Nearly blind from the spray of dust, Nico only saw a muddy blur,

301

but in the distance he heard a new voice...a voice he knew...running toward him.

"*Don't hurt him!*" Dr. Gosling yelled in his familiar southern accent. "*He's not fighting you!*"

Gosling was right. The fight was over. Even for Nico, four against one was too much.

"*Nico, listen to me—he's gone,*" Rupert said, down on his knees, holding on to Nico's shoulder and working hard to keep his voice calm. It was the only way to talk to Nico. "Whoever that was... whoever you're chasing...he's gone. *Look...*" Grabbing Nico by the ear and lifting his head, Rupert pointed him to the main road. Nico blinked hard to see. There was no missing it. Beecher's car blew past the guard gate and out from the hospital grounds.

With a final snort, Nico let his head collapse back into the gravel. His body went limp.

So did the rest of the group.

"Action's over! Let's get him inside!" Rupert called out.

In a mess of murmurs and curse words, the guards slowly and angrily peeled themselves off the pile.

"Nico, you're a real pimple on my ass," one of them said as he accidentally stepped on Nico's fingertips.

Nico didn't yell or complain. Behind him, as he lay there in the gravel still buzzing from adrenaline, he heard the sound of Velcro straps. They were bringing the stretcher. The one with the restraints. Nico knew the consequences of fighting, just like he knew what else was coming.

A mosquito bite of pain pricked him in the thigh. At the nurses' station, they called it a "B-52," a mix of Haldol, Ativan, and a few other antipsychotics that put you to sleep for the next eighteen hours.

"*Find out who that was!*" a guard shouted on one side of him.

"*I don't care how dangerous the job is!*" Dr. Gosling shouted on the other, more pissed than ever. "*You know our regs—there's no manhandling the patients!*" From the proximity of his voice, Nico knew Gosling was the one administering the shot.

"You got the other arm secure?" Rupert asked, still kneeling next to him.

The Velcro bit hard against Nico's wrist. He stared up at the gray sky, waiting for the foggy light-headedness that came with the sedation.

It never came.

"Nico, close your eyes," Dr. Gosling said, warmly patting the chest of his most famous patient.

Nico did what he was told. He closed his eyes. Yet as the stretcher tipped forward, then back, then was lifted in the air—as the nurses carried him back toward the building—Nico was surprised that instead of feeling groggy he felt wide awake. And better than ever.

86

Now

B ut how're you—? How can—?" I stop myself, pressing my phone to my ear and looking around my kitchen like I'm seeing it for the first time. "You're a *woman*?"

"The front door, Beecher. Grab your stuff and get outside," says the woman who, for two months now, has been calling herself Immaculate Deception. From the way she says my name—*Beech-ah*—she's got a hint of an old Boston accent. The fancy private school kind.

Rushing to the kitchen table, I hunch over my laptop and enter her name into Google. *Grace Bentham.* I add the words *computer expert* to narrow it down.

"Don't Google me, Beecher."

"Wait . . . are you . . . ? You hacked *my* computer too?"

"No—I hear the clicking of your keyboard. I'm not deaf," she tells me.

She says something else, but I'm too lost in an online profile from the *Boston Herald.* According to this, Grace Bentham is . . .

"I'm seventy-two years old," she adds. "I met Tot during my navy days."

I continue reading. A seventy-two-year-old former navy officer. Rear admiral. Bigshot back in the day. As I skim through the article, it says she was a pioneer in the computer field . . . one of the first programmers of the Harvard Mark I computer, whatever that is. Earned her the nickname *Amazing Grace.* In fact, according to this, she's the one who actually invented the term *debugging* when she found an actual moth in a Harvard Mark II computer and then pulled it out. But if that's who's looking out for me—a bunch of seventy- and eighty-year-olds...

"How many people are in the Culper Ring?" I ask her.

"Beecher, this is a conversation that's better saved for—"

"*How many!?*" I insist.

She goes silent. But not for long. "Seven."

"*Seven!?*"

"Seven. Including you. That's all that's left."

That means there were more. "Did something happen to the rest of them?"

Like before, Amazing Grace doesn't answer.

"What happened to them, Grace?"

Again, no answer.

"Grace, is someone hunting the members of the Culper Ring? Is that what this is about?"

"Beecher, don't forget that one of the key strengths of the Ring used to be its small size. George Washington barely had half a dozen members. Then over time, there were dozens of us, nearly a hundred at our height. But don't you see? That's why Tot picked you. As they hunted us down, Tot was determined to rebuild."

A needle of pain pierces my throat at just the mention of Tot's name and everything he's done for me. No way will his work stop here.

"There's four of you: Tot, you, the Surgeon, the one you called Santa...plus me is five. Who are the others?" I demand.

"Listen, I know you're upset."

"No, upset is what happens when you get a speeding ticket, or your girlfriend dumps you. I risked my life here! I risked my life thinking I was being protected by the team from *Mission: Impossible*! Instead, I got invited to an AARP meeting!"

"Beecher, don't underestimate us. You have no concept of the battles we've fought. And won. So I hear every word you're saying, but *please*... What matters right now is getting you to safety. If you want to have this argument, grab your stuff, run out the front door, and head for the safehouse that Tot showed you. At the post office. Let's have this fight from the safety of your car."

"But you just said . . . at noon today . . . That's when the Knight—"

"Marshall. The Knight is *Marshall.*"

". . . that's when Marshall is going to kill President Wallace," I add, saying the words for the very first time. And finally believing them.

"So what do you propose we do?" Grace asks.

"*Me?* I have no idea. But at the very least, we need to report this. Call the Secret Service. Tell them what's going on."

"And you think that'll help?" she challenges. "Beecher, if you call the Secret Service and tell them you know about an impending attack, there's only one thing I can guarantee: By the time you hang up, a set of Secret Service agents will be driving to your house and *you'll* be the number one suspect. And in two hours, when the Knight finally pulls that trigger and your prediction comes true, *you*—Beecher White—will be the very first name linked to that attack."

"That's not true."

"It *is* true. And y'know what'll make it even more true? When they find the security footage—which you know exists—of you sniffing around that restaurant in Georgetown yesterday. I told Tot not to let you near Marshall—but you couldn't see it, could you? When you trailed Marshall to Café Milano, that was *exactly* what he wanted. He had you—on camera—right at the potential murder scene the day before the President was scheduled to be there. And he had you there for the same reason he let you into his apartment . . . and let you put your fingerprints all over that Abraham Lincoln mask that you so conveniently thought you 'found.' And then, when you put that all together—the video, the fingerprints, the Lincoln mask, plus this phone call you're about to make—you know what they call that in court? *Exhibit A. Exhibit B. Exhibit C. Exhibit D.*"

I start to say something, but as we both know, there's nothing left to say.

"Tot said you're a smart person—and a good person, Beecher. I have to believe he's right. But since the moment this started—whether it's from guilt or just regret—whatever happened with Marshall when you were little...whatever you built into his life, you can't see what he's been building around you: a spider web. And the more you tug, the more it's going to strangle you."

"So that's it? I run to the safehouse, and we just give up?"

"Sometimes it's like that oxygen mask on an airplane: You've got to put the mask over your own mouth first and save yourself before you can save anyone else."

"What about you, though? You're the computer whiz. Can't you do something? Hack something? Alert the Secret Service anonymously?"

"Who do you think sent them the reports on the recent attacks? I sent them Marshall's name and his photograph. We're doing our job, Beecher. It's time to let the Service do theirs."

I think back to what Nico said when I was at St. Elizabeths: that I was the Knave. That when it came right down to it, I didn't actually care about saving the President. But I also remember what I told Tot. We need to be the good guys. Always.

"We need to do more," I insist, reaching for my winter coat.

"Beecher..."

"I mean it, Grace. You're acting like our hands are tied. We need to tell them ourselves."

"And how do you plan on doing that, Beecher? You think you can just drive to Camp David?"

"I don't know. I haven't—" I cut myself off, still thinking of what happened all those years ago to Marshall in the basement. There's a cost to doing nothing. I'm not paying that cost again. "All I know is this: What doesn't make sense is sitting here and doing nothing when we know exactly *where* and *when* he's pulling that trigger," I say, yanking the ace of clubs playing card from the Tupperware full of urine and running it under a quick blast of water. The words *Camp David* begin to fade, but you can still read them on the card. "You heard that story Tot told, about Marshall breaking into the army base. The Service has no chance against him. Not when they don't know who they're facing."

"Then let me share this fact with you: If you get anywhere near the President or the White House or Camp David, they're going to pull every gun they have and aim it at your head."

"That's fine, because you know what else'll happen? They'll grab the President, take him into whatever saferoom they have out there, and at least he'll be safe. Think about it, Grace. If you could go back in time and you knew about Lee Harvey Oswald, would you be content with just sending the Secret Service a telegram—or would you drive down to the Book Depository and do everything in your power to make sure the assassination didn't happen?"

Slapping my laptop shut and tucking it under my arm, I grab the car keys, fly through my living room, and race for the front door.

"Beecher," she pleads, leaning hard on her Boston accent, "I don't think you're thinking this through. What if you're doing exactly what Marshall wants you to do?"

"Then I guess I'm in—"

I yank the front door open and stop midstep. Blocking my way is a tall man with dyed black hair and the most exhausted eyes I've ever seen. He lowers his chin like he's turning away, but all it does is call attention to the rose-colored scar on his neck. The one he got on the day I saw him die.

"Just hear me out," Dr. Stewart Palmiotti says. "I have a proposition for you."

87

They grabbed the chaplain first.

The paramedics, the nurses...they knew she was dead the moment they saw her. Chaplain Stoughton's skin wasn't pink anymore. It was ashen and dark gray. No one comes back from that. But they still scrambled, lifting her body, which hit like deadweight, onto the gurney.

Running and ripping away her blood-soaked shirt, they rushed her out of the hospital chapel and across the hall to the emergency room. Chaplain Stoughton was still a member of the hospital's staff. How could they not grab her first?

It was a younger doctor—an Orthodox nephrologist who'd come down to say a prayer for his sick niece—who was the first on scene. Stepping into the chapel, he saw the puddle of blood pooling across the light cream carpet.

This was still a hospital. Within seconds, gurneys were rolling, IVs were flowing, and the emergency room staff mobilized, filling three side-by-side rooms and trying to bring one of their own back to life. They didn't have a chance.

In the first room, a trauma nurse called the time of death for Chaplain Stoughton. In the second, an attending physician and a handful of nurses were literally holding Tot's skull together. As the doctor looked into Tot's wide-open eyes, only one of them was reacting to light. He'd blown a pupil and his brain was now herniating, shifting to the other side of his skull. They started prepping him for surgery, but already knew the outcome. And in the third room, Pastor Frick—the pastor who was shot yesterday, and who had just gone to say goodbye to Chaplain Stoughton—was still in shock, his eyes dancing back and forth as doctors and nurses shouted questions in his face.

"*Sir, are you okay!? Can you hear me!?*" someone yelled.

"He spared me...he said my time had come," Pastor Frick kept whispering, over and over. As his foot tapped against the floor, the digital step counter on his shoe clicked upward.

"Did you get a good look at him? Did you see *anything*?"

Pastor Frick nodded, a thin splatter of blood running diagonally across his nose.

"You saw the shooter!? What'd he look like!?"

Frick glanced up, his chin quivering. He could barely get the words out.

"Like Abraham Lincoln."

88

Beecher," Palmiotti pleads, "before you say anything—"

I hit him as hard as I can.

It's a quick punch. And a brutal one. A total sucker punch that catches the President's former doctor just above the eyebrow and sends a shock of pain ricocheting through my fist and down my elbow.

The corner of my phone nicks Palmiotti's cheek as the impact knocks it from my hands and sends it crashing to the ground.

Palmiotti stumbles backward, holding his face.

"Ow! That's— *Ow!*" he yells, more annoyed than hurt. But as he blinks away the pain, he starts nodding. Slowly at first, then faster. "Okay, I deserved that, Beecher. I did."

"Stay the hell away from me," I warn him.

"I know you hate me, Beecher. I don't blame you for it. But if you just listen—"

"Listen to *what*? Another trainload of lies and bullshit!? You're a killer, Palmiotti! We both know you're a killer! In fact, you're so full of crap, you can't even *die* honestly!"

"That's clever, Beecher. But I thought you'd be a bit more surprised to see that I'm still alive."

"You think Clementine didn't tell me? She trusts you even less than I do. I figured it was only a matter of time until you showed up with some new threat. So what's it gonna be? You still mad that Clementine shot you in the caves? Or now that your pal the President brought you back from the dead, you got some new message for us?"

Before he can answer, I step out onto the porch, reaching down to pick up my phone. From what I can tell, it's still connected to

311

Amazing Grace. I angle it so Palmiotti can't see what's onscreen. Better to have someone listening in than to be here alone.

"Beecher, despite what you think, Orson Wallace isn't my friend. Not anymore."

I look up, tightening my glare.

"In all your anger, have you really thought about why I'm standing here? It wasn't to threaten you, Beecher. After what happened... after what I've seen... I understand the benefits of seeing the President dead."

"What're you talking about?"

"You think Wallace doesn't know about the pastors' deaths—or your friend Tot? He may not know who, but he knows someone's trying to kill him."

"But what you just said—"

"No, it's what *you* said, Beecher. That Wallace brought me back from the dead. And he did. But that doesn't mean he gave me my life back. In fact, he's still holding it, letting it dangle in front of me while trying to use me for his own benefit. I understand now. I know what kind of man he is."

My skin turns brittle, like it's made of eggshells. "So now I'm supposed to believe *you're* the one trying to kill him?"

"*Me?* No. I don't want Wallace dead. But after what he did—what he took from me—" For a moment, Palmiotti lowers his chin, which pinches the scar on his neck. "I don't care what his title is. Orson Wallace needs to answer for his actions."

I cock a skeptical eyebrow. "Okay, so even though I think you're a lying piece of garbage, I'm supposed to believe this sudden conversion and the fact that you want to go after the Presi—"

"*He took my life from me, Beecher! Not just my family! Not just my love! He took my life!*" Palmiotti explodes, his voice booming down the block.

"Only because you let him."

He grits his teeth. His chest rises and falls from the outburst. "You're right. There's plenty I let him do," he finally says. "But there's so much more you have no idea about, Beecher. Beyond what happened years ago...beyond the attacks and everything we did with Eightball. Whatever you think of me—whatever you want to believe—let me show you the proof. I have everything we need."

"Everything for *what*? I'm still not even sure why you're here. If you have the proof, and you know what he's done...why not just take him down yourself?"

Palmiotti shakes his head, forcing a nervous laugh that freezes like cotton balls in the cold morning air. "I know you're not stupid, Beecher. People love to point at Woodward and Bernstein, but they were just lucky that Nixon was such a cocky, lazy ass. These days, only a fool tries to take on the President of the United States— especially this President—by himself."

"And assuming I even believe all this, you think *I'm* the solution?"

"No. I think your group is." He pauses again, just to make sure I hear him. "I know about the Culper Ring, Beecher. The President told me. So if I help you with this, if I tell you what I know about Wallace and let you put the truth out there, I need the kind of help that only the Ring can muster."

"Palmiotti, you do realize we live in the twenty-first century, right? If you want to put the truth out there, all you need is an Internet connection."

"You misunderstand. I don't need help hitting the *send* button. But once I hit that button," he explains, his voice slowing down, "I need someone protecting me."

I look down at my phone and see that I'm still connected to Amazing Grace. Her words continue to echo in my brain. Seven members. With Tot shot, we're down to six.

"Doc, I'm not sure the Ring is the solution you think it is."

"I know you can't talk about them, Beecher. I know how it works. But I've seen their work firsthand. I know what they're capable of."

"You're not hearing me."

"No, Beecher, you're not hearing *me*. I'm offering to help you. With what I've seen...I can get you into Camp David."

I look up, but don't say a word.

"That is where you're trying to go, isn't it?" he challenges. "That's where you think your friend Marshall is striking next. You think we didn't know about him either? Or that Clementine's still unaccounted for? Wasn't she with you, Beecher? Why's she not by your side? For all you know, she's there right now."

He points down at my closed laptop. No. Not at my laptop. At the playing card that, as I grip the laptop, is still held in place by the palm of my hand. On the ace of clubs, the light purple words are easy to read: *Camp David*.

I look over his shoulder, still instinctively searching the empty street for Clementine. Even Nico asked her if she was the Knight. Of course she denied it. But Palmiotti is right about one thing: I have no idea where she is.

"Don't overthink it, Beecher. I was there last Christmas, and on those recovery days after the President's surgery, and even on the night Wallace had that surprise party for the First Lady. It's a simple choice, really. You can either stay here and let the President get gunned down, or try to save his life and make sure he's properly punished for everything he's done. This is where you find out who you are, Beecher. No one can get you closer. Now do you want to get into Camp David or not?"

89

Nico kept his eyes closed. For nearly an hour.

He kept them closed as they carried him from the parking lot, back into the new building.

He kept them closed as they patted him down, pulled out his shoelaces, and even as they checked his mouth, rectum, and under his fingernails.

He listened carefully as they talked about him. "...*recent increase in antisocial behavior*..." "...*broke Cary's finger*..." "...*should put him down once and for all*..." And he kept his eyes closed as they undid the Velcro restraints and rolled him off the stretcher, onto the thin mattress.

From there, as the nurses left the room and bolted the door, he couldn't hear anything. Not even an echo as they disappeared up the hallway.

Nico didn't like that. With his hearing, he wasn't used to such intense silence. But at least now he knew where he was. Whatever room they put him in, it was soundproof.

Still, just to be safe, Nico kept his eyes shut.

"*I think you're clear,*" the dead First Lady finally said.

Squinting carefully, Nico looked around. The room was narrow but tastefully painted in the same calming celadon green color as the check-in area that they entered through yesterday. He was on a thin blue mattress that was on the floor. There was no furniture, no TV, nothing he could hurt himself with. On his right, one of the walls—the one with the door on it—was made of solid, thick glass that looked out into an empty hallway and allowed the doctors and nurses to look in. And for Nico to look out.

Decades ago, they'd have put Nico in a straitjacket and tossed him in a rubber room. But in today's modern institutions, restraints were frowned upon and rubber rooms didn't exist anymore. Now they were called "Seclusion Rooms" or "Quiet Rooms"—places where the patients could find their own calm and "help themselves."

"*So the drugs they gave you… They didn't work?*" the First Lady asked.

Nico shook his head, slowly sitting up. His fingers were stiff and his body was sore from the fighting. As he peered into the empty hallway, no one was there. He wasn't surprised.

For weeks now, he knew *someone* had to be looking out for him. The Knight had shown up once, months ago. But after that, he was too smart to return to St. Elizabeths. Indeed, as Nico thought about it, with all the messages that the Knight was able to send—with the invisible ink playing cards that had been tucked into the old books—those messages didn't just deliver themselves. Someone inside the hospital was helping the Knight communicate with Nico. Someone was on his side.

"*You think that's who gave you the injection, don't you?*" the First Lady asked.

"The Knight told me… He told me he would provide—that we wouldn't be alone," Nico said as he replayed the past few days and thought about the one person who always seemed to be showing up, again and again.

"*I know who you're thinking about,*" the First Lady said. "*But you still need to be careful.*"

Nico *was* being careful. That's why he was staring at the back corner of the room, where a surveillance camera sat inside an octagonal-shaped metal wedge with scratchproof glass. No question, the camera watched every part of the room. It watched Nico. But to Nico's surprise, unlike every other camera in the new building, the little red light on top of the camera wasn't glowing.

"*Is it possible to shut off just one camera?*" the First Lady asked.

"The Knight said he'd take care of us. That he'd provide," Nico said, slowly climbing to his feet. He was still wary—but he was getting excited. Everything the Knight had said... it was all coming true. Destiny.

Pressing his face and fingertips against the glass, Nico checked the dark hallway. The lights were off, and there were no nurses. No orderlies. No one.

"Looks like God's looking out for you, Nico."

"Not just God," Nico said as he reached for the door. "The Knight looks out for us too. The Knight *provides*."

With a tug on the doorknob, Nico waited for the standard metal *tunk* that came with a deadbolt. Instead, the door swung toward him, not making a sound.

Unlocked.

For an instant, Nico hesitated. But not for long. The Knight was definitely looking out for him. Plus, someone else was too.

Stepping out into the hallway, Nico was on his way.

90

S o who do you think's helping him?" Palmiotti asks, glancing over at me from the passenger seat.

"Helping Nico? Not sure," I reply, holding tight to the steering wheel.

"Actually, I wasn't talking about Nico. I was—" Palmiotti stops himself. "You think this goes back to *Nico*?"

I go silent, my eyes locked on the small two-lane road known as MD 77. For most of the first hour, the game has been the same—he brings up small details, trying to pump me for information. But he's not the only one playing it.

"Who were *you* talking about then? You think the President's getting help?" I ask.

Now Palmiotti's the one who's silent. On both sides of us, the suburban strip plazas that lined I-270 have given way to huge swaths of snowed-over northern Maryland farmland and the rising Catoctin Mountain that's directly ahead. There's no one around—no one anywhere—but Palmiotti's still focused on our rearview mirror.

"How can someone be helping the President?" I add. "I thought Wallace was the victim here."

"He is the victim. But you have to understand, when you're President—just to communicate with the outside world... That doesn't happen without help."

"What kind of help?"

"Help from someone close."

"Like your old high school friend who happens to be the White House doctor."

"Or a trusted Secret Service agent," Palmiotti explains. "When

318

we get there, that's who we need to be looking for. A.J. Ennis. Find him and you'll find the President."

"So why not just call A.J.?"

Palmiotti turns from the rearview and shoots me a look. "I told you, Beecher. My direct line isn't as direct as it used to be." He pauses for a moment, like he wants to say something else, but it never comes. I see the loss in his eyes. All it does is make me think of Tot and everything I owe him, everything he's done. Grace said he picked me to help rebuild the Culper Ring...to help him do what's right. For that alone, it's enough to keep me going.

"So this guy A.J. That's who Wallace replaced you with?"

Palmiotti doesn't answer.

"You think A.J. might be a part of this?" I add. "I mean, if he is that close to Wallace, he'd be in the perfect spot to take a shot."

Before he can answer, I spot a yellow, diamond-shaped highway sign: *Watch for Ice on Bridge.*

It's the only warning I get. My chest flattens, pressing against my organs. Up ahead, there's no missing it: the small two-lane arched bridge that runs across a shallow ravine.

The metal bridge is old—bits of ice shine on the rusted archway—but it looks safe as can be. Still, at just the sight of it, my fists tighten around the steering wheel.

"Beecher, you okay?" Palmiotti asks.

I nod and hold my breath.

I don't like bridges. My father died on a bridge. But as we get closer and the tires thump across its threshold...

I'm not sure that that version of my father's death is true anymore.

Next to me, Palmiotti says something about President Wallace and how much he doesn't trust A.J.

I barely hear it.

Indeed, as the car's tires *choom-choom-choom* across the bridge's metal grated roadbed, the only thing going through my head is the letter from last night...

The letter Clementine showed me. My father's suicide note.

I fight hard to stare straight ahead—but in my peripheral vision, I still see the snow-covered rocks that lead down toward the frozen stream below us.

For as long as I can remember, I was told my father died on a bridge just like this one. Small bridge. Small town. Small death, so easily forgotten.

But like any son, of course I never forgot. For decades now, I've pictured every version of my father's death: his car plummeting because of an oncoming truck, his car plummeting because he had a heart attack, his car plummeting because he swerved to save a special old dog. I've seen my father die in every different permutation. But to read that note—to see his handwriting—and especially to see the date on that letter: one week *after* he supposedly perished...

Halfway across the bridge, Palmiotti's still talking, and I'm still holding my breath. My lungs tighten from the lack of oxygen. Blood rushes to my face, which feels like it's about to burst. But as we pass the midway point and the bridge's curved metal arches begin their angled descent, I—I—

I look around cautiously. The wheels continue to *choom-choom-choom* across the bridge's metal grating. And I still hold tight to the steering wheel. But not as tight as before.

"Beecher, you hear what I just said?"

"Yeah...no...you were talking about the President. That... that he's not the man you thought he was."

"You weren't even listening, were you? What I said was...when we were in seventh grade, Wallace ran for student government treasurer. Not even president. Treasurer. And he got beat. Miserably. The kids hated him back then. Do you understand what that means?"

"It means everyone's beatable."

"No. It means people can change, Beecher. Perceptions can change. For bad—or even good—not everyone is who they used to be. Just because something happens in your past, doesn't mean it defines your future."

He lets the words sink in as I think about my father, and Clementine, and of course about the President and Palmiotti. But I'm also thinking about Marshall and everything I did to him. So much that can never be undone.

With a final *ca-chunk*, the wheels of the car leave the metal bridge and I watch it fade behind us.

"But you are right," Palmiotti says, still staring in the rearview. "Everyone *is* beatable. Especially when you know where their weak spot is."

As the road weaves us through the small town of Thurmont, Maryland, and out onto the open road, a slight incline tells me we're beginning our ascent into the mountain. The next sign we see is a wooden one from the National Park Service.

Welcome to Catoctin Mountain Park

If we head right, to the eastern side, we'll find public camping grounds, hiking trails, and scenic mountain vistas. Instead, I turn left, toward the western side, where the road narrows even further—down to two thin lanes.

There's no more open farmland. No more small town. As we weave upward, slowly climbing the mountain, we're surrounded by steep slopes, rocky terrain, and thick swaths of towering oak, poplar, hickory, and maple trees. We can't see more than a few feet in any direction.

Still, we both know what's up ahead, hidden deep within the park. I glance at the car's digital clock. We still have a half hour.

"We'll make it," Palmiotti says. "But whatever happens from here on out, no more blaming yourself. What matters is you tried, right?"

Of course he's right. But that's exactly why I can't stop thinking about that night in the basement. I know who Marshall used to be. I know what I did to him. And in less than a half hour, I'm about to come face-to-face with exactly what I turned him into.

* * *

321

91

Eighteen years ago
Sagamore, Wisconsin

I t's dark down there."

"He'll be fine," Timothy Lusk said from his wheelchair, rolling to the edge of the steps and looking down, down, down into the dim basement. "You'll be good, right, Marsh?"

Holding the pushbars of his father's wheelchair and peeking over his father's shoulder, young Marshall took his own look down the unfinished stairs with the rusted metal treads. The black basement floor seemed to sway and move with a life of its own.

"I can get you a flashlight," Pastor Riis's wife—a woman everyone called Cricket—said.

"If you want, *I* can go," Pastor Riis added.

"He'll be fine," Marshall's father said. "It's just water."

Pushing his glasses up on his face, Marshall stepped backward, which sent a small, inch-high tidal wave flowing back through the kitchen. It *was* just water. And thanks to a cracked drainpipe that kept the pastor's dishwasher running during the entire weekend they were gone, it was everywhere: in the kitchen...in the living room...and, with some help from gravity, in the basement, which now looked like a dark black cesspool. When Marshall and his dad first arrived, Pastor Riis said it was knee-high down there. That meant even deeper for Marshall.

"Here...here's a flashlight," the pastor's wife said, handing the light to Marshall, who shined its beams down the steps, though it barely penetrated the dark.

"Don't worry, we'll be right here," his father said, pivoting his wheelchair and motioning Marshall forward.

Before Marshall could argue, a flashbulb went off, and his father's Polaroid *vrrred*, spitting out an instant image.

"Don't forget—you need this," his father said, handing Marshall the camera. "Get pics of everything."

Marshall nodded. For six months now, since his dad had been hired as an insurance adjuster, that was the job: take photos, document the damage, write up the report.

Of course, Marshall knew his dad got the job as a favor—even insurance companies feel bad for an unemployed guy in a wheelchair. But as the company quickly found out, so did claimants, who had a tough time complaining about how bad their damage was when they were talking to a double amputee who would never walk again.

"I told him not to run the dishwasher before we left. Didn't I tell you that, dear?" the pastor's wife asked, putting a hand on Riis's shoulder. Quickly catching herself, she glanced at her guests and added, "I'm sorry— I didn't mean to snap at my husband like that."

"You call that *snapping*?" Timothy laughed, motioning his son to the edge of the steps. "They should come to our house, right, Marsh?"

Staring down into the darkness, Marshall didn't even hear the question. Over the past six months, he didn't mind being dragged along with his dad. In fact, he liked it. There was something nice about being alone in the car with your father as the radio played and the wind whipped through your hair. Plus, when there were places his dad couldn't go—when the accident happened on the second floor of a house and there was no stair-lift, for instance— Marshall was the perfect assistant, grabbing the Polaroid and using the climbing skills he got from the treehouse to scurry up into attics or even out onto roofs. It didn't just make him feel good. It made him feel useful. Special.

But even twelve-year-olds know...attics and roofs are very different than a dark basement.

"If he's scared, I really don't mind going," Pastor Riis said for the fourth time.

"He's not scared. He loves the dark, right, Marsh?" his dad insisted, rolling his wheelchair forward, using the empty footplate to give Marshall one last shove.

Aiming the flashlight at the stairs, Marshall took his first step down.

"There you go. Toldja he liked the dark," his dad added.

For Marshall, this was about far more than just the dark. For years now, he'd heard the gossip about Pastor Riis. Two years ago, Bobby McNamera used to take a private Bible class that Riis used to teach in this basement. Soon after, Bobby abruptly moved away without saying goodbye, never to be heard from again. Every kid in seventh grade knew: Don't go down into the pastor's basement.

"Just be careful," the pastor's wife called out as Marshall took a few more steps down, the damp air clogging his nose. No doubt, the water was high, covering at least five steps from the bottom. Tucking the flashlight under his armpit and holding the camera over his head, he aimed and shot. A flashbulb popped and a quick photo popped out. He didn't even bother looking at it.

As he took another step down, his foot was swallowed by icy water, which filled his sneakers and made a sponge of his socks. With another step, the water was over his ankles, then up to his calf, his knee, his thigh. By the time he reached the final step, holding the camera even higher above his head like an army grunt trudging through a river, the water covered his thighs, skimming the edge of his testicles. It was freezing, but Marshall was sweating.

"Make sure you shoot it all! They need to see how bad it is!" his dad called out, though all Marshall was thinking of was Bobby McNamera, who he heard was put in a mental institution, though no one could confirm it.

Wading through the water, which tugged at his thighs and slowed him down, it wasn't as if Marshall expected to find human bones, or chains that hung from the wall. But as he glanced around he couldn't help but wonder what else was buried under all this water.

In every direction, loose papers, the lids to cardboard storage boxes, a plastic garbage can, even an old piece of luggage floated through the room, which had less than three feet of headroom because of the basement's low ceiling and a maze of high piping. Barely ten seconds had passed, and Marshall was breathing heavily. He knew the main water line was turned off, but that didn't stop him from thinking about what would happen if the water got any higher. Looking up at the ceiling, with the camera still over his head and the flashlight jerking back and forth in its own crazed light show, he could feel his sweat spreading, his glasses sliding down his nose.

On his left, from the banister, a thick black bug with the body of a spider and the legs of a cricket hopped through the air, landing in the water. Spider-bugs, Marshall called them, knowing them from every local basement, including his own.

From what he could tell as he looked around, the basement was divided into two rooms. This first was all mechanical. A flashbulb exploded as he took a picture of the half-submerged water heater on his left. Another bulb exploded as he snapped one of the nearby boiler, an old 1920s metal beast that barely broke the surface of the water.

"And get the boiler and water heater!" his father added as Marshall waded through the doorway that had no door on it, into the next room, which for some reason was better lit. On his right, he saw why: There was a narrow basement window, no bigger than an air-conditioning vent, that looked out into the backyard, but was covered in so much dust, the light barely got in. As for the room, it didn't look much different—lots of floating papers and debris—but instead of machinery and pipes, it had a chest-high built-in bookcase along the back wall.

The water had already risen to ruin half the books. But as Marshall snapped a photo and another Polaroid spit out, he saw that on the top shelf a large framed picture leaned diagonally against the wall.

"Marsh, how you doing!?" his father called out.

"Almost done!" Marshall called back, still holding the camera over his head as his glasses slid even farther down his nose. "I found this big picture frame down here...!"

"That's from my parents' wedding! Please don't tell me it's underwater!" the pastor's wife called back.

"No, it's good! I'll bring it up!" Marshall said, slogging forward toward the bookcase as the cold water nipped at his testicles. As he placed the camera and the flashlight on the top shelf, a trio of spider-bugs hopped through the air, skimming across the water and leaving a faint wake behind them.

Stepping up on his tiptoes, Marshall reached for the gilded frame that held the old black-and-white photo of a young man in a tux posed so elegantly with his new bride. Like in most old photos, neither was smiling, just staring, lips pressed together in that way that made them look like grandparents even when they were newlyweds. But as Marshall grabbed the bottom corners of the frame, unwedging it from its place, his fingers hit...*something*.

There was something behind it.

As he pushed the frame aside, he saw a neat stack of magazines, though he didn't even give them a second look. That is, until he saw...

Breasts. There were breasts. Big ones, cupped by a long-legged brunette with teased-out, tousled hair and a red headband. Kneeling on a pool table, she leaned toward the camera, but looked over her own shoulder, where a muscular, bare-chested man held her hips like he was— Oh jeez.

Marshall looked at the title. *Leg Show.* As he flipped through the photos inside, they revealed far more than legs. Lots more, including some wildly graphic shots of the woman on the cover and what she and this guy were doing on that pool table.

Marshall stood up straight, feeling something rise in his pants. Porn. Pastor Riis had porn. Lots of it.

Quickly thumbing through the stack, he found a half dozen more magazines, with titles like *Score, High Society,* and even one called *Bitchcraft*. Marshall laughed at that. If Beecher saw this—

"C'mon, Marsh, what's taking so long!?" his father called out.

Scrambling and still thinking of Beecher's reaction, he grabbed the stack of magazines and stuffed them in the waist of his pants. He was sweating so hard, they stuck to his doughy stomach as he tried to shove them in place. *"Almost done! Just grabbing the picture frame!"* he called back to his dad. But as he lowered his shirt over the magazines—

"Maybe I should help you with that," a voice asked behind him.

His body jolted wildly, his glasses almost flying from his face. He reached for the large gilded picture frame and spun around to find Pastor Riis standing there, knee deep in the water.

A single spider-bug leapt through the air.

"I-I was just coming up," Marshall said, holding the large frame.

"What about the flashlight? And your camera?" Riis asked, motioning over Marshall's shoulder. Both were still lying on the top shelf.

For a frozen moment, Marshall stood there. He could hand the frame to the pastor. But right now, that was the only thing preventing Pastor Riis from getting a good look at the outline of the magazines under Marshall's shirt.

"Sure. Of course. Here you go," Marshall said, tilting the picture frame toward the pastor, who grabbed it quickly, keeping it out of the water. With a quick pivot, Marshall spun toward the bookshelf, keeping his back to the pastor as he gathered the Polaroid and the flashlight.

"Y'know, some of the things down here," Pastor Riis began, "some of them have been here for years."

"That's what basements are for, right?"

"Of course. But in church... You wouldn't believe what people have given me over the years. And what I've had to confiscate."

A decade from now, a grown-up Marshall would've had the perfect retort. But right here, in this flooded, mildewed basement, with a glob of muddied light coming through the narrow window, young Marshall simply stared, frozen and terrified, at the pastor he'd known for his entire life.

"My dad's waiting for me," he blurted, pushing his glasses up on his nose and shining the light in the pastor's face, not even realizing it meant Riis couldn't see anything.

"Honey, the plumber's here with the shop-vac!" the pastor's wife called out. *"C'mon up, I don't want you getting sick down there!"*

And that was it.

At the top of the stairs, the pastor put the picture frame down on the kitchen table just as the plumber and his assistant joined them in the kitchen. Behind him, the pastor's wife wrapped a striped beach towel around Marshall, who used it to hide the rectangular bulge along his chest.

"Marsh, what the hell is *this*?" his father asked, flipping through the Polaroids and shifting angrily in his wheelchair. "You didn't let them dry! All the photos are stuck together!"

On any other day, Marshall would've apologized and offered to go back down. But today, as he stood there shivering in the kitchen with half a dozen porn magazines stuck to his chest, a twisted smile crept up his cheeks and only one thought filled his mind.

Wait till Beecher sees this.

92

*N*ico, you're not being smart," the dead First Lady warned.

Nico blinked a few times, walking quickly up the shiny new hallway. Since the moment he got out of the Quiet Room, the First Lady had been nervous. She thought it was a trap.

Nico knew she was wrong. With all that had happened—for the injection to have no drugs in it...for the door to the Quiet Room to be unlocked... No, this wasn't a trap. This was a message—a simple, well-planned message that stood out like a bright red thread and stretched out in front of him, down the stark hallway. Nico knew he had to follow the thread. Just like he knew that only someone in the hospital could've left it. Indeed, as he chased the thread up the hallway, he realized there was only one person who could've—

"*Nico, you hear that?*" the First Lady asked.

Up on his left, around the corner, two orderlies walked the main hall of the hospital, complaining about how slow the elevators were in the new building.

"*Nico, if they see you—*"

Nico never broke his pace, marching forward without a care. Sure, the orderlies were close. But Nico knew they'd never leave the main hallway. How could they? With everything that was now set in motion... Would God really have brought them this far to let them be stopped by something so mundane?

329

Sure enough, as quickly as the orderlies arrived, that's how quickly they disappeared, their voices fading into distant echoes.

"We're clear—hurry—go!" the First Lady said, motioning him toward the main hallway.

This time, though, Nico stopped.

"Nico, what're you waiting for? You know where we are?"

Nico knew exactly where they were. For two days now, since the moment they arrived, he'd been studying the new building. Yesterday, as they headed down to the labyrinth, he made note of the roving cameras and the sally port doors that secured each nurses' station. On his way back from the library, he'd memorized which entrances required just card swipes, and which required card swipes and keys. On his way out to see Beecher this morning, he counted three guards at the main check-in desk, but only two at the visitors' entrance.

Nico even spent an extra twenty minutes in TLC, pretending to relearn how to use a washer and dryer so he could listen in as the nurses bragged about the triple layer of security that now encased the back of the building and all the patient units. The first layer—on the exterior fire doors—was a silent alarm so that none of the other patients would know anything was wrong. The second layer came from thin wire fencing that ran horizontal with the ground. Yes, it looked easy to climb, but the moment you touched it, a hidden fiber optic wire sensed the shift in weight and sent every nearby camera spinning your way. And if by chance you got past that, the third and final layer was a twenty-foot-tall non-climbable fine-mesh fence that was woven so tight, human fingers couldn't fit in the holes. Back in the army, Nico had learned his way around that: Grab two screwdrivers, stab the fence, and scale your way to the top. But as he well knew, why risk going over a fence when you can walk right through the side door?

Up ahead, the hallway cut to the right, revealing the brand-new U-shaped desk and swinging double doors that led out to the loading dock. He had been here yesterday. But today one of the double doors was propped open with a wastepaper basket.

"*Nico, what're you waiting for?*" the First Lady asked. "*Here's our way out!*"

Like before, Nico just stood there.

"I hear you breathing," Nico announced.

The First Lady looked around. "*Nico, what're you talking about?*"

"I know you're here," Nico added. "I hear you. You know I hear everything."

Across the hall, past the U-shaped desk, a shadow shifted in the threshold of what looked like a bathroom, but was really a shower stall for patient delousing. Nico knew who was hiding inside. The friend who had left the bright red thread...and who was always looking out for him.

"Dr. Gosling, I need you to come out now," Nico said.

Without a word, the shadows shifted again and Nurse Rupert stepped out into the hallway.

Nico blinked quickly, then cocked his head, confused.

"*You're* not Dr. Gosling," Nico said.

"Nico, please don't make this harder than it is," Rupert pleaded. "Now do you want to escape or not?"

93

W e need to hurry," Rupert insisted.

"But how could—? It doesn't even—" Nico tried to get the words out, still staring at Rupert. "Dr. Gosling was the one who handed me the books, and was in my room—"

"It's time to go," Rupert said.

"But I saw Gosling put the needle in my thigh. He gave me the shot!"

Rupert lowered his chin, offering a dark glare as the daylight reflected off the bridge of his plastic eyeglasses. "And who do you think mixed that shot, Nico?"

Nico's thick caterpillar eyebrows merged together. "So you serve the Knight?"

"Please don't talk like *Lord of the Rings*. And don't call him some stupid name like the Knight. He—"

"Call him the Knight. You work for the Knight!"

"He paid me to do a job; I do the job. That's all it is, Nico. Now please prove to me you made progress here. I know you're not a killer. Not anymore. Don't prove me wrong."

"But for you to risk your job like this—"

"Nico, two months ago, for a stupidly small amount of money that I thought would help my nephew, I snuck five hundred milligrams of methylphenidate out of the hospital's pharmacy. Needless to say, the wrong people found out about it, including your so-called Knight. So this isn't about my job anymore. This is about me staying out of jail."

Nico blinked hard. He looked around, searching for the First Lady, but now…he couldn't find her. Instead, all he saw was

Clementine and the blonde wig that sat askew on her head. He closed his eyes, knowing that his fate, it was changing even now. Forget the Knight. Forget Wallace. Forget everything. After all these years, there was something else waiting for him on the other side of the hospital walls: his daughter. Clementine. For Nico, no other reward came close.

"Last chance, Nico. You want freedom or not?"

Nico turned toward the propped-open door that led out to the cement pad of the loading dock. Yes, the door was open, but through the doorway, past the cement pad, the exterior roll-top garage door was still closed. A high-tech keypad was embedded in the wall. To truly get outside—to open the garage door—he'd need an ID.

Nico glanced back at Rupert, noticing the ID badge that hung around Rupert's neck.

"You do what you have to," Rupert said, motioning down to the plastic-covered U-shaped desk. On top of the plastic was a single pencil. Freshly sharpened.

Nico hesitated. But not for long.

He reached down slowly for the pencil. Like a doctor choosing his favorite scalpel.

Rupert squinted, bracing himself. "Just do me one favor: Make it look like I gave you a good fight, okay?"

In one quick movement, Nico grabbed Rupert's wrist and stabbed the pencil down toward Rupert's forearm. There was a *ftt* as it bit through the hairy side of Rupert's forearm, and a *ttt* as it burst out the bottom, looking like a trick arrow you find in a magic shop. A spray of blood hit Nico's chest, the last few bits flicking two tiny dots on his chin.

"Nuuuhh!" Rupert screamed, thrashing wildly as his knees buckled.

Nico held tight to Rupert's wrist, fighting to keep him in place and pulling the wound close to examine it. Maximum blood without hitting any major arteries, organs, or blood vessels.

"Don't pull it out. It'll make it bleed more," Nico warned, lowering Rupert into a nearby desk chair.

"Th-That girl you were talking to this morning…that's your daughter, isn't it?" Rupert asked, his voice fading. "Is that what this's really about?"

Nico looked down at Rupert, realizing he knew nothing about the President and what was coming. With a quick tug, Nico ripped the ID from Rupert's neck and fished through his pockets, finding a set of keys. Now he had something to jam into the neck of the guard at the hospital's main gate.

He headed for the open door of the loading dock.

Rupert clutched his own punctured arm, with the pencil still in it, toward his chest. "Y'know, Nico—even with all this, there's only one thing I never lied to you about: You're *still* a pain in my ass," he called out, forcing a labored laugh.

Nico swiped the ID through the high-tech keypad. As the roll-top garage door slowly opened its mouth, a swirl of cold wind twirled through the loading dock. The sunlight was blinding as Nico strolled outside. Didn't matter. Sliding one of the keys between his knuckles, he knew exactly where he was going.

94

One hour later

Make a right here," Palmiotti says.

"You sure?" I ask, squinting through the windshield at yet another unmarked turnoff.

"Yes. I'm sure. *Here,*" Palmiotti insists.

I turn the wheel as hard as I can, nearly missing it. But as I'm learning, everything in the park is easy to miss. Indeed, as we weave our way up the mountain, there're no warning signs, no directional signs, not even one of those diamond-shaped ones that reads *Authorized Personnel Only*. In fact, when it comes to the secrets of Camp David, the clearest secret is simply that if you don't know where Camp David is, you have no chance of finding it.

"And another right here," Palmiotti says as we turn onto another narrow road that's just as perfectly paved as the last one. In a clean, straight line, all the snow is meticulously pushed to the sides. No question, Palmiotti knows where he's going.

Originally built back in 1938 as a summer camp for federal employees, Camp David first came on the presidential radar when FDR's doctors said that the White House was too hot for Roosevelt—that the President needed a cool-weather retreat. As they looked around, they realized that the camp, because of its elevation in the mountain, was always ten degrees colder than downtown D.C. Right there, the employees lost their camp and FDR gained what he called "Shangri-La," naming it after a mountain kingdom in one of his favorite novels.

To no one's surprise, when Eisenhower took over the presidency, he loved the retreat. But he hated the name, rechristening it after his grandson David. By now, Camp David has become far more than a presidential weekend house. In today's world, it's one of the only places where the President of the United States can truly leave the chaos of his life behind.

When it was first opened, FDR made twenty-two trips to Camp David. Ronald Reagan made one hundred and eighty-seven—and it wasn't just because travel got easier by helicopter, or because the place has its own golf green, driving range, movie theater, swimming pool, and bowling alley. For any President, Camp David's best perk is simply this: There's no press allowed.

When Bill Clinton took office, he said his allergies prevented him from visiting Camp David. But when he heard that the press was barred from the retreat, his allergies were cured. It was no different for Barack Obama or George W. Bush, who personally spent well over a full year up here with no one watching.

Well, almost no one.

Up ahead, the empty road straightens out. But as we approach a patch of particularly tall trees, the sun gets swallowed by the treetops and a long shadow crawls over us. Within seconds, my ears are so cold they start to ache. But it's not until I glance to my left that I feel the real chill.

I spot it immediately—in the forest—just beyond the first line of trees: a tall metal fence. Chain-link. Coated brown so it blends in with the forest.

I hit the brakes just to get a good look. According to Palmiotti, there are three different fences that surround Camp David's one hundred and eighty forested acres—plus marine guards, Park Service guards, and of course the Secret Service. So the fact we're even seeing this first fence . . .

"We're close, aren't we?" I ask Palmiotti.

He doesn't answer.

I look at the clock. Twenty-five minutes to go.

As I turn toward Palmiotti, he's once again staring in the rear-view. But the way his eyebrows dive... He definitely sees—

A loud knock on my driver's-side window makes me jump in my seat. I catch sight of someone else in the rearview.

They're behind us. And on the sides of us. Within seconds. Two men in dark green parkas and matching dark sunglasses. The logos on their chest say *National Park Service*, but I've never seen Park Service guys with guns on their belts.

"Can I help you?" the officer outside my window asks in that tone that feels like a punch. He pulls off his sunglasses, revealing a scattering of acne on the bridge of his nose.

"We're here to see the President," I tell him.

Now he's even angrier. He shoots a look at his partner, then back at me. "I need to see some ID. Now."

"Actually, Officer, I think all you need to see is *him*," I say, pointing to the passenger seat.

Next to me, Palmiotti ducks down just enough so that the officer gets a good look at him. Acne-face goes white, taking a full step back. To work security at either Camp David or the White House, they make you memorize flash cards with photos of every VIP. Even the perimeter guards know the President's dead best friend when they see him.

"This is the part where you call your boss," Palmiotti says.

The officer nods and pulls out his walkie-talkie.

95

Eighteen years ago
Sagamore, Wisconsin

And this was *his*?" Beecher asked.

"It *was* his," Marshall said, sitting on the edge of the treehouse's foldout bed and flipping through the pages of a magazine called *Escort*. "Now it's *ours*."

"So you're telling me Pastor Riis likes to look at *that*—at some fake-boobied woman who plays tennis without her top on?" Beecher asked, a deep crinkle in his forehead as he sat next to Marshall and pointed at the photo of a woman pressing her breasts against the strings of a tennis racket.

"Beecher, please don't ruin this for me. We're twelve-year-old boys and I found a stash of porn. I want to keep looking at this until I'm blind."

"That's fair, but—" Beecher leaned in slightly as Marshall turned the page . . . to a shot where the tennis player was now completely nude. "Y'know, I understand why you'd take your *shirt* off to play tennis—but there's something that makes no sense about taking off your *bottoms*."

"Maybe it's hot out there."

"Maybe. But your bottoms . . . ? There's something that— Maybe it's me, but that doesn't seem very hygienic."

"No, I agree. Especially when . . . look . . . that's a clay court."

The two of them leaned in, squinting to see.

"Definitely clay," Beecher agreed, though the crinkle still

338

wouldn't leave his forehead. "Marsh, can I just say: I love that you found us all these free nudie shots, but we need to be smart and get rid of it."

"What're you talking about?"

"I'm talking about if Pastor Riis realizes we have these—"

"Then what? What's he gonna do? Come and take them? He can't do anything, Beecher! At least not without letting everyone know that they were his in the first place, which I guarantee he doesn't want!"

"Maybe. But I'm telling you right now: No good can come from having the pastor's collection of porn."

"Will you stop worrying? No one even knows we have it."

A loud thud hit the treehouse as Vincent Paglinni shoved the plywood door open, barging inside. "Hey, Marshmallow, heard you got porn," Paglinni barked, pumping his bushy eyebrows.

Behind him, he led three other kids—two of them a year older—into the treehouse. For a moment, Beecher thought Paglinni might've come to steal it.

"Y-You wanna look?" Marshall offered, handing him a copy of *Leg Show*.

Paglinni stood there for a moment, personally deciding whether he'd be friend or foe.

To Marshall and Beecher, it felt like an hour of silence.

"Aw, why the hell not?" Paglinni eventually replied, plopping into one of the flat beanbag chairs as his three friends grabbed their own copies.

Within twenty minutes, the treehouse was crowded again, crowded with more teenage boys than when it was first built almost a year ago. Good news traveled fast. But porn at puberty? That moved at light speed.

"Marshmallow, you are one righteous nutjob!" Paglinni's best friend, a skinny redhead named Paul Mackles, announced as he flipped through a copy of *High Society*. In twelve years, that was the very first time Mackles ever spoke to him.

*   *   *

96

Today
Camp David

The agent with the small ears doesn't say a word to us.

Instead, he motions for me to extend my arms outward, then waves a handheld metal detector up the back of my legs and along my back. He's the second guard to wand me.

The first was at the front entrance to Camp David. Those guards didn't say a word to us either, even when I told them that someone was going to try and kill the President in twenty minutes. They looked at Palmiotti, then over at each other. When problems got this big, the decisions were made elsewhere.

From there, the agent with small ears put us in a souped-up golf cart with all-terrain wheels and weaved us between trees and along a macadam hiking path to our current location: a modest ranch-style house with freshly painted shutters. At the front door, instead of house numbers, there's a carved wooden sign that reads *Elm*.

I know where we are. Nearly every cabin in Camp David is named after a tree: *Laurel, Hickory, Birch, Dogwood. Elm* is home to the Secret Service command post. That means...

I glance over my shoulder. There are more ranch-style cabins in every direction. The whole place looks like Boy Scout camp. But directly across the snow-covered field, there's a perfect view of one bigger cabin: a rustic but elegant California-style bungalow with a low-pitched gable roof, tall brick chimney, and wide bulletproof windows. Even without the four agents in winter coats standing

340

along the front steps, there's no doubt that I'm looking at the cabin known as *Aspen*. The President's house.

"They're gonna try and kill Wallace. In seventeen minutes," I tell the agent in the sweater who's watching Palmiotti.

"Stewie, tell him to keep his mouth shut," the agent with small ears warns, running the metal detector up the front of my legs, toward my chest.

"Beecher, let them do their job. They'll get us to who we need to see," Palmiotti insists as Small Ears grips my shoulder and spins me back toward him, away from the President's cabin.

At my chest, the detector *beep-beep-beeps*. The other agent, a tall Muslim man, pulls his gun, pointing it at my heart. In the distance, through the bare trees, two different snipers—one on another cabin's roof... one in a tree—appear from nowhere.

"Whoa—no—it's a key. *Just a key*," I tell them as I pull out the old skeleton key that I wear around my neck. The Muslim agent lowers his gun. It doesn't make anyone unclench. The snipers stay where they are.

There's a loud *zuu-zeee* as the detector curves up my neck, to my chin. Wanding complete.

"You should wand him too," I insist, pointing at Palmiotti. I'm done taking chances. He may've been helpful getting us here, but that doesn't mean I trust him.

Palmiotti raises his hands, knowing the Service think the same. But it's not until the agent steps toward Palmiotti and moves the buzzing wand away from my ears that I realize just how quiet it is here. And how alone we are.

I shift my weight, hearing the crunch of rocks below my feet. There's a high-pitched hum that always lurks around campgrounds, and a far-off squawk of a distant bird. I glance around, but there are no staffers, no bigshots, not even a stray golf cart. This place feels like a ghost town. In fact, as I scan the compound and check each residence, every single cabin has its lights off... except for Wallace's. A wisp of smoke twirls from his brick chimney. It's just him and his family.

Across the snow-covered field, all four of the agents outside the President's house are staring only at me.

One by one, I search each of their faces. They're all wearing winter coats and khakis. None of them match A.J.'s description. That means A.J.'s inside, closest to the President. But for the first time, I wonder if that's good or—

"He's clear," the agent with the small ears calls out behind me as he finishes wanding Palmiotti.

Up on our left, toward the porch, there's a low metal thunk. Like a bank vault unlocking.

At the top of the concrete steps, the front door of the Secret Service's Elm cabin swings open, revealing a Secret Service agent with thin curly hair that's graying at the temples. He's not in sweater and khakis. He's suit-and-tied. We're moving up the chain of command.

"Reed, before you say anything," Palmiotti pleads.

Reed shoots him a look that's usually saved for drunk relatives. "Get them inside," he barks to his agents as they fall in behind us and usher us into the cabin. For a full thirty seconds, I think everything's going perfectly.

97

Inside the Secret Service house, it's no different from any rustic foyer. Hardwood floors. Wood-paneled walls. There's even an iron umbrella stand in the corner. But as I look to my left, in what was designed to be the living room, there are two side-by-side desks. Both are covered with an array of high-tech radio consoles and TV monitors. From the bird's-eye view of the cameras, these are the feeds from the hundreds of security cams throughout Camp David.

"This way," Reed says, leading us away from the surveillance room.

There's a Secret Service agent at the desk with more TVs. The other desk—the one with more radio equipment and views of the President's helicopter—is manned by two uniformed marines, one of whom is wearing headphones and presumably scanning marine frequencies. Forget the three outdoor fences. *This* is why Palmiotti said Camp David was safer than the White House. Even assuming you get past the Park Service...even if you fight your way past the Secret Service...you still have to take on the marines.

"They ready for us?" Reed calls out as we follow him into the room on our right. I've read about rooms like this: a Secret Service *down room*. Filled with old couches, folding chairs, and a small TV, it's where the agents rest and relax when they're not on post. But what catches my eye is what's at the back of the room: a heavy steel door with a high-tech card swipe, and next to it, an old gray phone built into the wall.

It reminds me of the SCIFs we have at the Archives—the bombproof saferooms where the most classified documents are read. Like ours, this one has redundancies built-in: In addition to swiping your card, you also have to be cleared in manually.

On cue, Agent Reed swipes his ID through the scanner and then looks up toward the ceiling. A thin security cam, like the ones in the White House, stares down at us. "Viv, coming down," he announces.

Down?

There's a pregnant *poomp*—my ears pop—and the airtight steel door opens toward us. The foul whiff of— I can't place the smell, but it's awful as it wafts through the room.

I look back toward Palmiotti, who nods that it's okay.

Before I can change my mind, Agent Reed grips my shoulder and adds a not-so-subtle shove. As I near the threshold, I finally place the smell. Burnt hair.

With our first step through the doorway, automated lights blink awake. Another burst of foul cool air belches from below. Industrial metal stairs go at least two stories down.

This isn't a saferoom. Or a SCIF. Or even a basement.

This is where they brought President Bush after 9/11. One of the safest places in the entire United States. The real hidden tunnel below Camp David.

98

Eighteen years ago
Sagamore, Wisconsin

B y now, it ran like clockwork.
The school bell rang at 3 p.m., and most kids reached
the schoolyard by 3:05. Of course, there was always some
screwing around in the schoolyard...a quick game of boxball or
off-the-wall...and then the extra lingering that weeded out anyone
with after-school commitments, tutors or piano lessons.

By 3:20, the group was set. There were sometimes a few varia-
tions, but like any neighborhood bar, the regulars were the regulars: Marshall, Beecher, Paglinni, Lee Rosenberg, Paul Mackles,
and the rest. Every day, they'd gather around Marshall, humming
impatiently in place until they found the critical mass that sent
them weaving back across the six-block, eight-minute trip to their
final destination: Marshall's treehouse. No two ways around it, the
Watchtower was finally living up to its name.

"Dibs on the beanbag!" Paglinni called out.

"I get the other!" Paul Mackles added as the rest of the group
spread out, taking seats on the foldout beds, on the floor, or, as Lee
Rosenberg (in his Lee jeans) always did, alone on one of the milk
crates.

Otherwise, as Marshall gathered the porn from the hiding
spots—in the Lucky Charms box...under the mattresses in the
foldout beds—there was no arguing. As he handed out copies, they
all knew the math. There were seven magazines in total, so the

345

group would peacefully, without fuss, silently pair off into seven smaller factions. Paglinni usually got his own. Same with Mackles and any of the other older ones. The rest would share.

At this point, after nearly two weeks with their X-rated contraband, every member of the group had been through the photos hundreds of times. But that didn't mean they were finished. Like the pubescent vultures they were, they scoured every single page for something new, something unseen. They read the articles, the ads, the interviews, even the letters page, in the hopes it would contain some new piece of illicit information.

On this day, Eddie Williams realized that in *Chic*, at the bottom of every *Letter to the Sexpert*, they'd print the letter writer's full name and address, prompting Paglinni to wonder what would happen if they wrote a letter to Coco Bean.

"We should tell her we're tall. She likes tall men," Paul Mackles said.

"Are you illiterate?" Paglinni asked with a laugh. "She likes *big* men. When she says *big*, she doesn't mean *tall*."

"Then what's she—? Oh. *Ew*," Mackles said as the group piled on, their laughter echoing through the treehouse. Then, at precisely 5:15 p.m., Marshall's mom would get home from work at the church and yell up to the treehouse that it was time for everyone to go.

On this night, though, Marshall's mom was working late. So whatever they were laughing at, it continued well into the dark. Beecher was laughing. Paglinni was laughing. Even Lee Rosenberg, still in his Lee jeans, still sitting alone on the milk crate in the corner, was laughing.

In twelve years, most of them had shared nothing in common, but tonight they were one unit. And at the center of it, finally the ringmaster, Marshall relished every second. Even Beecher couldn't argue with the uncontainable joy that lit up his friend's chubby face.

They had porn; they had friends; they had laughter.

By tomorrow night, it would all be gone.

*　　*　　*

99

The clanging is loud, like we're in a submarine, as we descend the metal staircase.

Agent Reed leads the way, followed by me and Palmiotti. Behind us, there's another loud *pooomp* as the agent with the small ears yanks the steel door shut, sealing all four of us down here as we head for the hidden tunnels below.

I'd heard rumors they existed. In the Archives, we have most of Camp David's building plans. According to some, the tunnels are part of an underground shelter that connects with the President's cabin and has its own secret entrance that's built into the President's bedroom closet. If there's an emergency, the Service can burst out of his closet and grab him at a moment's notice.

"So this'll take us to Wallace?" I ask.

Reed doesn't answer.

I don't mind the silence. What I mind is the smell, which is stronger than ever. My stomach lurches with each whiff of it.

Burnt hair.

You okay? Palmiotti asks with a glance.

I nod, trying to keep pace, but I know something's wrong.

From the industrial design of the staircase, the cinderblock walls, and the buzzy fluorescent lighting, the whole place feels like a 1960s bomb shelter. But there's no missing the recent additions: motion detectors in the corner...a chemical sniffer that I

347

spotted when we first walked in...and a thin plastic sheath—like flypaper—that coats the metal banister. I don't even want to think what it's for. What really matters is, if the world goes boom, this is where they'll rebuild it from.

As we reach the first landing, an open door reveals a narrow hallway, like an old hospital, lined with doors on both sides. Agent Reed keeps going, down toward the lower level. My ears again tighten and pop. By my count, we're at least two or three stories underground, and all I can think about is that when Richard Nixon's secretary, Rose Mary Woods, transcribed the Nixon tapes and famously lost eighteen and a half minutes, it was at Camp David, where no one would see the crime.

With a final *thump*, Reed slams down on the final metal step, his feet slapping against the concrete. We're at rock bottom, or at least the bottom of the stairwell.

Reed's pace never diminishes. As I follow him through the threshold and into a hallway that's lined with closed doors, the ceiling gets lower, but the fluorescent lighting stays bright.

"Here, we're in *here*," Reed says, leading us into the first room on our left. Like the stairwell, the walls are cinderblock and bare. There's not much inside: an army barrack metal bed, a matching government-issue dresser, and in the corner, a new Secret Service agent—a pale Irish-looking man with a pointy nose—who sits at a wooden desk and is watching something on TV. This isn't like the surveillance room, though. As far as I can tell, these are sleeping quarters.

"We're all clear, sir," the Irish agent calls out, standing up as we enter. "He's on his way."

I hesitate, staying back by the door, still unsure what's really going on. But I know what *he* means. *He* is always the President.

"Relax. Take a breath, Beecher," Reed says, his voice now warm and friendly. "You did good."

He gives me a small smile and I can't help but smile back, feeling strangely comfortable as I step into the room. "So Wallace is safe?" I ask. "You got him covered?"

"You have nothing to worry about," Reed says. "The President has never been safer."

Behind him, on the TV, I catch a glimpse of a waving American flag. But as the camera pulls out, I see that it's one of the tiny flags on the front of the President's private limo, the black Cadillac known as the Beast. The way the handheld camera's shaking...this is the Service's live surveillance footage.

As the door to the car opens, President Wallace steps out, followed by his young daughter. They don't wave or look around. They head straight for their destination. But from the background, from the black pavement where they're parked—

"President and his daughter on her school trip," one of the agents announces.

School trip? But wasn't that—? I squint at the TV, confused. I thought they canceled the school trip. Wallace took a helicopter *here.* So how'd—? I don't understand. "Wallace brought the school trip *here?*"

Reed looks over at Palmiotti, then back to me. "I'm sorry, Beecher."

From behind, the Irish agent grabs my arm, nearly pulling my shoulder from its socket. There's a loud *kk-kk-kk* as something bites my wrist. A handcuff. Then another *kk-kk-kk* and a metal clang. I look down as— I'm handcuffed to the metal foot of the bed.

"What're you—? Get these off me!" I shout, trying to tug myself free. The cuffs bite deeper into my wrist. The bed's bolted to the floor.

"You're not listening, Beecher. You can wait here until he's done," Reed says. "Our job's to keep him safe."

"Safe!? I just told you someone's gonna try and kill him here in the next ten minutes! Why would you suddenly let him walk around Camp David!?"

"Camp David?" Reed asks, his lips curved in a thin smile. "You really think we'd let you through the gates if the President was still at Camp David?"

Onscreen, the camera cuts to a wide shot of familiar marble

columns and the wide steps that run up to it. Everyone knows that building.

"Breaking news," the agent at the TV teases. "President Wallace surprises daughter at Lincoln Memorial."

I tighten my glance, making sure I'm seeing it right. Wallace holds his daughter's hand as they make their way toward what looks like the back of the Lincoln Memorial. But this event...this tour of the Memorial...they said it was canceled. The press said he was coming to Camp David. I saw the footage of them all getting on board the helicopt—

No. I saw his wife get on board. And their son. Then the helicopter took off. Which means—

"President Wallace was never on that helicopter, was he?" I ask, trying to step toward him as the handcuffs tug me back. "You never had any intention of bringing the President here!"

"We've got four deaths mirroring four different assassinations," Reed explains. "You really think we're gonna sit on our thumbs and let there be a fifth?"

"But if you—"

"I told you, Beecher, our job is to keep the President safe. And do you know the best way to do that? You take him to a place where no one knows he's coming. Or at least...well...where *most* people don't know he's coming," he adds, tossing a quick thank-you look at Palmiotti, who grins back, gloating like a toad with newfound flies.

A flush of blood runs through my ears. My wrist swells from the bite of the handcuff. He *knew*. He knew all along. That's why he took me here—he knew Wallace was somewhere else.

Palmiotti stares at the TV, refusing to look my way. "You protect your friends; I protect mine," he tells me.

"You think Wallace is your friend? How many times can he chew you up and crap you out before you realize you don't owe him anything?"

"Think whatever you want of me, Beecher. What Wallace and I have been through... When I buried my father and had to identify the body, he was the one standing next to me. In his will, I was the one named to take care of his kids in case he died. He was the same for mine. When that person leaves your life, you have any idea how bad you want him back?"

As he says the words, all I can see is my own mental image of Tot in the hospital, lying there with a bullet in his head. *No brain activity.* The anger hits so fast, I nearly bite through my tongue.

"*YOU SPINELESS TOADY! YOU KNOW HOW MUCH PAIN YOU CAUSED!?*" I scream, lashing out with my free hand and grabbing his neck. I dig my fingers into his scar. I don't let go. My fingers burrow down. His scar goes purple as I press even harder. No question, his skin's about to split—

Puuum.

The punch clips me in the back of the head, knocking me to the ground. The Secret Service are all over me.

"*Get off me!*" I scream, thrashing and kicking wildly as flecks of spit fly from my mouth.

The Irish agent grabs my free arm; Small Ears grabs my legs. I fight hard, refusing to let them take hold, but . . .

I have no chance. They're the Secret Service. They train for this every day. Without a single word uttered—without even a grunt—the Irish agent presses his thick forearm across my neck. As I gasp for air, they pin me to the cold concrete ground, my handcuffed arm still hooked to the bed and raised, like a kid in junior high asking a question of the teacher.

"You done yet, Beecher?" Reed asks, standing over me as they cuff my other hand to the bed.

My chest rises and falls, but no words come out. I show enough calm that Agent Irish lets go of my throat and the air returns to my lungs. "*Huuuh huuuh,*" I pant, fighting to catch my breath.

Palmiotti holds his neck, annoyed at the pain.

"It's time to stop lying, Beecher," Agent Reed adds, still standing over me. "We know who sent you. Just like we know who gave you the ace of clubs with *Camp David* written on it. Enough bullshit, son. Tell us why you're helping the Knight and working with Nico."

*   *   *

100

Eighteen years ago
Sagamore, Wisconsin

aybe you misplaced it. Did you misplace it?" Beecher
whispered, careful to keep his voice down.

Kneeling in the treehouse, Marshall replied with an
anxious look as he shook the box of Lucky Charms cereal. There
was nothing inside. Even the bra advertisements were gone.

"Maybe someone took it," Paglinni scolded.

"No one took it," Marshall insisted, pushing his glasses up on
his face as he scrambled toward the foldout bed and ran his hand
underneath the mattress. Nothing there either.

"Someone definitely took it," Paglinni said as an infection of
moans spread throughout the treehouse.

On this lazy Saturday morning, they were all here for the same
reason. Now, that reason was gone.

"I told you you should've put a lock on this place. I bet Claudio
snuck in and took it," Paglinni said, referring to a seventh grader
even he didn't mess with.

Marshall shot a look at Beecher. *Claudio didn't take it.*

"Guys, just give us a sec," Beecher said to the group. Pulling
Marshall aside and cornering him by the treehouse's Plexiglas window, he whispered, "What're you talking about?"

"I don't hide the magazines up here," Marshall whispered
back. "At night, once everyone's gone, the porn goes back to my
room."

"Your room? Why would you—?" Beecher stopped himself. "Don't answer that. I don't wanna know."

"Will you stop? It's me being smart. Those magazines are gold. How stupid would I be if I left them unprotected up here? In my room, at least they're safe."

"And they're not in your room?"

"I thought they were. I could swear I brought them there, but when I checked..."

"You think your mom took them?"

"My mom?"

"No offense, but you've seen how she's been since she started working at the church. She's like a second pastor. If she found your porn, you really think she'd let you keep it?"

Looking over Marshall's shoulder, Beecher saw how restless Paglinni and the rest were getting.

"Guys, give us two minutes—I think I know where it is," Beecher added, heading for the treehouse door and down the ladder rungs that were nailed into the tree.

Hopping down from the final rung, Marshall chased behind Beecher. "What're you—?"

"Double-check your room," Beecher said as they tugged open the screen door, ran inside the house, and raced upstairs.

Like any kid's room, there wasn't much to tear through. Desk, bed, dresser...

"Toldja, it's not here," Marshall said, approaching the set of encyclopedias that filled two rows of a bookshelf in the corner. Pulling a chunk of encyclopedias out from the top shelf, he pointed to what was hidden behind the volumes. Nothing. "See? All gone."

"And that's where you hid them all? Behind the encyclopedias?"

"Don't judge. At least I'm putting my encyclopedias to use."

"Yeah, as a hiding spot."

"And a good one at that. They were tucked behind F. Get it? For *Finally.* And *Friends.*"

"I get it," Beecher said, following Marshall out of the room and into the hallway. "But for someone to break into your roo—"

"You boys doing okay?" a female voice called out.

On their left, halfway down the worn carpeted hallway that had two matching grooves from wheelchair traffic, Marshall's mother was dressed in a freshly pressed black skirt, white gloves, and her favorite lemon yellow blazer. Church clothes, or more recently, work clothes.

"You said you'd be home today. It's Saturday," Marshall said.

"Just a few hours. Just to get everything set for tomorrow," she explained. "Oh, and sweetie, I'm supposed to tell you: When your father gets back, he wants you to go with him to Dr. Pollack's house. There's a nest of dead rats in the attic and he needs you to climb up and take pictures."

Marshall nodded as Beecher nudged him from behind.

"Mom, before you go: Has anyone been in my room?"

"In your room?" she asked, clearly confused.

"Or even at the house? I don't know, maybe last night . . . or even this morning . . . Did any friends come over to visit?"

Marshall's mother did that thing where she tapped her pointer-finger against her nose, lost in thought. "I don't think so. I mean, except for Pastor Riis."

Marshall stood up straight. "Pastor was here?"

"Just for two minutes. I think you were in the shower. He was dropping off a draft of his sermon he wanted me to look at."

Beecher shot a look at his friend, who didn't need to hear anything else.

"Did I say something wrong?" Marshall's mom asked.

"No, that's great. Thanks, Mrs. Lusk," Beecher said, tugging Marshall by the front of his shirt and pulling him downstairs. Neither of them said a word until they reached the kitchen.

"That skeevy sonuva— He stole my stolen porn!" Marshall hissed.

"I'm more skeeved out that he went in your room."

"Plus he went in my room! Plus he went through my stuff! Isn't it bad enough he's trying to screw my mom?"

"Marsh, whoa. That's not even funny."

"I'm not deaf, Beecher. I hear what people say. You see how she was dressed today? How many church secretaries get personal visits at home from the pastor?"

Shoving open the screen door and following Marshall back into the yard, Beecher didn't argue. He'd heard the same rumors. But in all their time together, this was the first time he'd ever heard Marshall broach the subject.

"The real question is, without the porn, what do we tell *them*?" Marshall added, motioning up to Paglinni and everyone else in the treehouse.

"Actually, I don't think that's a problem anymore."

Following Beecher's sightline, Marshall glanced diagonally upward toward the treehouse. From this angle, between the Plexiglas window and the open treehouse door, they could see inside. It was empty. Paglinni, Mackles, even Lee Rosenberg. All their newfound friends were gone.

Marshall's eyes went wide and he started to sway, staring up at the treehouse and looking like he wanted to crawl out of his own body.

"Y'know what the saddest part is?" he finally said. "I didn't even mind them using us for the porn. It was better than being by ourselves."

"They'll be back."

"They won't, Beecher."

"They will. Especially if we—if we—" Beecher's voice hung in the air, filled with a dangerous mix of promise and desperation. "What if we steal it back from him?"

"*What?*"

Beecher paused a moment as the pieces of the plan began to knot together. In a few hours, when he thought back on it, he'd tell himself that he just *reacted*...that he didn't like seeing his friend so lonely and heartbroken. But even now, as the words left his lips, Beecher knew he wasn't doing this just for Marshall. Beecher was doing this for *himself*.

"If Pastor Riis has the porn... You know where his hiding spot is, right? So what's stopping us from grabbing it back?"

"How about him catching us? And throttling us? And telling our parents?"

"Marsh, he's not telling anyone. You said it yourself—the last thing any pastor wants is to have his congregation find out he's got a stash of porn in his basement. Even if he knows we snuck in and grabbed it, he can't do anything. Weren't those your words? *He can't do anything.*"

Just from the look on Marshall's face—and the way his swaying started to quicken—Beecher knew he was close.

"You really like porn, don't you?" Marshall finally asked.

"C'mon, you know it's not just about the porn. Over these past few weeks, you saw what those magazines did for us. They were— They were like airline tickets to the cooler versions of ourselves."

"Now you're overstating it."

"I'm overstating nothing. We're not popular, Marsh. We're not good at sports. Face facts: Without those magazines, there's no way Paglinni and the rest are coming back. So either we find our way to those magazines, or we go back to our old lives. And no offense, but I don't want to go back."

Standing there in his own backyard, Marshall kicked down at nothing in the dirt, making his double chin become a triple.

"You really think we can do this?" he finally asked.

"Do I look scared to you?" Beecher said, already getting excited.

"I'm serious, Beecher. Whatever James Bond theme song you're now hearing, I'm not just going in there by myself."

"Can you please not worry for once? I promise you, Marsh. I'll be right there with you."

101

Y ou're serious?" I ask. "You think *I'm* working with Nico?"

"Beecher, we saw him slip you the playing card!" Palmiotti says.

"What're you talking about?" I ask as I climb to my feet, both arms still chained to the bed. "He didn't slip me anything!"

"We have it on video," Agent Reed interrupts, his tone always even. "You think with all these murders—and with the Knight copying Nico's old kills—we wouldn't be looking at St. Elizabeths' security tapes? We saw you there this morning, Beecher. We saw you bring Clementine there and we saw Nico slip you that playing card in his old book."

"No, you saw me *stealing* that playing card! I took it from Nico and—" I stop myself, replaying the moment. Nico dropped his book; I picked it up. I thought I was being so clever. But as I think about that ace of clubs . . . and the message hidden in it . . . That card was the only reason I raced here, to Camp David. But if President Wallace is actually somewhere else . . .

Onscreen, on the small TV, Wallace and his daughter are still hand in hand, his daughter's black hair dotted by a light mist of snow. They don't walk up the main public steps. Because of the security threat, they stick to the back of the Memorial, to what I'm guessing is some hidden VIP entrance. As they disappear, the camera cuts to a close-up of their eventual destination: the enormous sculpture of Abraham Lincoln sitting in his—

357

Oh God.

"*Nico knew*," I whisper.

"Beecher, don't try to shift blame to—"

"What time is it? I need to know what time it is!" I ask, pulling again on the handcuffs and trying to get close to the TV. In the corner of the screen, it says 11:57. Barely three minutes...

"Beecher, I asked you for an answer," Reed repeats. "Tell us where Clementine is! Tell us why you're helping Nico!"

"Don't you see? Nico doesn't need my help. He doesn't need *any* help. He knew all along," I insist. "Look at the video. He didn't drop the book by accident—he dropped it on purpose. He knew I'd steal the card and that I'd—" The room starts to spin, but then stops just as fast.

"Don't you see? He wanted us to come here so we wouldn't be *there*!" I add, tugging even harder on the handcuffs as I point to the TV. Onscreen, the camera cuts to the tall pillars in front of the monument. If Marshall's there... "You need to get Wallace out of there."

"There's nothing safer than an off-the-record movement."

"You're telling me Marshall and Nico couldn't predict that Wallace would insist on keeping his noon Presidents' Day event with his daughter and her class? Reed, this is his life on the line. Can't you just—?"

"We're done, Beecher. And you're done," Reed says. "The President's safe where he is. We've got him covered."

"What if you're wrong?" I challenge, turning solely to Palmiotti. "He's your *friend*. Isn't it worth holding Wallace in some back room until you know the truth?"

On TV, the camera shows Wallace's daughter's fifth-grade classmates gathering at the foot of the Lincoln statue.

"Is A.J. here at Camp David, or with the President?" I ask.

Palmiotti stares at the TV. A.J.'s with the President.

"Stewie, you know Beecher's trying to manipulate you," Reed warns Palmiotti.

"That's not true. This is—" I cut myself off as I see what's onscreen. Slowly, the camera pulls out on the eleven-year-olds, revealing a wider shot of the Abraham Lincoln statue. My mouth gapes open. "No. Nono..."

"What? What is it?" Palmiotti asks.

"Listen to me, you need to get the President out of there," I insist.

"Beecher, this isn't—"

"I'm telling you: Marshall isn't coming to Camp David. He's waiting for the President right now inside the Lincoln Memorial!"

"What're you talking about?" Palmiotti asks.

"Look at the murders. Look where they took place. St. John's Church... Foundry Church... even the chapel at the hospital..."

"I get it," Reed says. "They're all places of worship."

"Exactly. And do you know what *that* building is?" I ask, pointing back to the TV and the wide shot of the Lincoln statue. The fifth graders are getting excited, bouncing on their heels. Wallace is close. I've got less than a minute to go.

"People don't worship Abraham Lincoln," Reed says.

"No—forget Lincoln! Look at the building! When the Lincoln Memorial was first designed, do you know what it was built as?" I ask as the camera jerks left. Along the bottom of the screen it says, *POTUS Arriving*. "A temple!" I tell him. "It was modeled on a giant Greek—"

I stand up straight as a frozen calm presses against my face.

I know who did this "I know who the Knight is," I blurt.

Next to me, Reed cocks his head, holding his finger to his ear. So does the Irish agent and the one with the small ears. Something just came through their earpieces, but from the way they're looking at each other...

"What? What's wrong?" Palmiotti asks.

"Shots fired," Reed says. "At the Lincoln Memorial."

*   *   *

102

Eighteen years ago
Sagamore, Wisconsin

They waited until dark. Not midnight dark. They were still twelve-year-olds; there was a limit to how late they could be out before their parents started making phone calls. But at a quarter to nine, as Beecher and Marshall hid behind the narrow dogwood tree in Darlene Signorelli's front yard and squinted diagonally across the street at the modest arts-and-crafts-style house with the low-pitched roof, it was dark enough.

At the front door, hammered copper porch lights were filled with yellow bulbs, giving the 1930s house a golden glow. In the distance, there was a steady *rrrrrr* of a faint lawn mower. Everyone in town knew Tom Sable only mowed his lawn at night, thinking it was better for the grass. But all that mattered now was that house across the street. The home of Pastor Riis.

"You sure you can fit in there?" Beecher asked, staring up the driveway at the small rectangular basement window that sat just above the grade of the lawn.

"It's bigger than it looks," Marshall said, hunched just behind Beecher and looking over his shoulder.

"You homos humping back there or what?" a familiar voice called out.

Beecher jumped, the back of his head slamming into Marshall's jaw. On their right, halfway up the block, Vincent Paglinni pumped his bushy eyebrows, laughing that laugh that stabbed like a blunt screwdriver.

"Not funny!" Beecher yelled. "What're you even doing here?"

"Y'mean besides *living* here?" Paglinni shot back, tugging on a retractable leash and revealing a small fluffy dog—a brown bichon—that let out a defiant yip.

"Murphy, *no! Sit!*" Paglinni commanded, though the dog hopped frantically, letting out another yip. "She's just excited—she hates everyone," Paglinni explained, scooping the dog up and letting Murphy lick his face and lips, adding his own machine gun of puckered kisses.

For a moment, Beecher forgot. Paglinni's family lived around the corner.

"So that's your dog?" Marshall asked.

"No, I stole it. Of course it's my dog, dumbass. Now who you two watching undress?" Paglinni asked, still cradling his dog.

Beecher looked down at the pavement. But Marshall was still glancing diagonally across the street.

"*Nooo*," Paglinni gasped. "Pastor Riis's *wife*? You know how nasty-brained you gotta be to see her naked?"

"Can you please keep your voice down?" Beecher pleaded. "We're not trying to see her naked."

"We're here to get our magazines back," Marshall said.

Marsh, don't! Beecher said with a scolding look. Too late. Paglinni already had that smile that came with feathers in his mouth. "*Our magazines...?*" He looked across the street. The house was mostly dark, with one light on in the back room, by the kitchen.

"*That's* who took your porn? *Pastor Riis?*" Laughing out loud, Paglinni added, "Lemme guess: Marshmallow's mom gave it to him."

In his head, Marshall wanted to race at Paglinni. He wanted to scream, *Don't talk about my mom!* And he wanted to shove Paglinni in the chest, knocking him back on his ass.

Instead, Marshall just stood there in the dark, his gold eyes locked on the ground.

"Do you even realize how out of your league you are?" Paglinni laughed.

"You're wrong," Beecher blurted. "Marsh already broke in there once before."

Paglinni wheeled around, excited by the challenge. "What'd you say?"

"In Riis's basement. Mallow was there. Ask him."

Paglinni looked at Marshall.

"I *was*," Marshall said.

"And when exactly did this fantasy take place?"

"Two weeks ago."

"Same day you started visiting our treehouse," Beecher added, now the one wearing the smile that came with feathers.

Even for Paglinni, it didn't take long to do the math. "Wait... so that was..." Paglinni's eyes went round. "*Leg Show*! Sonuva—! Don't tell me *that's* where you got all the porn!"

"Fine, I won't tell you," Beecher teased.

"I'm serious, Beech Ball. You expect me to believe Pastor Riis really keeps a secret smut stash?"

"Not only does he keep it; Marsh *stole* it. And unless you want to keep wasting our time with dumb questions, you're gonna miss him stealing it again, because he's about to sneak back in for round two. Isn't that right, Mallow?"

Marshall nodded hesitantly, even as he shot Beecher a look. *I thought we were* both *going in. You're not coming?*

You don't need me. You'll be great, Beecher replied with his own quick look, meaning every word.

Across the street, the light in Pastor Riis's kitchen went dark, while the one in the living room blinked on, dim and flickering behind the lowered vinyl shades. The upstairs was still black. As was the small basement window.

"I think he's watching TV. C'mon..." Beecher whispered, tugging Marshall by the shirt, leading him across the dark street. "Let's get you in there. If he goes to bed, it'll be too quiet."

"You're serious? You're really doing this?" Paglinni asked as they took off without him. For a few long seconds, he stood there, alone in the dark, still cradling his dog. A chorus of crickets sang out, harmonizing with the *rrrrrr* of Tom Sable's distant lawn mower. Paglinni looked around. No way was he missing this.

Catching up with them at the curb, Paglinni's dog let out another loud yip. "Marshmallow, I gotta say, you even pretend to pull this off and you're officially fifty times more whacked in the head than I ever thought you were," Paglinni added, patting Marshall on the back with one hand and still holding his dog with the other.

For Marshall, though, it wasn't the thundering back pat that kick-started a sudden flush of confidence. Sure, peer pressure was a potent social lubricant. But as any seventh grader knew—especially when it came from Paglinni—nothing emboldened a teenager more than simple admiration.

"Marsh, you're gonna be town hero after this," Beecher added as they reached Riis's driveway, whose only light came from the nearby porch lights. They glanced around again, checking the street, the sidewalks, even nearby windows. No one was in sight.

"He's right," Paglinni said, a newfound excitement in his voice. "You pull this off, we'll have a victory parade. They'll make a statue of you. You're like the Hugh Hefner of seventh grade."

"I know you're just saying that to get me in there," Marshall said.

"Think whatever you want," Paglinni shot back. "You're clearly not the pud I thought you were."

Standing there in the dark, Marshall didn't move.

"That's a compliment, jackass," Paglinni added.

Pushing his glasses up on his nose, Marshall smiled. Looking over at Beecher, he gave his friend one last chance to come along.

Beecher stayed where he was. By Paglinni's side.

"So I'll see you soon," Marshall said, though it sounded like a question.

"I'll be right here," Beecher reassured him, adding a final nod for him to get going.

"You heard it here first: *Hugh Hefner of seventh grade!*" Paglinni whisper-yelled as Marshall took off up the driveway, ducked low like a waddling ninja.

Marshall was chubby and wasn't a great runner. "He gonna fit through there?" Paglinni asked.

"He said it's bigger than it looks."

For about thirty seconds, Beecher and Paglinni stood there silently in the dark, watching Marshall's pudgy silhouette get swallowed by the black shadows of overgrown shrubs.

Double- and triple-checking in every direction, Beecher again studied the house, the empty sidewalk, every nearby window. At one point, a car rumbled down the block but passed without incident. Even on Saturday night, Sagamore didn't have much nightlife.

At the back of the driveway, down on his knees, Marshall pulled out the Swiss Army knife that one of his dad's clients had bought him as a thank-you gift, then wedged it into the cracks at the base of the window. Old hinges shrieked as he tugged the low awning window toward him, flipping it upward.

"I think he's... He's *inside*..." Beecher whispered as Marshall disappeared down the rabbit hole and the window flapped back into place, snapping shut like a car trunk.

Next to Beecher, in the dark, Paglinni grinned, letting out a barely audible chuckle.

"*What?* What's funny?" Beecher asked, smiling along, but knowing that look on Paglinni's face. Something was wrong.

"You're kidding, right? You didn't see it?"

"See what?"

As his grin spread even wider, Paglinni held his pup and gave her another kiss on the head.

"Vinnie, if you know something—"

"All I'm saying is, don't be so sure Marshall is the only one visiting the pastor tonight..." Taking a step toward the sidewalk, he pointed at the tan Honda that was parked up the block—just far enough that it didn't look like it was in front of Pastor Riis's house.

Beecher's teeth began to hurt as soon as he saw it. The tan Honda. He knew that car.

That was Marshall's mom's car.

Turning back to the pastor's house, Beecher studied the dimly lit living room window and the way its shadows flickered against the shades.

Oh, God. If Marshall's mom . . . if she's inside—

"How long's the car been there?" Beecher blurted.

"What'm I, a meter maid? I thought you saw it too. I figured you didn't want him to wuss out or—"

"And you let him go in? What's wrong with you!? If Pastor Riis . . . if they're alone . . ." Beecher could barely get the words out. "How could you *do* that to someone?"

"I want the porn," Paglinni said matter-of-factly, his eyes cold and his grin long gone. "Besides, even if it all goes wrong, can you imagine? Marsh walks in and finds his mom bent over? Beech Ball, this is gonna be *theater!*"

Shaking his head, Beecher studied the closed basement window at the end of the driveway. If the porn was where they thought it was, Marshall would be out any second. Any moment now, Beecher told himself, his teeth feeling like they were about to drop from his mouth. The window didn't move.

"We need to tell him!" Beecher said, heading for the house.

Paglinni grabbed his arm, holding him back. "Tell him what? That his mom's got her panties off in the living room? He's already inside. He'll be done any minute."

"What if he's not?"

"Beecher, look around. There are only two options here: Either Marshmallow rescues the porn and gets out . . . or Pastor Riis catches him and gives our boy the shock of his life. But I promise you, if you race in there making noise and trying to warn him, you'll guarantee that the second one is the one that takes place. And even worse, you're gonna get caught along with him."

Focusing on the distant buzz of Sable's lawn mower and swaying from one leg to the other, Beecher didn't respond. If he wanted, he could go help Marshall in the basement. He could scramble through the window and be right there, right by Marshall's side.

Even if everything went wrong and they got nabbed by Pastor Riis, at least they'd be together and Marshall wouldn't be alone.

That's what a real friend would do.

Indeed, as Beecher swayed there in the darkness, he could see in his mind's eye just how much better it would be for Marshall to at least have a friend by his side.

But as he stared across at that small basement window—as the buzz of the lawn mower grew louder than ever—Beecher just stood there. And did nothing at all.

It was a decision he'd regret for the rest of his life.

103

One hour ago
Washington, D.C.

The Knight knew how it would end.

Today was a perfect day to kill a President. And in less than an hour, as a fine mist of snow tumbled from the sky, that day would come.

But as the Knight squinted at the silver-and-red tour bus at the end of the block, he understood that the President wasn't the only one who would die today. No. Today was the day that the Knight would die too.

There was no arguing with it. From John Wilkes Booth, to Charles Guiteau, to Leon Czolgosz, to Lee Harvey Oswald, the four men who successfully murdered the President of the United States were all men with a cause. And when their task was complete, all four—every single Knight of the Golden Circle—lost their lives.

At first, the Knight thought he'd find a way around it. That somehow he'd be the one who'd figure out how to escape. But the more he studied his predecessors, the more God's will became clear. Every fraternity had its rituals. And its rites of initiation. Indeed, if Nico had succeeded in killing the President, he'd be dead now too. There was no choice. To join this brotherhood, the cost of admission was life itself. But the reward? As others had said: Blood alone moves the wheels of history.

Up the block, a young couple walked straight at him, hand in hand, both of them looking at their own cell phones. Like every one of his predecessors, the Knight was careful, cautious. On his head, he wore a checkered newsboy cap. On his face he'd glued a fake gray beard. In his shoe he'd tucked a single small pebble, which gave him a convincing and realistic limp. It was an old CIA trick. Changing your face made you hard to spot; changing your walk made you an entirely new person.

Sidestepping the couple and heading farther up the block, the Knight checked every nearby bench, every tree, every parked car. No Secret Service. No undercover agents. And as far as he could tell, no sign of Beecher or any of Wallace's staff.

He could feel it now. It wouldn't be long until his initiation was complete.

For weeks, the Knight had been dreaming of this moment—truly dreaming of it. As he eyed the tour bus in the distance, he wondered if President Wallace had had similar dreams. Wallace wouldn't be the first. Throughout his life, Abraham Lincoln was obsessed with his own dreams. Indeed, on the day he was shot, at what became his final Cabinet meeting, Lincoln told his Cabinet members that the same dream preceded "nearly every great and important event of the war." It was a water dream.

In it, Lincoln said he was in some "singular and indescribable vessel" that was moving fast toward an indefinite shore. He told his Cabinet that he had the same dream that very night, and that it meant great news was coming soon. Within hours, John Wilkes Booth entered Ford's Theatre. Great news *was* coming. Just as it would today.

At the end of the block there was a loud mechanical belch as the silver-and-red tour bus opened its front door and spit a mob of Dutch tourists onto the sidewalk. Taking it as a sign, the Knight lowered his head and slipped into the group's jet stream. As they shuffled diagonally across the street, he walked right past a uniformed member of the Park Police who was standing guard on the corner, near the entrance to the Vietnam Veterans Memorial.

On his right, at the sight of the Lincoln Memorial's grand marble staircase, the Knight's skin began to prickle. In his jacket pocket he fingered the brand-new gun he'd bought for the occasion. In his other pocket was a hunting knife, a set of old playing cards, and the plaster Lincoln mask that he knew was now his totem.

Scanning the crowd and its steady stream of tourists, the Knight picked out two other members of the Park Police, but still no Secret Service agents. For a moment, he was worried he might've misjudged the President—but as always, he trusted in his predecessors.

When the third Knight, Leon Czolgosz, was a boy, he used to go hunting with his brother. Leon always carried the gun. But it was his brother, armed with only a stick and a burlap sack, who was the smart one. Approaching a rabbit hole, his brother would set a small fire on one end of the hole, then cover the other end with the burlap sack. Once the smoke started, like clockwork, the rabbit would take off, scurrying right into the sack. Best of all, there was no blood. Until later.

It was a lesson not lost on the Knight. For days now, from the murder at St. John's to this morning at the hospital, everyone thought these were copycat crimes or some sad tribute to Nico's early days. But for the Knight, each attack was simply a small fire.

At this moment, he'd sent Beecher scurrying down one rabbit hole, and the President down another. All the Knight had to do was hold tight to the burlap sack.

"*U ziet de architectuur,*" the Dutch tour leader announced, leading the crowd along the main plaza and pointing out the Reflecting Pool on their left. Just ahead, a tourist carrying a tennis bag glanced around, pretending to enjoy the sight. Undercover Secret Service, the Knight knew. Tennis bags were where they hid the M-4 assault rifles.

Sticking to the base of the famous steps, the group of Dutch tourists headed for the open door on the far left side of the monument.

Just ahead, a small sign showed pictograms for men's and women's restrooms and a bright white arrow that pointed dead ahead. Through the open door, beyond the restrooms, was a small museum exhibit and a wheelchair-accessible elevator for those who couldn't walk the steps to the statuary chamber. But what the sign didn't say was that there was also a mechanical and electrical room that ran underneath the monument and out the back of it, making it the ultimate private entrance for a President who wanted to make a surprise unannounced visit.

Feeling his skin prickle more than ever, the Knight closed his eyes for a moment, thinking back to the original Knight—the Sacred Knight known as Vignolles. For centuries, he'd been credited with creating the suits that we still see on modern playing cards. Spades, hearts, clubs, and diamonds, each one representing a part of medieval society. But what had been lost to history was the fact that, from the start, there weren't just *four* suits. There were *five*.

Opening his eyes, the Knight still felt the aching soreness from the white ink tattoos he'd drilled into his own body. Four symbols—from his four predecessors—marked his back, his thighs, and his left hand. He did the last ones this morning. All were invisible to the naked eye. But now, as he pulled his left hand from his pocket and looked down at his open palm, he saw the bold black ink (there was no hiding now) of the final symbol—the secret symbol: a small crescent moon. Yes, the four suits represented the parts of society, but it was the moon that represented the final part, the part that made the circle complete: the Enlightened.

"Let's keep it moving!" a member of the Park Police called out, motioning the line forward.

As the Dutch crowd shuffled through the open door, the Knight stood just outside the entrance, waiting patiently to go inside. Looking diagonally upward, toward the very top of the grand marble steps, he couldn't see the statue of Abraham Lincoln. From this angle, it was hidden by the Ionic columns. But the Knight knew what was carved into the marble wall just above Lincoln's head:

IN THIS TEMPLE

AS IN THE HEARTS OF THE PEOPLE FOR WHOM HE SAVED THE UNION

THE MEMORY OF ABRAHAM LINCOLN

IS ENSHRINED FOREVER

Unwrapping a butterscotch candy, the Knight tossed it into his mouth and stepped inside.

He knew how it would end.

In a temple. Just as it was supposed to.

PART V

The Fifth Assassination

"Didn't you ever hear what Queen Victoria wrote to her daughter?

It is worth being shot at—to see how much one is loved."

—*President Orson Wallace, joking around,
two minutes before the gunshot was fired*

104

Eight minutes ago

Soon, they'd all be screaming.

It always started with screaming—then running and scrambling, then the inevitable stampede that the Secret Service had no hope of containing.

But right now, as the heavy bulletproof door of his SUV was tugged open and a light mist of snow tumbled into the car, President Orson Wallace stepped out, all smiles.

His good mood had nothing to do with their current location or the fact that everyone thought he was still at Camp David. It had to do with who he was *with*.

Behind him, following him out of the SUV, Wallace's eleven-year-old daughter, Vanessa, stuck her head outside, instinctively looking around. Their SUV had stopped along the edge of the road on the D.C. side of Memorial Bridge. But to her surprise, there was no crowd waiting, no one cheering, no cell phone flashbulbs popping. It was the same trick they used for Obama's surprise Christmas visit to Iraq . . . and for sneaking President Bush to his daughter's rehearsal dinner before her wedding. Instead of a motorcade, they put the President in a pair of jeans, the leather jacket he never got to wear, and an unmarked black baseball cap—then tossed him in a single SUV that no one would look at twice.

On her far left, pulled up on the grass, was an ambulance parked under one tree, and a black van tucked behind another. The Secret Service had prepositioned a few assets, but all were far enough away that father and daughter truly had something they never got to have: peace and quiet.

"It's just us," Wallace promised, which, really, was the point.

The President was determined not to miss this day. He'd missed so many already. Not the big ones, of course. Nessie's birthdays, her elementary school graduation, even the spring piano recital—those were easy to block out on his calendar. But the small, everyday ones—like Fifth Grade Art Night or the softball game where they gave her a chance to pitch and she struck out two hitters!—those were the days he'd never get back.

When Wallace had first taken office, he heard the stories—about how Chelsea Clinton learned to drive from her Secret Service agents at Andrews Air Force Base. Wallace swore he'd do better than that. But as he learned during the very first days on the job, if you want to be the leader of the free world, sometimes the fifth-grade field trip needs to go on without you.

But not always.

"So. You *excited*?" the President asked, kicking himself for sounding so much like his own overenthusiastic father.

Nessie didn't answer, shooting him the kind of preteen-daughter look that even the Secret Service can't protect you against. Still, as Wallace reached out to help her from the SUV, Nessie reached back, taking her father's hand and holding it in her own.

In just a few minutes, Nessie would be sobbing uncontrollably as a Secret Service agent carried her, clutching her to his chest. But right now, as they walked hand in hand—her thin fingers intertwined in his—the President's day couldn't possibly get any better.

"Sir . . . Miss Nessie—this way, please," A.J. called out, pointing them toward the narrow path that led through the wide-open, snow-covered field behind the Lincoln Memorial.

"Not as good a view as the front, is it?" Wallace asked.

"I like it better from back here," his daughter said, looking up at the enormous symmetrical columns that lined the back of the Memorial. "It's quieter—like it's ours."

"Mmm," the President said in a wordless hum that encompassed the pure joy of simply being alone with his daughter. Or as alone as a President gets. In front of them, a casually dressed Secret Service agent and a similarly dressed military aide—both in unmarked baseball caps—walked at least twenty yards ahead so they wouldn't look like bodyguards. In back of them, A.J. brought up the rear, keeping a similar distance. For a full two minutes, as snow tumbled from above, father and daughter were just two more tourists exploring the nation's capital. Nearing the back of the monument, A.J. whispered something into his hand mic. The President couldn't help but glance over his shoulder. A.J. shot him a knowing nod.

Wallace knew what it meant: Palmiotti had put the meat in the bear trap, and it had finally snapped shut. They had everything they needed at Camp David. Soon, they'd have the rest: Beecher, Nico, Marshall... The President still wasn't sure *how* or *why*—but he knew they were all tied together. And now, whatever fight they were picking, one by one, they'd all go down.

"Sir, this way please," the lead agent called out as he and the military aide approached the back of the Memorial and stopped a few feet shy of the granite base. On cue, from the ground, bits of snow popped as two metal cellar doors opened and a rusted old platform rose upward on an industrial scissor-lift. When the Lincoln Memorial was built back in the 1920s, the scissor-lift helped them lower electrical, mechanical, and plumbing equipment down to the basement level. These days, it lowered Presidents and visiting VIPs.

"Your chariot," the President teased, motioning his daughter toward the steel platform with its three-sided railing. It wasn't big enough to hold all of them. The lead agent and the mil aide went first, thinking they were being safe.

"So you think your friends will be excited to see me?" the President asked as the platform's scissor-lift grunted and screeched, swallowing the first two members of their party.

"Dad, I hate to break it to you, but my friends didn't vote for you."

"That's only because they're eleven," Wallace said as the now empty platform churned upward. When it stopped, the President and Nessie stepped onto it. Joining them, A.J. glanced around, doing his usual recon.

"Goliath and Glowing moving," A.J. said into his hand mic as he squeezed next to Nessie. With the press of a button, the platform rumbled, and all three were eaten, slowly sinking underground.

105

Eighteen years ago
Sagamore, Wisconsin

The drop was longer than he thought.

He was on his stomach, lowering himself feet first through the basement window. While the top half of his body held his weight, his legs kicked in every direction, searching for something to stand on. Chairs. Suitcases. Anything to break his fall.

Finding nothing, Marshall didn't panic. Even if it was four feet...five feet...the basement ceiling wasn't that high. The drop couldn't be that bad. With a quick shove, he slid down on his stomach, like a child on a steep playground slide. But as he picked up speed and the ground still hadn't arrived...the drop was farther than he anticipated.

Off balance, Marshall tumbled on his ass, crashing to the concrete, which, in the dark, felt like it was covered with a thin membrane of fine dirt, the last remnants of all the filth washed up by the dishwasher flood.

Two weeks ago, this room was filled with water. Today, it was dry but smelled of wet books...and something else. Something old.

Climbing to his feet and readjusting his glasses, he reached into his pocket and pulled out a small penlight, trying hard not to think of Pastor Riis entertaining young Bobby McNamera down here. By now, Marshall was sweating, though he didn't think too much of it. Marshall was always sweating.

"Get in, get out," he whispered to himself, remembering Beecher's rules and heading for the bookcase. As the penlight cut through the dark, spider-bugs hopped in every direction. Last time, there were three or four. Now there were dozens, pinging from the floor to the walls and back again. But in the half an eyeblink that it took for Marshall's eyes to adjust, all he cared about was the built-in bookcase, where he saw . . .

Nothing.

The books were gone. The case was picked clean. Forget the porn, even the shelves were taken out.

It was the same with the rest of the room. The file boxes, the folding chairs, the luggage, the brooms, the mops, the milk crates—every single thing that had been stacked up around the room—with that much water damage, it was all removed. That's why the drop from the window was so— Oh jeez.

The window.

Spinning back, Marshall looked up at the small rectangular window that he'd just snuck through. Not only was it shut. It was high. Way above his head.

Panicking, he looked for something to stand on. The room was empty. He reached up, but the way the window was perched just below the basement ceiling, it was too far. As he added a quick jump, his fingers skittered at the ledge, but not enough to take hold. He even tried running at the wall, jumping up and— "*Uff.*"

His chest crashed into the concrete, and the result was the same. The window was too high.

"*Beecher . . . !*" he whisper-hissed. He gave it a moment.

"*Beecher, I'm stuck!*" he whispered again.

But even as he said the words, as he looked up at the closed window like he was praying to God Himself, he knew there'd be no answer.

Sweating hard now, and finally starting to notice, Marshall spun back around. On his left was the doorway that led into the basement's main room. *In there.* Maybe there'd be something to stand on.

Wasting no time, he darted next door, looking for a stepladder, a mop bucket, for anything to boost himself up with. But as he skidded to a stop and another swarm of spider-bugs pounced toward the walls, it was more of the same. Except for the boiler and water heater, the place was picked clean. Even the stairs— He stopped again, doing a double take.

The stairs.

There it was. His way out.

No, don't be stupid, Marshall told himself, knowing better than to take that kind of risk. The last thing he needed was the pastor grabbing him in the kitchen.

Darting back into the other room, Marshall again headed for the high window.

"Beecher, please!" he called out, up on his tiptoes and waving his penlight back and forth like a lighter at a rock concert.

The only response was a skittering noise down by his feet.

The shadow moved fast, disappearing in the corner. Marshall jumped at the sound, spinning with the penlight and barely spotting it. But there was no mistaking the *tkk-tkk-tkk* of tiny claws clicking and scratching against the concrete. Whatever it was, it was way larger than a spider-bug. One thing was clear: Marshall wasn't the only one in the basement.

And that was it.

"Gaaah!" Marshall whisper-yelled, scrubbing at his own skin and racing for the stairs as fast as he could.

He didn't go up. He just stood on the first step, anxious to get on a different plane from whatever it was that had just run through the room. But as he looked up—as the shine from his penlight ricocheted off the stairs' metal treads—he saw that at the top of the stairs, underneath the door to the kitchen, the lights were off. No one was there.

Doesn't matter. Stay where you are, he told himself, shutting the light so the pastor wouldn't see him either.

But the longer Marshall stood there in the dark, reality was sinking in. Beecher wasn't coming. Neither was Paglinni. Plus, it wouldn't be long until his mom started panicking, wondering why he wasn't home. Unless he planned on sleeping with the spider-bugs and whatever animal was running around down here, he was running out of options.

Glancing toward the top of the steps, he could hear the rise and fall of his own breathing. The sweat was pouring down his chest, making his shirt stick to his stomach.

He wished there was another way. But there wasn't.

Slowly and carefully, he shifted his weight to the second step, whose old wood let out a loud creak. Marshall stopped in place, his eyes locked underneath the kitchen door. Still dark. No one there.

Taking a breath, he gently made his way to the third step, then the fourth.

Step by step, he climbed slowly in the dark, listening for even a hint of anyone upstairs. At the top, on the second-to-last step, his heart sank as he grabbed the wooden doorknob. What if it was locked? What if it was...?

Kllk.

The latch gave easily, pulling its tongue from the strikeplate and freeing the door to open. Gently...carefully...Marshall eased it open, pressing his face so close to the threshold, the corner of his glasses scratched against the doorframe.

The smell of fresh bread hit him first. At his feet, a lone spider-bug pounced out onto the worn linoleum.

Otherwise, the kitchen was dark and empty. The only sound was—

"*Oh, God...Oh, Lord...*"

It was a woman's voice—faint—coming from one of the front rooms. At first, Marshall thought it was a prayer...someone was hurt.

To be honest, Marshall didn't care. He was moving too fast, already eyeing the back door, ready to shove it open and escape through the yard. But as he took his first steps, he couldn't help but turn. That voice...

He knew that voice.

Stopping on the linoleum, he glanced over his shoulder, back toward the living room.

That sounded just like his mother.

106

Six minutes ago
Washington, D.C.

You okay? the President asked his daughter with just a look.

Nessie nodded, but was still holding tight to the railing of the scissor-lift. As the platform descended underground, below the Lincoln Memorial, a dark shadow rose up, enveloping them.

"What is this place?" Nessie asked, her eyes squinting and adjusting as the white brightness of the snowy day was replaced by a damp, poorly lit basement that smelled of mud, rainwater, and oil. With a final *thunk*, the platform locked into place and the cellar doors in the ceiling clamped shut, stealing the gray sky with it.

"Mechanical room," A.J. explained, pointing around at the roomful of huge industrial equipment. "These are the generators that light up Lincoln and his famous columns. Plus you need a boiler, chiller, and a water supply in case there's a fire or other emergency. Every tourist attraction in the world—from the Eiffel Tower to the Pyramids in Egypt—they've all got one of these below it," he added, trying to be reassuring.

Nessie still didn't release her grip on the railing.

"Don't worry, there're no spiders," her father finally said. Turning to A.J., he added, "She's not worried about the dark. She hates spiders. Always has."

Following them off the platform, Nessie didn't argue. She was too busy looking around at the peeling ceiling, the cracks along the

383

concrete wall, and even some old graffiti. The machinery was relatively new, but the room hadn't been updated in nearly a century.

"Nessie, I promise you—if we see any spiders, I'll have A.J. shoot them," the President said.

Not amused, Nessie let go of his hand. "Just FYI, Dad, one of the other chaperones...Emily Deutchman's dad...she said her father didn't vote for you either."

Wallace grinned his presidential grin. "You saying I need to turn on the charm?"

"No, I'm—" Nessie caught herself, knowing her father too well. "Dad, *I'm serious*... If you— Don't even talk to him, okay?" she threatened, following the lead agent and the mil aide up the room's main aisle. Behind them, A.J. brought up the rear.

With the twisting pipes and enormous machinery, plus the natural darkness of the basement, the room was truly a metal maze. Making a sharp right at a giant water tank, the mil aide stood still, waiting for the President to pass as A.J. rotated forward. Now A.J. and the lead agent were in front, and the mil aide was in back. Upside-down triangle formation.

At each twist and turn, the triangle shifted again, so someone was always on watch as the President turned a dark corner. They still had no idea how soon the screaming would start.

"So this girl Emily's father, is he the one I met at parent-teacher night...with the thin blond hair?" the President asked.

"Dad, I'm not joking. If you say something..."

"A.J., did you just hear that? Nessie was about to threaten me."

Ignoring the joke and reaching the end of the room, A.J. and the lead agent climbed a set of cracked concrete steps toward a thick metal door that was marked *Plaza Level*. The President had come this way before during the concert for his Inauguration. Through here was the small museum exhibit and the elevator that would take them up to the statuary chamber. A.J. disappeared through the door, checking the hallway.

"Y'know, you really should be nice to me," the President chided his daughter. "Today *is* Presidents' Day."

"That's only for dead Presidents," Nessie teased back. "And good Presidents...like Lincoln and Washington."

"You're joking, right? Do you have any idea how many people want me dead?"

At that, Nessie tucked her chin down, pulling away. "Dad, that's *not* funny."

"What're you talking about? Didn't you ever hear what Queen Victoria wrote to her daughter?" Putting on a quick British accent, he added, *"It is worth being shot at—to see how much one is loved."*

"Sir, we've got the all-clear," the lead agent called out from the top of the stairs, cracking the door slightly wider. Fluorescent light from the hallway lit the left side of his face. "Right this way."

Heading up the concrete steps with the mil aide behind him, the President placed his hand on the small of his daughter's back, ushering her in front of him. At the top of the steps, the open door led out into a short, perpendicular hallway. The Service had blocked it off, probably with something simple like a *Wet Floor* sign. But from the far left of the hallway, they could still hear the echoes of bustling tourists making their way back and forth toward the restrooms and the exhibit.

"We've got the elevator. Sharp right, sir," the lead agent whispered to the President as he approached. Like before, at the open door, the lead agent held his position and let Wallace, Nessie, and the mil aide pass as the triangle once again shifted.

In a quick, almost balletic movement—while keeping his head down and using his baseball cap to hide his face—the President of the United States followed his daughter out into the hallway, holding her shoulders and steering her to the right. They pivoted quickly, leaving just enough room on their left—back where the tourists were—for the mil aide to follow them into the hallway, where he used his body to block any clear view of the President.

"You're getting the hang of this, Nessie," A.J. said as they joined him on the waiting elevator, followed by the mil aide and the lead agent. As the doors began to close, Wallace and his daughter were at the back of the elevator. Still, the President couldn't help but stare out at the empty hallway—and the perpendicular one at the far end of it. Just as Wallace lifted his cap, a black woman in a black winter coat turned his way. Their eyes locked as the doors chomped shut.

"She *saw* you." Nessie laughed.

"She didn't. Not with my awesome baseball cap on. This thing is satellite-proof."

For a moment, the five of them smiled to themselves as the elevator silently rose toward the statuary chamber. In less than a minute, Nessie's classmates would all stop and turn, making her the true center of attention and the envy of every kid there. Nessie would never have said it, but this was one of those moments where she was happy—truly happy—that her father was the most powerful man in the world.

Feeding off his daughter's excitement, the President nodded a quick thank-you to A.J.—for taking care of everything with Beecher.

In thirty seconds, the screaming would begin.

"You know what you're gonna say?" Nessie challenged.

"What kinda tour guide do you think I am? I did *research*," Wallace said, patting his jacket pocket at the one-sheet his staff had prepared for him. "Did you know that Lincoln's statue was carved from twenty-eight blocks of Georgia marble? Or that there's a U.S. flag draped across the back of his chair? Or that his head is slanted down so that his eyes meet yours? Trust me, this President knows his Presidents' Day facts," he said as Nessie's smile spread even wider.

The elevator slowed, bobbing to a stop. A.J. and the lead agent angled forward. They'd be the first ones out, vetting the crowd. With surprise visits like this, it took at least four minutes before strangers realized what was going on, and even then, they didn't believe it. With the baseball hat and the crowd of kids around him, it might take even longer than that. No one looks twice at school field trips.

In that pregnant moment when the elevator had settled but the doors still hadn't opened, Wallace lifted his smile into place. Through the doors, he could hear the crowd outside, their voices bouncing through the limestone chamber.

"Dad, just promise me . . . about Emily's father," Nessie said, tugging at his arm.

Looking down, he shot her a playful look, a look she knew well. He didn't have to say it. He'd never do anything—in this entire world—to hurt his daughter.

With a clank, the elevator doors parted. The President lowered his cap and again put his hands on his daughter's shoulders, steering her behind A.J. As they stepped outside, the cold wind felt good against their faces, and they blew right past the few people waiting to get on the elevator. Not one of them noticed that the man with the lowered baseball cap was the President of the United States.

Across the chamber, an undercover Secret Service agent sat on one of the marble benches, pretending to read a newspaper. Another stood in the corner, and another on the right side of the statue, both carrying tennis bags. On the left side of the statue, but at least ten feet away from it, a crowd of ten- and eleven-year-olds bounced on their feet, in the exact spot where they had been told to wait.

On cue, a few kids started to turn. One of them—one of Nessie's friends—began to point as she realized who was coming. *"Nessie!"* another girl yelled as Nessie's smile bloomed wider than ever. They were yelling *her* name. Not her dad's. One by one, the rest of the kids began to turn . . . began to look . . . began to smile.

Yet as Wallace made his way through the chamber, he wasn't looking at the kids. Or the hidden agents. Or even at any of the dozens of tourists snapping photos in every direction. No, at this moment, with his head craned upward, with two agents in front of him and the mil aide behind him, the only thing the President of the United States was looking at was the towering 175-ton white marble statue of Abraham Lincoln clutching the armrests of his chair.

He didn't even notice the bearded old man in the checkered newsboy cap who was standing to the side of the elevator.

As Wallace passed by him, the man leaned forward, like he was finishing a sneeze. But as the man stood up straight, what Wallace and his agents missed was that he was now wearing a plaster mask.

"Dad, lookit," Nessie said, pointing back over her own shoulder. "That guy...he's actually dressed like Abraha—"

President Orson Wallace turned. So did the mil aide.

Neither was fast enough.

The Knight reached into his pocket.

There was a soft *pffft*. Like a muffled gunshot.

Then a burst of blood.

Then there was nothing but screaming.

107

Eighteen years ago
Sagamore, Wisconsin

Marshall should've never turned the corner.

He knew it too. He knew it from the moment he heard that noise coming from the living room. He knew it the moment he left the kitchen. Indeed, as he tiptoed down the hallway that was lined with vacation photos of the pastor and his wife, he felt the universe pushing him back, warning him away.

The problem was, he knew that voice.

Every child knows his mother's voice. Just like they know their mother's sneeze. And even the sound she was making right now— an indistinct moan that sounded like she was mumbling in her sleep, or twisting in pain.

Hours from now, as the tidal wave of gossip plowed through the town, everyone would say that Marshall knew...that he came here because he was angry and suspicious of his mom and Pastor Riis. But right now, as the chubby twelve-year-old reached the end of the hallway, about to step into the dimly lit living room with its flickering TV lights, anger was nowhere in Marshall's makeup. No, as he swallowed hard, feeling like his tongue was stuck in his throat, Marshall was worried. He was confused. That noise his mom was making...

He just wanted to make sure she was okay.

"Mom, are you—?"

As Marshall turned the corner, his mouth was still open, mid-syllable. The first thing his brain registered were two candles, side by side, their flames flickering as they burned on the end table, next to the floral-print sofa. That's why the room was so dim.

But as Marshall entered the room, he saw more than the end table. He saw the sofa. And who was on it.

Marshall froze. He saw her bare back first...and the beauty mark just below her left shoulder blade. She had no top on. But what made him completely confused were the two arms wrapped around his mother's neck. Someone was hugging her. Someone with freshly painted pink nails. And pale breasts.

"Mrs. Riis...?" Marshall stuttered, staring at the woman everyone called Cricket.

"Cherise, move...!" the pastor's wife exclaimed, pushing Marshall's mother aside.

"Mom...what're you—? What's happening?"

His mom twisted to face him as she struggled to cover her bare breasts with her hands. Their gazes locked—mother and son—both their eyes wide with terror that slowly shifted to—

"What're you doing here!? Get out!" his mom exploded, stumbling, spinning, grabbing clothes to cover herself. She was naked. Naked with Pastor Riis's wife.

"You didn't see this! You hear me!? You didn't see this!" his mom shouted in a tone Marshall had never heard before.

"Get him out of here!" the pastor's wife screamed, grabbing sofa pillows to cover herself.

Marshall tried to turn and run. But his feet were locked, like they were bolted to the carpet. His eyes swelled with tears.

"Oh, Lord, we're dead..." the pastor's wife whispered, now starting to cry.

"You didn't see this!" his mother kept yelling, racing toward him. She pressed her shirt against her chest with one hand. With her other, she clumsily pulled on her skirt.

Across the room, Marshall just stood there, horrified by the shadowy glimpse of his mom's pubic hair.

"They'll call us abominations. We're abominations," the pastor's wife sobbed.

"Did your father send you here!?" his mother shouted as she threw on her blouse and snatched her bra and lemon yellow blazer off the floor.

"No, I—"

"It's okay. It'll be fine," his mom insisted, her voice softening but still racing. "We'll go home and it'll be fine."

She grabbed Marshall by the back of the neck, twisting him around and shoving him back up the main hallway, toward the front door.

"You didn't see this," she added, still holding her bra against her chest. "If you didn't see this—if your father doesn't know—we're okay."

"Dad didn't do nothing!" Marshall pleaded, crying, stumbling, barely able to stay on his feet. His mom's blazer fell to the floor. She didn't stop to get it.

As they reached the front door, his mother let go of her son for the three seconds it took to fight with the doorknob. "Don't run away. Come back," she said, gripping him again. "It'll be fine—"

She was still yelling as the door flew open, bathing them in yellow porchlight. But as they crashed down the front steps and into the warm night, Marshall's mom was moving so fast...and holding Marshall's fat neck so tight...and still clutching her bra in her hand...

...she didn't even notice that Beecher and Paglinni were standing right there, watching everything from the driveway.

108

Two minutes ago
Washington, D.C.

The Knight didn't rush.

He was patient, with his head down, pretending to look at his watch as the elevator doors slowly opened.

The President exited calmly, without a fuss, stepping off the elevator and making his way through the small crowd waiting to take it down. Well past the crowd, midway through the chamber, the Knight still didn't look up. He saw it all out of the corner of his eyes, counting three agents plus Wallace's daughter.

The Knight's skin tingled. He didn't have to approach the President. From where he was standing, Wallace was approaching him.

The Knight had practiced for this moment. Prayed for it. Like his predecessors, he had run through every detail. *Every* detail, including putting on the mask. For hours, for days now, the Knight had taken out the mask and slipped it on, taken it out and slipped it on, over and over, until he had it down to one quick movement.

Seeing President Wallace delivered to him like this, the Knight knew his prayers were about to be answered.

The President was about to pass him. Leaning forward, the Knight reached into his pocket, palming the front of his plaster mask. At just the touch of it, as his fingers scraped against its chalkiness, muscle memory took over. Time froze. Life moved frame by frame as the two agents in front of the President seemed to float by like life-size parade floats. Two steps behind them, as the Knight pulled the mask from his pocket, the President and his daughter floated by too. Same with the mil aide in back of them. As they passed, the Knight couldn't help but grin. He was diagonally behind them all now. None of them had even noticed him.

They were all locked on their destination—on the group of kids across the chamber. As the President got closer, a few kids began to turn. One of them, a girl with big cheeks and brutal-looking braces, lifted her hand, beginning to point as she realized who was coming. Another began to mouth the President's daughter's name. One by one, the rest of the kids began to turn...began to look...began to smile. The Knight's plaster Lincoln mask was firmly in place.

"Dad, lookit," Nessie announced, pointing back at the Knight. "That guy...he's actually dressed like Abraha—"

President Orson Wallace turned. So did the mil aide.

The Knight reached into his jacket pocket, where his gun—

No. His gun was gone. How could that—?

Pffft.

Something with burning teeth bit into the Knight's lower back.

Grabbing at his own back and clutching at the pain, his finger hit a hole. In his back. There was a hole in his lower back.

He looked down at his stomach. It was soaked...and red... Blood. His *own* blood, seeping and spreading down to his waist.

He'd been shot. Someone...someone...

"Why?" a barbed wire of a voice growled closely behind him.

The Knight teetered, spinning to face his shooter, who was holding the Knight's gun. The man wore a bright red scarf that covered the lower half of his face. But under the scarf...there was something wrong with the shooter's skin. Like it was melted.

Cocking his head, the Knight felt his eyesight go blurry, then come back again. He knew the man—the man with the melted skin—the man who had just shot him and saved the President's life: That was Marshall.

"Why did you kill Pastor Riis!?" Marshall demanded, reaching for the Knight's mask.

The answer never came.

People were screaming, scattering in every direction.

"*Shots fired! Shots fired!*" someone yelled.

In a blur, undercover agents plowed into Marshall and the Knight. Both men went limp, their heads snapping sideways and backwards as they plummeted like tackling dummies. Yet as Marshall fell—the Knight could see it on his face—he was calm, unconcerned. It's what made Marshall so dangerous. He didn't care about himself.

As he hit the floor face-first, the Knight's mask shattered. Half its pieces skittered outward; the other half chewed into the Knight's face, peeling away the fake beard, finding blood, and revealing a man with a dimpled chin and a boxer's nose.

Chestdown next to him, Marshall knew him immediately—from the shooting at Foundry Church: the pastor. The pastor who was shot...who fell to the carpet...and who lived. The same pastor who took the Christmas photo with the rabbi and the imam... and who was in the hospital chapel when both the chaplain and Tot were attacked.

"I didn't do anything!" Pastor Frick yelled as they tore through his pockets. "*He* shot *me!*"

"*Knife!*" a Secret Service agent shouted from the dogpile that smothered Pastor Frick. From Frick's pocket, he pulled out the hunting knife with the curly birch handle.

"*Go, go—move!*" an agent yelled across the chamber.

In the distance, a group of agents formed a human wall around the President, gripping him by the elbows, lifting his feet off the ground, and rushing him to the preselected saferoom. At the back of the statuary chamber was a door that led to the Park Police's breakroom. Racing behind them, A.J. scooped Wallace's daughter into his arms.

"Your dad's fine. He's fine," A.J. whispered, following the group to the saferoom as, shaking, she sobbed into his chest.

Still pinned facedown, Pastor Frick let out a wordless howl as the Secret Service drilled their knees into his lower back—into his wound—and cuffed his hands behind him. They didn't care that he'd been shot—or that he couldn't feel his legs—or that unlike the wound he'd so carefully inflicted on himself in his office, this wasn't the kind of attack he'd walk away from. Marshall had gone for vital organs.

Across from him, under his own dogpile and with his own hands cuffed behind his back, Marshall didn't struggle...didn't say a word. Chin to the ground, he simply stared at Pastor Frick—his gold eyes burning with that first question he'd asked: *Why did you kill Pastor Riis?*

Still on the ground, with his bloody cheek pressed against the bits and pieces of his mask, Frick could barely see anything. The world was still blurry, the edges of his vision ringed by a red circle that began to shrink and tighten, leaving only black. Frick tried to answer...he looked at Marshall and said the words: *Nico told me to.*

Nico told me to! he insisted.

But all that came out was a wet gurgle. It came up from Frick's chest, up his throat, rattling like a bag of teeth.

Indeed, as the red circle continued to tighten and blackness filled his peripheral vision, Pastor Frick's final thoughts were of the simple fact that, all this time, he had it all wrong.

For years now, Frick had heard the rumblings and rumors about the Knights and John Wilkes Booth. But it wasn't until four months ago, when the church picked Associate Pastor Frick and put him *here*—right in Abraham Lincoln's church that he began to understand God's message. Surely, this was fate.

And then, to get the call that President Wallace was coming to visit. Frick had known the President wasn't a churchgoer. Wallace attended on Easter, on holidays...only when there was a camera around. But now, with the President coming, here it was. Every life exists for a reason. This would be Frick's chance to bring faith to millions.

Yet what Wallace did on Christmas—using Frick's church and Frick himself, bringing the rabbi and imam, then parading the three of them together like cheap interchangeable toys, as if one size would fit all. For the millions watching, and for Frick himself, it *was* a blasphemy.

During those days, Frick understood the real reason why God had sent him to Lincoln's church. Here in D.C., he could feel the church's greatest threat raising its head once again. Every President has power; so too does the church. But to Frick, it was now clear why the balance between the two was shifting. Rather than looking to the church for moral guidance, the world watched as the President trivialized the name of Christ and everything it stood for.

Was it any wonder that congregations were shrinking, members were disengaged, or that some refused to believe altogether? Today's church was being reduced to a community center where people were bribed with Date Nights and fruit smoothies. It was time for the pollution to stop, for the sacrilege to end, and for the pure church, with its intended purpose, to make its return.

The President didn't even hide his goal—he said it right to Frick's face: He would bring all three voices...Christian, Jewish, Muslim...the President would do everything in his power to bring the country together. *Like Lincoln! Like JFK! Like every king whose growing influence would challenge church power.* The church had lost so much lately. It couldn't afford to lose more.

Frick knew he'd need help. He knew he couldn't do it alone. That's what made him seek someone with experience and inspired him to reach out to Nico. And then to learn that one of his congregants—that Rupert—that Rupert worked with Nico... And to hear Nico's stories and all that had gone before...

Centuries ago, Vignolles created the Knights to protect the Name of God. But even Vignolles knew that what he was really protecting was the church's power. When that power shifted between church and state, Knights like Booth, Guiteau, Czolgosz, and Oswald stepped forward to restore a proper balance. Now it was Frick's turn. Someone had to stop this civil war and end this blasphemy.

With Nico's help, it was all so clear. How could this not be Frick's mission? *He thought he was chosen! Frick was the final Knight!* But to look at it now, to look around and see the pieces that remained . . . No, now Frick understood: It was never *he* who was Chosen. From the start, he had it wrong. The Chosen One was always . . .

Nico.

Nico was the final Knight. And his mission was just beginning.

It was that final thought—of Nico and the mission still to come—that sputtered through Frick's brain as the red circle shrank into a pinhole and the world went black. That and the fact that he'd been right about one thing: He wouldn't survive this day.

109

I t was a small funeral. Not by choice.

In a town as watchful and religious as Sagamore, judgments moved even quicker than gossip. Especially gossip like this.

At the close of the funeral, they called on Marshall as one of the pallbearers. His father too. But since a twelve-year-old and a double amputee can't be relied on to lift anything heavy, he and his dad simply put their open palms on the back of the coffin as it was rolled on the metal scissor-cart out to the hearse.

That was this morning.

It was dark now, nearly ten o'clock. Yet for Marshall, who was sitting alone on the treehouse carpet, in the glow of one little lantern, glaring down through the Plexiglas window at the last few visitors leaving his house, that wasn't even the hard part. The funeral was already a blur. It'd been nearly a week since his mother crouched down in her walk-in closet, prayed the rosary, then put a gun in her mouth and pulled the trigger. At this point, filled with so much anguish and rage, he just wanted everyone to stop telling him that it would all be okay. Even twelve-year-olds know when they're being lied to.

"Knock, knock, Marsh—you there?" his father called, rolling out to the treehouse when everyone was finally gone.

Marshall didn't answer.

"Buddy, you okay? You been up there all night," his father added.

Still no response. And unlike the past few nights, when Marshall insisted on sleeping in the treehouse, his father didn't press. Plus, as Marshall knew, even if he did, it wasn't like his dad could climb up and bring him down.

For that reason, twenty minutes later, Marshall sat up straight in his beanbag chair when he heard someone climbing the ladder rungs nailed to the tree.

"Whoever it is, I hear you," Marshall warned.

No one replied.

"Beecher, if it's you, get the hell out," Marshall added even though he knew that while Beecher's mom had let him attend the funeral, she had forbidden him to pay any more visits to the treehouse. It was the same with Paglinni. And the rest. No one told him directly, but after a week of sitting alone in a beanbag, Marshall got the point.

"You taking visitors?" a familiar voice asked.

From the ladder, Pastor Riis peered over the floorboards, his normally neat hair looking scruffy and overgrown in the dim light.

"Go away," Marshall said, disgusted.

"It's a hard day. I came to see how you're doing."

"You shouldn't be here."

"Says who?" the pastor challenged.

Shifting in his beanbag chair, Marshall thought about it. He didn't have an answer.

"I heard the funeral was . . . *uff* . . . I heard it was beautiful," the pastor said, hoisting himself up and climbing into the treehouse.

"No one showed," Marshall said, refusing to look up. "It was practically empty."

"I heard. And I'm sorry I couldn't be there. I really wanted to."

Rolling his eyes but refusing to turn and face him, Marshall stared down at the worn and filthy carpet.

"Marshall, you know I couldn't be there, no matter how much it hurt me. And I promise you, it hurt me."

Hearing a crack in the pastor's voice, Marshall looked up. Not out of concern. Or sympathy. Marshall was damaged goods, his eyes filled with a darkness that came from getting a good hard look at what life eventually offers all of us. When Pastor Riis saw those eyes, he knew it was a darkness that Marshall would carry forever.

Riis took a seat on a nearby milk crate. When he was on the pulpit, the pastor stood tall and vibrant. Today he looked ten years older, hunched forward as he fidgeted with a stray thread that dangled from the wrist of his sweater.

"I heard they fired you from the church," Marshall finally offered.

"They had no choice."

Marshall nodded, though it still made no sense. What Paglinni saw, when he ran home and the word got out... He told his parents it was Pastor Riis and Marshall's mom. But the pastor wasn't even there. It was Riis's wife who— Marshall closed his eyes. "Why didn't you tell them the truth?" he said.

"She's my wife, Marshall."

"But she's the one who—"

"She's my *wife*. Bound by God. To care and protect," he insisted in that voice that could keep an entire town quiet for hours at a time. "Nothing would've changed if people heard the truth. Not for any of us." Pausing a moment, he added, "That includes your mom too."

Grabbing the side of the beanbag chair, Marshall pinched it until he was squeezing just a single bean of foam between his thumb and his forefinger.

"I know you're thinking something, Marshall. Just say it."

Marshall squeezed the bead of foam even tighter.

"You want to know about my wife, don't you? And what she and your mom—"

"Don't talk about my mom," Marshall growled.

"Then tell me what you're thinking. Tell me something."

Twisting lower in the beanbag, Marshall felt a swirl of questions racing through his brain. He *did* want to know about the pastor's wife. He wanted to know how long it went on, and how serious it was, and if anyone else knew. But more than anything else, he wanted to know if his own mom...what she did with the gun... He wanted to know if she was in love, or did she just hate having to take care of him and his dad?

But instead, Marshall said nothing, squeezing the bead of foam so hard, it flattened in his fingertips.

"Marshall, I can't pretend to have known your mom very well," Pastor Riis finally said. "But I do know this. Your mother loved you. And despite what you're so intensely feeling, she loved your family."

"That means you don't know the answer."

"No. It means everything is complicated. No one has all the answers."

It was as true a statement as Pastor Riis had ever uttered, but that didn't mean it helped Marshall, who was still glaring down at the carpet.

"Let me ask you this, Marshall. When a tornado hits, which is a better use of your time: wondering why your house blew down—or figuring out how to rebuild?"

"You gave that speech this past Easter. This is where I'm supposed to say that I need to rebuild."

"You disagree?"

"If you don't figure out why the house blew down, how can you rebuild it so it's strong enough so that it won't happen again?"

"You're missing the point, Marshall. Even the strongest house can be knocked down by a big enough tornado. And those really big ones? There's no predicting their path, or trying to understand, much less control, what can't be."

"So you're saying my mom's a tornado?"

"No, what I'm saying is, you already have all the tools to build your house. And I promise you one thing: It'll be a great one."

Marshall gave no answer.

"I found a new parish. It's a small one," the pastor finally said. "In Toledo."

Marshall nodded.

"And I heard you're moving to Michigan," Riis added.

"My dad's sister. If we stay with her, she said she'd help with my dad."

"Family's important," the pastor agreed.

Shifting again in the beanbag, Marshall slowly looked up, glancing over at the pastor.

"Y'know that day when your basement flooded," Marshall began, "I stole a stack of magazines that were down there."

"I know. I saw you," Pastor Riis said. "They weren't mine. We confiscate them every few months and just toss them down there. Cricket's always worried about people seeing them in the church trash."

"You're not listening," Marshall insisted, his voice starting to speed. "When I came back last week…to your basement…it was because I thought you snuck into my room—"

"Marshall, I'd never—"

"I know. I know that now," Marshall stuttered, feeling the tears swelling behind his eyes, but refusing to let them out. "I found them a few days ago in my dad's closet…when I was helping him clean up. *He's* the one who took them from my room. But if I didn't go back to your house…back into your basement…If I didn't see my mom and Mrs. Riis—" Fighting the tears, he started to gasp, struggling to catch his breath as a week's worth of horrors cracked the dam in his chest, flooding forward. "*Oh, God, don't you see what I've done!? I killed my mom!*"

"Marshall, this is not your fault. Your mother killed herself. You're not responsible."

"No, that's not true! This is God's punishment. *This is for what I did…! I'm so sorry…!*" he said, sobbing and sinking downward.

Pastor Riis knelt by the beanbag, taking Marshall in his arms. "That's not how God works, Marshall. Are you hearing me? God doesn't work like that," Riis said as Marshall crumpled against his chest.

For several minutes, Marshall sobbed, sniffling over and over. Finally, the storm subsided. He was exhausted.

"I will say, though, I think you ruined my sweater," Pastor Riis joked, pointing to the gob of snot that was now on his chest.

Even Marshall had to laugh, pulling away, lifting his glasses, and wiping his eyes with the heel of his hand. "I'm—I'm just so sorry I caused so much pain for you."

"You owe me no apologies," the pastor said. "The experienced life is far more fulfilling than the blissful and innocent life. Y'know who said that?"

"Jesus."

"No, not Jesus. William Blake. He's pretty good too."

Marshall smiled at that. "Still doesn't change the fact that my mom's gone. I ruined my life."

Taking a seat back on the milk crate, Pastor Riis gave a sharp tug to the thread at his wrist, snapping it from the sweater. "Marshall, y'ever hear of Harry Houdini?"

"Of course. I did a book report on him last year. World's greatest magician."

"And escape artist. Magician and escape artist. And did you know he was from Wisconsin? Not far from here."

"In Appleton—I know. That was in the report too."

"Then you know that after his father died, his mother wanted him to take a factory job that would help support the family. Instead, Houdini followed his heart, literally joined the circus, and eventually became the most famous performer of his time. Such a great story, right? But of all his achievements, you know what Houdini's greatest escape was?"

"The one where he's in a coffin at the bottom of a pool for an hour and a half?"

"That's the trick that killed him. Not his finest."

"What about the water torture one, where he's tied up and lowered into a fish tank?"

"Nope."

"I don't know... The one where he jumps from the bridge... or where they stuff him in a milk jug... They're all the same."

"You're right. They are all the same. But y'know which escape is his best, Marshall? When Houdini left Wisconsin. And moved on with his life."

Turning toward the pastor, Marshall sniffled hard, sucking

everything inside. He stared down, through the Plexiglas window, at the roof of his house. His old house.

"Pastor Riis, can I ask you a dumb question? How far is Toledo from Michigan?"

"Barely an hour. Why?"

"No, no reason. I was just thinking, if you're ever bored or something, I dunno... Maybe you could come for a visit. Or something."

Sitting on his milk crate, Pastor Riis leaned his elbows on his knees, and grinned with just his eyes. "I'd like that. And even when I'm not bored, if you ever need anyone to talk to, or want to hear me steal quotes from my old sermons, just let me know and I'll be there too."

He meant it.

Over the course of the next decade, Pastor Riis would stay in touch with Marshall, offering advice, visiting Michigan, and (though he never told Marshall) helping out financially when Marshall's dad got sick and the hospital bills again began to pile up. Even when Marshall's dad got better, and a teenage Marshall got arrested after that incident in East Lansing, and arrested again in his twenties, Pastor Riis would check in, still write, and still work to keep Marshall out of the trouble that always seemed to find him.

Indeed, it was Riis who would first suggest that Marshall enlist with the military, since Riis was a military man himself. It was a decision that would change Marshall forever.

So, three weeks ago, when Marshall heard about Pastor Riis's death, and found out that someone had shot him in the chest with an obscure old gun, Marshall swore he would tear the gates of hell off their hinges to find the person responsible.

"Maybe we can plan something for Christmas break. Or even earlier," Pastor Riis offered, standing from the milk crate and ducking down slightly in the treehouse.

"Sure," Marshall said, watching Pastor Riis climb down the ladder rungs, not really believing he'd ever see the pastor again.

*   *   *

110

Today
Camp David

My wrists hurt.

So does my back.

I've lost track of time. It feels like seven or eight at night, but since the shelter has no windows, it's hard to know for sure. I'm still hunched on the edge of the bed, my hands still cuffed to the metal footboard.

For the first few hours, they asked questions nonstop: about Marshall, and the Knight, and about what I knew and didn't know about the foiled attack on the President. I saw most of it onscreen, including Frick and Marshall. When the Service finally left, I knew we weren't done. But when an hour went by and no one returned, it made no sense. Then a second hour went by. Then a third, making me wonder if they'd forgotten about me. It's almost nighttime now.

Leaning toward the metal door, I listen, trying to see if anyone's coming. The problem is, the whole shelter has an odd metallic hum, most likely from whatever generators are down here. Closing my eyes, I focus harder, listening through the noise. Above me, a wisp of warm air blows from the air ducts. Every once in a while, there's a *click-clack* of someone walking the hallway. But from the faint rumble of voices coming from the room across the hall, at least half a dozen agents are still gathered together in one place.

Until they're not.

The rumbling comes quick, pounding out into the hallway, toward the metal stairwell. They're moving fast, with purpose.

"Viv, stay here," Agent Reed calls back as the stampede rises upward. Within seconds, the submarine door slams shut, everything goes silent, and I'm still alone, handcuffed to the bed.

I'm tempted to scream for someone to let me out. But in the underground shelter below Camp David, the Secret Service only moves like that for one person.

All this time, I thought they were working me over. What they were really doing was making me wait.

For him.

From above, the submarine door again opens with a loud pop. There's no stampede this time, just a lonely *ting-ting* of footsteps clanging against the metal treads. These aren't the steel-toed boots that most of the agents wear. The sound is softer, like dress shoes.

There's a long silent pause. I lean toward the door, trying to hear, but my heart is drumrolling too loudly.

With a soft *click*, the lock unclenches and the metal door to my room swings open, revealing a man wearing a black leather jacket and palming a cup of tea in fine bone china. He looks down at me with the world's most famous gray eyes.

President Orson Wallace.

"Sir, if you need us..." Agent Reed announces, sticking his head in and making sure I'm still handcuffed to the bed.

"He'll be fine," insists a younger agent, who fits the description of A.J. As the President steps into the room, A.J. stays in the hallway. Whatever's about to happen, it's not happening in front of anyone.

Shooting a final look at the President, A.J. tugs the door shut but doesn't lock us inside. I get the message. If anything bad happens, they'll be in here within seconds.

Taking a sip of tea and letting the silence take hold, Wallace is unreadable as always. As he walks toward the center of the room, it's the first time I realize his other hand has been in his pocket the entire time.

"Y'know, most people stand when I enter a room," the President says.

I stay where I am, shackled in a sitting position at the foot of the bed.

"That was a joke, Beecher." He shakes his head. "Would you like me to have them get you some tea?" the President adds. "Red robe oolong. The Chinese government always brings it as a gift. It's quite good."

I pull on my handcuffs just hard enough that he knows what I think of his oolong tea.

Next to the bed, the President spots a metal chair, but he stays where he is, taking another sip of tea and standing over me.

"What do you want from me, Wallace?"

"I want you to know, I'm not your enemy, Beecher."

I'm silent.

"I realize you want to see me as the bad guy, but I'm not the bad guy here. Not in this one."

I study his face, then look away.

"Actually, I came to say thank you," he goes on. "For trying to save my life. And my daughter's too." Taking a final sip, he sets his teacup on the edge of the metal chair. "Whatever else you think of me, Beecher, I know that's the reason you drove to Camp David. To keep me and my family safe."

I shift in my seat. It's the one point even I can't argue with.

"I assume you also had something to do with sending Marshall there," the President says. "He's an old friend of yours, yes?" When I don't answer, he adds, "I owe you for that, Beecher. I wouldn't be here without you."

I keep my eyes on the floor, refusing to look up at him.

"They said this Pastor Frick... They said you figured out he was the Knight," the President says. When I still won't look at him, he adds, "The Secret Service has the body. When they ran a black light over it, he was covered with white ink tattoos, including one on his hand with the initials *J.W.B.* John Wilkes Booth."

I nod as if it makes sense.

"You're a smart guy, Beecher. And I know this wasn't an easy one. They told me about your friend, about Tot. I already placed a call to the doctors at the hospital. He'll get the best help anyone could ask for."

"He doesn't need your help. And we don't want it."

"You sure about that?"

I look up, hearing that tone in his voice. It's not a threat. He's actually concerned.

"I know how hard you're fighting for this country, Beecher. And how much the Culper Ring's lost," he says. "But if you let me help you...if we put our heads together...this is our chance to build it back. Stronger than ever."

"You're serious? You want to help rebuild the Culper Ring?"

"Stronger than ever," he says, moving the teacup to the floor, taking the seat opposite me and crossing his legs. "I won't interfere, Beecher. You keep doing everything you need to. But if you get in trouble or need help, do you have any idea of the resources I can bring? In fact, just today, when Nico escaped—"

"Nico *escaped*?"

He sits up straight, enjoying the slight advantage that comes with being a step ahead. "He walked right out through the St. Elizabeths loading dock. Stabbed a poor nurse to do it. Apparently, someone who looked like his daughter, Clementine, was spotted there too," he says, reminding me of the fact that I still have no idea where Clementine is or what she's up to. "But when they checked the list of visitors, you know who Nico's last official visitor was? You, Beecher. That's what it said in the computer. Until about an hour ago," he adds, flashing the insta-grin that convinced sixty-eight million people to vote for him. I know he's the President of the United States, but sometimes I forget how charming he can be. Still, it doesn't erase what I found out months ago: that as he climbed the rungs of power, he and Palmiotti were part of a ruthless attack and at least two recent murders.

"So whattya say, Beecher? Stronger than ever?"

"It's a generous offer, Mr. President. And I'm thankful for you looking out for me. But when it comes to the Culper Ring, I think it's better if it stays independent."

"Now you're talking like a politician. I'm offering you a chance to help the Culper Ring reach its true potential. Isn't that why George Washington created it? To arm the President with a fighting force no one else would see coming?"

"You make us sound like a weapon."

"And you make it sound like you're in charge," Wallace says, his insta-grin now gone. "Or that I'm asking your permission." He lifts his grin back in place, hoping it'll intimidate. Last time, it worked. But this time isn't last time.

"Sir, what you said about George Washington... You're wrong," I tell him, trying to keep the conversation upbeat. "He didn't create the Culper Ring to protect the President. He created it to protect the Presidency. Especially from those who might do it harm."

"You think that's clever, Beecher? Let me say this as clearly as I can: I'm currently extending my hand to you. If you refuse it, this offer, this opportunity I'm offering right now... it'll never come back."

"I appreciate that, sir. And I also appreciate that you're not used to people saying *no* to you. But let me remind you," I tell him, leaning forward so we're only a few feet apart. "I know who you are. I know what you've done. And just so we truly understand each other, the Culper Ring doesn't work with murderers."

"Then you should talk to your friend Tot," the President shoots back, keeping his voice steady, his legs still crossed for teatime. I forgot how he fights. No matter how hard he's hit, he never loses his composure. He just keeps acting like he's in control. Until he is.

"You just made that up about Tot to get in my head."

"You keep telling yourself that, Beecher. But don't be so sure you know who you're working with."

"Tot's not a murderer."

"If you say so," he says, resting both palms on his crossed knee. "I'm just sorry we won't be working together." Calmly reaching down toward the floor, he picks up his teacup and tosses me one last false grin. "So. We're done here, yes?"

"Y'know, you said that to me two months ago. That we were done. But we're not, Mr. President. Not yet. In fact, do you remember what else you told me last time? You said this was a prizefight. And near as I can tell, we just finished round two."

"From where I'm sitting, you lost round two."

"Maybe I did. But next time I see you, Mr. President..." I tug hard on the chains, pulling them tight against the footboard. "...I'm not gonna be in handcuffs."

"Good news for me, then. Because the next time I see you, Beecher, I most definitely won't be offering you tea," he says, toasting me with his teacup. Standing from his seat and heading for the door, he adds, "Be sure to say hi to Tot for me. And if I were you, I'd get there as quickly as I could."

111

Three hours later, I'm staring at a set of closed doors with frosted glass squares cut into them.

"I'm sorry, visiting hours are done for the day," the nurse tells me, her voice coming through the in-house phone that's next to the doors.

"Is this Angelica? Angelica, my name is Beecher White. I was told to ask for you."

There's a pause. Without another word, the closed doors of the ICU swing open. It's nearly midnight, but as I step inside, a chorus of pings and beeps swarm like a hornet attack.

At the nurses' station, behind the main desk, Angelica doesn't say a word. Like most nurses, she knows the emotional risk of eye contact; she also knows what happened here today. Two people were shot. Their hospital chaplain was killed. Keeping her head down, Angelica points me around to the left and I start reading room numbers.

There, midway down the hall: Room 214—home of the Knight's final victim. And my best friend.

Still thinking of the President's warning, I slow down, my stomach hollowing out from the terror that comes with most hospital visits. The room is sealed by sliding glass panes, frosted at the bottom and transparent up top.

As I look through the glass, the lights are dimmed and a mass of red and white dots glow inside. They warned me before I came that there'd be lots of machines...and that they had to shave his head for the surgery...but to finally see him... The lump in my throat makes it hard to catch my breath.

I slide the glass door open and the lump expands. His beard...

They shaved his beard, trimming it so the accordion feeding tube could be inserted in his neck, where bits of dried blood mark the entry point. His eyes are closed and his color's gray, like a corpse, which only makes the nasty black scar on his head stand out even more. The scar's stitches and knots are thick and black, arcing down the side of his head like a jagged roller coaster that dead-ends at the pillow of gauze covering most of his ear.

But the worst part is the other half of his head, where his silver hair is still long. They only shaved *half* his head, making Tot look like a baseball that has patches of gray yarn sprouting from it. His mouth hangs open like a urinal. His palms are up, facing the ceiling, like he's begging for death.

"I wish they hadn't shaved his beard," a soft female voice whispers.

I spin, following the sound. At the foot of the bed, in a wood and vinyl hospital recliner, sits an older woman with a wide nose, unpierced ears, and horn-rimmed glasses that weren't stylish even in the 1950s. Her silver hair is in a bob that grazes her chin, and on her wrists are two carpal tunnel Velcro braces. Of course. She's on the computer all day. Immaculate Deception.

"Grace," I say, though it comes out as more of a question.

She nods, blinking enough that I can tell she's been crying. And though she barely fills out the black sweater she's wearing, there's nothing frail about her.

"He doesn't look good," I say.

She tries to reply, but when nothing comes out, I'm hit with that feeling you get at a funeral, where the dread rises off the mourners, engulfing everyone nearby. But what I'm really seeing is relief.

"They said he'll make it. They said he's strong," Grace says, nodding and trying to smile.

"So the doctors—?"

"They're on it. They've mobilized half the hospital for this. Apparently, President Wallace called them personally," she says as I picture him toasting me with that teacup. "They said when Tot was shot, the bullet hit him in the bone behind his ear. It kept the bullet from his brain. They called it a miracle. They said when the swelling goes down, they can check the rest of his functions."

"But he'll be okay?"

She nods, her whole body shaking. "They hope so...they think so."

I close my eyes and whisper a quick thank-you. As I open them, I see Tot's open mouth and the way he's barely moving. I replay Grace's words: *He'll make it.*

"He's tougher than they think," I insist.

"You have no idea."

Standing from her chair, she smooths her skirt and approaches the bed. She adjusts one of the Velcro straps at her wrists. "How long did the Service keep you locked up for questioning?" she asks.

"What're you—?"

She motions to the red marks on my own wrists, from the handcuffs.

"They wanted me to see Wallace," I tell her.

"And did you?"

I nod.

"He do anything but hit you with veiled threats?"

I shake my head.

"That's his style. He'll never change. That's why, back at your house, I told you not to go with Palmiotti."

"You didn't tell me anything."

"I did. You stopped listening. Once he said the words *Camp David*, you were out the door and—"

"Grace, is that really the best use of our time right now? You gloating that you were right about Palmiotti?"

"I'm not gloating, Beecher. But I *was* right about Palmiotti."

"And you were wrong about Marshall. So was Tot." I look over at the bed. From this angle, the way Tot's head is tipped back with his mouth agape, I see he has no teeth. They took out his dentures. But at least he'll survive. "It doesn't feel like much of a win," I say, my voice catching.

"*Win?*" Grace shoots back. "You think this is a *win*? Look

413

around, Beecher: We lost! The Culper Ring lost! We didn't stop the Knight, Nico escaped and is God knows where. And worst of all, the President, who we all know is a monster, is now taking a victory lap and is more beloved than ever, thanks to surviving this assassination attempt. The only good news is that Tot won't be using diapers and bedpans for the rest of his life."

"We still found out about Palmiotti. We can prove he's alive."

"And where does that get us?"

"It'll show what a liar Wallace is. Isn't that the real goal? Tot told me you've been trying for years to build a case against Wallace. Palmiotti's the way to finally put it together."

"And again, where does that get us? They'll either deny it, and people will believe them, or they'll make up some excuse and no one will care. Either way, Palmiotti only gets us so far. To topple a President, you need to get the President, not his childhood pal."

"But if the rest of the Ring—"

"The Ring is decimated, Beecher. You're looking at most of it right now."

"But I'm not looking at *all* of it, am I? You said Tot was starting to rebuild."

For once, Grace stays quiet. Reaching down, she takes Tot's open hand, holding it between both of her own.

"Grace, Wallace is the one who's been hunting and killing the Culper Ring, isn't he?"

This woman's been doing this since before Kennedy was President. She's no novice. But as I watch her holding Tot's hand, the way her thumb gently brushes circles into his palm...I don't know how far it goes back, but something tells me that when Tot's wife was alive, she wasn't Grace's number one fan.

"So that's it? We just sit here and wait until Tot's better?" I ask.

"Beecher, did you ever hear that Winston Churchill quote, the one where he says, *Never give in. Never give in. Never, never, never, never—in nothing, great or small, large or petty—never give in, except to convictions of honor and good sense?*"

"What about it?"

"This is the moment of *good sense*." Still holding on to Tot's hand, Grace turns my way, her dark eyes looking even smaller through the thickness of her horn-rimmed glasses. "The Culper Ring didn't last this long because we're the toughest, Beecher. We lasted this long because we're the smartest."

"But if we stop fighting now..."

"...then we'll survive. And regroup. And try to figure out what the hell just hit us. That's how we rebuild. We've done it before and we'll do it again. I'm sorry, Beecher, I know it's not as satisfying as punching someone in the face and yelling a good catchphrase, but that's how this chapter ends."

Standing on the opposite side of the bed, I don't say a word.

"Don't look at me like that, Beecher. We don't have a choice. The fight's over. There's no one left to send in the ring."

"Maybe," I say, glancing through the sliding glass door into the empty hallway. "But maybe not."

"Beecher, wait—! Where're you going?"

112

By the time I get home, all the adrenaline is gone.

It's nearly 1 a.m., my wrists are even more sore, my toes are frozen, and my body temperature is plummeting from exhaustion and hunger.

Unlocking my front door, I flick on the lights and bathe in the calm, familiar smell of my townhouse. As I look around, the sofa's still made up like a makeshift bed, and across the carpet, I spot a few remnant strands of Clementine's blonde wig, but it's all untouched. Not a single thing is out of place.

"Marshall, I know you're here," I call out.

As the kitchen door swings open, I spot my best friend from childhood.

"How'd you know?" Marshall asks in his raspy voice, joining me in the living room and still wearing his wool peacoat.

"I didn't. But I know you."

He goes to say something, but for some reason decides against it. As he gets closer, his posture stays perfect, but he keeps his head slightly down and turned away. He doesn't like being looked at.

"Can I get you something to drink or—?"

"Sorry about your wrists," he says, motioning to the red marks from the handcuffs. Forever the wolf, he doesn't miss a detail.

"Why'd you come here, Marshall?"

"You called me three times in the last half hour."

"You could've just called me back. Why'd you really come here?"

He takes a deep breath through his mangled nose, and I can't tell if he's annoyed or just upset. "I wanted to know if they killed you."

416

"What?"

Pretending to stare at the three framed black-and-white photo cards that hang over my sofa, he presses his lips together, his sagging skin shifting in one large chunk. "They *are* going to kill you, Beecher. I called a friend in the Service who's stationed up at Camp David. They know who you are. From here, it's just a matter of time." Letting the statement sink in, he adds, "So tell me, Beecher: Why'd you call me three times in the last half hour?"

"Because we need your help."

"We?"

"The group I work with."

"The Culper Ring?"

I shoot him a look. Of course he knows their name.

"They're the ones who gave you that tracker you put in my car," he reasons.

"They're good people, Marshall. Smart too. And I was thinking ... with your skills ... plus their resources ..."

"Don't ask me to be part of your group, Beecher."

"But if we—"

"There is no *we*. I'm not for sale. And I'm not some cheap grenade you get to toss at your enemies."

I stand there a moment. I expect him to leave, but instead he stays where he is, still staring at the framed photos.

"That's Saggy, isn't it?" he asks, referring to our hometown.

"From back in the 1920s," I explain as he takes a step closer to the three side-by-side photo postcards showing men, women, and children waving American flags and marching down the street in front of Cannell Park. "They're from an old firemen's parade that the town used to have."

"They're nice," he says.

"Yeah, when I put them up, I told myself they were my daily reminder that if I screwed things up here, that's where I was going back to. But I think it's finally time to admit, I just like them because they remind me of home."

Marshall looks my way. "Home is terrifying for some people."

"It can also be a reminder of where you came from. And how far you've traveled."

He turns back to the photos. "You're still a cornball, aren't you, Beecher?"

I laugh at the comment, studying my old friend and once again trying to see the old chubby, glasses-wearing version of himself. Tot said that was my problem, that I can't stop remembering. He may be right. But some things are worth holding on to.

"Marsh, I'm sorry for thinking you were the one who killed those pastors."

Still staring at the images, he doesn't respond.

"It's just that when I saw you had that Lincoln mask and those old playing cards, plus your history with Pastor Riis..."

"You were investigating the case, Beecher. You did everything you were supposed to."

"That's not even true. I got fooled by Nico. I couldn't save Tot. I fell into every trap the Knight left for me. If it wasn't for you, we'd be watching the President's funeral right now."

"So you think you lost?"

"You telling me I didn't?"

Turning away from the photos, Marshall stands there, eyeing me. "Beecher, how'd you know Pastor Frick was the Knight?"

"Excuse me?"

"My friend in the Service. He said you figured it out right before the shots were fired."

I take a breath, staring down at the carpet and reliving the moment. "The real assassinations. When all this started, I told Tot that when President Garfield was shot, he should've lived. It was medical malpractice that killed him, not the bullet. I figured that's why Pastor Frick was left alive. But when I started thinking about how meticulous the Knight was—always killing in temples, using the old guns—it reminded me that Garfield *did* die. So for Pastor Frick to still be alive and walking around...and for him to be at the same hospital for the third and fourth attempts... That was it. But it still didn't make me fast enough to save the President. Without you, Wallace would be dead right now."

"You're wrong."

"Marshall, I appreciate the pep talk, but—"

"Do you have any idea why I went to the Lincoln Memorial?" he challenges.

I shake my head.

"Because you sent me there, Beecher."

"What're you talking about?"

"From the very start, I was trying to find the person who killed Pastor Riis. So when that first rector was murdered at St. John's, the only pattern I saw was someone killing *pastors*. That is, until you came in and found all those links to John Wilkes Booth: the peephole in the wall, and the piece of wood in the umbrella stand. Once I heard you and Tot talking about that—"

"Wait. You bugged me?"

"In your wallet. Right after you bugged my car," Marshall shoots back. "But the fact remains, without you spotting that original Abraham Lincoln connection, I would've never found the pattern of dead Presidents. That's when I started looking at Wallace, and his schedule, and all the places he was supposed to be."

For thirty seconds I stand there, still digesting his words. "I still don't understand how you knew the Knight would be at the Lincoln Memorial."

"I didn't. In fact, I thought it was A.J. who was doing the killing. So when it came to the Memorial, I figured I had a fifty-fifty chance. And even if I was wrong, I had you at Camp David," he says, his voice warming up as much as his voice can ever warm up. "You understand what I'm saying, Beecher? I may've grabbed the gun and shot the Knight, but when it comes right down to it, *you're* the one who actually saved President Wallace. That was the job, right? You did everything the Culper Ring couldn't. That's why they picked you."

I look straight at Marshall, who, for once, doesn't look away. Though I try to fight it, I feel a grin lifting my cheeks.

"Beecher, you truly don't make any sense, y'know that?" Marshall adds, sounding mad. "I thought you hated Wallace."

"I do hate him."

"So you'd rather save his life now, and then hope to take him down fair and square later?"

"There's a right way and a wrong way to do things, Marshall."

"You sure about that? Because when I was up by that big Lincoln statue and the Knight started reaching for his gun... God, I took joy in pulling that trigger. Real joy." Reading the look on my face, he adds, "Don't look so shocked. You know how many people he might've killed if I didn't take that shot? Y'know how many kids were up there?"

"But that's not why you took the shot, is it?"

"What're you talking about?"

"You weren't at the Lincoln Memorial to protect Wallace, or even to save a bunch of kids. You said it just now. You were after the Knight because he killed Pastor Riis."

"What's your point, Beecher?"

"I'm not— I just—" I cut myself off, still wondering whether to touch the subject we've both avoided for so long. "It always goes back to that night, doesn't it? With Paglinni and the basement... when we... when I—" My voice cracks. I fight to catch my breath, still terrified that the words I've waited so long to say will never repair this pain. "Marsh, I'm sorry I sent you in there. I was a coward that night. I never should've let you go down there alone."

"Beecher..."

"No. I need to say this, and you need to hear it. I'm sorry for the pain I caused you. I'm sorry I wasn't strong enough to stop it."

"Beecher, there's nothing you could've stopped."

"That's not true. If you never went down there... if you never saw your mom with Pastor Riis—"

"Don't blame Riis. It wasn't him."

"How can you say that?"

"It wasn't *him*."

"But he's the one who—"

"Listen to what I'm saying, Beecher. It. Wasn't. *Him*."

Struggling to read Marshall, I replay the night. I can still see the yellow tint from the porch lights. Still see the view from the driveway. And still see the front door flying open as Marshall's mom, holding her bra in her hand, shoved Marshmallow outside.

"Pastor Riis wasn't even there," Marshall insists.

I hear the words, but they don't make sense. Marshall's mom was half dressed. She was with *someone*. But if Pastor Riis wasn't there—

Oh.

In front of me, the yellow porch lights fade, leaving me staring back at Marshall's gold eyes, which drill at me in my living room.

"*Mrs. Riis?*" I blurt.

Marshall doesn't move, but I feel him nod.

I nod back, my mind still processing. "But even so . . . if we— If I didn't send you down there—"

"Beecher, do you know how I got into your house tonight? I picked all three of your locks. Easily. And back when I was in the military and finishing the training that taught me how to do it, for the final exam, my squad leader gave us one final lock that we'd have to pick. In the corner of the room, he'd lock you in one of those diver's cages like you see during Shark Week. In your pocket, he'd give you a bent piece of metal, then he'd point at the rusted old lock and tell you it should take you three minutes or less to pick your way out. 'Go,' he said, slamming the cage shut and hitting the stopwatch.

"Within the first few minutes, the lock didn't budge and I knew I was in trouble. As ten minutes went by, I started to sweat. By the thirty-minute mark, I'm flipping out and still can't open the door. Finally, after an hour of trying to pick this lock . . . in total frustration, I collapse against the door, which swings open. The squad leader shoots me a grin."

"The door was unlocked the entire time," I say.

"Completely unlocked. But in my mind, it was locked—and that was enough to keep me from opening that door and getting out."

"What're you trying to say?"

"You didn't put that gun in my mother's mouth, Beecher. Or pull the trigger. It's time to let yourself out of your cage."

Staring across at my old friend, I try to swallow, but my throat expands with a ball the size of a grapefruit. I had no idea until this exact moment, but I've been waiting eighteen years to hear those words. "Marsh..."

"Don't thank me, Beecher. And don't cry either," he says, serious as ever. "If you cry, I'll stab you."

"Yeah...no...I'm not crying," I say, fighting hard not to laugh. "But y'know what's funny? I think I remember Pastor Riis telling a story just like that during one of his sermons. But when he told it, it was Harry Houdini who was in the cage."

Staring back at me, Marshall presses his lips together, unreadable as ever. "It's still a good story," he says.

"I agree." Nodding to myself, I'm amazed how much it makes me think about the still missing Clementine.

Stealing one last look at the black-and-white photos, Marshall turns toward the door and reaches into his pocket. "By the way, here you go..." he says, tossing me a small black object.

"What's this?" I ask as I catch the outdated, flip-style cell phone.

"It's a phone."

"I can see it's a phone."

"It's a clone of the one Palmiotti uses to call A.J. When Palmiotti's phone rings, so will that one."

"Where'd you get this?"

"I told you. My friend in the Service. Not everyone there is a scumbag. Anyway, you listen to it long enough, you might hear something interesting."

I glance at the phone, then at Marshall, who's nearly out the door. "But you'd never join the Culper Ring, right?" I call out to him.

"I don't like bullies, Beecher. Especially presidential ones."

"I'm taking that as a *yes*!"

Stepping out into the night with his head ducked down, Marshall doesn't answer.

* * *

113

Three hours earlier
Washington, D.C.

At first, the dark blue car just circled the block, around and around, slowing down as it cruised along Pennsylvania Avenue, then speeding up again as it approached the corner and made a sharp right on 6th Street.

Over and over, the driver retraced the circle, but not for too long. There was nothing suspicious about pretending to look for a parking space. But this close to the White House, which was barely ten blocks away, only a fool thinks he can circle the block too often without being noticed.

Quietly settling into an open spot on 6th Street, the driver shut the engine, looked around, and eyed the two or three nearby pedestrians.

Nothing so far. It was almost time, but the driver still knew it was best to be patient.

The only problem was, the driver hated Washington, D.C.— especially this part of D.C., diagonally across from the National Archives. Too many bad memories.

After a half hour, the car pulled out of the spot and started circling again: looping around the block, slowly rolling down Pennsylvania Avenue, and speeding up on the corner of 6th Street.

These days, the northeast corner of 6th and Pennsylvania held a modern glass-fronted building that was home to the Newseum, a museum dedicated to news and media. But what the driver really

423

cared about—aside from the two uniformed guards who stood just inside the glass doors of the museum—was what *used* to be here. Years ago. Nearly a hundred and fifty years, to be precise, which is when the National Hotel used to occupy this exact corner.

Founded in 1827, the National was so popular that sitting Presidents from Andrew Jackson to Abraham Lincoln used to leave the White House and spend a night there, enjoying terrapin dinners and rare old wines. Indeed, Lincoln even had his post-Inauguration banquet there. In 1852, Henry Clay died in Room 116. But of all the great secrets contained in its halls, none was greater than the one that was hatched on the second floor—in Room 228—where John Wilkes Booth stayed while he plotted to assassinate President Lincoln.

Glancing down at the car's digital clock, the driver pumped the brakes and again searched the sidewalk as the car rolled slowly along Pennsylvania Avenue. A young woman with a forceful gait and a Justice Department ID leaned forward as she plowed against the wind tunnel created by the canyon of tall buildings that lined the block. In the opposite direction, a middle-aged couple held hands as they headed for the Metro.

But as the car reached the end of Pennsylvania Avenue, what caught the driver's eye was a homeless man approaching the corner of 6th Street.

He was no different from most of the homeless people on the street tonight. His knit cap was tattered and old, he wouldn't make eye contact, and his crumpled jacket and torn pants looked like they were fished from the garbage. But as he reached the northeast corner of 6th and Pennsylvania—just as his foot touched the edge of the curb where the National Hotel used to exist—the driver couldn't help but notice the time: 10:11 p.m.

The exact moment John Wilkes Booth pulled the trigger on Lincoln.

Hitting the brakes on the corner of 6th Street, the driver lurched forward as her car bucked to a stop. The homeless man didn't look up.

"You're not alone," the driver of the car called out as she lowered the passenger-side window.

"Clementine?" the homeless man asked, staring at the woman behind the steering wheel.

Clementine nodded, staring back at the so-called homeless man. At Nico, her father.

"Nico, you need to get inside," Clementine added, popping the locks.

Turning to the side, Nico muttered something as if he were talking to someone next to him. His imaginary friend.

"Nico..."

Adding a quick prayer, he pointed a thank-you up to God and mouthed a silent *Amen*. Pulling open the car door, he slid into the front passenger seat, smelling of fish and wet garbage.

As her fingers curled around the steering wheel, Clementine couldn't take her eyes off him, overwhelmed at how simultaneously old and young she felt every time she was in her father's orbit.

"How did you know I'd be here?" Nico blurted, drilling her with a look that felt like he was trying to break her down to a chemical level.

"I'm your daughter," Clementine offered.

Nico almost turned away. But he didn't.

"I thought you'd be with Beecher," he finally said.

"I'm not."

"He'll be looking for me. They'll all be looking for me."

"I understand," she insisted. "I'm still your daughter."

Clicking his front teeth together, Nico felt his cheeks rise into a crooked grin. "I need a razor," he insisted.

"We can get it later," she replied, kicking the gas and twisting the wheel as the car took off up 6th Street.

"I need it now. I need a razor right now," he told her, staring up at the passing storefronts and streetlights. It'd been so long since he'd been outside the hospital.

Ten minutes later, after a quick stop at a nearby CVS while Nico waited in the car, Clementine handed her father a can of shaving cream, a set of disposable plastic razors, and a bottle of water.

"You don't have to do this now," she said, sending the car racing up the street. Next to her, Nico popped open the shaving cream and sprayed it into his hand.

With a quick smudge, he spread the cream into his black hair and tore open the bag of razors with his teeth.

"You need to use the water," she told him.

Nico didn't care. Starting at the back of his own neck, he pressed the blade to his skin and tugged upward, taking out a square of black hair and leaving a tiny nick of...

"You're bleeding," Clementine said, turning quickly and pulling onto a quiet side street where they'd be better hidden. "Please... can't this wait?"

But it couldn't. If Nico was in pain, he didn't show it. Rinsing the blade with a dump of bottled water, he started again, working his way upward.

Shutting the car and watching him, horrified, Clementine assumed he was worried about being seen or recognized. By now, his picture was all over the news. But as the clumps of hair fell away, she noticed there was something else besides stripes of shaving cream and streaks of blood on the back of his head. At first, she could only see the edge of it: a thin line. It was muddy and pale green.

"Is that a tattoo?" Clementine asked, mesmerized as she studied its curved lines. Slowly, Nico worked the razor upward, shaving his own head.

"No," Nico said. "It's a symbol."

With a sharp tug, the metal blade swallowed a final chunk of black hair from his nearly bald skull, which was shaved down the center like a lawn mower plowing a jagged line through a black forest. But it wasn't until Nico lowered the razor and turned toward the passenger window that Clementine got a good look at what—for decades now—he'd kept hidden underneath. The final secret Nico Hadrian had kept from them all, even the Knight: a small tattoo that dated back to the Renaissance, where it was the fifth and final suit in certain decks of cards: a crescent moon.

The final suit of the final Knight. And the clear sign that—dear Lord, he had no choice but to admit it now—this mission had always been his.

His body shook, fighting to contain the tears he was keeping inside. In that moment, his entire life made sense. This was why he was chosen. Fate had led him to so many places—and now, once again, it had led him back here. Back to the original mission. Like his predecessors, like his fellow Knights, it was his destiny to kill the President of the United States.

The Knights of the Golden Circle would live again.

Facing the back of her father's head, Clementine studied his reflection in the passenger-side window. "You know you don't have to do this," she told him.

Nico raised his close-set eyes, staring back at her. "That's what you've never understood. I don't have a choice."

Knowing better than to argue, and wondering if he might actually be right, Clementine continued to study her father's reflection. The more hair he took off his head, the more he looked like Clementine without her wig.

"Were you being honest before?" Nico asked, running the razor up the side of his head. "Do you have my cancer in your body?"

Clementine nodded, feeling her blonde wig clamped against her skull. But as she started the car, she didn't want to talk about cancer, or killing, or anything else. For the first time in her life, Clementine just wanted to enjoy a quiet night with her father.

114

One week later
Camp David

W hat about meatballs. You like meatballs?" the President
asked.

"You know I like meatballs," eight-year-old Andrew
replied, trailing behind his father through the cabin's rustic living
room.

"And do you like hamburgers?"

"Maybe."

"Don't say *maybe*," Wallace told his young son, heading into the
bedroom, toward his closet, where he pulled out a fleece pullover
with the presidential seal on it. "That's a rule for life. When someone asks you a question, say *yes* or say *no*. Stand for something.
Now, do you like hamburgers?"

"Yes," Andrew said assertively.

"And do you like taco meat?"

"May— Usually," the boy said.

"*Usually* counts as a yes," the President pointed out, sliding his
arms into the fleece and pulling it on. As his head popped through
the neckhole, Wallace's hair was still perfectly in place. "Then you
should like steak. Meatballs, hamburgers, taco meat...that's all
steak is, just in a different form."

"But it's harder to chew," the boy countered.

Making his way back to the front door of the cabin, the President of the United States stopped and looked back over his shoulder

at his son. "You really are going to be a politician when you grow up, aren't you?"

"I don't like what I don't like," Andrew said.

"That's fine. Tell Suzanne to make you some spaghetti instead. And tell your mother we're not having any more children."

Grinning at the victory, Andrew ran toward the kitchen.

"I'll be back," the President called out, still amazed, after the recent horror, how quickly life could return to normal.

For nearly a week now, the Secret Service had kept them all at Camp David, not just to help Wallace relax, but to let the nation catch its breath after the shooting. With no press to bother him, and barely any staff, Wallace played air hockey with his son, taught his daughter how to shoot a proper free throw, and spent his nights either watching a movie in the private theater or simply reading in front of the stone fireplace with his wife. Even when they were just having a meal together, his family was acting like a family again.

Still, that didn't mean he couldn't squeeze in a few business meetings.

Kneeling down on one knee, he double-knotted the laces on his running shoes. As he tugged open the front door, the frozen air chilled his cheeks, reminding him just how unforgiving the mountain winds could be. And how invigorating.

"Did you stretch?" he called out.

If Wallace were in the White House right now, there'd be a small army of staffers waiting, plus a half dozen uniformed and plainclothes Secret Service agents.

Today, at the foot of the porch, among the poplar and hickory trees of Camp David, there was just one. A young agent in a faded Duke sweatshirt.

"I'm all set, Mr. President," A.J. replied.

Without another word, President Wallace began to run, slowly at first, giving A.J. a chance to join in. In no time, they were jogging side by side, away from the cabin known as Aspen, and away from the Secret Service command post.

As their breath snowballed from their lips, they followed the main path, then a narrower path that broke off from it. The ground was hard in the cold, but it didn't take them long to enter the southern part of Catoctin Mountain Park, where they picked up a trail known as Hog Rock Loop.

When George W. Bush was President, he used to love running Hog Rock, which was filled with beautiful streams and a nice big hill that put your calves and quads to the test. To this day, the Secret Service still joke that every time Bush was halfway toward the peak, he'd say the same thing to whichever agent was his runner: "Seemed like a good idea at the time."

It *was* a good idea at the time.

Just as it was for Wallace and A.J. today.

Feeling the pitch steepen and his lungs tighten, the President still had a half-step lead. He knew A.J. was taking it easy on him, letting him set the pace. That is, until they spotted an old, warped picnic bench that sat under a towering tupelo tree. Picking up speed and checking over his shoulder, A.J. pulled ahead of the President and made a sharp left downhill, off the path, a clump of wet leaves shifting with his heel. Wallace followed him into the forest.

For nearly half a mile, the two men continued to run downhill side by side, cutting between trees, neither saying a word. Unlike the mostly paved path, the ground here was covered with snow, making it far more slippery. Every few yards, A.J. would scan the area—left to right, then up and down—making sure they were alone as he searched for...

There.

Up ahead, hidden by a thicket of mountain laurel bushes that were hardy enough to still be green in the winter, was a tall man in a dark overcoat. The President slowed down, eyeing the man's black dye job. But even if his hair had been pink, Wallace would still know his oldest friend a mile away.

"Not even huffing and puffing, huh? Your color's better too," Dr. Palmiotti said.

"Y'know I still hate your hair like that," the President teased, bending over and catching his breath.

"Nice to see you too, sir," Palmiotti replied, his wide smile revealing just how happy he was to be back in the mix. Better yet, in over a week, his name still hadn't appeared in the papers. At least that secret was safe.

"I take it things are going better?" the President asked.

Palmiotti knew what his friend was talking about. Lydia. "I appreciate you doing what you did. She sends her best."

"You're just happy you're getting laid again," Wallace said.

"Sir, we really need to make it quick," A.J. interrupted, talking to the President, but shooting a scolding look at Palmiotti. This wasn't a social call.

"So we're back on track?" the President asked.

"Why don't you ask the man himself?" Palmiotti replied, stepping aside and motioning to the thicket of mountain laurel behind him.

From behind the bushes, a man with thin, burnt-away lips stepped out as javelins of sunlight stabbed down from the treetops at his candlewax skin.

"Here he is, America's unsung hero," the President said, offering Marshall a toothy grin.

Marshall didn't grin back, his gold eyes glancing around the empty forest. "You sure there're no cameras here?"

"No cameras," A.J. insisted.

It didn't make Marshall feel any better.

"What's wrong, son?" the President asked. "You look miserable, even for you."

"I don't like being second-guessed," Marshall said.

"Pardon me?" the President asked.

"You said you trusted me."

"I do trust you."

"But yet you still thought I was the Knight, didn't you?" Marshall challenged. "That I was the one who killed those pastors."

"Marshall . . ."

"Don't insult me by denying it. Palmiotti and A.J. both said as much."

"What'd you expect us to think?" Palmiotti asked. "First you get caught at the scene of the crime, then the police find Beecher's name in your pocket—"

"Stewie, stop talking," the President scolded. Never taking his eyes off Marshall, he put a calming hand on his shoulder, massaging it with the same reassuring confidence that convinced Syria to sign last year's peace accords. "Marshall, this lunatic we were fighting... this Knight who was trying to murder me... I'm sorry he killed your friend."

"Pastor Riis wasn't a friend. He was like a father."

"And I know how precious fathers are. I do. Mine walked out when I was in my teens. My mother still used to kiss his picture every night before bed. But we picked you for a reason, Marshall. I hired you to do a job, not to race off on your own investigation."

"Well in this case, you got a twofer," Marshall shot back.

"Watch your tone," Palmiotti warned.

"Then use your brain," Marshall said. "You really think Beecher would've come along if I just showed up and said, *I really missed you, old pal*? That trick might've worked on him once, but it wasn't gonna work again. Beecher needed to feel like *he* found *me*. And it worked. In fact, the way I see it, you got what you wanted *and* you're still alive. So forgive me if I'm having a little trouble understanding why you're still complaining."

Palmiotti started to say something, but the President cut him off with a glance. Same with A.J. On a day like today, the time for fighting was over.

"Y'know, one of my agents, when he tackled you and the Knight to the ground," the President began, his hand back on Marshall's shoulder, "he kept it out of his report, but he said that you were talking to Frick, asking him why he killed Pastor Riis."

"What about it?" Marshall asked.

"He said Frick died without replying. That you never got your answer."

"Again, what about it?" Marshall repeated.

"I'm just saying, if you've been reading the papers, or at least the bloggers..."

"I don't read bloggers."

"That's smart of you, Marshall. But even the mainstream press, well... at this point, it's just conjecture, but considering the way the Knight was communicating with him, plus his recent escape from St. Elizabeths, and his ties to your hometown..."

"Are you trying to tell me that Nico was the one who sent the Knight after Pastor Riis?"

"Son, how could I possibly tell you that? The only person who knows that is Nico himself."

"I'm not sure I understand your point, sir."

"All I'm saying is, whoever catches Nico first—be it the Secret Service or anyone else in law enforcement... Well, it wouldn't surprise me if Nico fights back with such ferocity, he takes a bullet to the neck and, like John Wilkes Booth or even Lee Harvey Oswald, never even makes it to trial."

For a long moment, Marshall stared across at the President, who was a full head taller than him. "I appreciate that, Mr. President. But when do I get what we talked about?"

"When you're done," Palmiotti replied. Nothing had changed since he first approached Marshall two weeks ago. In return for Marshall's help with Beecher, they'd give him all the details of what happened all those years ago in the military to Marshall's father.

"How's your dad doing these days?" the President asked.

"He's dying," Marshall said, remembering the lie he told Beecher.

"Then I guess you should work quickly," the President of the United States said, staring back at Marshall's face. "So that's it, yes? You think we're in good shape?"

Marshall nodded. When Palmiotti had first reached out to Marshall, the President wanted the name and identity of every last member of the Culper Ring. Right now, thanks to Beecher, Marshall was their newest recruit.

"I just need to remind you of one thing," Marshall said. "I know your feelings about Beecher, but—"

"You don't know anything about me and Beecher," the President said.

"I know he saved your life. So you need to know that too, sir. Without that brain of his, I would've never been at the Lincoln Memorial, and your daughter would still be picking pieces of your skull out of her hair."

"So now I'm supposed to be scared of Beecher?" the President shot back. "You're talking about someone who let us lock him up in Camp David."

"That's because he's new. But I'm telling you, he learns faster than anyone I've ever seen. He's learning right now. So if you think this is going to be easy, or you take your eyes off him, that'll be the worst mistake you'll ever make."

Biting a speck of chapped skin from his lips, Wallace didn't respond.

"Then it's good we have you," the President finally said, looking uphill and pivoting toward the path that would take him back to Camp David. "Though I appreciate the warning."

Following his own snow footprints back up the hill, the President began to jog, slowly at first, then faster as A.J. fell in next to him, the President always leading by an unmistakable half step. As they reached the top and rejoined the Hog Rock Loop, the President glanced back over his shoulder. Downhill, Palmiotti was still standing by the mountain laurel bushes. Marshall was already gone.

A half-smile crept up Wallace's face.

For over a week now, as the details leaked out, the press had been fixated on the set of ancient playing cards that were found in the Knight's pocket. But as the President picked up his pace and followed the path back to Camp David, he knew that when it came to kings, queens, jacks, and the rest—and especially when it came to Beecher and the Culper Ring—nothing beats a wild card.

434

AUTHOR'S NOTE

I've been working on this book for almost four years now. That means I've spent four years surrounding myself with presidential deaths. And yes, the death of a President shouldn't be any more compelling than the death of anyone else, but when I hear that John Wilkes Booth used a mysterious card to get into Ford's Theatre, my eyebrow starts twitching and I get obsessed.

And so, let me answer the number one question that the proof-readers kept asking me when they finished reading: *How much of this is real?* The question took many forms. *Did John Wilkes Booth really have that creepy tattoo? What about the second killer? Did he have that tattoo also? And what about the playing cards?*

I love doing the research and including as much real history in my books as I can (even as it consumes me). To that end, the scenes with the Presidents' deaths are as accurate as could be. That museum in here that has pieces of Lincoln's skull and John Wilkes Booth's bones? That place is real too and has even more cool stuff that I didn't have room for. And those tunnels under Camp David? I changed a few security details for safety purposes, but yeah, those are pretty darn real too.

But as you know, this is still a work of fiction. So yes, John Wilkes Booth really did have a *JWB* tattoo on the web of his hand, but he didn't have an ace of spades. The playing card details came from a tattoo on a leathery piece of skin that I found in an old museum box. Inside the box were many artifacts that purportedly belonged to presidential assassin Charles Guiteau, including the bones of his trigger finger. As it says in the novel, those bones were stolen from the museum and then returned. When they came back, that piece of skin was with it (and yes, the tattoo is exactly as I described, including the eagle and the red diamond with the knife in it). To this day, no one knows where the skin came from or if it's Guiteau's or not, but the moment the museum folks put it in my hands, the lightbulb went off and I started researching playing cards (and yes, George Washington really did order playing cards by the dozens).

If you want to know more about the other historical details—or ask a question about anything else—then let me invite you to BradMeltzer.com. You'll see answers to tons of questions there, including ones about the secret code that I hid in the pages of *The Inner Circle*. Crack the code and it'll lead you to the location for a hidden "treasure" (no one's found it yet). Even the *Decoded* folks haven't uncovered it.

Other than that, let me say the most important thing of all: Thank you for reading to the very end (or at least skipping to the end and ruining all the good parts).

See you in the Archives.

AMERICAN MANUFACTURE